Alive?
Copyright ©2018 Melissa Woods
All rights reserved.
Printed in the United States of America
First Edition: October 2018

Clean Teen Publishing
WWW.CLEANTEENPUBLISHING.COM

Summary: Everyone knows the first rule of the zombie apocalypse: Don't. Get. Bitten. Too bad Violet has never been great at following the rules. She manages to let one of the Dead take a chunk out of her only hours after they've begun walking again. Fortunately for Violet, she doesn't die. Unfortunately for Violet—she's not exactly alive either...

ISBN: 978-1-63422-310-2 (paperback)
ISBN: 978-1-63422-311-9 (e-book)
Cover Design by: Marya Heidel
Typography by: Courtney Knight
Editing by: Cynthia Shepp

Young Adult Fiction /Apocalyptic & Post-Apocalyptic
Young Adult Fiction / Zombies
Young Adult Fiction / Action & Adventure / Survival Stories

COVER ART
© NEOSTOCK: BILLIE-URBAN-FANTASY-13
© FOTOLIA/ СЕРГЕЙ КУЧУГУРНЫЙ
© FOTOLIA/ PHOTOMINUS21
© FOTOLIA/ HERSCHEL HOFFMEYER
© FOTOLIA/ LUCHIYAPOSTIKE

Dedicated to Ray Winter, the best father, teacher, advisor, and giver of hugs anyone could hope to have. You touched the lives of all who were lucky enough to meet you. I hope I made you proud.

VIOLET WINTER WAS DEAD.

Probably.

Possibly.

To be honest, she wasn't quite clear about it yet. All she knew was that ever since being bitten by the zombie, things had started to get weird.

As she stood there with warm blood drying on her fingers and bits of someone's face in her teeth, she decided that making the choice to take the shortcut through the woods might not have been the best one.

O
N
E

VIOLET'S PHONE BUZZED ANGRILY IN HER POCKET. She groaned, pulling it out and jabbing at the buttons. It was her alarm, playing the irritating tune that came pre-programmed, which, after three years, she still had no idea how to change. Violet had never been exactly blessed when it came to understanding technology.

After at least forty-five seconds of the jangly tune, she finally managed to silence the thing. It was only then she began to take in her surroundings. Simultaneously, she realized two very important facts; she wasn't in her bedroom, and that wasn't her hand resting on her thigh.

1

Violet wriggled free of whoever had passed out beside her, and then climbed off the couch she'd been sleeping on. The snoring man didn't wake up. Violet groaned, running her hand through her tangled brown hair. This party had certainly not been her idea.

"It'll be fun," her best friend had promised. "And you owe me after going to that weird fetish thing with you."

"That was a sci-fi convention! You enjoyed it," Violet had protested.

"No, Violet, it was weird. Some man dressed as a bear kept trying to pick me up and carry me around."

"You know he was a Wookie."

Amy had waved her hand at that. "In any case, you owe me. You're coming to this party!"

And so Violet had gone to the party. She had worn a dress and pretended to have fun, when all she'd been thinking about was getting back to her room and losing herself in a horror movie or playing a video game. But she supposed she'd experienced one of the things that seventeen-year-old girls were supposed to do. Even if she never planned on doing it again.

Violet glanced around. The whole living room looked like something out of a disaster movie. Bottles and cans littered the floor, as well as every available surface. Food, drink, and what was almost certainly vomit were soaked into the carpet, which appeared to have been expensive before.

Probably not so much now.

The walls were covered in... Violet didn't want to think about what the walls were covered in. Whatever it was, it probably wasn't going to impress Fiona's parents when they got back from their weekend away. Violet got to her feet, deciding it was probably best not to be there when they returned. She grabbed her sweater and hurriedly pulled it on, not thrilled with the fact it was damp—for some reason she didn't want to ponder.

Amy wasn't one of the two people asleep on the couch, and she wasn't on the floor with the three other sleeping bodies either. Violet wondered whether Amy might've been upstairs, but she was in no hurry to explore whatever delights might be found in the rest of the house.

Maybe some lovely used needles or a corpse?

She decided to leave without her friend. Amy was a big girl, and a veteran of parties like this. She'd be able to get home without Violet's help. Amy wasn't exactly in her good books after the events of the previous evening anyway. She had decided to trust her 'good friend' and come to the party. She also trusted Amy when she handed her a glass of purple liquid, looked her dead in the eye, and said, "Trust me, Violet, it's practically lemonade now; they've watered it down so much!"

It seemed Amy's definition of 'lemonade' wasn't the same as hers. She had no memory of anything that had happened after her first cup.

Violet began a brief search of the vomit-room for her handbag. She saw it caught underneath a sleeping man with blond dreadlocks and a plaited beard. When she gently pulled at the strap, the bag seemed to be lodged securely under his stomach. She sighed, pulling harder. Still nothing. She wasn't overly keen on waking him up, but she needed her bag. Violet gave one last tug, as hard as she could, and it finally flew out from underneath him. He groaned, but didn't open his eyes.

"Not cool," he mumbled, rolling onto his side and beginning to snore.

The hallway was in no better shape than the living room. There were more mystery stains on the walls, and a sour smell in the air: a mixture of vomit and urine. She shuddered to imagine what happened last night.

Never again. Next time Amy tries to convince you to go to a party, tell her the truth—you'd rather stick pins in your eyes.

She found the front door and stepped into the fresh air, shivering slightly at the cold. The damp sweater wasn't much help, but it was at least hiding part of the sequined monstrosity Amy insisted she wear. Amy had said everyone would be dressed up. She'd lied.

Violet turned back to the house once she reached the road, pulling the short dress down self-consciously. From outside, the damage didn't seem too bad. The windows were intact, though one of them was wide open and had a roll of toilet paper trailing from the second floor to the garden. The garden itself was a little torn up from the number of cars that had been parked the night before. There weren't many vehicles left. Most people had gone home hours ago, with only the most hardcore group staying. And Violet. But that wasn't exactly a testament to her staying power; she'd just passed out in the first available space. At ten PM.

The street was quiet. Violet glanced at her watch. Eight o'clock. It was Sunday, too, so she wasn't really surprised to be standing outside alone. She planned to be home and in bed herself within twenty minutes, so she decided to take the shortcut through the woods. The entrance was only a few meters from the house, but upon reaching the tree line, she suddenly found herself frozen in place. The morning was dark, the clouds heavy and ominous, and the woods felt more than a little uninviting. Violet scolded herself. She walked through the woods to school every day, but something felt wrong this morning. Shaking her head, she tried to clear the thoughts, before heading down the familiar path.

She felt her phone vibrate again. It was a message from Amy.

Amy: *Sorry I disappeared! Not feeling well, so I'm going home. Don't worry, I've got someone with me. Couldn't find you, so guessing you're still having fun! Call me later. XX*

The message had been sent hours ago. Why had she only just gotten it? She was glad Amy was okay, but couldn't help but be a little annoyed her friend hadn't made more of an effort to locate her. When Amy had sent the message, Violet wasn't 'still having fun'. She was where she'd been for most of the night—passed out on the couch. And surely Amy knew her well enough to know she would never be able to outlast her at a party. Violet continued into the woods, mentally composing the sarcastic reply she would send later.

Her thoughts were interrupted by something bumping into her leg. She looked down, more than a little surprised to see a small white dog sitting at her feet. It had scruffy fur and huge brown eyes. She smiled, momentarily forgetting the empty threats she'd been making about Amy, and knelt to stroke its head. She'd always liked dogs.

This one was covered in dirt, and had several twigs entwined in its fur. Violet read the tag on its collar—Ben. The dog wagged his tail as she said his name. "Where's your owner, then?" she asked, scanning the trees. There was no one around, and she couldn't hear anyone calling his name. She got up and continued a little further, Ben trotting beside her.

After a few minutes, and with no sign of an owner, Violet was beginning to wonder what to do with the dog. Should she take him home? It didn't feel right to leave him. She reached for her phone, deciding to call the number on the collar, but there was no signal.

Stupid nature blocking the satellites.

She glanced up, realizing Ben had trotted on ahead. She decided to follow. It wasn't like she had any other plans for the day.

Or tomorrow.

Or any other day.

Okay, Violet, we get it, you're a loser.

After several more minutes, Violet and the dog reached a fallen tree. She noticed a strange smell in the air, something she didn't recognize, thick and terrible. Ben moved behind the tree, and Violet followed. When she saw what he found, she felt like the air had been kicked out of her. On the ground was a woman, lying on her back in the dirt. Her stomach had been ripped open so wide Violet could see every organ left in her body. There weren't many. Some were scattered around her; the rest were just gone. The woman's bloodied fingers were curled, as if she'd been trying to fight back. Her eyes were open, and her mouth was wide, contorted in an expression of pure horror.

Violet choked, not even realizing she'd been holding her breath, and sucked in a huge lungful of air. The dog sat beside the woman, whimpering quietly and pressing its nose against her hand. For a few minutes, Violet couldn't move, frozen in place. Coming back to reality, she grabbed her phone and dialed 911. She still had no signal, but remembered reading somewhere an emergency call could be made without it.

It was busy.

How can it be busy?

Violet suddenly felt furious. Then scared. She had no idea what to do. She'd been prepped on 'strange men,' and 'keeping safe when walking home,' but no one had ever given her the 'so you've found a dead body in the woods' talk.

Violet's next thought was to run home and get her parents, before remembering they were visiting family in Australia. She groaned loudly, trying 911 again and getting the same busy tone.

As she frantically tried to decide what to do next, a terrible thought occurred to her.

Whoever killed that woman could still be in the woods.

Her heart began to race. She spun around, searching for any sign of movement. There was nothing, but she wasn't going to wait around to be ripped open. The dog whimpered again, pawing at the woman's arm. Violet moved closer, as close to the body as she was willing to get.

"Come on," she whispered, barely hearing her own voice. "Come on, Ben."

I'll take the dog home, and then call the police. I can bring them here, but I'm not staying alone.

But the dog wouldn't move. Violet bit her lip before spotting a blue leash on the ground. She grabbed it and clipped it to the dog's collar. A snap behind her—a twig? Had Violet trying to turn so fast she stumbled. She fell forward, holding out her free hand to stop from falling straight onto the corpse. Her hand touched the dead woman, and she recoiled as if scalded.

It was still warm. The woman hadn't been dead long. Whoever killed her had to be close by.

Violet staggered to her feet, pulling Ben away from the body. He fought against it a little at first, but soon fell into step at her side. She tried to retrace her steps back to the main path, but it was hard to focus because her mind was such a mess. Every noise set her heart racing.

The killer is still in the woods.
The killer is still in the woods.

She tried to keep calm and think about anything that wasn't the dead body behind her. The most complicated thing she could conjure up to distract herself was a movie she'd watched a few weeks ago with Amy called *Shadow Ghosts*. It had made no sense, and it had been so full of twists the two girls had got completely lost. This seemed to work as a distraction, and Violet managed to keep her mind off her possible impending death. Mostly.

Soon, she was back on the path, feeling a little less stressed about the mutilated corpse. Until another sound, a rustling, broke through. But it wasn't the wind; Violet was sure of it. She didn't think it was an animal either.

Something's behind me.

She wanted to run. Or at least start walking. In fact, any kind of movement would've been preferable to her chosen action, which was to stand still and do nothing. But that appeared to be all she was capable of at that moment.

Great. Just pretend to be invisible; that'll keep you safe.

So there she was, excelling at doing nothing, when Ben turned around to face their follower. He began to growl. Violet, realizing she could not simply freeze her way out of this one, turned around, too.

It was a man. He wasn't the large, imposing Jack-the-Ripper type she'd been half expecting. In fact, he was almost the exact opposite. Thin—scrawny, really—with unkempt red hair and pimpled skin. He wore a shirt with the name of an obscure band on it, and was missing a shoe. He didn't seem to have a weapon, but Violet knew he was the killer. She could just sense it.

Plus, his shirt, hands, and mouth were stained with blood.

Boom. You've just been detected, murderer!

Her heart began to race as she came to the realization this man might just decide to kill her, too.

Be calm. He doesn't know you know.

But then, he dropped his gaze to the dog.

He'll recognize the dog.

"I...I just found him in the woods," Violet stuttered, trying to make her voice sound calm. "I'm trying to find his owner. Have you seen anyone?"

Have you, perhaps, killed and eaten anyone?

She knew he didn't believe her. His glazed eyes just stared, unblinking, into her own. He swayed slightly, like he was drunk. Then his lips curled upward to reveal his bloodstained teeth.

Run.

The word popped into her head, surrounded with flashing neon lights, and booming out as though someone were shouting it. She did as she was told, running as fast as she could in the opposite direction. Ben was faster, practically pulling her along with him. She could hear the man chasing her. Violet had never been a particularly good runner, but she knew she was almost at the main road. Surely he couldn't hurt her if there were witnesses?

It was a nice thought, but when Violet cleared the tree line, she realized just how wrong she was.

It was chaos. The street was awash with crashed cars, people running into or out of their houses, fighting, screaming. So much screaming. There was smoke coming out of a house a few doors down. She could see people trapped inside. Just a few feet away from where she stood, there was a woman on the ground. There were four people around her, ripping her open just like the body in the woods. They were pulling out her insides and eating them. Violet had watched enough zombie movies to know what this was, but she couldn't believe it.

Her hand slackened, and the leash whipped through her fingers. She watched, numb, as the dog ran to the corner and disappeared. There was a hiss from behind her, and she turned just in time to see her drooling friend from the woods. He was so close, seconds from grabbing her. She ran, stumbling past other people. No one stopped to help; everyone was too busy trying to save themselves. Violet saw a family up ahead fleeing toward a house, and she called out for them to hold the door, to let her in. But they slammed it shut as she approached, so she had to run again.

She jumped over an overturned stroller, and then past a group of zombies hammering on the windows of a car. There were two men in the front, and a woman in the back. The engine was spluttering and gurgling, but wouldn't start. As she passed, she heard glass breaking.

Violet could see another house with its door open, but no sign of anyone nearby. She ran as fast as she could, her legs starting to give out after a whole thirty seconds of cardio. She made it up the path and inside, turning to slam the door. But the man was close, and he got halfway through before she could close it fully.

Zombies are meant to be slow, she thought angrily.

She pushed against the door with all her might, screaming with the exertion it took. Finally, he was shoved outside. She managed to close the door, sliding the lock into place and leaning her back heavily against the wood. Sweat poured down her forehead. She felt sick. Violet closed her eyes, wondering if her heart would ever stop racing. She could still hear the screams outside. There were cars crashing, alarms going off, crying and terror and the kinds of noises she never thought she'd hear when she woke up less than an hour earlier.

A creak of floorboards. Violet opened her eyes just in time to see a woman lunge. She was wearing a white lace nightie, offset slightly by the gaping wound in her stomach. Violet held out her arms, pushing back with all her strength. She barely had any left, but it was just enough to keep the zombie at bay. The woman's eyes were almost white, and her teeth snapped in Violet's face. Though she had no idea what caused this or why it was happening, she knew this thing wanted to kill her.

Her arms were hurting, but she continued to fight. The zombie moved her head suddenly, sinking her teeth into Violet's left arm, just below the elbow. She screamed as teeth tore through her skin.

It was worse than any pain she'd ever experienced—sharp and brutal. She kicked out, catching the woman in the stomach and pushing her back. Violet ran, clutching her bleeding arm against her chest. She had no idea where the back door was, so she ran up the stairs. When she saw the bathroom up ahead, she threw herself inside.

The door slammed shut, and Violet saw a man click the lock into place as she dropped onto the floor by the sink. He was normal, not dead like the others. There was a hammering at the wood, rattling the frame. The man grabbed a towel, hurriedly wrapping Violet's arm. She wanted to thank him, but her eyes felt heavy. Within seconds, everything was black.

WHEN SHE OPENED HER EYES, IT TOOK HER A FEW minutes to realize she wasn't in the bathroom anymore. She was lying on the floor of a bedroom. Her arm hurt. A lot. In fact, everything did. She sat up slowly, letting her eyes adjust to the space around her. It was a large bedroom with floral wallpaper and a wooden dressing table. She was alone.

Violet leaned forward and threw up, managing to avoid getting it on herself. Mostly. When she was finished, she wiped her mouth with the back of her hand, with all the dignity that action allowed. Catching sight of the large bruise on her wrist—her now incredibly pale wrist—Violet started to get nervous. She had never exactly been tanned, but she didn't remember being *that* white.

She looked at her other arm. The bite mark had been stitched, but the veins underneath were now dark black, and she wondered briefly if she might have blood poisoning.

If only.

She noticed a couple of other abnormalities as well. Like the scratches on her arms. As she got to her feet to examine herself in the mirror on the wall, she saw bruising on her face, too. Her very pale face with bloodstains around the mouth.

I must've cut my lip.

Her eyes were different, too. She moved closer to the mirror to investigate more closely. They had always been brown, but were grey now, with just a couple of streaks of brown across the iris. Her hair was matted and dirty, like she hadn't washed it for days, but that couldn't be right because she had the morning of the party.

Cautiously, Violet made her way to the open door. There was no sign of the man who saved her, or the woman who bit her. She crept to the bathroom, but realized it was different. She wasn't in the same house she'd passed out in.

How did I get here?

Her stomach growled. She felt hungrier than she'd been in a long time. And thirsty, too, with an unpleasant taste in her mouth. Violet went downstairs to the kitchen, which was deserted. She drank water straight from the tap, and then searched the cupboards. She found a packet of chips, and then began shoveling handfuls into her mouth. Stomach revolting, she stopped to throw up again, but at least managed to make it to the sink.

Her vomit was black.

Violet raised her head, taking her first glance out of the window. The street was quiet, the same one she'd been on when she left the woods, except this house was on the other side. There were no people outside anymore, no walking ones at least, but there were bodies. There were also more crashed cars and debris, along with a pile of rubble where the burning house had been.

How long have I been in here?

She heaved, vomiting more black liquid, hot and acidic as it came up her throat.

What happened to me?

T W O

VIOLET MANAGED TO GET MORE VOMIT ON HER sweater than she'd anticipated, and though she hated the sequined dress, she didn't love the idea of smelling like puke all day. She tossed the sweater into the garbage can, searching for a jacket that fit well enough. After she found one on a hook by the back door, she slid it on. The dress was bloodstained, but she didn't want to waste time rooting through a stranger's wardrobe for something else to wear. She wanted to get away from this place as quickly as possible, but couldn't find her bag or cell phone anywhere.

Just leave it; you need to go.

Violet glanced out the window. The sun outside was low, so it was probably early in the morning.

After drinking a little more water, she made her way to the front door. It was open. She'd been lucky none of those things had come inside.

But why am I here?

Did the man who saved me bring me here?

The sky was cloudy, and there was a heaviness in the air, as if a storm were approaching. Violet couldn't shake the feeling she'd been in the house for more than a couple of days. The appearance of the street outside suggested things had been bad for a while.

She continued, her shoes on the pavement the

only sound in the quiet street. There were no screams now, just the silent bodies. Violet felt almost numb as she passed them, as though they weren't real. She felt a little like she was on the set of a movie. When she glanced to her right, she could see the woods, her quickest route home, but there was no way she was going back in there again. There was a dog barking somewhere, and Violet thought briefly of Ben. Would he still be alive? She hoped so.

Violet's foot hit something soft. She'd been so focused on the woods she'd not been paying attention to where she was going. She'd walked right into a dead body. It was a woman in a blue dress. Or at least, it used to be blue. The dress was stained from the large open wound on her chest. Most of her face had been chewed off. She had a jagged piece of glass sticking out of her skull. It was while Violet was gaping at this body that the realization of what was happening finally hit.

These are all people. Dead people. They've been ripped open and left to rot out here.

What if I'm the only one left? What if no one else made it?

I was bitten, so what does that mean?

Violet fell to her knees, her heart racing, beads of sweat prickling on her skin. She didn't know what to do, couldn't even think straight. The road around her seemed to be spinning out of control, and it was all she could do to put her hands onto the tarmac and try to hold on for dear life. She closed her eyes, put her head down, and rested her forehead on the ground. Tiny bits of concrete dug into her skin, but it was good. The pain reassured her that she was still alive.

I'll go home. Try to make sense of all this in the safety of my house. Lock all the doors, climb into bed, and try to come to terms with this nightmare. In my pajamas.

As usual, Violet was handling things calmly and maturely. She opened her eyes, grateful her surroundings seemed to have stopped spinning at least. Slowly, carefully, she got to her feet. She moved past the woman, past the other bodies, and on toward the main road. There was smoke in the distance, coming from several different places. She supposed more houses had caught fire.

Violet screamed as fingers curled around her ankle, and she tried to yank away. Something that used to be a person had grabbed hold of her. It must have come from the burned-down house, because it was scorched all over and missing both legs. It held tightly onto her ankle, growling and snapping its teeth. She lost her balance and fell.

"Get off!" She kicked out, trying to free herself.

The man, zombie, whatever it was, held on tightly. Violet kicked out again, catching it right in the jaw. It knocked the scorched head clean off its shoulders.

"Oh my god!" Violet wriggled back, away from the body. The hand detached from the arm, and she roughly pried the blackened fingers from her skin. The head was a few feet away, snapping its jaws as though nothing had happened.

Violet got to her feet, wiping the dirt and ash from her body, her heart rate slowly returning to normal.

"Gross," she muttered, staring at the head.

Violet glanced around, confirming no one had seen her slight overreaction to a creature that pretty much turned to dust when touched, then headed toward the main road. There, she found more cars. Some were crashed, some abandoned, some burned out. But up ahead, she could see the shape of a person still inside one, someone moving. She hurried over, praying it would be a living human. But of course, today was not her lucky day.

The dead one in this car was a man in relatively good condition. His face was devoid of scratches or marks, and his pale, dead skin actually complemented his shiny blond hair. He looked almost Scandinavian—strong, muscular, handsome.

Not that she was attracted to him. He was a zombie. That would be weird.

She moved a little closer to the window, trying to get a better idea of what she would be up against, and also coming to the bitter realization that even though this guy was dead he was still out of her league. His beautifully shaped eyes were devoid of all color. His perfectly straight teeth were gnashing hungrily. He had a large bandage wrapped around his muscular arm. It was soaked in dark red blood.

He was bitten.

The thought appeared in her mind immediately. It made Violet jump back from the window, but it didn't make sense. If being bitten turned people into one of those things, why was she still okay?

But you're not okay; you can't even remember when you arrived in the mystery house.

Violet shook her head. She couldn't know for sure it was a bite mark on the man's arm. It could've been anything under that bandage.

She moved on, quickening her pace down the quiet street, the sound of the man's movements drifting away behind her.

As she rounded the next corner, Violet came face to face with another one of the creatures. Unfortunately for her, this one was neither an attractive man, nor separated from her by a pane of glass and a seat belt. It was a female feeding on a corpse on the ground. Violet's eyes widened, and she froze where she stood. The woman made horrible noises as she fed, slurping and smacking her lips together.

Go, a voice yelled in her head. *Go now while it's distracted!*

Of course, when put under pressure, Violet screwed it up. As she backed away, a piece of broken glass crunched loudly under her shoe.

Great.

The woman jumped up, a loud growl escaping her lips. She ran, forcing Violet to spin around and head down a road to her left. She moved as fast as she could, skidding around another corner. A huge truck had overturned, blocking most of the road. Three cars were crashed together, filling in the only gap.

I could climb over the cars?

But it was no good. There were four more zombies already doing just that, heading toward her. Violet let out an angry cry, changing direction and cutting through a narrow road between the houses. She didn't look back, not wanting to fall over, but she knew there were now at least five of them close behind. She also knew she wouldn't be able to keep up this pace for very long. She'd never been a good runner, and her legs were already tiring.

As she passed a house on the left, she could see two zombies hammering on the door. The people inside watched her from the window, but they couldn't do anything. Unfortunately for her, however, it seemed she could help them, because when the zombies caught sight of her, they joined the ones who were already chasing.

Oh sure, come along, too!

Violet had no idea where she was going; she didn't know this neighborhood. Up ahead, she could see a small convenience store. There was movement inside. She knew she had to take a chance, since her energy was almost depleted. Forcing herself to speed up, she hurtled toward the door, pushing the full weight of her body against it.

Yes!

It opened! Violet threw herself inside, slamming it shut behind her. When the zombies arrived, they banged heavily on the glass, throwing themselves against it. She found the lock, hurriedly sliding it into place.

"What have you done?"

Violet spun around. There was a man standing behind her. He was short, skinny, and probably in his early twenties. He wore glasses and held a baseball bat, watching her from behind the thick lenses with an anxious suspicion that didn't make her feel altogether comfortable. She tried to catch her breath, heart still hammering in her chest.

Sweaty, out of breath, and at least seven zombies trailing behind you. What a treat for this guy you are, Violet.

"Why have you brought them here?" he asked, eyes on the shaking door.

A bit taken aback, she paused, trying to think of the most polite way to say, *I was trying not to get killed, you moron!*

"They were chasing me," she began, attempting to

keep her tone even. "I saw someone in here, so I came in. I had to get away. I couldn't run any longer."

"You need to get out."

Violet wasn't sure she had heard him correctly. "What?"

"You need to get out."

She slowly pivoted back to the door, which was still shaking under the weight of the zombies pressed against it, before turning back to the man.

"I'd rather not."

"You need to leave!"

Violet shook her head. "No, you don't seem to understand. What we need to do is barricade the door. We need to stop them from getting in."

"I'm not going anywhere. This is my store, but you need to leave. You need to take those things with you. Get them away from here." His voice was frantic, as if he were putting the plan together in his head as he spoke.

Okay, my mistake—you're clearly insane.

Violet spoke gently. "Okay, that's fine. I'll leave. Where's the back door?" If she could get out that way, she could hopefully get a head start before the zombies saw her. It would give her a chance at least, and it was a more appealing option than staying in the store with Crazy McCrazerson anyway.

But Crazy wasn't on board with that plan either. "No, you need to go that way." He pointed to the front door, where the nearest zombie was smashing its head violently against the strong glass. "You need to take them with you."

Violet shook her head. "Out there? I don't think you understand—"

But he wasn't listening, babbling to himself as he paced back and forth. "You need to get them away from here. Yes. Draw them away. Then I'll be safe again. Safe and sound."

"They'll kill me," Violet insisted, taking a tentative step toward him. "I won't get one foot out the door."

"They'll be busy with you, and I'll be safe." He wasn't even talking to her now; his eyes were focused over her shoulder.

Violet shook her head, desperately trying to convince

him. "As soon as you open the door, those things will come in here. They won't just take me; they'll kill you, too. Surely you can see that?"

But his mind was made up. He moved closer to Violet, using the baseball bat to force her toward the door. Violet's back hit the glass. She could feel it vibrating as the things outside hammered against it. She knew it wouldn't hold much longer. The man leaned over, reaching for the lock. Violet pushed him as hard as she could, fighting with all she had left to keep him from the handle.

"It's the only way," he panted, his free hand on her neck, holding her at arm's length.

He's going to open the door! Do something, anything!

She bit him on the wrist. Not exactly the actions of a sane person, but it was the only thing she could think to do. Her hands were busy trying to hold him back, and she knew she only had seconds to act. She'd only meant to shock him, to force him away.

It worked. He released his hold, crying out in pain.

But from the moment the blood hit Violet's tongue, the whole world around her seemed to change. Everything became black and white. Except the blood. The blood pouring out of his wrist was a glorious, beautiful crimson. She felt strong, unstoppable, and something else.

⌁〜〜

WHEN VIOLET WOKE UP, IT WAS RAINING. SHE COULD hear the drops falling heavily against the windows. She was lying on her back on the cold floor, her arms and legs wide as though she'd been making a snow angel. A rather macabre one, since the floor was slick with blood.

Her head felt heavy, and was throbbing painfully. She reached to feel it gingerly. There was no cut at least. The zombies had gone. There was no sign of them at the door. She didn't know where the man was. Carefully, she sat up, glancing around the store.

Oh, there he is.

This doesn't bode well for me.

Most of his arm, the one she had bit into, had been

chewed away, right down to the bone. So had his nose and the majority of his left cheek. Violet anxiously scanned the room, panicked that one of the zombies was inside the store with her. But she was alone. She looked down at her hands; they were covered in blood. There were dry flecks all over her skin, and she could taste iron in her mouth. All too suddenly, she knew.

I ate him.

She vomited again. And again. Blood, skin, bone fragments, hair—she could see it all as she spluttered and wretched onto the floor. Every time she thought she was done, there was more.

Finally, there was nothing left. Violet was sweating, exhausted, and sore, but finished.

What am I? What's wrong with me?

She needed to work this through in her head. Needed to put the pieces of this gross, blood-covered puzzle together. Quite obviously, the flesh-eating thing was a new phase in her life. It had to be connected to the bite. The taste of the man's blood had made her lose control and blackout. She'd become like the other zombies, but now she was fine again. Was this happening to all of them? She doubted that.

Violet shook the thoughts away. She couldn't deal with them now. Not here, not with the dead man beside her. She straightened out her dress. It was dry, so she must've been passed out for a while. Head spinning, she moved toward the door, sliding the lock to one side and opening it cautiously. No sign of the zombies, but it was getting dark. She supposed she could stay in the store for the night, but she didn't want to stay with the corpse; she wanted to go home. Stepping out into the rain, she began to walk.

THE RAIN WAS HEAVY, AND THE SKY SEEMED TO BE GETTING darker by the second. Violet was soon soaked to the skin. Her hair fell like a heavy curtain around her face, and she shivered. The blood from her dress, diluted by rain, dripped onto the concrete as she walked.

There was a sound behind her, and she turned to see a can rolling across the ground.

Where did that come fro—

The thought was interrupted by the sight of three of the dead, almost right behind her. The rain had disguised their footsteps. She had never even heard them.

Oh, come on!

She ran as fast as she could, water splashing up from the cold ground. Her wet clothing slowed her down, but she kept going. She arrived on George Avenue, and then darted into the first house she saw. The door was open, and she slammed it shut behind her. She didn't think they'd seen her come in.

There was a sound from her right, and Violet spun around. A figure stood in the doorway to what she assumed was the living room.

"Please don't be another zombie," Violet wheezed.

The figure moved forward, and she breathed a sigh of relief. He was definitely alive. Though there was little light in the room, she could see he was tall with dark brown hair. In fact, not only was he alive, but he was also someone she recognized.

"Wait, I know you," Violet began. "Matt, right? We used to go to school togeth—" She was interrupted as a zombie appeared behind Matt, grabbing hold of his arms. He staggered backward, forcing the creature into the wall as he attempted to shake it off. They struggled for what felt like the longest time, though it could only have been seconds, before Matt broke free and slammed a knife into the creature's skull. It fell to the floor with a thud. Matt was breathing heavily, blood spattered on his face. He stood up straight, staring at her now.

"Violet?" He said her name with surprise, as though the sight of her standing in front of him was completely unbelievable.

"Nice to see another person alive," Violet breathed, smiling. "How are you? It's been a long time."

"Yeah, it has."

"What are you doing with yourself now?"

Matt was currently leaning down to pull his knife out of the skull of the thing on the floor. He lifted his head, quirking an eyebrow.

"Oh yeah...right. Zombies."

There was a crash as the front door began to buckle. The dead had found them.

"Run," Matt ordered, heading toward the back of the house. Violet followed him into the rain.

"Where?" she called as they ran. Matt pointed to a large building up ahead. It was the high school. She tried to keep up as Matt charged for the open gates. The doors were strong, and if they could get inside before the zombies, they should be able to keep them out. Matt waited for her at the entrance.

"Duck," he instructed, swinging his bat over Violet's head to hit the zombie behind her. She hadn't realized it was so close. Using her last burst of energy, she sprinted to the main doors of the building, rattling the handles.

Locked.

Of course they're locked.

"Do you have the keys?" Violet asked frantically as Matt caught up. The dead were getting closer.

He reached into his pocket, then swore loudly.

Great.

"This way," he said, moving toward the side of the building, scanning the walls as he ran. He stopped, pointing at an open window. It wasn't too high. Violet chanced a look behind her; the zombies were close, but they had enough time. Matt had reached the window first. He climbed into the building, then held out his hand to help her inside. She grabbed it, and he began to pull her up and in.

The window was smaller than she'd anticipated, and it wouldn't open any more than it already was. Violet's head and shoulders were in, but her bottom half was dangling. It might've been her dress catching, but she couldn't help but feel that getting stuck in a half-open window during the zombie apocalypse was enough of a reason to start feeling bad about her body shape. Matt was still pulling, and she began to move forward into the school. The dead had arrived now. One grabbed hold of her leg. She kicked out violently, managing to free herself, and was finally yanked into the room.

She and Matt stood in the darkness for a moment, both struggling to catch their breath.

"Are you okay?" he asked.

Violet nodded, bending over and taking a big lungful of air. The building was dark, but within seconds, she realized they weren't alone. Someone else had entered the room through the door in front of them.

Oh crap.

"Violet?"

Amy's face was just visible in the fading light. Her expression was a mixture of shock, joy, and fear. She grabbed hold of Violet, pulling her in for a hug.

"I can't believe you're here," Amy whispered when she finally released her friend.

Violet shook her head. She couldn't believe it either. Had all of that really just happened? Had she just escaped the dead for the third time? Fourth? She couldn't even remember.

"Come on," Matt said, as the zombies continued to pound on the glass. "We should get out of here before the sound draws more of them."

Amy took Violet by the hand, leading her from the dark classroom. Matt shut the door. The three of them made their way through the hallways, now almost completely black, up a flight of stairs, and into a small room. The lights were on up there, and Violet could see several people dotted around inside. She recognized the room as the teachers' lounge, though it had changed since the last time she had seen it. Several of the chairs and couches had been moved around and turned into makeshift beds. There were cans of food piled on one of the kitchen units, and a few bottles of water on another. By the state it was in, she guessed it had been lived in for at least a week.

**T
H
R
E
E**

I need to find out how long I was unconscious.

There were five other people inside, all staring at her with shocked expressions. Violet supposed a new arrival covered in blood would hardly be a comforting sight. She was just grateful her bite was hidden by the coat.

Violet was able to see Amy more clearly now that they were in the light. She appeared tired. Her blonde hair was limp, tied roughly with an elastic band. Her eyes were red, with large bags underneath. She was thinner, and her usually clear skin had broken out in pimples.

Ha! Who's smug about their perfect skin now?

That's horrible; you're a horrible friend.

Now that she could see properly, she could also take in Matt. She'd had some classes with him at school, but he'd moved a couple of years ago. He wasn't much different than last time she'd seen him: skinny, unkempt dark brown hair, bright green eyes. Violet always thought they were the kind of eyes that seemed to see right into her soul.

Violet might've had a crush on Matt at school. Though she wouldn't have admitted it, of course, because Amy wouldn't have let her forget it.

Apparently feeling her scrutiny, Matt smiled and said, "It's good to see you, Violet."

Thankfully, Violet was too exhausted and emotionally drained to take part in her go-to response when a boy she liked spoke to her—blush profusely or do this weird laugh-snort—so she simply nodded.

Amy addressed the rest of the group. "This is Violet."

The others moved closer. The first to speak was a tall guy with brown hair and warm eyes. He was probably a couple of years older than her.

"Joe," he said with a smile, speaking with a strong English accent. "Nice to see someone else avoided the biters." He thought for a moment. "So far, anyway."

"Comforting, Joe," Amy muttered.

Violet was introduced to another guy—Sam. He was shorter than Joe, muscular, and had short brown hair. Sam seemed like the kind of guy who was probably used to using a lot of product to keep that hair in check, and it had become a little messy after some time in the zompocalypse.

No one ever thinks about the effect the undead uprising has on your hair.

There was a red-headed girl—Maggie—who was probably around fourteen or fifteen. An older woman—Emily—had caramel skin and beautiful dark eyes. She had a familiar face, and Violet recalled she'd been a teacher. Not one of hers, though. The last was a man—Tom. He had blond hair, and an expression she couldn't help but think was rather smug.

Amy shook her head. "I still can't believe you're here. Violet, I was so worr... Is that my dress?" She eyed the bloodied, sequined monstrosity and scowled. "I told you to be careful with that."

Violet raised an eyebrow. "Really? Now? We're doing this now? I almost got eaten by dead people."

Amy shook her head. "Sorry."

"That's okay—"

"It's just my favorite dress, and I thought—"

"Yeah, I got it."

Sam, clearly feeling the vibe of the room, stepped a little closer.

"Have you been out there all this time?" he asked. He meant outside, out with the dead, alone. Violet nodded. Sam seemed surprised, but also a little impressed.

"You must be fast."

You literally could not be more wrong.

Violet shook her head. "Just lucky."

"She's covered in blood," Tom said. He pointed at Violet accusingly. "She's been bitten."

Her heart began to race. She knew the coat was covering the bite, for now, but she didn't like the certainty in Tom's voice. What if they found out? Everyone was staring at her now, and Sam moved forward.

"Show us." It wasn't said unkindly, but it was firm. Violet was suddenly aware of the baseball bat he held casually in his left hand. It was still down at his side, but he seemed to be gripping it more tightly.

Amy stepped in front of her friend. "Don't," she said

to Sam.

"I'm not going to do anything," he replied. "We just need to be sure. You know the rules. If she's been bitten, she can't stay."

"Why?" Violet asked, though she was sure she already knew the answer. "What happens if you're bitten?"

The group looked confused, as though the question made no sense. When Sam finally spoke, it was slowly, as if to a child.

"You turn. You become one of the biters."

Violet felt a lump in her throat. "How long does it take?"

Matt shrugged. "An hour. Sometimes a few more. Not long, though. I've seen it happen even faster."

Sam regarded Violet carefully. "Have you been bitten, Violet?"

What could she say? If she admitted she had, they would throw her out. She wouldn't last another day outside. Even if she managed to explain, which would be practically impossible, would they believe it? What would she even say...

Yeah, I was bitten, and I think I might be dead, but I'm not sure. I've definitely eaten at least one person, though. Anyway, where shall I sleep?

No, that response pretty much guaranteed being kicked out at best, getting beaten to death with Sam's baseball bat at worst.

"No," she lied. "I haven't been bitten." It was easier than she'd expected; the words slipped right off the tongue. The others seemed happy enough with it, though Sam kept his eyes fixed on her. It was Tom, however, who shook his head.

"How can we trust you? Show us!"

Matt held up a hand. "If she says she hasn't, that's good enough for me."

Violet felt a huge flood of gratitude toward Matt, even though he was technically making a catastrophic mistake.

"It won't be good enough when she's chewing your face off," Tom continued. "Get her to show us!"

Violet scowled. *Someone just got himself to the top of*

the face-eating list.

Joe raised an eyebrow. "What do you want her to do, strip in front of all of us?"

"Amy," Sam began, his voice gentle. "She's your friend. We'll give you some privacy, but you need to check her."

"This is stupid," Amy protested, but Sam held up his hand.

"We have to know for sure."

She sighed. "Fine."

The others turned away, and Violet's heart began to race again. Amy caught her eye with a puzzled expression. Slowly, understanding washed over her face. Violet unzipped the coat, and then pulled her arm free to show the bite. Amy stared at it for several seconds. She reached out and gently felt the stitches, moving the arm to inspect it closer before looking up into her friend's eyes.

"Well?" Sam asked, his back still to them.

"She's fine," Amy replied, without breaking eye contact with Violet. She put her friend's arm back into the coat, squeezing her hand as she did so. When the others faced them again, the mood was immediately more relaxed.

"Good," Sam said. "Sorry we had to do that, but we had to be sure."

Violet nodded, not trusting herself to talk.

"Where's the blood from?" Tom asked.

Violet caught sight of a few irritated glances in Tom's direction, and couldn't help but wonder whether he was a particularly popular member of the group. She already knew she didn't like him; though probably because he was the only one who seemed to think there might be something a little 'off' about her.

"I was with someone who died," she replied. It wasn't technically a lie. She had just decided not to add, *And I was the one who killed him.*

"I'd rather not talk about it," Violet continued.

Sam seemed to understand. "We've all got stories like that."

I'm pretty sure you haven't.

"If you want to go and clean up, the showers are still working," Emily said. "I can wash your clothes for you and find you some clean ones to wear in the meantime."

"Thank you," Violet nodded.

"I'll take her down," Amy offered, taking her by the arm and leading her from the room.

THE GIRLS CHANGING ROOM WAS LARGE, WITH LOCKERS and benches on one side, and showers on the other. Though Violet and Amy had made their way down through dark hallways, Amy flicked the lights on when they got inside.

"We only use the lights in rooms with no windows, or where we can block them," she explained.

Violet remembered how the blinds had been drawn upstairs. "Are they drawn to the light?" she asked.

"Yes."

For a moment, neither of them spoke. Finally, Violet took Amy's hand.

"Thank you."

"I know you wouldn't try to put us in danger, so I need you to explain to me why you didn't say anything. If you're going to turn—"

"I'm not," Violet interrupted.

"How can you know that?" Amy asked. "Everybody does."

"I was bitten on the first day. I'm fine." Violet chose her words carefully. She didn't want to tell Amy about the man she had killed. Not because she didn't trust her. Amy was, and had always been, fiercely loyal. She'd keep her hideous secret. But Violet couldn't tell her because she didn't want her to worry, or worse, be afraid of her.

"I'm not going to turn," Violet repeated.

Amy's whole body seemed to relax. "Wow," she breathed. "So you must be immune to it? To whatever this thing is?"

"I don't know. I think I'm infected with...something."

"Why?"

Violet took off her coat, holding out her arm. "The veins around the bite are black. *Something* has happened. I'm infected; I'm just not like them."

"But they're dead." Amy paused, eyes widening. "Are *you* dead?"

"I don't know." Violet ran her hands through her hair in frustration. "It's not like I can google my symptoms."

Amy punched her on the arm.

"Ow!"

"So you felt that?"

"Yes!"

"Maybe you're not dead?"

Violet scowled. "Thank you, *Doctor*."

Amy crossed her arms. "I'm just trying to help." She sighed. "Okay, well, what do we know? The infection kills people. They die, and then they come back to life. What happened after you were bitten?"

"I blacked out," Violet admitted. "For a while, I think. How long have you been here?"

"Ten days."

Violet's eyes widened. "I only woke up today. So I must've been unconscious ever since the day it happened, the day after the party."

Amy sounded surprised. "You didn't eat or drink for nine days?"

God, I hope not.

"I don't know. How can we find out if I'm dead?" That was a question she'd never imagined herself having to ask.

Amy thought for a moment, and then her eyes lit up. "I could cut your wrists?"

Violet paused, eyes narrowing. "Okay, good idea. Can you see any problems with that?"

Amy seemed to be thinking, then bit her lip, "Oh, yeah."

"Yeah, what's the best that can happen in that scenario? I find out I'm not dead...and we celebrate in the ten minutes it takes for me to bleed out all over the floor."

"Okay, it was just an idea."

"Yeah, well, it was terrible."

Amy rolled her eyes. "Okay, so we can't find out if you're dead or not. How do those things act around you?"

"They try to eat me."

"That's good!"

"Not really."

"No, but I mean, if you were really one of them, they wouldn't try to kill you. You obviously aren't completely infected like they are." She smiled. "And it's not like you're eating people!"

"No. Definitely not. That would be so gross." Violet laughed nervously. "Anyway, I just need to get clean and get some sleep."

Amy gestured to Violet's clothes.

"Give me those. The water is still on, for now. But it's cold, I'm afraid."

Amy was lying; it was freezing. Violet gasped as the icy water hit her skin, but it was also oddly soothing. It was like she was washing away the horrors of the last few hours.

Amy made no effort to leave the room; she'd never exactly been one for privacy. Violet decided to start a conversation. At least then, they would be two people talking while one of them showered, and not two people standing in silence while one showered and the other watched. That was weirder.

"What happened to you?" Violet asked.

"After I left the party, I was walking home with Harry. Do you remember him, the one with the eyebrow piercing?"

"The one with the tattoo of a knife on his cheek?"

"Yeah."

"Yeah, he seemed...nice."

"Don't be a snob. Anyway, we were walking home with his friend, Dan, and we found some of those things. They killed Dan, and we had to run. We saw the school and the open gates, so we took a chance. It was still pretty dark, so the biters didn't see us go inside."

"What happened to Harry? Is he here, too?"

Amy dropped her gaze, shaking her head. "There was someone else. She'd come in to hide. But she turned, and she bit him."

"I'm sorry."

Amy shrugged. "It's okay. I barely knew him."

"Did he turn, too?"

"Yes. He died really fast, then he came back." Amy

handed Violet a towel, which she wrapped around herself.

"What happened? How did you get away from him and the woman? Did you have to—"

Amy shook her head. "No, Matt arrived. He did it. He saved me."

"So he's been here with you? He was outside earlier."

"He went out to find supplies, but he's been here since the start."

Emily appeared a moment later, and Violet hurriedly hid her bitten arm behind her back.

"Spare clothes," Emily offered, holding them out. Amy took them quickly, before Violet had to attempt to grab them with one hand.

"Thanks, Em. We'll be up in a minute."

VIOLET MADE HER WAY BACK TO THE TEACHERS' LOUNGE with Emily and Amy, her mind still racing. She had no idea how she was going to hide her bite from the group long term—surely, they'd find out sooner or later? Her thoughts, however, were interrupted. The moment the three of them stepped through the door, everything went dark. For one horrible moment, Violet was sure she'd blacked out again, but then she felt Amy's fingers close on her arm.

"What's going on?" Amy asked into the darkness.

"Power's gone out," Sam replied simply. "We knew it was going to happen sooner or later. It just happens to be the worst timing."

"Nah," Joe replied. "Could be worse."

"How?"

"The biters could choose this moment to break inside. Then we'd be in the dark *and* running from the unde— Ow!"

Violet guessed Joe had just received a swift kick from someone, because he didn't finish his sentence.

"Okay," Sam began. "We need flashlights, or at the very least, some candles. Let's split up and look around."

"Said no one who's ever seen a single horror movie,"

Joe added sarcastically.

Sam continued as if he hadn't heard him. "We know this building is secure. It's locked up, and we've swept it several times. We're safe; we just need some light. We can wait until morning?"

"No, let's get it done now," Matt said from somewhere to Violet's left.

"I agree," Violet added. She didn't like the idea of spending the night in the pitch black.

SAM PAIRED EVERYONE UP: VIOLET WAS WITH MATT, TOM with Maggie, Joe and Amy, and Emily and himself. Matt and Violet began to check the classrooms off the main hallway, which was a tricky task in almost complete darkness. There was, at least, some moonlight coming in through the classroom windows. The two of them held their hands out in front of them as though they were blind, and Violet was not immune to the bitter irony. They were doing a pretty good impression of every zombie cartoon she'd ever seen.

"Are you okay?" Matt asked as they went into the next classroom.

"Yeah, just trying not to trip over stuff."

Matt shook his head as he opened one of the drawers on the teacher's desk and began to root around inside. "No, I mean, you were out there on your own for a long time. It must've been horrible."

"Yes, but I was fine."

A little light illuminated Matt's face, and he grinned. He'd found a lighter, and showed it to Violet victoriously before continuing his search. "I've been here since the start, and that's been hard enough. Those things have tried to get in so many times."

"Have they ever done it?"

"Not so far. They seem to lose interest after a while if they can't see you anymore."

"We need to find a way to lock the gates," Violet said. "Then we won't have to be scared to walk past a window."

"Yeah, you're right." Matt stopped rummaging through the drawer, his eyes flicking to the window. "Do you hear that?"

"What?" Violet followed his gaze. She heard it that time. Barking. It sounded close. Going out into the hallway, she followed the sound until she reached a classroom at the end. She moved inside and headed to the window.

You've got to be kidding!

It was the dog from the woods; his leash was tangled around a small tree just outside the window. He barked in frustration as he struggled to get free.

"I know that dog!" Violet pressed her hands against the glass as Matt approached. "We have to get him."

"He'll be fine." Matt's response was so quick, so casual, that it surprised her a little. She couldn't help but feel a wave of something unpleasant and scowled.

"Those things could kill him!"

Matt leaned closer to the window, the moonlight illuminating his face. Violet could see that he appeared completely unconcerned, and this made her even angrier. He seemed to sense this, holding up his hands as he explained.

"They don't eat animals. I've seen them pass dogs and cats like they aren't even there. They're not interested in eating anything that's not human." He nodded at Ben. "He'll be okay. We can get him in the morning. It's not safe to go out there in the dark."

Violet was sure he was telling the truth. He didn't seem like the kind of person who would happily watch an animal get torn apart, but she still didn't feel okay about leaving Ben outside.

"Maybe *they* won't hurt him, but he could still *get* hurt." She gestured to where the dog was still fighting against his leash. "He could strangle himself out there. Please, we need to get him."

Matt looked again and sighed.

"Okay. But we need to do it fast. It wasn't long ago that those things were out there. We haven't given them enough time to get bored and leave. They could still be around."

Violet climbed onto a nearby table to open the window. This one was bigger than the last, though still relatively high. Matt got up beside her. "I'll go, and then pass him up to you."

Violet shook her head. "No, he might run away when you untangle him. He knows me; I'll get him. Plus, I'll need help getting back inside, and I won't be strong enough to pull you up."

She could see in Matt's eyes he knew she was right, but he wasn't happy about the plan. Regardless, he agreed, and Violet climbed out into the night.

She landed with her usual grace and elegance— stumbling into a puddle and soaking her new clothes. It had at least stopped raining. She moved toward Ben as quickly and quietly as she could.

He saw her coming, almost strangling himself as he jumped up in excitement. She crouched beside him, hurriedly untangling the leash and taking it in her hand. He seemed okay—no bites, no scratches, maybe a little thin, but otherwise unscathed. She didn't know if animals could get infected like humans, but he appeared healthy enough.

"Looks like you've had better luck than me," she muttered.

Ben continued to wag his tail, then sniffed cautiously at her arm. Violet's heart began to beat a little faster. What if he blew her cover? A dog constantly sniffing at the same spot on her arm could draw suspicion. But he lost interest, beginning to lick her face. She smiled, stroking his tangled white fur. For a minute, she forgot where she was, and why she'd been in such a hurry to rescue him.

Until she heard them coming.

They were down by the gates, far away for the moment, but there were five of them and they were heading straight for her. Ben barked, and Violet hurriedly pulled him toward the window. Matt was leaning half out, reaching for the dog. She held him up, and Matt pulled him inside. Then he was back, holding his hands out for her. He looked up, eyes widening, pulling his hands back inside the moment their fingers touched.

"Run!"

Violet turned. They were so close! She wouldn't have time to try for the window. She dodged to the right as they closed in, continuing to run. She heard Matt calling out after her.

"Get to the cafeteria!"

She knew where it was, and she was going in the right direction. Her eyes were streaming from the cold air, and she slipped and almost fell over more than once. Rounding the corner of the building, she saw the fire door to the cafeteria up ahead, but it was still closed.

"Matt," Violet cried when she was just a few feet away. "Open the door!"

But there was no one there.

JUST AS SHE WAS ABOUT TO PASS IT, THE DOOR SWUNG
open. Matt was there, and he grabbed her by the
arm, wrenching her inside and pulling the door
shut behind them. The dead hammered their hands
against the wood, but they couldn't get in.

We're safe.

Violet dropped down onto her knees, exhausted.
Her heart was hammering, and her shirt stuck to her
skin. Ben began to lick her face enthusiastically. She
stroked his back with clammy hands. Matt sat down
beside her, out of breath.

"Are you okay?" he asked.

Violet gave him a thumbs-up, too out of breath
to speak.

The two of them sat in silence, the sound of
banging outside eventually slowing before stopping
altogether.

"They'll stand around for a while," Matt said,
nodding to the door. "Then they'll wander off. They
usually do."

"This is so messed up."

"I know."

Violet found herself shaking her head in disbelief.
"How did this even happen?"

Matt leaned against the wall behind him. "I have
no idea. None of us do. One minute, everything was

F
O
U
R

fine. The next... How did it spread so quickly?"

"The bites, I guess."

"But it was so fast."

She shrugged. "Those things don't need to rest. They just bite and feed. I suppose it doesn't take too long to spread over a small town like this."

Matt thought for a moment. "Do you think this is happening everywhere?"

"You mean the rest of the country?"

"The rest of the world."

"I have no idea."

"It must be," Matt concluded. "It's been ten days. Surely the army or someone would've come by now? If no one's got here yet, maybe they're not coming at all?"

Violet rested her head in her hands. "Well, that's a cheerful thought."

MATT, VIOLET, AND BEN MADE THEIR WAY BACK UP TO the teachers' lounge. They hadn't found anything of use besides the lighter, but the others had found candles and flashlights, so the trip wasn't a total loss. Everyone seemed happy to see the dog, and he got a great deal of attention from everyone except Tom, who muttered something about having another mouth to feed before skulking over to the window.

There was more good news. Sam and Joe had found a heavy chain and padlock to secure the school gates, as well as spare keys to make up for the ones Matt had lost.

"We'll lock the gates first thing tomorrow," Sam said. "At least then we won't have to be too scared to walk past the windows, and we'll actually be able to spend some time outside."

"Sounds good," Matt said. He glanced briefly at Violet, and she knew what he was thinking. Hopefully the dead would be gone from the grounds by the morning. They didn't tell the rest of the group about the ones outside, or about Violet almost getting eaten for about the millionth time. There was no sense worrying them, not now that everyone seemed a little more relaxed.

"That's not all," Sam continued. "We need to secure the rest of the school—the other buildings. No point locking ourselves in if there are biters hiding anywhere inside. We'll make sure the whole place is safe, and then we can start to make it more like a home. Until we get rescued at least."

She knew Sam was right, though the idea of exploring the other buildings with no clue what was out there didn't exactly fill Violet with excitement.

THE GROUP WOKE UP EARLY, AND SAM WENT OVER THE plan. The school was made up of three buildings. The main block was where they currently resided, which contained classrooms, the cafeteria, school hall, and changing rooms. There was also the art block, and the science block. There were several small huts scattered around the grounds, too, which were used as extra classrooms.

The group knew the main block was secure, so split into groups to check the others and the rest of the grounds. The school was surrounded by a high brick wall at the front, enclosed at the sides by chain-link fences, and had hedges planted in front for privacy. The only way for the dead to get in and out, provided there were no gaps in the fence, was through the main gate.

Sam and Amy went to the science block, with the plan to lock the gates on the way. Maggie and Joe checked the perimeter for gaps, and Tom and Emily went to the huts. Matt and Violet were given the art block. They took Ben, too. Violet had a weapon now, a baseball bat. It didn't exactly scream 'zombie exterminator,' but felt heavy enough that it could do some damage if brought down on a skull.

The art block was dark, and Violet almost jumped out of her skin when they first entered the textiles room and came face to face with five mannequins. Luckily, however, the building was completely empty. They checked the whole thing in less than twenty minutes, with only one room left. It was the boys' bathroom. Violet stood by the door, waiting for Matt to go in.

"You're not coming?" he asked.

"I'm not a man."

"I'm not sure that's relevant."

Violet was less than convinced. "It's going to be gross in there."

Matt raised an eyebrow. "So you're willing to let me get ripped apart by the undead because 'it might be gross' in there?"

"I think that's pretty accurate, yeah."

Matt laughed. "Fine." He went in alone, flicking on the light switch out of habit.

"Oh, right, no power," he muttered.

Luckily, the art block was set on one level, and the bathroom had a skylight in the roof, which let in a little natural light. Violet propped the door open with her foot as Matt moved further inside.

"I'll be right here, holding the door open."

"How comforting."

Matt disappeared. Violet wasn't worried. If he hadn't encountered one of those things by now, it wasn't in there. Still, she'd feel better when Matt gave the all clear. She could hear him pushing the cubicle doors open with his bat as he passed.

"Huh," she heard him mutter.

"What?" she asked, leaning a little further into the room. 'Huh' wasn't typically the reaction of someone who was getting torn apart by a zombie, so she still felt pretty relaxed. He didn't answer, so she sighed, moving further into the room. It wasn't so bad; clean enough, anyway. Matt was standing at the end of the line of stalls, peering into the last one. Violet joined him. Every inch of that stall was covered in writing. Years and years of graffiti, squeezed into one small space.

"Why is it all in here?" she asked, examining the other stalls, which all had spotless walls.

Matt shrugged. "I know when I went here it was like this—the janitor only kept the ones near the door clear, since the principal never checked further in. Over the years, the guys just stuck to writing in this one."

Violet briefly glanced over the writing. It was the usual stuff she'd expect to see in a school—names written in different styles, phone numbers, kids insulting each other, her name.

My name?

"My name is on here," she exclaimed, swiveling toward Matt. Was he surprised? He didn't look it. In fact, he looked like he was trying not to laugh. She turned back to the wall, reading aloud.

"'Gary's list of hottest eighth graders.'" She rolled her eyes. "How charming."

Matt grinned. "I know."

Violet examined the list. "Eighth grade...this is old." Amy was there, of course. She was second. She'd hate that. Amy hated not being first in anything, even if it was a gross list on a bathroom door. Violet found her own name again.

"Twentieth." She couldn't help but laugh. "Twentieth on a list of twenty."

"At least you made the list." Matt shrugged, smiling. "Lots of girls didn't make the cut."

"Lucky me," Violet replied sarcastically, but she couldn't help but feel a little lighter. It was almost like things were normal; this was the kind of thing two friends might laugh about. Much better than remembering how they had almost died the night before after being chased by flesh-eating monsters.

Violet smiled at Matt, but suddenly felt aware of how cramped it was in the small stall. She was practically standing on his feet.

"Sorry," she spluttered, clumsily tripping over him in her haste to get out.

Smooth, Violet, very smooth.

ON THEIR WAY BACK TO THE TEACHERS' LOUNGE, MATT and Violet ran into Tom. He was standing on top of the wall at the front of the school. He faced the street, holding several small rocks in his hand. Matt caught Violet's eye and raised an eyebrow.

"What are you doing?" Matt called over.

"Practicing," was Tom's lazy reply. Matt climbed onto the garbage can by the wall, joining Tom at the top and holding out a hand to help Violet up, too. She looked down at the street. It was empty except for one zombie—a woman. She had no legs and was on the ground by the wall, reaching out her arms and hungrily snapping her jaws. Tom threw another rock, which hit the side of the creature's head. She hissed, but continued to reach up toward him.

"Practicing for what?" Matt asked.

"Just practicing. You never know when we'll next have to fight these things."

"I'm not sure throwing rocks at one that can hardly move is that useful," Matt replied, watching the creature almost pityingly. "Where's Emily?"

Tom shrugged. "Went inside, I think."

"Can't imagine why," Violet muttered.

"We should go, too," Matt began. "Doing this will just bring more over."

"So?"

"We don't want a big crowd of them outside."

"We've locked the gates. It doesn't matter."

Violet frowned. "Listen, Tom, I don't want to sound rude, but what you're doing is weird and creepy. If you want to be weird and creepy on your own, go ahead, but we don't want the dead piling up at the gates."

Tom glanced at her momentarily, then threw another rock. Matt sighed, motioning for Violet to climb down.

"He's a jerk," Violet whispered.

"Yeah, he's been through a lot."

"So have all of us."

"It was a nice touch to say you weren't being rude before you called him creepy." Matt sounded serious, but there was a smile playing on his lips. "Otherwise, it could've sounded really mean."

"I do what I can."

THE SCHOOL WAS SECURE, WITH NO BITERS INSIDE. SAM had locked the gates, and the group came back to the teachers' lounge to eat. There wasn't much: a few packets of chips, cans of beans, and candy bars taken from a pried-open vending machine. Violet wondered how long they had been surviving on stuff like this.

She was hungry, which was something she added to her *'things that prove I'm not dead'* list. It wasn't very long. In fact, it was the only thing on it so far. And she'd had to add *'food has no taste'* to the other list she was mentally compiling of *'things that suggest I might be dead.'* Everything she put in her mouth had virtually no flavor whatsoever. Still, she tried not to think about it, and was just grateful she hadn't accidentally eaten anyone today.

Sam sat forward on his chair, clearly about to speak. Everyone looked over, and Violet realized he was the leader of the group. No one had said it—not Sam, not the others—but they didn't need to. He could hold their attention without saying a word.

"We're safe here now," he began, meeting each of their eyes. "The school is clear of biters, and the gates are locked. Now we need to think long term."

"Long term?" Amy asked. "Aren't we waiting to get rescued?"

"The chances of that get smaller every day. Of course, being rescued is the ideal scenario, and we'll keep waiting, but we need to take steps to make sure we can survive here in the meantime."

Matt nodded. "I agree. We don't know how far this thing has spread. Probably across the whole state by now. Otherwise, we'd see signs of rescue, or at least quarantine. But there are no road blocks, no helicopters. Nothing."

"It could be even further," Joe suggested. "Might have spread across the whole country. Maybe the world."

"Let's not think about that right now," Sam interrupted. "We need to focus on making this place somewhere we can call 'home'. For now, at least. So let's talk about what we need."

Violet spoke first. "We need more water. It may still be running at the moment, but the power's off and we don't know how long it'll be before the pipes run dry."

Sam began to write on a notepad. "Okay, so we'll set up buckets to collect rainwater, as many as we can get."

"We also need more food," Matt suggested. "We've got enough for a little while longer, thanks to Emily finding those boxes in the storeroom, but not enough. We could get bottled water, too."

Joe nodded. "We could start to think about places to go for this stuff. Matt said most of the houses around here haven't got much. There are a few stores in town. Those are probably our best bet, but we should draw out maps to find the best route away from places we know there are likely to be more biters." He looked at Violet. "You've been out there. Maybe you could help."

"I didn't see much. I was too busy running," Violet said doubtfully, not wanting to get his hopes up.

"Anything's better than nothing."

"Sure, okay."

"We should also make a sign, put it on the roof or something," Amy added. "For when the rescue comes. We want them to know we're here."

The others murmured their agreement, but Violet wondered if they were thinking what she was, which was whether there was anyone left to rescue them at all.

Good. Let's keep that positivity going.

JOE AND VIOLET WERE SEARCHING FOR ANY CONTAINERS they could put outside to try to catch rainwater. They grabbed a cart from the science block, then began their hunt. So far, they had three buckets, some jugs, and a couple of mugs.

"I always hated biology," Joe muttered, passing Violet another measuring jug.

"I was never very good at it," she admitted.

"I was okay, but Mrs. Addams hated me."

"How do you know?" Violet asked, examining a coffee

mug, then putting it back with a grimace. She wasn't sure any amount of soap would get rid of that much mold.

"She always used to give me bad grades," Joe continued.

"Maybe you're just not that clever?" she teased.

Joe smiled. "Nah. Well...maybe. But I remember one time I didn't study for a test, so I copied Sam's paper. Literally copied every answer, yet I got a D and he got a B!"

"Really?"

"Yeah."

"And she didn't say why?"

Joe waved his hand absentmindedly. "I don't know, something about some of my answers being put on the wrong questions. I wasn't really listening."

Violet laughed, finding another bucket and adding it to their collection. Joe picked up a couple of test tubes. "Do you think these would be any good?"

He reached to put the tubes in the cart, but then lost his balance, tripping over his own feet and stumbling into the table in front of him. One of the glass tubes shattered in his hand as he reached out to stop himself from falling. Joe swore, dropping the bloodied pieces. He examined his hand before grinning at Violet.

"I bet that looked pretty cool. No woman can resist a man who struggles to stay upright when standing completely still." He laughed, but Violet barely heard him, unable to tear her eyes away from the blood dripping from the cut on his palm. He followed her gaze, misinterpreting the stare.

"I'll be okay. Can you pass me that cloth?" He gestured over her shoulder.

Violet could barely think straight. Everything was becoming hazy. Her head was pounding, and she could hardly breathe.

No. No, not this. Not again.

She grabbed the cloth, threw it at Joe, and then ran from the room, barely able to put one foot in front of the other. Fighting every instinct she had, she ran from the building, not stopping until she was at the edge of the playing fields. The cold air whipped around her face, and slowly things began to come into focus. Violet dropped down onto the wet grass, her head in her hands. That had been too close.

Okay, so now I know. If I want to avoid zombieism, I need to keep away from blood.

F I V E

VIOLET HAD BEEN IN SELF-IMPOSED ISOLATION FOR A week. She'd found a classroom down in the art block, and spent her days alone, other than for Ben. Amy usually came down once a day to paint in the room next door, but the others had kept away. Violet might've felt hurt by that, if it wasn't for the fact she was terrified she'd lose control and eat them if they got too close.

Violet filled her days with reading. She'd grabbed a suitcase full of books from the library, setting up in one of the smaller studios, and had barely left since. She slept down there, too. So far, no one had really questioned it. The rest of the group stuck together, sleeping and eating up in the teachers' lounge. She ate alone, which was less depressing when food had no taste anyway.

She'd finally completed her '*am I or aren't I dead*' list, but had yet to come to any conclusions. Things that suggested she was dead included the change in her skin tone and eye color, food having no taste, and the small fact that she'd killed and eaten at least one person.

Then, on the opposing side, were the few things that suggested she was alive—like the fact the zombies still tried to kill her, she could feel her heart beating, and she still bled. She'd tested that last one the old-fashioned way—with a knife. A small cut on her arm was enough to check, and though the blood had been darker than she remembered, it was warm and flowed quickly. The fact she still ate and still went to the bathroom also suggested she wasn't full-zombie. However, proving she might still be alive didn't change the fact that she wasn't altogether 'normal'.

Living or not, eating people was a switch, and it meant that whatever infected the biters had done something to her, too. At least the others didn't suspect anything. Amy knew about the bite, of course, so didn't question Violet's change in appearance. She seemed to assume it was a harmless side effect of being 'immune' to the virus. It hadn't put her friend off coming down to eat lunch with her most days. Violet knew Amy wanted to ask why she had suddenly shut herself away, but she didn't. Perhaps she was frightened about what the answer might be. Maybe that was why she mostly left her alone.

Until now.

Violet raised her head at the sound of the door opening. Amy and Matt stood in the doorway, both observing her as though she were a sick relative they were visiting. They approached tentatively.

"Hi?" Violet began.

"We thought you might like some company," Amy said. "We brought breakfast."

Violet smiled, trying to seem grateful for the candy bar she held.

Mmm, unflavored. My favorite.

Violet had run out of water, so Matt went to get some. The taps ran dry a few days ago, so they'd had to resort to the buckets and containers spread around outside. After he left, a guilty expression crossed Amy's face.

Violet scowled. "Why are you really here?"

"Like I said, we thought you might like company."

"You know I don't. I've been alone for the past week."

"Yeah, and it's not healthy. I don't know what's wrong, but you need to snap out of it. We miss you."

Violet lifted a brow skeptically. Amy continued, her tone changing a little. "Matt insisted. He's worried about you; we all are. I know you want space, and I managed to keep him away so far. I told him you had diarrhea."

"Oh, thanks."

Amy missed the sarcasm. "You're welcome. I said it was really bad, and you'd be mortified if you had an accident in front of him."

"What an awesome thing to share."

Amy was still oblivious, beaming at her ingenuity. "I know, and it seemed to work, but he wouldn't take no for an answer today." She grinned. "I think *he* missed you the most."

Violet groaned. It was like they were back in Amy's room again—Amy teasing her about boys, Violet denying they even existed. She didn't get a chance to argue, though, because Matt reappeared with three cups of water.

"Did I miss anything?" he asked, sitting beside her.

"No," Violet insisted before Amy could embarrass her even further.

"How are you doing?" he asked, looking more than a little concerned.

Violet glared at Amy. "Fine."

The three of them ate in comfortable silence, though Matt watched her closely and kept asking how she was feeling.

"Make sure you're drinking lots of water. You can get dehydrated when you have di—"

"Thanks, Matt, but I'm fine," she interrupted, plotting all the ways she could punish Amy for her 'helpful' lie.

When they were done, she noticed Amy and Matt giving each other sideways glances.

"What?" she asked, feeling like she was missing some secret. "Do I have something in my teeth?"

Amy laughed, but Matt looked serious. When he spoke, his voice was full of concern.

"Why are you down here?"

Violet was momentarily surprised by his bluntness. Even Amy hadn't asked outright. She didn't really know what to say.

I'm here so I don't eat you.

"I just..." Violet searched for an answer. Amy offered

no help, smiling a little at Matt's forwardness. Violet scowled at her before answering: "I needed some space. To take everything in." It was a weak answer, and even she could hear how unconvincing it sounded. Matt was nice enough not to probe any further. However, Amy seemingly couldn't resist the opportunity to push it.

"But you're ready to come back now, right?"

Violet shot daggers at her. "I guess so."

It'll be your fault if I eat you, Amy Lowe.

Matt smiled, "That's great! Anyway, we should get upstairs. Sam wants to have a meeting."

"What about?"

Matt shrugged, "Not sure, but maybe it's about the food situation. There's barely anything left."

BACK IN THE TEACHERS' LOUNGE, THE REST OF THE GROUP were already gathered in the seating area. Eyes were on Sam, but heads turned when Violet walked in. She supposed she had been a bit of a ghost recently. Sam smiled at her, and then addressed the group.

"Okay, as I was saying, our best option is the supermarket in town. We know it's guaranteed to have lots of food, and it's unlikely to have been fully looted yet."

"Yeah, and we know why," Joe piped up. "Emily said when she was out there, she passed loads of biters outside the front doors."

Emily nodded. "There must have been almost a hundred."

"There's a back entrance," Sam continued, undeterred. "If we go in that way, they'll never even know we were there. We just make sure we steer clear of the front of the building, it's made of glass."

"This sounds super fun," Joe said sarcastically.

Sam shrugged. "I know, but we have no choice. Not only is it the nearest place, but it's our best chance at getting a good amount of supplies. I don't want us to have to go out again for as long as possible."

"There's another place," Violet said. "There's a

convenience store not too far from here. I was in it the morning I got here. It has food." She shuddered, remembering the man she killed. He would still be on the floor.

Matt cocked his head. "Are you okay?"

"She's still getting over her illness," Amy piped up helpfully.

"What illness?" Joe asked.

"She had diarr—"

"I'm fine," Violet interrupted, shaking her head. She continued, "It's not as big as the supermarket, nowhere near, but last time I was there, it was clear of the dead. It's got food, water, and a few other things we might need."

"Candles?" Sam asked. "Batteries?"

Violet struggled to remember. She hadn't had much time to browse before she'd started eating the guy who lived there. "Maybe. I'm not sure."

"It's worth a try," Joe said to Sam.

Sam considered this for a moment. "Okay, let's give it a shot. Now for the big question. Who's coming?"

There was a silence. Violet knew none of them were exactly keen to go outside again, back into the unknown with the dead.

"I'll go," Matt said, raising his hand.

Joe sighed. "It's not like I've got anything better to do." Sam smiled.

The three of them turned to Tom, who had been silent throughout the whole discussion.

"Me?" Tom asked, almost incredulous that anyone would suggest he should go.

"I need at least one more person," Sam explained. "It will mean more supplies, and keep us safer." Tom said nothing, and Violet couldn't help but bite her lip when she saw the expressions on Joe and Matt's faces. Clearly neither of them was thrilled with the idea of spending the day outside with Tom.

"Fine," he finally gave in.

Sam grinned. "Good, okay, the rest of you stay here. We'll probably be out most of the day, but we'll be back before dark."

"Unless we get eaten," Joe added, and Emily slapped him on the arm.

The guys made to leave, but Violet stepped in front of Sam. "I want to come, too."

"You don't need to," he replied. "You can just tell us where the place is."

She shook her head, not entirely sure why she was pushing this, but feeling like she needed to. "I'm the only one who's been out there recently. And I can't sit around here waiting." She didn't break eye contact. "Please."

Matt shook his head, but Sam agreed. "Okay. Grab your weapon."

Sam and Tom left the room, but Matt and Joe stayed behind. Both looked nervous.

"We'll be fine," Violet said, sounding more confident than she felt.

"This is going to be hell," Joe groaned, sounding like a little boy.

"It might not be too bad out there," Matt suggested.

Joe shook his head. "No, a whole day with Tom. If anything, I'm praying for zombies just to give us a break from his voice." He winked and headed out of the door. Violet laughed so hard she snorted.

Attractive. Good one.

Matt's eyes were still on her. "I'll be fine," she insisted.

He didn't look convinced. "Stay close to me."

Violet raised an eyebrow. "Of the two of us, who lasted outside for the longest? I think I can handle myself."

No, Violet, you got bitten on day one by the second zombie you met.

Sam unlocked the gates, handing the chain and padlock to Amy. He, Violet, Tom, Matt, and Joe stepped outside into the cool air. According to Matt's watch, which he held out for Violet to read, it was only eleven. They had the best part of the day to hunt for supplies. Ben stood at Violet's side. He wasn't on his leash anymore. She thought he'd probably be useful to have around; he might be able to warn them about the dead before they got too close.

Sam had wanted to find a car, but it was easier said than done. None of the group exactly had any experience jacking a vehicle. Their best bet was to find one with the keys still inside. Sam was glancing in the windows, trying the doors of each one they passed. They'd been walking for a while now, and so far, no luck.

"Violet, you said we should avoid South Street, right?" Joe asked, looking at the map they had constructed before leaving.

"Yes. We might just about be able to get past now. We could climb over the wreckage. But if we do find a car, there's no way we can get through."

"Getting a car seemed like such a simple idea," Sam muttered, trying another locked door. "Not having any luck with these."

"It's weird that no one was considerate enough to leave their cars for us to steal after the dead came back to life..." Joe mused.

"Let's just see what happens," Matt said. "We're not too far now if I'm thinking of the right place?"

Violet looked ahead, pointing with her baseball bat. "It's just over there." She could see the store in the distance, so she needed to come clean. Not completely—she wasn't insane—but she had to let them know what they were about to find.

"There's something I should tell you all about this place."

"There's a dead body in there?" Sam guessed immediately.

"Yes."

"Someone you knew?"

"No." That was true at least. "He was dead when I arrived." That part was less true.

"Any biters around?" Joe asked. "He didn't get bitten, right?"

Uh-oh, getting into dangerous waters here. Time to get a little vague.

"I think he did," she began. "I'm not sure, but he was definitely dead. Like, not-getting-up dead."

The others seemed happy enough with that, which was good, as they were now at the store. Sam went first, cautiously opening the door. The rest of the group followed behind. Violet was last inside. She could see him now. The corpse looked even worse in such bright light. The blood had pooled around his body, and the remains of his face stared at her accusingly. There were bite marks all over his face and neck, as well as on what was left of his arm. Violet sucked in her breath, hearing Joe do the same.

"Wow. Yes, Violet, I'd say he was definitely bitten."

"I tried not to look," she muttered, heading to the back of the store and beginning to load up her bag with food.

"On the neck as well," Sam was still examining the remains. "And the wrist, but it's the head injury that killed him. My guess is he fell onto part of a broken shelf—the metal went straight through the back of his head, which is why he hasn't turned. Violet, you didn't see any biters in here when you arrived?"

She shook her head, not able to meet his eyes.

Sam continued, "Hopefully whoever chewed up this guy's face got distracted by something else and left, but I'll check the back of the store just in case. Joe, come with me?"

"Great, love to, thanks."

Violet turned in time to see Joe grab a candy bar, rip open the packet with his teeth, and follow Sam out of a door behind the counter and up a set of stairs. She, Matt, and Tom stayed downstairs, splitting up to collect supplies. Violet was confident Sam and Joe wouldn't find any biters—seeing as the zombie who chewed the guy's face off was currently in the store loading up on cans of soup—but she knew they had to be sure.

Ben sat beside her as she filled the bag with as much as it would hold. She glanced over at Tom, who appeared to be trying to reach the dirty magazines on the higher shelves. Matt came over and stood on her other side.

"Are you okay?" he asked.

"Yeah, fine. It seems to be going pretty well."

"Oh yeah, of all the group pillages I've been on during the countless undead apocalypses, this is at least in the top five." He grinned. "How long were you here? The first time, I mean."

"Not long. I came in to get away from the zombies...I mean, the biters."

"Zombies. I suppose that's what they are," Matt considered. "I haven't been able to call them that; it just always sounded weird, like the ones you see in films where they're all green and eat brains."

"And walk slowly."

"Yes!" Matt agreed enthusiastically. "Why are these so fast?"

Violet shrugged. "I guess we—"

"Get out! Get out! Get out!"

Sam and Joe came barreling into the room at full speed, both shouting for the others to run. Violet soon saw why; there were three biters close behind them. The guys were already at the door, running back out into the street. Violet forgot about her bag, sprinting for the exit, too. Ben darted ahead, slipping out first. Tom and Violet reached the door at the same time, and he shoved her aside to make sure he got out first. Matt swore at him loudly, pushing Violet through next. Then he was out, and Sam pulled the door shut behind them. He and Joe held it closed as the creatures pounded against it.

"Why the hell did you open that door?" Sam asked Joe angrily. "It was covered in blood!"

"I forgot!"

"Who forgets not to open a door covered in blood when there are monsters literally everywhere?"

"I don't know why you're asking that question, because we both know the answer is obviously me!"

"Wait." Matt eyed the glass door, interrupting the heated exchange. "I think you can move away."

Sam followed his gaze, and then seemed to understand. He and Joe both stepped away. The door only opened inwards. While the creatures threw their weight against it, they had no chance of getting it open.

"I guess they haven't mastered handles yet," Joe noted.

"Where were they?" Violet asked, trying to catch her breath after ten seconds of cardio.

"Up in a room upstairs" Sam said, without so much of a bead of sweat on his forehead. "Might've been his family." He motioned toward the store, to the dead man on the floor. Violet took another look at the ones by the door: a woman, an older man, and another one about the same age as the one she'd half eaten.

"No chance of getting the food now." Tom groaned. "Our bags are still inside."

"But..." Sam said, a trace of a smile on his lips. "All is not lost." He held up his hand, jangling a keychain from it. On it was an electronic car key. Violet felt her whole body lighten; she'd feel safer in a car. Sam pressed the button triumphantly.

Nothing.

He frowned, pressing it again.

Still nothing.

"This is a little anti-climactic," Joe muttered.

"It might not be parked here," Matt suggested.

"It could be close," Violet said. "Those keys don't have a long range. Let's check the cars over there." She pointed to a cluster further down the road.

Sam agreed. "It's got to be one of those. Things are looking up. Our luck's changing!"

The positive mood was immediately broken by the sound of glass breaking. The group spun around instinctively, but the door to the store was still intact.

What was it?

Then she saw it; a nearby house had a broken downstairs window. There was someone on the ground—a living person. The woman was getting to her feet. Violet realized she must've fallen through the window. Or maybe she threw herself out, because she had her eyes fixed on the house, as if terrified she would be followed.

"Why did she—"

Before the question had left Violet's lips, it was answered when one after the other, several biters jumped out of the window after the woman. They forced her to the ground, then proceeded to rip her apart. She screamed, but only for a second.

Violet and the others said nothing. As if they were

too frightened of making a single sound. They couldn't do anything but watch. At least until the biters saw them. It was just one at first, but it screeched loudly, and then the others snapped their heads up. They forgot their meal, jumping to their feet and flooding toward the group.

"Go!" Sam yelled, and they ran for the parked cars at the end of the street. Sam held out the keys, pressing the button repeatedly. "Come on," he cried, his voice full of exasperation. Violet's legs were already beginning to wobble, and she felt the familiar burn in the back of her throat.

If I survive this, I need to start running laps. This is just embarrassing.

Sam was still jabbing at the button on the keys. Success! One of the cars suddenly lit up, unlocking.

"Get in!"

"Hurry up!"

"They're almost here!"

"Move!"

Matt opened the back door, letting Violet get inside first with Ben. Sam and Joe got into the front, with Sam behind the wheel and Joe riding shotgun. Tom ran around the other side, getting in to sit beside Violet. Matt climbed in last, sitting on her right. Matt slammed his door just as the creatures arrived. They pounded on the glass hungrily.

"Go!"

"Sam, drive!"

"Go!"

"Come on!"

"Why aren't we moving?"

"Driving would be good, Sam."

"Shut up, Joe!"

The car wouldn't start. Sam swore loudly, trying again. Nothing. It choked and spluttered, but wouldn't move. There were more zombies now, drawn by the noise. They surrounded the car. Ben whined on Violet's lap. Joe and Tom were still yelling at Sam, but Matt just looked at her. She knew what he was thinking.

We're going to die in here.

"TRY AGAIN," JOE CRIED.

"Turn it slowly," Tom shouted.

"No, slow and then fast!"

"Pop the clutch first!"

Sam pounded his hands on the wheel in exasperation. "Do you want to drive? Just shut up!"

Matt was holding Violet's hand. She couldn't remember when he had taken hold of it, but she was clutching his just as tightly, aware she was probably cutting off his circulation.

Finally, after what felt like an eternity, the car spluttered to life, and she took a breath for probably the first time since they'd gotten inside. Sam edged the car forward, pushing back the dead. Once he had cleared a little room, he accelerated, leaving the monsters behind. Violet's heart rate finally began to return to normal. She glanced down at her hand, realizing she was still gripping Matt's. She smiled awkwardly, letting go. His lips curved up, but she caught sight of him stealthily rubbing his hand, as if trying to get the blood to flow back into it.

"We'll have to try the supermarket," Sam said. "We can't go back with nothing."

The others agreed, and they spent the rest of the journey in silence. Violet couldn't help but think they had just been incredibly lucky to get out with no one

S
I
X

being bitten. Would they be that fortunate again?

SAM DROVE INTO THE SUPERMARKET PARKING LOT, WHICH was surprisingly full.

"End of the world and we can't even find a parking spot," Matt muttered. "Now that's depressing."

Violet shook her head. "Not as much as you calling it the end of the world. Don't do that."

Sam stopped the car at the edge of the parking lot, and they all climbed out, heading silently toward the back of the store. There was a door next to the huge shutter at the back. Violet knew from her brief time working there the summer before that the shutter was for unloading deliveries from the large trucks. The back door was shut and locked, but there was a small gap under the shutter.

"What do you think?" Violet asked.

Sam studied the gap, considering it. "I doubt the biters would know to squeeze under that. It could be clear. Still, let's be careful." He went first, laying on his stomach and sliding into the darkness. The rest of the group followed.

It was pitch black inside the warehouse. "Let's go into the store," Sam whispered, "I don't like the idea of stumbling around back here. It'll take us five times as long to find what we need."

Plus, we don't know what's hiding in the darkness.

He didn't say it, but Violet knew it was what he was thinking. It was what they were all thinking.

When Sam opened the door to the store, the smell hit like a wave. Each of them clapped their hands over their noses. It was rotten and putrid—the foulest thing Violet had ever smelled—and she'd eaten a dead person before. The air seemed to hang, sour and heavy, all around them.

"What is that?" Tom choked.

"Power's out. It's the food rotting," Sam replied, moving his hand away from his nose and gesturing to the lights on the ceiling with his bat. "It's not too bad when you get used to it." He paused. "Be right back."

He quickly moved out of sight. Slowly, the others

took their hands away from their noses, tentatively taking small breaths. The smell was still there, of course, but Sam was right. It wasn't so bad after a little while.

Sam reappeared.

"Where did you go?" Violet asked.

"The front of the store is all glass," he explained. "I wanted to make sure none of them were out there." He gestured for the others to follow before heading back in the direction he just came. They fell into step behind him.

"And we're okay?" Violet asked.

"Yeah, I can't see anything. I did a quick sweep of the aisles, too. There aren't any of them here. Besides, Tom would've led them straight to us with all his heaving."

Violet glanced over her shoulder. Tom didn't seem to have heard. He was still holding his nose, his eyes darting rapidly back and forth. Sam led the group to a small collection of carts at the front of the store, and they each took one. Violet glanced outside; it was completely deserted. A few of the bordering stores had their windows smashed, and there was a lot of garbage blowing around in the wind. There were corpses, too, or what was left of them, rotting on the ground. But no walking ones, at least not yet.

"Our priority is food and water," Sam began. "We're fine for water right now, thanks to all the rain we've collected, but we won't always be so lucky. Get as much as you can." Violet and the others nodded. Sam continued. "There are the other things almost as important. Matches, candles, batteries, anything you can think of." He addressed Violet. "You're in charge of those."

She nodded again. They dispersed, all heading in different directions. Joe whistled for Ben to follow him. Violet knew the sorts of things Sam wanted her to get, but she also had a very clear idea of the other things they *needed.* Her first stop was the magazine section. She didn't check the covers, just grabbed one of everything and threw it into the cart. She suddenly had the feeling she was being watched, so she turned to find Matt regarding her with a strange expression—half smiling, half confused.

"Can I help you?" she asked, raising an eyebrow.

"What are you doing?"

"I need more reading material. *We* need more reading material."

"Right, it's just that we live in a school. There's a library."

Violet smiled. "Matt, I'm not sure you understand. Amy and I need to know what the celebrities are doing...or *were* doing. We need to read seedy real-life stories like..." She grabbed the nearest magazine and read aloud. "*My boyfriend stole my kidney and ran away with my sister.* We need those to be entertained. I'm afraid our library is severely lacking in material of this caliber."

Matt considered this for a moment, then grabbed at least five different music magazines. "Okay. In that case, we need these, too." He gestured toward the back of the store. "I'm going to get as much water as I can. Then I'll take it to the car and come back for more. Sam's going to come with me."

Violet felt a slight pang in her stomach. "Be careful."

After giving her a reassuring smile, he headed off.

She picked up another magazine. Reading them wasn't just about entertainment—it was escapism. If she could read about what celebrities wore to a party 'last week,' she might be able to kid herself they weren't drooling monsters right now.

As she made her way toward the batteries, Violet passed Sam. He was loading up on canned food, and his cart was practically groaning under the weight of the cans, bottles of sauce, and dried pasta.

"This is great," Violet said. "All that stuff should last forever."

"Going to try to take as much as possible, especially now we have a car. We don't want to have to come back. Joe found a camping stove, too, so we'll be able to cook." He began to push his cart toward the back doors. "I'm going to take this to the car with the water Matt's got, then we'll be back."

Violet hated the idea of the two of them leaving, but it wasn't like they had a choice. Besides, if anyone was able to take care of himself, as well as Matt, it was Sam. She could see why the others respected him so much. He was a born leader.

Violet moved on to the next aisle, which was pet food. Ben was already there, shredding some poor toy that happened to be on a low shelf. Violet put three huge bags of dried dog food into the cart, as well as some treats. Sam might argue it wasn't 'essential,' but she was willing to fight her corner. She unwrapped a bone and passed it to Ben, who wagged his tail excitedly and ran off with his new prize.

In the next aisle, Violet grabbed eight toothbrushes and at least forty tubes of toothpaste. She threw in as much shampoo as she imagined Sam would allow without it being 'a waste of space,' reasoning that being able to have proper showers would at least bring a touch of normality back into their lives.

Plus, there was the smell.

Following that theme, she also piled in soap, razors, shaving cream, and deodorant. She was pretty sure Sam wouldn't fight her too much over the last one. With eight people living practically on top of each other, things weren't exactly daisy fresh.

Violet heard footsteps behind her. She turned to see Joe approaching with his cart, which he purposefully crashed into hers. He grinned, examining what she had so far.

"You know what? I think you win the award for 'worst looter'. We're living through the apocalypse, and you stock up on magazines, dog food, and shampoo." He was speaking in a serious voice, but Violet knew he was joking. She smiled, taking the opportunity to scrutinize his own cart.

"Okay then, what do we have here?" She picked up various items. "Wine, vodka, string, and..." She leaned further into the cart to pick out the small box. "Condoms? Why?"

Joe snatched them back with a laugh. "Oh, come on, Violet. We've been locked up together for over two weeks. Hormones have been going crazy. Don't you feel it?"

He raised an eyebrow in a mock-seductive fashion, but she remained stone faced. Joe continued, "So I decided to get some alcohol so we could have this wild party. But what happens if things get out of hand—which is likely in the situation we're in. Everyone's getting hot and heavy, but thinking, 'We can't do it. What if I get pregnant and my baby is this weird zombie thing?' That's when I walk in, condoms in hand, and am, therefore, the savior." He finished his speech with a little bow. Victoriously, he threw the box back into the cart.

"Okay, let's pretend for a second that what you just said is even the smallest bit possible—which it's not—why have you only got one box?"

"I'm not a machine."

Violet finally cracked, giggling at his serious expression. Joe grinned, taking the box out of the cart and tossing it over the aisle.

"Okay, fine. That all makes perfect sense. What's the string for?"

Joe shrugged. "I don't know. You always need string, right?"

Rolling her eyes playfully, she moved on, pushing Joe's cart out of the way with her own. She grabbed as many batteries, boxes of matches, and candles as she could, reasoning it would be good to get a least a few things from Sam's list, then moved to the next aisle. She passed Tom, who was loading his cart up with toilet paper. They'd been okay so far, but Violet didn't look forward to the depressing day when they'd have to start rationing that, too.

Who said the apocalypse would be glamorous?

"Hey, everyone come here!" It was Sam's voice. He was back. Violet left her cart behind, jogging in the direction of the sound. She arrived just after the others. Sam was standing next to a puddle of blood.

"How did we miss this?" Violet asked. "We've been walking around in here for at least half an hour."

"It was behind that." Sam pointed at a huge metal container full of cartons of milk. "I wouldn't have thought to move it if Ben hadn't been sniffing around so much."

"Is it fresh?" Matt asked.

Violet couldn't tell by sight. By the looks of it, neither

could the others. But she was still in control of herself at least. It must only be when someone was actively bleeding that she started to lose it.

Well, isn't that comforting?

No one made any motion to answer Matt's question. So she sighed, kneeling and putting her finger into the puddle. She pulled it out to examine the blood. Joe sucked in his breath behind her.

"Violet, that's really gross."

She ignored him. "It's not congealed. This happened recently." She took a breath, reassured that even with relatively fresh blood on her finger, she was still in control.

"Look." Sam pointed to the right of the puddle, where there were more spatters of blood. They formed a trail, which lead to a door by the fridges. "It goes through there."

Joe backed up. "Cool. Let's go the other way. Nothing good ever comes from following a blood trail."

Violet couldn't help but think Joe might be on to something, but Sam was already pushing the doors open, Ben trotting beside him. Violet caught Joe's eye. He shrugged defeatedly before following Sam through the door. Tom, Matt, and Violet were close behind.

There was something in the air now, a smell that crept up on Violet, settling over her like a warm blanket. It was intoxicating—like baking bread, maple syrup, and every other mouthwatering smell she could imagine. None of the others seemed to have noticed it, and this made her more than a tad nervous about what they were heading toward. She paused, standing still for a moment, and Matt seemed to mistake her action for fear of the dead. He gave her hand a little squeeze, then stepped in front of her so she didn't have to be first into the next room.

Oh, Matt, if only you knew. I'm not scared of finding a zombie. I'm scared of becoming a zombie. I'm pretty sure that will get in the way of our future hand holding.

The door led to a small and grubby breakroom. There were a couple of couches, some vending machines, and a bulletin board. Ben moved ahead of the group, sniffing at another set of doors. Violet already knew where they needed to go without his help. She was following the smell, too, but she kept back. Sam reached for the handle, pushing one of the doors open.

There was a new smell. Not of sour milk and rotting food, or the delicious one from earlier. This was decaying flesh. On the floor lay a man. He wore cleaning overalls, and a fire extinguisher for a hat. Technically, the fire extinguisher was lodged in what was left of the top of his head, but Violet thought her description was a little nicer.

The blood had pooled around his body. Violet looked at the dark blood around the man's head. "This is old. It's not the same as the stuff we're following."

Sam nodded in agreement. The delicious smell was still there, in the background, and Violet realized it was coming from a door to her right. She saw the trail of fresh blood also continued through this door. *Security* was written on the frosted glass.

Violet moved to open the door, but was gently pushed aside by Matt, who went in first. He was closely followed by Sam and Joe, with Tom behind them. Violet found herself at the back of the line. She took a breath, not altogether disappointed to be going in last, and stepped inside.

There was a man sitting at a desk, facing at least twenty small screens. None of them were switched on. He had very short hair, as though he used to shave his head but hadn't been able to for a while. He appeared strong, but had clearly let himself go over recent years and developed quite a beer gut. His right arm was held close to his chest, and Violet could see blood seeping slowly from the wound, which was half hidden by his other hand.

Stepping back, she hit the door roughly. She knew she shouldn't be so close; there was too much blood. She should run, get away before she lost control, but she couldn't. The others might start to wonder what was wrong with her.

They'll also figure it out when you eat him, Violet. Get out of here!

I can't. As long as I'm not too close, I'm safe. They're safe.

The room had a small window, which was cracked open. She moved a little closer to it, trying to breathe in the fresh air rather than the tempting smell. She glanced around the room—looking at everything except the man—and saw it had clearly been lived in for a while. There were empty bags of potato chips, candy wrappers, sandwich packages, beer, and soda cans everywhere.

"So," the man began, making Violet jump a little after such a long silence. He didn't face them, his eyes still on the blackened screens. "Stealing from me? Going to take what you want and leave me with no food?"

Sam opened his mouth like he was about to interrupt, but the man cut him off. "I knew it would come to this—gangs of looters roaming the streets, taking what they want and leaving everyone else to rot. That's what this world is now. As if it was ever any different..." He swiveled the chair around, surveying the group with anger and disgust. Violet couldn't help but picture a villain from an old spy movie, and half expected to see him menacingly stroking a fluffy cat.

"Please," she insisted, seeing where this was going. "We had no idea there was anyone here. We've been living in the school, but we've run out of food. Can we take some of yours? We'll leave you with plenty for yourself."

The man didn't reply. Matt moved a little closer. "Do you want us to have a look at your wound?"

"It's fine," he said, but held his arm out all the same. It was a bite. They all knew what that meant. He was infected. He would turn. Even now, the smell in the air was changing. It was still pleasant but becoming weaker. Another was taking its place, one of damp leaves and rotting fruit. The temptation Violet had felt when she stepped into the room was dying, and she was able to move a little closer.

"When did you get bitten?" Matt asked.

"Not long. About an hour ago?"

Sam and Joe glanced at each other, and Violet saw Sam tighten his grip on the baseball bat. He raised an eyebrow at her, but she shook her head. The man hadn't turned yet. Sam didn't need to end it. Not right now.

Maybe he won't turn at all? Maybe he's like me?

You know he's not. He smells like the dead.

"If you were bitten, it means—" Tom began, but Violet interrupted.

"It means you're bleeding. We should cover the wound before it gets infected." She moved closer still, taking some bandages and gauze from the table in front of him. She threw a look at Sam. *Don't tell him,* she pleaded with her eyes. *He doesn't know what it means. There's nothing we can do, but don't let him suffer knowing what's coming.*

Sam gave a small nod. Violet wrapped the man's arm, unable to ignore the fact that the damp smell was getting stronger, while the pleasant one became more faint.

"What's your name?" Matt asked.

"Steve. I worked here, was doing the night shift when it all went to hell." He pointed to the door, to the room with the dead body. "That thing out there, he was fine when I arrived, but when I went to open the store the next morning, he attacked me. I used to be in the army, so I had no problem restraining him, but I knew there was something weird going on. No matter what I said or did, he kept trying to hurt me. Eventually, I couldn't hold him down any longer. I had to cave in his head with the fire extinguisher."

"But that's not how you got the bite," Matt continued, gesturing to his bandaged arm. "This is new."

An emotion Violet didn't recognize crossed Steve's face. "A few days ago, I decided I couldn't take it anymore. I tried to leave. I wanted to go home, see if...see if there was anything still there. I opened the shutters at the back and went out. I saw someone I knew. I wanted to trap her out there, so she would be safe. I was thinking if they found a cure... Anyway, she bit me."

"There is no cure," Sam interrupted. "Those things have lost their minds. They have no memories, no thoughts, no soul."

Gee, thanks. Even though the words stung, Violet worked hard to keep her face blank.

"They're infected," Sam continued. "They're dead."

At this, Joe piped up. "Am I the only one who thinks it would be easier to just call them zombies? Why are we using all these different words? They're gross, terrifying, eating the living—clearly, they're zombies."

"I call them zombies," Violet offered.

Joe gestured to her. "She gets it."

But Violet was preoccupied. Something didn't add up. "You went outside a few days ago, but earlier you said you were bitten an hour ago. Which is it?"

Matt continued the thought for her. "And there was no blood in the warehouse, or outside by the shutters. You must've been bitten inside..."

Violet noticed Ben sniffing around a closed door at the other side of the room. Steve's eyes were also fixed on it. Matt picked up his bat from the table before moving over. He swung the door open. There was a woman inside the small room, tied to a chair. She'd been quiet while they were in the office, but as soon as the group entered, she began to snarl. Her hair was ragged, her face pale and sunken, and she mashed her bloodstained teeth together furiously. She probably used to be pretty. It was hard to tell now that one of her eyes was missing. She struggled so wildly against her restraints that she knocked her chair over. Ben whimpered, hiding behind Violet's legs.

Steve's voice came from behind them.

"I brought her inside. It didn't feel right to leave her out there. She's been in this room for a few days. I was in here an hour ago when I made a mistake." He moved closer to the woman, closer than Violet would've been comfortable getting, restraints or no, and continued.

"Maybe it's because I haven't slept properly in weeks, I don't know. I just lost concentration, and she took a bite out of my arm. I panicked, then ran back down to the store to grab some bandages. Then I heard movement, and I knew someone was inside. I froze, didn't realize I was bleeding out so much. I was too worried about who was inside. I thought it might be more of those things, or a gang of looters, so I pulled the milk across to cover the blood, then came back up here."

The woman continued to writhe on the floor, snapping her jaw hungrily. She was trying to free herself, but couldn't. At least not yet. Everyone was quiet for a minute, just watching her. But Violet didn't like this. She didn't feel safe. What if more of the dead had followed under the shutters? How long did they have until Steve turned? What about their friends back at the school? Were they okay?

"We should go," she began, her voice little more than a whisper. "We've been gone too long."

"Okay, yeah, I agree," Sam mumbled. He seemed unable to tear his eyes away from the woman.

"Will you be okay?" Matt asked Steve. Violet knew he wouldn't be. Of course he wouldn't. He was already infected, and it was spreading fast. The smell of his blood was becoming foul. They needed to leave, right now.

"I'll be fine," Steve said, his breathing becoming much heavier. "You should go. Get back to your friends. Take whatever you need, and feel free to come back. We'll still be here."

That's reassuring.

--\^-\/\|\|\^\w\w\~\~_____

BACK IN THE STORE, SAM QUIETLY BARRICADED THE DOOR with the huge container of milk.

"It won't be long," he muttered. Hurriedly, they bagged their supplies and went back down to the warehouse. They couldn't raise the shutters, and the carts wouldn't fit under the small gap, so they needed to make multiple trips. It took several journeys, but they eventually carried the final supplies back.

They didn't talk, moving silently through the parking lot. As they approached the car, there was a bang. They all dropped their bags in unison, raising their weapons defensively. The banging continued. It was close.

Violet turned around, coming face to face with a biter.

Tom screamed from his place behind her.

"Don't be such a girl," Sam hissed. Violet clamped her hand over Tom's mouth. Sam walked over to the parked car, where the dead woman snapped at them from behind the glass. He tapped the window with his bat, which seemed to make her even angrier. She drummed her hands against the glass with more force. She was still strapped into her seat, and her movements were restricted by the belt. It was frayed, as though she'd been trying to chew through it. She was relatively young, and in pretty good condition thanks to being trapped in the car. She had brown hair, and Violet tried to shake the idea that they looked similar.

That could've been you. She looks just like you.

Except a bit more dead.

Violet uncovered Tom's mouth, and he stomped away. She made her way over to Sam, giving him a push. "Don't call him a girl."

"He screamed at a biter...in a seatbelt...behind a window." Sam rolled his eyes.

She pushed him again. "*He's* a wimp, not a girl. *I'm* a girl."

"All right, point taken."

Tom screamed again. Sam looked ready to bash his head in, until he saw why the kid was yelling. Tom was fighting off a biter. It had approached so fast none of them had even heard. It forced him against a car, setting the alarm off. The noise rang out in the silent parking lot.

Violet and the others hurried over. Joe got there first, grabbing the biter by the collar and wrenching him off Tom. Sam swung his bat, cracking it against the zombie's skull. Blood sprayed onto Sam's face, and he hit it again. It went down, but now two more were approaching, screaming as they ran. Matt took out one, bringing his bat low and smashing the knees of a woman in a wedding dress.

"Violet!" Sam threw her a knife, which she, of course, didn't catch. But she picked it up from the ground, then brought it down into the skull of the blushing bride.

Sam and Joe fought against a huge man in overalls. They both knocked him to the ground, hitting him with their bats again and again until he stopped moving.

Violet glanced around. No biters close by, but there was movement from the nearby houses.

"We need to go," she yelled over the sound of the car alarm. The group quickly climbed into the car, heading out of the parking lot as more of the dead began to arrive.

VIOLET SURVEYED HER FRIENDS AS THEY HEADED BACK home. Most were splattered with blood and exhausted, yet also triumphant. Today had been good. They'd gotten food and personal supplies, no one had died, and she'd been able to be around blood without eating anyone.

"I think that went well," Joe began, as if reading her mind.

Sam and Matt agreed, but Tom looked incredulous. "How the hell did you come to that conclusion?"

Joe's tone was casual. "We got the stuff we needed, and you know what? We made some memories."

"I almost died!"

Joe smiled. "And I'll cherish that one the most."

Violet tried not to laugh, keeping her eyes fixed out of the window. Joe was right; things were okay now. They could go back to the school, eat, and wash. She could try not to kill anyone, and it would all be super.

Violet's positive attitude lasted around ten minutes. Right up until they arrived back to find the school gates wide open, swinging back and forth in the breeze.

AMY WATCHED THE OTHERS DISAPPEAR OUT OF THE gates with a sense of impending doom. She didn't have a good feeling about this. Something bad was about to happen.

She shook the thoughts away. She was being ridiculous; they would be fine. Sam was more than capable of taking care of the others. But for some reason, she couldn't convince herself. Violet had already been bitten; she was just lucky enough to be immune. Amy was relatively sure the others wouldn't be as fortunate. And what if they got overrun? Violet's immunity would mean nothing if she got ripped to shreds.

Amy wasn't great at being positive.

The morning air was crisp, and she hurriedly wrapped the chain around the gates. A sound caught her ear—was that crying? Amy froze. For a moment, the noise didn't compute. It seemed so unnatural in this world. Then she saw the kitten. It stood on the other side of the street, meowing right at her.

Amy smiled. She couldn't remember the last time she'd seen a cat. She knelt. "Come here," she called. Her voice was louder than she intended it to be, too loud for this quiet road, but she wasn't thinking about that. The kitten meowed again, slowly padding toward her. Then it stopped, raising its haunches. It hissed

SEVEN

71

and ran away. Amy got to her feet, listening desperately. She couldn't hear those things, but that didn't mean they weren't around. She kicked herself for being so loud, for not being careful. Hurriedly, her eyes still on the road, she snapped the padlock on and walked back to the school.

What she didn't see was that she hadn't secured the chain correctly. It snaked its way off the bars seconds after she went inside, landing neatly on the ground. Moments later, the gates opened.

SAM PARKED THE CAR AND LOCKED THE GATES BEHIND them. Slowly and silently, Violet and the others entered the school. She told herself she was worrying over nothing; Amy was probably just careless locking up. It wouldn't be out of the question; her friend was notoriously unreliable. She told herself when they got upstairs, they'd find the others and everyone would be fine. But she didn't believe it.

Carrying only their weapons, they made their way down the hallway toward the stairs to the teachers' lounge, leaving the food and supplies in the car. Violet didn't imagine she'd be much good fighting off the dead with a baseball bat in one hand and a bag of magazines in the other. She had no idea what to expect as they continued through the silent building. Would they turn a corner and find hundreds of biters? Would her friends be in pieces? Or would there be nothing at all?

"We need to split up," Sam whispered. Joe's expression suggested that once again, he knew this was a terrible idea, but it wasn't like they had any other choice. "Tom, Matt, and I will check the library. That's where Maggie and Emily were going. Violet and Joe, check the teachers' lounge."

Violet didn't mind being part of a smaller group; she knew Tom would be less than useless if they ran into the dead. In fact, based on his behavior today, she had no doubt he'd be the first to push her into a horde to save himself.

I must remember to have a little chat with him about that.

They split up, and Joe and Violet crept up the stairs toward the door.

"I can't take this silence," Joe whispered, but Violet shushed him. The door to the teachers' lounge was wide open, and the two of them crouched at the stop of the stairs, neither wanting to step inside.

Violet eyed Joe, knowing he was thinking the same thing. There was a good chance they were going to go in there and find something horrible. Was she ready for that? As she tried to force herself to get moving, Ben passed the pair of them, heading through the door as though nothing was out of the ordinary. There was no sound—no whimper or bark. Violet caught Joe's eye, and he shrugged. It seemed like they were good to go.

They got to their feet and entered the room.

Everything is fine!

The window was open, and several of Amy's drawings sat on the table. It looked like she'd spent the day sketching. There was no one in the room, but no biters either. Violet supposed Maggie and Emily were in the library, and Amy was maybe using the bathroom, or even painting in the art block. She turned back to Joe, smiling.

Joe wasn't looking at her. His horrified gaze was locked on a body by the couch. It was female. Her insides were on the outside, spread all around her. There was blood. So much blood that Violet couldn't even tell what color her hair was. She felt no temptation whatsoever; the red liquid smelled of nothing but death. Ben sniffed at the body, pushing gently against it with his snout. She was face down, but Violet knew who it was. She couldn't believe it, though. She wouldn't. Stumbling across the room, she knelt beside the body, turning it over heavily. The face was different. Her eyes were wide open and terrified. Her cheeks were scratched and bleeding. Once-beautiful lips had been ripped open, and blood was smeared on her mouth like crude lipstick. Violet brought the body close, ignoring the cool blood on her knees. She buried her face into the hair of the dead girl, sticky and matted from where her head had cracked against the floor. She'd seen death, but not like this. Not her.

She heard the others arrive at the door. They were talking about not finding anything. Then silence. She felt hands on her shoulders, trying to get her to stand up, but she couldn't let go.

Eventually, she was pulled from the body and led to the couch. The shaking in her legs wouldn't stop. Blood dripped from her hands and knees.

That's her blood.

Matt knelt in front of Violet, talking, but the words made no sense. It was like being underwater. He put one warm hand on her face, then the other. He pulled her head close so their foreheads were pressed together. She put her hands on his, smearing blood all over his skin. He didn't push her away.

There was a noise. It came from the coat closet. Matt got to his feet, holding his weapon and stepping in front of Violet protectively. She saw Sam walk to the door. He glanced at the others, and then flung it open.

THE THREE LEFT BEHIND HAD BEEN IN THE TEACHERS' lounge for several hours, killing the time in a variety of ways. Amy had been alternating between drawing and reading. She was supposed to be by the window, but she was at the table. She couldn't bear to just sit and watch the road. If she had, she might've known what was about to happen. She might have been able to warn the others that one of them was going to die.

Maggie had been reading a book about gardening, checking the clock every five minutes and wondering if it was possible for time to be running backward.

Emily had been painting her nails, using one of the jars found in the box of 'banned items' the teachers had collected. There was a surprisingly large selection. As well as nail polish, there had been cigarettes, some dirty magazines, earrings that went over the penny size limit, and rather alarmingly, several knives. Emily knew about the box, having taught at George Avenue for the last year. She'd collected some of the items herself.

Around the time Violet and the others found the puddle of blood, Maggie heard a noise. It wasn't much, something she only noticed having become so accustomed to silence. She glanced at the other two; they'd heard it as well, and stared at each other anxiously. Amy got to her feet first, and moved to the door. The others watched as she disappeared, heading down the stairs.

There was no sound for several moments, but just as Maggie started to wonder whether she'd imagined the noise, there was a scream. It echoed off the walls, so loud she could swear the screamer was right beside them. Emily jumped up, but Maggie was frozen where she was.

"Stay there," Emily ordered, though Maggie knew she was incapable of doing anything else. She ran for the door and leaned over the railing. What she saw would forever be stained onto her eyes. She hurried back to the room and grabbed Maggie by the hand, remembering the bolt on the door, the one Sam had installed the day after they arrived, too late. The creature was close. She could hear it coming up, coming for them.

Emily pulled Maggie toward the closet, swung the doors open, and pushed her inside. Seconds later, she was in, too, closing the doors behind them. For what seemed like an eternity, nothing happened, and there was no sound but their breathing. Then there were steps again, heavy breaths, and a bloodied figure stumbled into the room. Something about the way it was breathing made Emily open the door just a crack. It was Amy. She was bloody and limping, but alive. Emily opened the door a little wider, unable to get up because Maggie was practically on top of her.

"Amy," she hissed.

Relief flooded Amy's face. She stumbled over just as a second figure appeared at the door. It was a man. He was tall, muscular, and dead. Amy heard him coming, turning to face him the moment he reached her. Emily wanted to cover her eyes, but she couldn't. She knew she had to witness it, even if she didn't understand why. She could hear Maggie sobbing, could see her friend—for they had become friends over the past few weeks, despite the decade between them—cover her own mouth to silence herself in the darkness.

Emily watched as the creature wrestled with Amy. She had no chance. Amy was weak from the first attack, and Emily could see the bites on her neck and arms. She wanted to help, but she was frozen with fear. Her whole body felt like lead.

It was brutal. The way it tore at her body with teeth and fingers was more than just animalistic; it was vicious, cruel, hateful.

Within seconds, Amy was on the floor on her stomach, the monster ripping at her back. She reached out her arm toward the closet, reaching for help. Emily felt something overcome her, and moved to open the door further. She knew she had to do something; even if it was killing the monster and putting Amy out of her misery.

A sound escaped Amy's torn lips. She moved her hand as much as she could. It looked like a wave.

"She's telling you to close the door," Maggie breathed.

Amy gestured again.

Emily realized she was telling them not to come out. She was telling them to stay hidden and save themselves.

Emily nodded slowly, blowing a kiss to Amy and pulling the door closed.

MAGGIE AND EMILY WERE IN THE CLOSET. THEY BOTH had their hands over their ears and tears on their cheeks. As the doors opened, they opened their eyes. Relief flushed their faces, and Sam and Matt helped them out. Maggie flung her arms around Matt's neck, Emily doing the same with Sam. But her eyes never left Amy's body. Finally, she stepped away from Sam, heading toward Violet, who got to her feet. Emily pulled her close.

"I'm so sorry," she sobbed. "I couldn't save her."

Violet just nodded, unable to speak.

"We need to go back out," Sam said listlessly. "Whatever did this to Amy is probably still in the school somewhere."

"You don't know that," Violet muttered, her voice thick. "The gates were open; it might've gone."

"We need to be sure. We'll find it quicker if we get into groups."

Violet sighed. She was so sick of being split up and ordered around, but too tired to argue. She did as she was told.

VIOLET WAS WITH JOE AGAIN, CHECKING THE MAIN BLOCK. Sam and Tom were starting from the other side, with the aim to meet in the middle. Matt and Emily were doing a sweep of the playground and other buildings, but Violet knew it wouldn't be there. It wouldn't have gone far. Maggie was in the staffroom with Ben. She hadn't stopped shaking since coming out of the closet, and Sam thought it'd be safer to leave her behind.

Violet felt as though she'd been cut in half. One side was distraught, feeling as though a part of her had been ripped out. The other side was numb. She knew she had to focus on one thing—killing the foul creature that had torn up her best friend. She could grieve after it was done.

"Amy and I dated once."

Violet paused, halfway through opening one of the classroom doors. She turned to Joe questioningly. Was this a joke? Amy was her best friend. Violet knew everything about her. Amy had never, not once, mentioned dating Joe.

"No, you didn't," she replied after a moment, checking the classroom. Empty.

"We did. I swear on my life. It wasn't for long. A month maybe?"

"No. She would've told me." Violet stopped walking and studied Joe's face. There was no sign he was lying, and he had no reason to. But it didn't add up.

"She didn't tell anyone," he continued. "Last summer, I went down to the beach with my family to visit my grandma. Amy was there, too, visiting hers. How weird is that? We met at some hideous 'disco' that our families dragged us to. I'm sure she wouldn't have usually given me a second glance, but seeing as I was the only guy there who was under fifty, we started talking. I made her fall in love with me through my amazing sense of humor and rugged handsomeness."

Violet's face was stone, and Joe smiled. "Okay, that bit wasn't true, but the rest of it was."

Violet supposed it was possible. She knew Amy went out to the beach every summer for a month or so. But why had she kept it a secret?

Joe continued. "I guess for her, I was probably just a way of getting out of the house and away from the endless games of Monopoly she had to endure. But for me...I don't know. It was something else. Don't get me wrong—Amy could be rude, flaky, and completely unreasonable at times, but she was funny. You know, in that mean, sarcastic way. And she cared about stuff. She was a good person."

Violet blinked back the tears that threatened. Joe had described Amy perfectly. She could come across as hard, even cold at times, but she had a good heart. She went out of her way to look after her friends, or even people who just seemed like they needed it. On the first day of high school, Violet knew no one, having only recently moved to town. Amy had invited the new girl to join her table, despite her other friends telling her not to. Amy didn't care that Violet had no clue about what to say to boys or about fashion. She pretended to be interested in the video games Violet played, or the weird cult movies she obsessed over. They were like sisters.

"So what happened?" Violet asked. "Between you two?"

Joe shrugged. "What do you think? Summer was almost over, and we were both going home. She didn't think we'd work out because we were too different. We both knew it was because she liked James Hobson, and I didn't even compare to him. I think she was a little embarrassed by me; I was making jokes all the time, whereas she was always cool about everything. We probably wouldn't have worked out."

Violet wasn't sure what to say. It did sound like a typical Amy break-up—none of her relationships lasted more than a month. She got bored relatively quickly—but the fact she had never told Violet about it might have meant something.

"I think she really liked you," Violet said.

Joe raised an eyebrow, smiling. "She didn't even tell you about it. That doesn't exactly fill me with confidence."

"No, but she told me *everything*. Every bad date, every weirdo she met, every single time a guy had embarrassed her and she'd had to dump him. That fact she didn't ever tell me about this... She must've felt bad about how she acted. It must've meant more to her than she realized."

Joe considered this, and Violet continued, "Besides, James asked her out and she said no."

Violet continued down the hallway. Joe walked quietly beside her, but now there was a small smile playing on his lips.

Each classroom was the same: look inside, see nothing, move on. Look inside, see nothing, move on.

Then it was different. The next one wasn't empty. There was a man inside, standing with his back to them and staring out the window. His hands were bloody, as were his clothes. His hair was brown, matted with dirt, and what could easily have been more blood.

Amy's blood.

Violet stepped forward, practically shaking with anger, but Joe put his arm across her stomach to prevent her from going any further. She knew what he was doing. He was trying to keep her back—he thought he should be the one to do it. She pushed him away.

It has to be me.

Violet silently made her way past the desks. She stood behind the creature, keeping her breathing slow. She was closer now than most people would ever get to one of the dead without being bitten or killed. She could smell the blood and decay—that familiar mixture of damp leaves and rotting meat. She could hear it breathing in raspy carnivorous breaths.

Why do they still breathe?

She raised the baseball bat high above her head. She was only just tall enough to reach. With one swift movement, she forced it down. The zombie's skull cracked, and he crumbled to the floor. He bled, though not as much as a living person. Violet watched, then brought the bat down again. And again. And again.

Blood spattered onto her clothes and face. She heard Joe moving over, saying her name, but she didn't stop. This was for Amy.

Joe grabbed her, pulling her close and forcing her to drop the bat. She clung to him, hot tears streaking down her dirty cheeks. She wiped them with the back of her hand.

Blood. She was crying blood. Violet's eyes widened. She pushed Joe away, running from the classroom before he could see the fresh blood on her face.

"Done. Now I'll just wrap this up... Don't want it to get infected."

Pain, pressure.

"Don't worry, it's just a scratch."

Something in the air. Something new.

"What are you doing? Get off me! Help!"

Violet awoke sweating and out of breath, the shadows of the dream still hanging over her. What was it? A nightmare?

A memory?

Her eyes scanned the teachers' lounge. Everyone else was asleep.

Not everyone. We're not all here. One of us is dead. Downstairs on the floor.

Sam said they'd bury Amy tomorrow, out in the field behind the basketball court. He, Matt, and Joe had spent the evening digging her grave. He said they could all say some words, but Violet knew she didn't have any. She rolled over, hoping to get a few hours' sleep before then. But in her dreams, she was haunted by blood, bites, and pain.

E
I
G
H
T

The next morning, they threw the corpse of the infected man over the wall. They buried Amy under a large oak tree. It was raining. No one said anything at first. They stood in silence around the mound of dirt for the longest time. Finally, Sam stepped forward. He cleared his throat.

"Goodbye, Amy. At least you're away from this now."

A WEEK PASSED. THE SCHOOL WAS SECURE AGAIN, AND everyone was attempting to get back to normal. Or at least their version of it. Things were different, though, and not just with Violet. The others had changed, too. They hadn't lost anyone since the first day. They'd thought the school was impenetrable. That feeling of safety had come crashing down on their heads.

Since Amy's death, everyone was constantly alert. Their lives were even quieter, conversations in whispers that seemed to last no longer than a few minutes. No one would sleep unless someone was keeping watch by the window. It was largely unnecessary, since the gates to the school were now securely locked, and the door to the lounge was bolted shut whenever everyone was inside. Still, every night they took shifts staying awake.

The air was constantly tense. Every now and then, someone, usually Joe, would try to lighten the mood with a joke, or casual conversation, but it always fizzled out. But despite all that, despite the tension and anxiety, Violet was at least beginning to get over her grief. She was starting to feel human again.

Revision: as human as someone who craves human flesh can be.

Yes, the hunger was still there, but she could control it, at least when there was no one actively bleeding out in front of her. That was part of the reason she was still trying to keep her distance from the others. It was safer if there was no temptation.

Today, Violet was down in the art block again. It was silent down there, but she wasn't afraid. She was used to it. She followed the long, yellow hallway, decorated with paintings and sculptures made by students. It seemed like they had been crafted a lifetime ago.

How many of them are dead now?

She entered one of the studios. This was the one Amy used, and Violet suddenly felt incredibly guilty that she'd never come in before. Every wall and surface was covered in Amy's art. They were mostly paintings, though there were sketches, too, hardly a surface not covered in them. There were even more balled up and thrown roughly in the direction of the overflowing garbage can. Violet was holding onto the last drawing Amy had been working on. It was on the floor next to where they had found her. Violet guessed it was going to be a picture of the two of them, but they were just outlines. They didn't have faces. Still, Violet had carried it around in her pocket like a talisman, not caring the lower left corner had soaked up a little of Amy's blood.

She put the picture down for the moment, walking the room as though she were in an art gallery. Amy's work was varied. The first few paintings she passed were calming: flowers in a meadow, a riverside at sunrise, some horses on the beach. Violet guessed her friend had coped with the walking corpses in the beginning by pretending they didn't exist. But slowly, the world outside began to creep into Amy's work: the painting of a beautiful flower, deep red and alone in the middle of the field, had black shadowy figures just visible in the distance. In the next riverside scene, the black figures appeared again, once more only just visible on the horizon, hidden slightly by the trees. The horses grazing in the next painting were stalked by the same shadows, the once-blue sky now dark grey, with streaks of red across the clouds.

Violet's heart felt heavy. Amy's art had always been so beautiful, but now it was tainted. She grabbed the painting of the horses and angrily crumpled it between her hands. She regretted this immediately, of course, and tried to smooth it out on the table. Something else caught her eye: a sketch of a group of people. This was unusual since Amy rarely drew people. She had always said that no matter how hard she tried, someone would always be unhappy with the way she portrayed them.

"But you draw me all the time," Violet had replied when she said this.

"Because I don't care what you think," Amy had said wickedly, not even looking up from her nails, which she had been painting a deep crimson. Violet had thrown a pillow at her, laughing.

She pushed those thoughts away, not ready to deal with those memories right now. Violet instead brought her attention back to the drawing. It was of all of them. Amy had made it seem like they were posing for a photograph, sitting on or around a large couch. Sam and Tom were smiling, standing just behind the chair —although Amy had managed to capture beautifully the fact that Tom's smile could more accurately be described as a smug sneer. Maggie and Emily were sitting on the couch together, smiling shyly. Joe was pulling a funny face beside Tom, which might've been directed at him. Amy and Violet were sitting on the other side of Maggie and Emily, with Ben on Violet's lap. Matt was next to Violet.

Wait. Violet peered a little closer. Were she and Matt holding hands?

She rolled her eyes. "Very good, Amy," she muttered. But she felt a smile cross her lips. Even now, Amy was still able to tease her. After she rolled up the drawing carefully, she secured it with a rubber band.

As she went to leave the room, she saw something different. It was a piece of paper with some writing on it. She picked it up curiously, reading the few words.

Amy. Amy Lowe. My name is Amy Ann Lowe.

The words were simple, probably testing out a new pen, yet they hit Violet like a truck. There was something about the writing, about the simplicity, that made Amy seem alive, if only for a second.

Violet left the room with the rolled-up drawing and the paper with Amy's name. Things felt like they were starting to spin. She needed to breathe—to go somewhere else, somewhere far away from the paintings her dead friend had created. Somewhere safe and small.

She found herself in the boys' bathrooms, in the stall with all the graffiti. Not the most glamorous place, but it felt somehow safe. Sitting on the closed lid of the toilet, she read the writing again.

Amy. Amy Lowe. My name is Amy Ann Lowe.

Is not *was.* When Violet read this writing, Amy was still alive. Her name *is* Amy. Not *was* Amy.

It seemed Violet hadn't cried all her gross blood tears after all. New ones began to prick viciously at the corners of her eyes. Hastily, she folded up the paper and stuffed it into her pocket. She took a breath. When she felt relatively sure she'd managed to hold back any eye leakage, she unfurled the drawing and tacked it up to the cubicle wall. No one else really came down to the art block, so Violet felt secure none of the others would see it. But she would know it was there, and that was enough.

New tears threatened, and Violet wiped her eyes, distracting herself with the writing on the walls. Most of it was run-of-the-mill, but there were a couple that made her smile. Her favorite was a short dialogue, beginning with:

I love Harry Nicks and I'm not ashamed! D.P.

Then below it: *We all know it's you, Daniel Parker.*

And below that: *You tell us all the time. We don't care.*

Then: *This is Harry. Still not interested.*

She smiled, but jumped as she heard the door to the bathrooms open. Violet held her breath, not sure what to say to anyone who found her sitting on the toilet crying blood. She roughly wiped at her face again.

They won't come this far down. Whoever it is will use a cubicle nearer to the door.

Violet was thinking this reassuring thought right up until the moment the door swung open and nearly hit her. Matt stood in the doorway, surprised.

"Jesus, Violet, you almost gave me a heart attack." He grinned. "What are you doing?" Suddenly, he looked down at the floor, and Violet thought he might actually be blushing. "Sorry, stupid question." He turned away, and Violet laughed.

"Unfreeze, I'm decent. Just sitting."

Matt turned back. "Oh right, so you are." He paused, raising an eyebrow. "Can I ask *why* you're hanging out in the bathrooms?"

What answer could she give? *I'm trying to avoid you guys in case any of you get a paper cut and I try to eat you?*

Yes, she was grieving Amy, but she knew her real reason for hiding away was more down to her fear of what might happen if she lost control. But she couldn't tell Matt that, so after an incredibly long and awkward silence, she decided to stall.

"Why are *you* in here?"

"Well, I actually need to go to the bathroom."

"Go then. I'm not listening."

Okay, that didn't sound incredibly creepy.

Matt seemed to consider it, but then sat down on the floor in front of her, letting the door close behind him. "I can hold it."

Violet lifted her legs, sitting cross-legged on the lid to give him more room. Matt regarded her more intently for a moment. "Have you been bleeding?"

Crap, blood tears.

"I had a nose bleed."

Matt seemed a little confused. "Oh...okay. It's just, it's around your eyes."

"I sneezed."

"Oh."

Great, Violet, that makes perfect sense. I'm sure there will be no follow-up questions to that.

"But how did—"

"That floor looks dirty," Violet interrupted.

"Yeah, it is."

"It's got to be full of bacteria."

"No doubt."

"They'll be burrowing into your skin as we speak."

"That's probably what that weird feeling is."

Violet raised an eyebrow. "So why are you sitting down there?"

Matt shrugged. "It feels like we haven't spoken in a really long time."

Oh no, this might be about to get heavy.

Violet kept her tone light. "I'm okay. I just needed some

space. You know, to deal with everything." Weak answer, but Matt was, as usual, too nice to call her out on it.

"Do you think you've had enough?"

No. "Maybe."

Matt smiled. "Good, I missed you. Well, we all missed you. Everyone. Not just me. I missed you a normal amount."

Another awkward silence, and Violet couldn't help but hope for a zombie to stumble in and give them something else to focus on. Luckily, Matt noticed the drawing.

"Wow, is that one of—"

"Yes," Violet interrupted. She didn't want him to say Amy's name. She didn't want to hear it out loud.

"It's amazing." Matt studied the picture for a long time, and Violet really hoped he didn't notice the hand holding. She pointed to the declaration of love on the wall beside the drawing, diverting his attention.

"Have you seen this one?"

Matt grinned. "Yeah, it's my favorite. Well, other than that one." He nodded to the one where Violet was listed as the twentieth hottest girl in eighth grade.

"That one's pretty funny, too."

Matt shook his head. "No, I didn't mean it like that. I just mean it makes me smile when I read it. I remember when it first went up."

"Really?" Violet asked. For some reason, she had assumed he saw it for the first time when she did.

Matt nodded. He spoke in a serious tone, but he was smiling. "Oh yeah, I was one of the contributors. You have no idea how much work goes into this kind of thing. There were drafts and re-writes." He looked Violet in the eye, lowering his voice to a serious whisper. "You know, it's permanent marker, Violet."

"It sounds like a big job."

"Absolutely. Although to be honest, I didn't get much of a chance to share my choices. I was just there to write it out. Apparently, I had the best handwriting."

"Wow, that's wild."

"Yeah, not exactly something the girls went crazy for."

"Why did they care about handwriting anyway?" Violet asked. "It's a gross list on a bathroom door."

"Violet. *Permanent* marker."

She laughed, a genuine, light, carefree sound she hadn't heard in a long time.

Matt continued. "Anyway, I wasn't allowed to actively participate in the order of the list. Let's just say I wasn't quite so cool back then as I am right now."

"No?"

"No, I'm at least..." He paused to consider this. "At least a third cooler than I was when I was fourteen."

"Wow."

"Exactly. So like I said, no one really cared what I thought. In fact, my choice for number one got pushed right to the bottom."

"Well, that must've been..." Violet trailed off, realizing what Matt had said. She felt her cheeks burn. "Oh...thanks." She didn't know what else to say, never knowing how to take compliments. On the rare occasion she had received them in the past, she'd usually made an awkward joke and scuttled away.

Luckily, she was rescued by Joe, who chose that exact moment to swing the stall door open, almost hitting Matt in the face.

"Well...this is cozy." Smirking, he eyed them with mock suspicion. He stepped into the cubicle, which was now a real squeeze. Despite this, Joe fought to close the door once more. He sat down beside Matt. "What are we doing in here?" He raised an eyebrow. "Is it a sex thing?"

"No!"

"Joe, one of us is sitting on the toilet. How could that in any way—"

Joe shrugged. "I don't know how you guys operate."

Matt scrunched up his face. "If you thought it was a sex thing, then why did you come in?"

"It's been a while. I don't mind being a third wheel."

After a rather awkward pause, Violet decided to blow past that one. "Why are you really in here?"

"I like having stuff to read when I pee," he explained. "Plus, I was trying to find you. Sam and I have noticed that things have been a bit...mellow, recently. We think it'd be a good idea to cheer everyone up, so we've created a game!"

"Is it called 'Let's see how many people we can fit into a dirty bathroom stall?'" Matt asked sarcastically. "Because I think we've exhausted that one."

Joe cocked his head. "No, but it might be fun—Sam!"

"Thanks, Joe." Violet rubbed her ears at the sudden outburst. He grinned apologetically. She heard the main door to the bathroom open, and Sam's voice drifted inside.

"Yeah?"

"Get over here," Joe called back.

"No, I'm not falling for that again. Whatever it is, I don't want to see it."

"Just come here!"

Violet heard Sam knocking open the other stall doors, muttering, "I swear, if this is the same as that thing you showed me last time—"

Their door opened, and Joe managed to catch it just before it hit him in the face. Sam looked down at the three of them, wearing a confused expression.

"What are you doing?"

"Explaining our game."

"Why are you doing it in the bathrooms?"

"I don't know. Violet and Matt were doing a sex thing in here."

"We were not—"

"Joe! That's so—"

"Anyway," Joe interrupted. "Sit."

Sam shrugged. "Okay." He dropped down, and Matt groaned uncomfortably.

"I still need to pee," he wheezed.

Luckily for Matt, it didn't take Joe and Sam long to explain the premise of their game. Soon, they were off.

The game involved a chair on wheels, some mannequins from the textiles room, and a person who didn't mind careening down a hallway and smashing into the wall at the end. It was a bit like bowling, but on a larger scale and a lot more painful. One member of the team sat on the chair, while the other members launched them into the mannequins. Whichever team knocked over the most mannequins won the round. Matt, Sam, and Violet were on one team. Joe, Maggie, and Emily were on the other. Tom didn't want to play.

"Great!" was Joe's reaction, which earned him a foul look from Tom as he stalked away. Joe sucked in his teeth. "I meant because the teams won't be odd," he explained.

"Sure..." Violet grinned.

They played best of five, then best of eleven, and then just kept going over and over again. Violet had no idea who was winning by the end, but couldn't remember the last time she'd had that much fun.

VIOLET WOKE FROM ANOTHER DREAM WITH A START. SHE was covered in sweat and shaking, but could remember nothing she had dreamed about. Only that there was blood, screaming, and something fantastic.

She really hoped all those things weren't connected.

Matt was keeping watch by the window. Something was different about him. As the room started to come into focus around her, she realized there was an orange light flickering on his face, even though the candles had been extinguished for the night.

Violet got off the couch, then padded across the room toward the window. She was cold, wearing a long-sleeved—but thin—shirt, and some shorts from the PE department. Both were a little small. Fine for sleeping in, but not ideal for nighttime walks. She halted beside Matt at the window.

"What is it?" she asked.

He started a little at her voice, having been so focused. "Sorry, I didn't hear you." He pointed to a spot not far in the distance. Violet followed his gaze. One of the houses on the street outside, the one where they had met, was on fire. It roared out of control, crumbling as they watched.

"How did it start?" she asked.

Matt shook his head. "I don't know. One minute it was fine, and the next it was up. I didn't see anything."

"Could it be the dead? Maybe they knocked something over?"

"Maybe, but what? There's no power anymore."

He was right. The more likely explanation was that it was people, living people, but why? To burn any biters in the house? For fun?

"You're shivering. You should go back to bed," Matt said, looking at Violet with concern.

"I'm fine. I can't sleep."

"Bad dreams again?"

That caught Violet a little off-guard. "Again?"

"Sometimes you make sounds in your sleep."

"What kind of sounds?"

"Just...sounds. Like you're afraid. I thought it was nightmares."

Violet nodded. "It is."

"I get them, too."

Not like this.

Matt got to his feet, offering her his place by the window. It was a comfortable spot with cushions propped against the side of the wall. Violet shook her head, sitting down on the other side of the ledge instead. But Matt wouldn't let her off that easily. He went to get a blanket, draping it carefully over her shoulders. Violet froze. She didn't like people to get this close, not anymore. She was terrified she'd lose control and do something. Matt's neck was just inches from her face as he placed the blanket. She knew she could bite him right then—tear out his throat before he could even scream.

Who thinks like that?

Violet swallowed the heavy lump in her throat. Matt moved back, his eyes meeting hers, and smiled. Something about the light flickering on his face made him look different. Softer. Almost like he wasn't real, like something from a dream.

"Thanks," she muttered.

He took his seat once more.

I could've killed him right there.

Or kissed him.

Not quite as bad, but still a terrible idea.

At least I know where I stand with killing him. Kissing him would make things a million times more stressful.

Good logic there, Vi.

"VIOLET, WAKE UP."

Violet blinked. Slowly, the room around her came into focus. She was still sitting up at the window beside Matt, but his face wasn't soft and dream-like anymore. It was etched with worry. He pointed outside. Dawn was breaking. The fire outside was dying down, but Violet followed Matt's gaze, her eyes widening. There was a large 4x4 parked outside the school. Five men were climbing out. She watched as they ran for the gates, rattling them frantically. She didn't have to be any closer to recognize that fear, that panic—they were being chased.

Without waiting another second, she dropped her blanket and sprinted for the door, grabbing the keys to the gate on the way. She heard Matt waking the others behind her.

Soon, she was outside, forgetting about her bare feet as they slapped against the cold, hard ground. One of the men saw her approach and called out.

"Hey, please let us in!"

"I'm coming," Violet called back, quickening her pace. She arrived at the gates, frantically searching for the right key in the dawn light.

"Hurry," another one pleaded, looking behind him. Violet managed to unlock the padlock, but struggled to untangle the chain. Luckily, Matt, Sam, and Emily

**N
I
N
E**

weren't far behind her. In no time, the chain was ripped off and the gates swung open. The men hurried inside. Matt quickly secured the chain back in place and snapped on the lock, just as they heard the telltale sound of pounding feet on tarmac.

"Inside," Sam ordered, leading them back into the school.

"They were right behind us," one of the men said once they were indoors. He was the tallest, with red hair and a sharp nose. His physique was strong, and made even Sam look like a little boy. "Thank you," he continued, introducing himself as John.

The second man, shorter but almost as muscular, was Edd. The third, Vince, was of a similar build with curly brown hair. The three of them appeared to be in their thirties, but the last two were probably about Violet's age. One had little muscle to speak of, dark skin, and anxious eyes. He introduced himself as Zack, and then said nothing else. The last was Daniel. He was similar to Tom in stature and appearance, though his hair was darker and reached his shoulders. By this point Maggie, Joe, and Tom had arrived, and everyone took a few minutes to introduce themselves to the newest members of the group.

"Thanks again," John said. "I don't know what would've happened if you hadn't let us in."

"Don't worry about it," Violet replied. She caught sight of the one called Edd staring at her, and was suddenly aware of how very underdressed she was. She crossed her arms across her chest self-consciously, wishing again that the shorts weren't *so* short. Matt seemed to sense her discomfort. When Edd took a step closer, Matt casually stepped out to intercept.

"How long have you been here?" Edd asked, addressing his question to Matt, as if that had been his intention all along.

"A few weeks," Matt said vaguely.

"So you've got food and stuff?" John asked.

"We went for supplies a week ago," Sam answered.

"Do you think we could get something to eat?"

"Of course." Sam gestured toward the cafeteria. Violet

took the opportunity to go upstairs and change, deciding that having a little less skin on show would be more appropriate now that there were strangers in her home.

EVERYONE ATE TOGETHER IN THE CAFETERIA, SOMETHING that usually never happened. With the increased numbers, however, it just seemed more practical than taking their food upstairs. Violet sat at the end of the table, watching the others talking. She tried her best to eat as much as the rest of the group, but eating somehow didn't feel right. It had nothing do with her nonexistent taste buds; something felt strange.

No one seemed to notice her hesitation. Everyone was laughing and joking, and all seemed to be getting on really well. This was the biggest the group had ever been, and Violet knew it should make her feel safer than before. She knew it *should*, but it didn't. She had no idea why, but that feeling of anxiety sat in her stomach like a rock. Everyone else had welcomed the newcomers with open arms. Joe and Sam were laughing loudly with John and Daniel, and Tom was talking with Edd.

Poor Edd.

Maggie and Emily were deep in conversation with Zack, and Matt was smiling at something Vince had just said.

Or was he? In one split second, Matt caught Violet's eye and gave her a look. She didn't know what it meant exactly, but it almost seemed like he was trying to say, *I know, I feel it, too.* But then he turned back and continued his conversation, and Violet wondered if she had just imagined it.

"So where do we sleep then?" Edd asked, bringing her focus back to the room. Sam seemed as though he was about to speak, but Violet cut in before he could.

"The library. We're a little bit crowded upstairs, but there's space down there. There are comfortable couches and lots of books if you can't sleep."

Sam caught her eye. They both knew there was plenty

of room upstairs, but he didn't call her out on it. Maybe he felt something weird, too. Or perhaps he just didn't want to make a big deal out of her lie in front of the newcomers.

"Sounds good," John said. "Do you mind if we go there now? After what we went through last night, I think we could all do with a rest."

Violet nodded, eager for a break. The feeling in her stomach was stronger than ever, but she couldn't put her finger on what it was.

$$\sim\!\!\sim\!\!\wedge\!\!\wedge\!\!\wedge\!\!\wedge\!\!\sim\!\!\sim\!\!\!—\!\!\!—$$

"*DONE. NOW I'LL JUST WRAP THIS UP. WE DON'T WANT IT to get infected.*"

"*Something doesn't feel right. I feel sick.*"

"*Put your head between your legs. You're probably just in shock. I think we all are.*"

"*Were you bitten, too? Your arm—*"

"*Don't worry, it's just a scratch.*"

"*It's bleeding.*"

"*I caught it on the door when I ran in. Could you pass me that towel? I'll try to clean myself up.*"

"*It looks deep.*"

"*I think it might be.*"

Something in the air. Something new.

"*What are you doing? Get off me! Help!*"

Violet woke up choking, barely able to breathe. Sweat poured down her face, and her T-shirt clung to her damp skin. She swept her hair out of her eyes, looking around the room. Everyone else was asleep. Their day had been long: meeting the men, getting to know them, showing them around, finding them new clothes and blankets, talking about how things worked at the school. They were all exhausted by the time they went to bed.

Yet here she was, waking up at dawn from another nightmare. Except now she knew it wasn't a nightmare. It was a memory. A memory of what she did. Violet got to her feet. She couldn't think straight. She needed to know what happened, to know what she did. The man in the store had been an accident; she'd been trying to stop him from causing her death, and had ended up causing his. But what happened to the man in the house? She had to know if she killed him, too.

Silently, she threw on some clothes, and left the teachers' lounge. She held the keys to the gate tightly in her hand. If everything went to plan, she should be out and back again before the others woke up. And if she wasn't, at least they'd be locked in and safe.

It was a cold morning, and the chain felt like ice beneath her fingers. She unlocked it quickly, stepped outside, and then secured the gates once more, slipping the keys into her pocket. She wouldn't take the car. It would be too noisy, and she couldn't risk drawing the dead to her. Besides, if something went wrong, she didn't want to leave the others without a vehicle.

Violet took a breath and headed off in the direction of the house, along the path she had traveled what felt like a lifetime ago.

SHE HAD BEEN WALKING FOR ABOUT TWENTY MINUTES, and hadn't encountered any biters. In fact, there had been no movement at all on the empty streets.

Until now.

Violet could see something up ahead, moving quickly along the road. It wasn't the dead though; it was people on bicycles! They were too far away to see her, and she knew she couldn't risk shouting for fear of drawing the attention of any nearby biters. Still, she couldn't let them just disappear. She wanted to see them. She *needed* to see them to prove to herself there were still others alive. There were so many, at least ten. Violet broke into a run, trying to catch up. She reached the corner just in time to see them disappearing into the woods.

They're kids. She was sure of it now. Her lips curled into a smile. There were still kids alive. Children out there in that nightmare, riding around on bicycles. She wanted to laugh at the pure absurdity of it. Part of her wanted to catch up to them, but she couldn't. She had other things to do. The spot where the kids had disappeared was where she'd stepped out of the woods, and over on the other side of the road was the first house she'd run into. Violet made her way toward it. She needed answers, and her racing heart and sweaty palms weren't going to stop her from getting them.

The front door was open, and she stealthily stepped inside. She had forgotten her baseball bat in her haste to leave the school, so grabbed a knife from the kitchen. The house was silent, but still she moved slowly, alert for any signs of movement. She could hear her own heart beating.

Violet went into to the living room. There was no sign of the woman who bit her, but there had definitely been a struggle. The glass coffee table was smashed, as though something heavy had been dropped onto it. Pictures had fallen from the fireplace, and couch cushions were on the floor. There was a brown stain on the carpet next to a broken mug. Violet tried to remember if the room had been like this when she arrived, but she'd not had much time to explore before being bitten and chased. She turned to leave, noticing another stain on the carpet. This one looked like blood.

It throws itself onto the man. He fights with it, throwing it down onto the coffee table, but it gets up and chases him from the room.

Her heart was racing. Where had that come from?

Was that me? Did I do that?

Nothing made sense. She needed to go upstairs, to the last place she remembered.

The stairs creaked beneath her feet, but Violet was less concerned now about the noise. There was no one here. The bathroom door was open. There was more blood. Handprints were on the wood of the door, dried streaks staining the white surface. She stepped into the small room. There was a first aid box on the floor, along with even more blood. More than her bite wound would've caused.

She sat down on the mat, in the spot she had been in when she fell into the room. Taking another breath, she closed her eyes, willing the memories to come back.

Eventually, they did. She soon wished they hadn't.

HE FINISHED STITCHING UP HER ARM. IT HURT, BUT SHE *knew it had to be done. The man spoke quietly, even though they were sure the thing had gone. It hadn't pounded on the door for a long time.*

"Done. Now I'll just wrap this up. We don't want it to get infected."

Violet's head was spinning. "Something doesn't feel right. I feel sick."

There was concern in his brown eyes. "Put your head between your legs. You're probably just in shock. I think we all are."

She was about to do what he said when she noticed he had his own wound. His right arm was bleeding. "Were you bitten, too? Your arm—"

"Don't worry. It's just a scratch."

"It's bleeding."

He examined it. "I caught it on the door when I ran in. Could you pass me that towel? I'll try to clean myself up."

She nodded, reaching behind her for one of the pink towels. For some reason, she couldn't take her eyes away from his wound. "It looks deep."

"I think it might be." He squeezed his arm slightly, causing more blood to seep out.

Something in the air. Something new. A smell. Violet felt something, something she'd never felt before. The man was staring at her, a worried expression on his face. He touched her forehead.

"Let me get something on here. You're burning up." He reached for another towel, his arm inches from her face.

It was too much. Violet didn't know what was happening, but her mouth latched on to his skin.

"What are you doing?"

The blood hit her tongue, and she felt fantastic. It was like she could feel every millimeter of her body getting stronger, and she needed more.

"Get off me!" He fought against her, but she was stronger

now. She needed to taste. Needed to bite.

"Help!"

It bit.

He pushed it off. Opened the door and ran. It chased. On the stairs, it almost caught him, but he pushed it back. It hit its head and could taste its own blood.

It followed him downstairs and jumped. He fought with it, throwing it onto the coffee table, but it got up and chased him out of the room.

He ran to a new house, and it followed. There were other its in there, too, but they were busy. He ran into a bedroom and through another door, slamming it shut. It hit the door over and over and over until its hands were bruised. But then things began to change.

She was falling. Then she hit the floor. She felt weak. Everything slowed down. Turned black.

AS THE MEMORIES FADED AWAY, VIOLET FOUND HERSELF on her feet in the bathroom. It was true. She had bitten him. He had tried to save her, and the infection in her blood or whatever else it was, came to life and tried to kill the first person who had tried to help.

She left the room. She was disgusted with herself. Hated herself. But she needed to know. She had to find out what happened to him after that.

She went back into the house where she had woken up and headed upstairs. To her right was the bedroom with the flowery wallpaper. She stepped inside, heading for the closed door from her memory. It looked like a walk-in closet. She paused, her hand on the doorknob. Violet knew what she was about to find, but she had to see it. It was her fault, and she needed to finish it.

She swung open the door. There he was—dead, just like the others. He spun around, hissing angrily at the sight of her.

"I'm sorry," she breathed.

He ran toward her, but Violet was faster. She stepped to the side, and then plunged the knife into the back of his head. He dropped to the floor, twitching for only a moment. His blood squirted onto her shirt, but she barely noticed. When he was still, Violet screamed. She couldn't hold it in, and it escaped even though she didn't want it to. It wasn't a scream of fear—it was anger. Anger at what she had done, at the hideous thing she had become.

What am I?

Violet pulled the knife out of his head. She turned it over in her hands, terrible thoughts running through her mind. She could do it, end it right there. Her friends would be safer without her around; she knew that. If she did it, she wouldn't be able to hurt anyone else.

"Violet?"

It was Matt's voice. It sounded like he was coming up the stairs. Violet got up and hurried to the doorway just in time to see him arrive on the landing. Relief covered his face at the sight of her, but it faded.

"Is that blood on your shirt?"

Violet looked down. "No?"

Matt's brows knitted together. "Right. Okay. I'll be honest, I'd be more reassured if I didn't feel like there was a question mark at the end of your answer."

Violet sighed, heading back into the room. Matt followed, frowning at the body on the floor.

"What are you doing here?" Violet asked, before he could ask her the same thing.

"I heard you scream." His eyes swept from the dead man to Violet, and back again. She still held the knife tightly in her hands.

"You followed me?"

He nodded. "I saw you opening the gates. I was worried, so I climbed over the wall. I lost sight of you, but I was just outside when I heard you screaming. What happened?" He swung his eyes back to the man on the floor again. "Did it attack you?"

"He saved me," Violet said quietly. "That first day. He saved me. I...I left him here, and he turned and now he's dead."

Matt moved closer, putting a hand on her shoulder. "You did the right thing."

Violet shook her head.

"Yes, you ended his suffering." Matt's voice was insistent, which made Violet feel even worse.

"No. It's my fault."

But Matt didn't understand. He simply pulled her closer to him, enveloping her in a hug. She could feel his heart beating against her chest, and allowed herself one moment to feel safe. Then she pulled away. "I can't stay."

"You're right; we need to get back."

"No, I can't stay with you. With any of you. It's too dangerous."

Violet watched the confusion spread across his face. "It's safer if we stay together. You know that."

"No. It's safer if I'm alone." She tucked the knife into her pocket, making the decision then and there, and headed for the door. Matt followed.

"If you leave, I'm coming with you."

Violet shook her head. "Don't be ridiculous. You said it yourself; it's safer in a group. Go back to the school."

"If you're going, I'm going."

"You can't leave your friends."

"Exactly."

Violet sighed. This was going nowhere. She knew Matt well enough by now to know he wasn't going to let her just wander out into the zompocolyptic wasteland alone. She also knew she shouldn't go back to the school to constantly live in fear that she was going to snap and eat someone. But if Matt followed her and died, that would be her fault, too. Or if something happened to the others because they didn't have enough people? There was no good option. Matt moved closer slowly, as if approaching a deer.

"No matter what, we'll keep each other safe. I'm not leaving you alone, so tell me where we're going."

THEY WENT BACK TO THE SCHOOL. WHAT CHOICE DID Violet really have? They made their way up to the teachers' lounge where the others were waiting. Sam and Joe hugged them both, relief on their faces.

"When we realized you were gone..." Joe began.

"Where were you?" asked Sam.

Violet got the feeling the concern in his voice wasn't solely centered on the two of them. Something else was going on. She looked around. Maggie and Emily were both standing anxiously by the window. Tom was pacing.

"What's wrong?" Violet asked, the vicious butterflies in her stomach rearing their ugly heads again.

"Our weapons have gone," Sam muttered.

Violet's eyes widened, automatically eyeing the table where the bats and other makeshift weapons were usually kept. Matt still had his bat and she had her new knife, but that was it.

"They must've gotten them this morning," Joe began. "After you left. The door was locked before then."

Guilt washed over Violet. She'd only been back for five minutes, and already something was her fault—she'd left her friends exposed! Joe squeezed her arm reassuringly. "Don't blame yourself, Vi. It's not your fault those people can't be trusted."

"I shouldn't have unlocked the door," she muttered, shaking her head. "It's my fault the weapons have gone."

Sam strode toward the door. "Let's go and get them back." He turned to Maggie and Emily, "You two stay here. Lock the door behind us."

Violet tossed over the keys, grateful Sam was letting her come along. Not only was this her fault, but she also wasn't ready to play damsel in distress while the men dealt with all the problems. Besides which, she didn't think many damsels spent their days stabbing zombies or eating flesh.

Tom stayed, too, because...well, Violet didn't really know why. But she was just happy he did.

Matt, Joe, Sam, and Violet headed to the library. The newcomers weren't there, but they'd certainly left their mark on the place. There was garbage everywhere: chip packets, cans, cartons. The couches had been moved around, and one had been stabbed repeatedly—the stuffing pulled out and thrown all over the floor.

"Looks like they helped themselves to more food after

we went to bed," Joe said, gesturing to the debris. There were also dozens of beer cans, more than Joe had collected from the supermarket.

"They must've brought their own alcohol," Matt suggested, pointing to the men's backpacks in the corner. Violet moved over to the bags. Most were empty now, but one was almost full to bursting with money. She picked up a handful of bills. "Where did they get all this from?"

"It's not like they can use it anymore," Matt replied.

"Guess we missed the party." Joe emptied out one of the other backpacks. Violet watched as several small, clear plastic bags fell onto the floor. Most were empty, but a couple still contained pills or white powder.

"Seems like it," Sam agreed. "I'm not sure things are going to be as smooth as we hoped."

THE FOUR OF THEM WENT TO THE CAFETERIA NEXT, where they found Tom, Emily, and Maggie waiting for them. Violet initially assumed they'd come of their own free will, but another look at Emily's face suggested they'd been forced out. The men were there, too, sitting at the table beside Violet's friends. And Tom.

John smiled when he saw the others approaching.

"Morning, we've been waiting for you. Breakfast?" He gestured to the food on the table. There was a lot—more than was needed. Violet knew well enough that their supplies wouldn't last long if they didn't ration them.

"Where are our weapons?" Sam asked. No one spoke for a moment. Violet crossed her arms across her chest in some effort to look as though she wasn't terrified. But she was.

The smile on John's face faded a little, but it didn't disappear. He held eye contact with Sam.

"We didn't think weapons were necessary." He nodded at Matt's bat. "Why don't you put that down? Wouldn't want there to be any accidents." At that moment, Violet was incredibly grateful that her knife was tucked away in the back of her jeans. Sure, it may have been ever so slightly stabbing her every time she moved, but at least John wasn't about to take it.

"If you don't think we should have weapons, why do you have a gun?" Maggie asked, her voice lacking its usual timid tone. John sighed, then reached into his pocket and took out a handgun. He glanced back at the rest of the group. "We're all friends here, so I'm sure I'll never have to use this. Sit down, have some breakfast." He grinned a yellow smile, gesturing for the group to join him at the table. None of them did.

John frowned. "Sit."

His tone was serious. Without saying a word, Violet and the others slowly lowered themselves onto the chairs in front of them. Her heart was racing.

"Good." John sighed. "See how easy that was." He wasn't smiling anymore, and he leaned a little into the table. "Now, let's discuss a few...changes. Things are going to be a bit different around here."

SURE, VIOLET, LET'S OPEN THE GATES TO FIVE STRANGE men and let them in to the only safe place in town during the zombie apocalypse.

It had been a week since the confrontation with John and the others. Violet had to admit she wished she'd ignored Matt's request and run away when she had the chance. Sure, she'd be alone. And sure, she'd almost certainly have been eaten alive by now. But at least she wouldn't have been spending her days cooking, cleaning, and washing the clothes of five men who seemed to have no idea how to get food into their mouths.

No, that wasn't fair. She didn't want to leave her friends behind. It didn't matter they'd barely known each other, or not known each other at all, before the world ended. It didn't matter they were all one hundred percent alive, and Violet thought she was about fifty percent there. They had become close. It was like she was living with family. And Tom.

John and the others were not part of her family. In fact, Violet knew she would happily chew their faces off without a second thought. These men had their own way of doing things, and seeing as how they were the ones with the weapons, they were the ones in control. The original group had been split in two and given different jobs accordingly. Maggie,

T
E
N

Emily, and Violet had their own routine, which had to be followed every single day. They cooked, cleaned, and washed clothes. It was hardly what Violet would've called 'empowering' work. The only time they saw Joe, Sam, Matt, or Tom was at meals, when they were made to sit at opposite ends of the table and listen to John and his friends laugh and joke while they ate in silence.

Whenever Violet or the other two finished their chores and were allowed some free time, they had to stay inside, within sight of John or his friends. At night, they slept in a locked classroom, while Matt and the others were shut in the teachers' lounge. John and his men still had the library.

The routine for Matt, Sam, Joe, and Tom was very different. They spent every moment outside, whatever the weather, patrolling the fences. They had no weapons, of course. Had been told simply to "handle it" if they saw anything. Violet sometimes caught sight of one of them out of the window. How had things changed so much and so quickly?

THAT MORNING, EVERYONE ATE BREAKFAST TOGETHER AS usual. There wasn't much food laid out, and John eyed the table disapprovingly.

"Where's the rest of it?" he asked Violet.

"We have to save some. We don't have much left."

He scowled. "Yeah, or maybe you're keeping more back for yourselves." His eyes swept across the group before settling on Edd and Vince. "Go check." They got up and headed for the kitchen, but were back within moments.

"She's right," Vince said. "There's hardly any food."

John turned back to Violet, and she held his gaze. If anything, she was angrier than he was. It wasn't her fault he and his men were such pigs. She kept her face hard, imagining what it would be like to chew his big nose clean off. The thought—hideous as it might have been— comforted her immensely.

Eventually, John spoke, addressing the rest of the

group. "Well, it appears that we need some more food." His eyes locked with Sam's. "You and your friends can go and get some for us."

Sam seemed unsurprised by John's proposal, and Violet supposed he'd probably been waiting for it for a while.

"We need the car."

John shook his head. "No, go on foot."

"We can't get much if we're walking."

"Improvise. I need that car. Ours is wrecked, and I'm counting on that one if we need to get out of here fast."

"So we just carry the food?" Sam asked through gritted teeth.

"You'll just have to find somewhere to put it."

"I can think of a couple of places," Joe muttered, and Violet snorted. She tried to cover it with a cough. Luckily, it seemed John hadn't heard. He kept his gaze fixed on Sam.

Sam looked angry, but eventually nodded. "We'll need our weapons."

"Why?" John asked. "Like you said, you're going to be carrying the food. Don't want space taken up with a baseball bat." He grinned, and then held out his hands. "Well? What are you waiting for? No time like the present."

Violet and the others got to their feet, but John shook his head, gesturing to the women. "No, not you. Sam and his merry men need a reason to come back. Otherwise, you might all just decide to run off into the sunset together."

Maggie and Emily sat down reluctantly, but Violet remained standing. John raised an eyebrow. "Something on your mind, princess?"

Princess? Let's see you call me that when I'm chewing your ears off.

"I want to go, too."

"We can't all get what we want," Edd sneered, but John held up a hand to silence him.

"Why? It's pretty scary out there. It might be too much for a young lady like yourself."

Violet scowled. "I've been out before, on the last supply run. And I was alone outside longer than any of these guys. I can handle myself."

Matt nodded. "She's useful. She's fast and knows her way around. We could use her."

Okay, I'm none of those things, but I appreciate the lies.

Violet could tell John didn't like being told what to do, but he was also no fool. If he thought she would be able to get him more supplies, he almost certainly wouldn't be stubborn enough to refuse.

Probably.

"Fine," he relented, gritting his teeth. "But hurry back. We wouldn't want your friends to worry." He meant Maggie and Emily.

Violet nodded, giving the two of them a reassuring smile. One that said, *We'll be back, I promise.*

THE FIVE OF THEM—VIOLET, MATT, SAM, JOE, AND TOM— moved through the streets in silence, none of them feeling safe enough to talk while still in view of the school. Sam led the group past the burned-out house, around the corner, and up the front path of another. The door was locked, but the yard was surrounded by a thick hedge, so it seemed a secure enough place to stop and talk.

"So... this is less than ideal," Joe drawled. "Violet, I'm starting to think maybe you *shouldn't* have let them in."

"I'm so sorry. I was such an idiot."

Sam shook his head. "Any one of us would've done the same thing," he said reassuringly. "It was the right thing to do. I guess we just have to realize that people aren't how they used to be."

"Maybe they are," Joe suggested. "There have always been scumbags like that; there just used to be others left to balance it out. They're probably the ones who died first."

"Cheerful." Matt's sigh was heavy.

"What should we do?" Violet asked, shivering as a bite of wind whipped across her face.

"We should just go," Tom suggested.

"What do you mean?" Sam asked. "They've still got

Maggie and Emily; how would we get them back?"

"We wouldn't. I know you don't want to hear it, but we have to think about our best chance for survival."

"Leaving the others behind?" Matt sounded angry. "That's our best option in your eyes?"

Tom nodded. "They won't hurt the girls. They're useful to them."

"That's comforting," Joe muttered sarcastically.

Tom continued. "But we're not useful, not really. They'll kill us when they realize that. Better we leave now." He looked at each of the group for approval, but Joe turned and began to walk back down the path.

"Where are you going?" Sam asked.

"To get the supplies so we can get back."

Tom's face flushed red, and he almost spat fire when he spoke. "You're not even going to finish hearing what I have to say?"

"No. I walked away mid-conversation because your ridiculous, cowardly speech was boring me to death. I suppose my survival instincts kicked in." Joe threw his hands up. "Leaving Maggie and Emily in that place is not an option, so why are we even talking about it?"

Sam nodded. "He's right. We have to do what they want. We keep them happy for now while we think of a plan. At the moment, we only have two options: either we leave the school together, or we make them leave."

"Or we kill them," Matt added. When everybody focused on him, he shrugged. "Not saying we should, just that it's an option."

Sam spotted a shovel against the side of the house and grabbed it. He spoke to Tom. "If you want to go, then go. We won't stop you. If not, then stop talking and let's get this done."

Tom didn't leave. Violet knew he wouldn't—he wouldn't last a day out there on his own.

When they reached the supermarket a while later, they found the shutter around the back completely closed.

"Great," Matt muttered.

"Let's try the front," Sam said.

Several of the huge windows at the front of the store had been smashed, and Violet could tell before they even got inside that the place had been ransacked. She stepped over the broken glass, trying to be quiet. Unfortunately, trying to be quiet when walking over broken glass was the most difficult thing in the world. As they entered, making as much noise as it seemed humanly possible to do, Violet knew the place wasn't safe anymore. The others saw it, too. No one grabbed a cart. They all just stood silently, listening for sounds of movement.

"Let's just fill our backpacks and get out," Sam whispered, and they all headed off in different directions.

SO MANY OF THE SHELVES WERE EMPTY NOW, AND THERE was food smeared all over the floors. Violet reached for a lone can of tinned tomatoes still on the shelf. Empty.

"What, you just ate the tomatoes and put the can back?" she muttered with a scowl, tossing it away. Sam appeared at Violet's side.

"This wasn't just people looking for supplies; they trashed this place on purpose."

"Why would they do it?" She picked up a can of tuna and put it in her bag.

"For fun?"

Violet sighed, grabbing another tuna can. The liquid inside immediately leaked down her arm and onto her shirt. She groaned.

"That's just great," she mumbled, trying to wipe away the fishy water, but only succeeding in spreading it further across the material.

Sam and Violet moved on to the end of the aisle, finding a small stand full of seeds. Violet eyed them for a moment. Most were for growing flowers, but there were a few packs containing vegetable seeds. She took every single one. She had no idea how to grow vegetables—and didn't know if it was the right season or if they had the right soil—but it would be worth a shot if it meant they could be more self-sufficient.

"Now all we need are some cows." Sam grinned. "I could go for a cheeseburger right about now."

"I'm a vegetarian," Violet replied automatically.

A vegetarian zombie, how ironic.

They turned onto the next aisle, and saw six bikes laid out on the floor. Sam raised an eyebrow. "Wha—"

"The kids," Violet interrupted. "I saw some kids riding bikes the other day when I came outside. They must be here, too!"

"Kids? On their own?"

Violet was only half-listening, counting the bikes. "There were more than this."

"Maybe they're somewhere else?"

"Maybe." She didn't think they were.

There were voices coming from a door to their left, the one that led to the dark warehouse. They were kid's voices, but not happy ones. They were screaming, crying out in fear and pain. She made to run for the door, but Sam pulled her back.

"We need to help them," she argued, fighting against him. The screaming got louder, closer.

"It's too late!" Sam kept hold of her, stronger than she was.

The doors burst open and three young boys ran out, each bloodied. They grabbed their bikes and climbed on. The first two peddled away quickly, but one paused.

"Get out," he ordered before following his friends. Sam and Violet didn't need to be told twice, turning tail and sprinting in the same direction. Violet heard the warehouse door open, and the screaming from inside got louder.

There are still kids down there.

She didn't let herself look back. Sam shouted to Matt and the others, telling them to run. Violet couldn't see where they were.

As Sam and Violet rounded the corner toward the front of the store, they saw Joe. His eyes widened as he caught sight of whatever was behind them, making Violet even more secure in her decision not to turn around. He shouldered his bag, sprinting toward the exit.

Matt was waiting by the smashed glass, Tom already outside. The kids were long gone. Violet ran until her legs felt like they were on fire, over the broken glass and out. Now that they were back together, they charged toward the alleyway that led to the parking lot. Tom was out in front, then Sam, Joe, Matt, and Violet at the back.

But Violet made her first mistake—looking over her shoulder. She couldn't see the biters yet, but that didn't mean they weren't close. Unfortunately, trying to do two things at once, like running and using her eyes, had never been her strength. She glanced back to see where she was going just in time to watch the ground fly out from underneath her. She hit the concrete with a thud. There was no opportunity to register the pain in her hands and knees, because she could hear them coming now. She scrambled to her feet, stumbling for the alleyway. Her friends were already disappearing down it, but she was too late. Her few seconds on the ground had given a zombie in a tuxedo the chance to cut her off. He shrieked, running toward Violet with his hands outstretched. She managed to dodge his crumbling fingers, but then made her second error—turning and going a different way.

It was a stupid mistake. She had enough time to follow Matt and the others, but she panicked. Still, it was too late now. She was pretty sure she knew another way to the parking lot, so even though she could hear Matt calling her name, she kept going. She reached another alley, one she knew would take her where she needed to go. But it was barricaded with half a dozen garbage cans and bits of scrap metal.

"Oh, come on." She glanced back to see more biters heading her way. There was a row of stores to her left, so she darted toward them. Three had their shutters down, no way of getting in, but the forth didn't. As she approached, she could see movement inside, and realized with excitement that the door was ajar. She had just reached the store and was wrapping her fingers around the handle, when she discovered the people inside were neither friendly nor alive. The two biters hissed, baring their bloodied teeth and throwing themselves against the glass door, forcing it shut.

She continued past the stores, not sure how much longer she could run, but knowing the alternative meant getting eaten alive. There was a narrow gap between two buildings, which at least provided a place to hide while she fought to catch her breath. She tried to think about where she could go, but was too exhausted to even know where she was right now.

"Hey!"

Violet raised her head, but there was no one around. Still, it had definitely been a voice.

"Go to the bike store!"

Violet knew where it was—just around the corner. She slipped back out onto the street, spotting six biters only a few yards away. She could probably outrun them, but she'd have to go now, before they saw her.

Too late.

Violet groaned as they began to run in her direction, screeching as they did so. She charged toward the bike store, and could see the shutter was raised a little off the ground. It was barely enough for her to fit under. Hurriedly, she took off her backpack, lay down on her stomach, and tried to ease herself under the tiny gap. She could hear the biters now. Her head and arms were inside, but the shutter was hard against her back. She was starting to worry she wouldn't fit. Suddenly, there was someone grabbing her arms, pulling her into the darkness of the store.

Then there were hands on her legs, too, trying to pull her back out.

"No!" she yelled, as if it were going to make any difference to a zombie. She continued to wriggle, kicking free of their grabbing hands. It worked. Finally, she was inside.

Violet got up on her hands and knees, no energy left to stand, and crawled away from the shutter. She could see the faces of two dead women, as they tried to follow her under the gap. A figure stepped between the nearest biter and Violet, then smashed the creature's head to pieces with a hammer. Seconds later, her hammer-wielding savior cracked open the skull of the second zombie, kicked the corpses back under the shutter, and forced it closed.

Violet collapsed, and everything went black.

VIOLET WOKE SLOWLY, HER EYES ADJUSTING TO THE SEMI darkness.

Oh no, please don't let me have killed anyone else. This zombie thing is making it hard to make new friends.

Cautiously, she took in her surroundings. There was a boy sitting not far from her. He was young, probably about eight or nine. He had white-blond hair that was splattered with blood, and a scratched and bruised face. He hadn't been half-eaten, which was a happy change of pace. He stared at Violet for a moment. Neither said anything. She gave herself a moment to take in her surroundings. The room was large and dark, with only a few slivers of light coming in through gaps in the barricaded windows. They'd been covered up with flattened cardboard boxes, stuck together roughly with tape. There were bikes on stands nailed to the walls, and many more shoved into a corner of the room to free some space. Just behind the boy was a large pile of blankets and pillows, as though a lot of people had been sleeping in the same space. There were also some comic books, empty packets of potato chips, candy bars, and other telltale signs of children living in a small place.

Finally, Violet broke the silence. "How long was I out?"

"Only a few minutes."

She nodded.

"Were you bitten?" The boy held the bloodied hammer tightly. Violet shook her head, praying he wouldn't want to check. Her scar may have been old, but it was clearly bite-shaped.

"Were you?" she asked.

Pausing, he shook his head. He moved to a table by the wall, picked up a bottle of water, and threw it toward her. Violet picked it up off the floor after missing possibly the easiest catch ever, and gulped down huge mouthfuls.

"Drink it slowly," the boy instructed. "You don't want to be sick."

She did as she was told, then put the bottle down. She was already feeling a little better, but still not ready to stand up yet. She realized for the first time that the boy was alone.

"The other two..." she began. He shook his head. Violet looked down. She supposed they had turned, or maybe been jumped on the way back to the store. Either way, they were dead.

"What's your name?" she asked.

The boy paused, as if unsure whether he wanted to answer. "Toby."

"I'm Violet. Thank you for the water. And for saving my life. I probably should've said that first actually."

He shrugged, fiddling with some little screws on the table beside him. Violet pressed on. "How old are you?"

"Nine."

"And your friends? They're the same age?"

"They were. They're dead now. All of them."

"I'm so sorry."

He shrugged again. Violet got to her feet slowly, surveying the dark store.

"Have you been living here this whole time?" she asked.

"We were all at Noah's house for his birthday sleepover. His mom was sick and went to bed early. In the morning, she tried to kill us. We ran away."

"And came here?"

He shook his head. "No, first we went to the woods. We have a secret camp. We stayed there for a while, but then we came back into town. The monsters chased us, and we hid here. We could fit under the gap."

Violet was impressed. A group of kids had managed to survive for so long, yet she had lasted less than a few hours before being bitten.

"How did you manage to stay alive?"

Toby shrugged. "We tried to stay out of sight. The monsters follow sound, so we kept quiet. The bikes are fast, but don't make noise like a car. We got food every couple of days and came back here. Most of the time, they didn't even see us. They're stupid. You can stay away from them easily as long as you're clever. It's not too hard."

All right, kid, I get the picture.

Toby's eyes flicked to the floor. Violet knew he was thinking the same thing she was—what would he do now since his friends were dead?

"Do you want to come back with me? We're living in the school."

"I know," he replied. "We see you sometimes. Your group, I mean. We see you standing by the gate. The other day we saw you let in the bad men."

"The bad men?"

"The men who trashed the supermarket. The ones who set the fires. We saw them kill a man and a woman and steal their food. They're worse than the monsters." He grabbed a towel, then wiped at the dried blood on his hands. "I don't want to come back with you. I'm safer here."

VIOLET HATED LEAVING TOBY BEHIND, BUT SHE KNEW HE was right. He was better off in the store, away from John and the others. A big part of her wanted to stay with him—she knew he would've let her—but she had to go. She couldn't leave her friends.

She hugged Toby goodbye, an action she wasn't altogether sure he enjoyed due to the strong smell of tuna that still lingered on her clothes, and then he opened the shutter enough for her to slip under. Violet held her knife tightly in her sweaty hand, tiptoeing out into the street. She still wasn't exactly confident in using it, but she figured that as long as she didn't slip over and stab herself, she'd be okay. Luckily, she didn't have to use it yet. The biters had left the outside of the store, and all that remained were the corpses that had their heads caved in by Toby's hammer.

Violet glanced from left to right, the gentle wind blowing her hair across her forehead. The backpack was where she'd dropped it, so she put it back on. Slowly, eyes and ears alert for the dead, she made her way back around to the main road. When she got to the front of the store, she heard the rumble of an engine. She instinctively hid behind a burned-out car at the side of the road. If the people driving it were anything like John, she didn't want them to see her. She saw the vehicle approach. It was a battered Ford with scratched white paintwork. The windows were down, and she chanced a look at the people inside.

"Sam!" Violet jumped up, recognizing the driver immediately. The car stopped, and Sam grinned.

"We were starting to get worried," he said.

Matt swung open the door and got out, hugging her tightly. Violet allowed herself to relax for the first time in hours, finally feeling safe, happy, and like nothing could destroy that perfect moment.

"Violet, you stink."

Joe had gotten out of the car and was standing beside Matt, regarding her with eyebrows raised. Matt stepped back a little, as if smelling her for the first time.

"It's fish," she muttered. "I spilled fish juice on myself, okay?"

Matt smiled, looking her up and down. "Are you okay?" he asked.

"Besides the smell?"

"Besides the smell."

"Yeah, I'm okay."

"We should get back," Joe said. "I don't like leaving the others for so long, and your stench is making me feel sick."

"Always the charmer," Violet drawled, rolling her eyes and getting into the car. Matt sat beside her, clearly caring less than the others about her smell.

Is he breathing through his mouth?

That doesn't matter. The point is he's being nice.

"Are you guys okay? Violet asked, surveying her friends. None of them appeared any worse for wear. Joe nodded from the passenger seat.

"No problems at all," he said breezily.

Tom scoffed from his place beside Matt.

"What?" Joe asked.

"You forgot me," Tom spat. "You literally got into the car and started driving."

"It was an accident," Sam replied airily.

"It was only for a second," Joe added. "Then we realized."

"You only remembered me because I threw that rock at the car."

Joe waved his hand. "The point is, we came back."

The car pulled away, and Violet glanced over at the front of the bike store. She could see Toby in one of the second-floor windows. He watched her nervously, as though he thought she would soon be dead.

Violet didn't blame him. She was halfway there already.

OH CRAP. OH CRAP. THIS IS BAD.

Calm down. It could be worse.

But as Violet stood over the corpse, the taste of his blood still fresh in her mouth, she wasn't exactly sure how it could be any worse than this.

It had all happened an hour ago. She was heading toward the library to pick up another load of dirty laundry, wondering bitterly how the men managed to go through so many clothes, when she'd heard a voice.

"So how's your day going?"

Matt was standing by the fire exit, smiling at her. The door was propped open slightly behind him. She could see the rain falling heavily outside. It had been raining all day, and it showed no sign of letting up. He was soaked to the skin, and water fell in heavy drops from his clothes onto the floor.

"It's going great," she replied sarcastically. "Just about to get another load of dirty socks and underwear to wash by hand in cold water. How's yours?"

Matt laughed. "It's fantastic. I'm just letting myself dry off a little before I head back out into the rain. I like to really *feel* how drenched I'm getting. The wind is super helpful, too."

Violet felt a smile creep across her face. Even though they were both miserable, Matt knew just how to cheer her up.

**E
L
E
V
E
N**

119

"I'm sorry you have to be outside," she said.

"I'm sorry you have to wash their boxers."

"It's worse than that."

Matt's eyes widened. "Oh no, not—"

Violet cringed. "Yeah. Briefs."

"That's so much worse."

"I know." Violet sighed, leaning against the wall. "Do you see any end to this?"

Matt moved a little closer. "I honestly do. We just have to be patient. I think Sam is putting something together. It's just hard to plan since they started putting one of their guys in the room with us at night. But don't worry, we'll figure it out." He put a hand on Violet's shoulder. It felt comforting, yet she was suddenly aware of how close they were, of how heavy his hand felt. Matt was gazing at her intently, as though he were about to say something else.

Then she smelled it—it was faint, but it was there. Blood.

Violet instinctively backed away from his touch, feeling her stomach start to churn. "You're cut."

Matt looked surprised, then lifted his sleeve to show a thin scratch on his arm.

"I caught it on some branches when I was walking the perimeter, just wasn't paying attention," he explained. "It's small; doesn't even hurt really."

The rain and his wet clothes had hidden the smell before, but now it was coming through so strongly that Violet had to force herself to take another step back. She shook her head, trying to focus on something, anything else. Her thoughts were getting harder to control, and things around her seemed to be taking on a soft edge.

"You should go," she stammered.

Matt glanced back at the door. It was still pouring. "Yeah, I will. I just thought while it was raining this hard, I might—"

"You should go, go back outside. We shouldn't be here together." Violet closed her eyes, trying to get everything to stop spinning.

Matt cleared his throat, stepping back. "Yeah, yeah, okay. It was good to see you, anyway." She heard him push the door a little wider, then it clicked shut behind him. Violet opened her eyes, exhaling loudly. That had been way too close. Where Matt had been standing was a small puddle of rainwater—the only evidence he'd been there. She suddenly felt guilty, worried she'd hurt his feelings.

Better his feelings hurt than his arm chewed off.

Violet took another breath as the spinning in her head subsided, heading into the library.

"Hello, there."

Daniel was sitting at one of the tables. He watched Violet enter the same way a cat observes a mouse. He didn't move, but his eyes never left her. She didn't know much about him; only that he seemed to spend most of his time reading or touching himself. She'd been lucky enough to walk in on him doing both. Thankfully, he'd been too absorbed in each activity to notice.

"Hi," Violet replied, reaching down to pick up the clothes the men had so helpfully left on the floor.

"Coming to get the laundry?"

Nope, just browsing.

"That's right," she replied.

Daniel got to his feet. "Which one are you again? Sarah?"

"Violet."

"Close enough."

Literally not one letter the same, but sure.

She finished picking up the clothes and made for the door, but Daniel stepped out to block her exit. He had small eyes, like a snake, and dried saliva at the corners of his mouth. His hair hung limply to his shoulders, smelling of grease and cigarette smoke. Repulsion for him skittered over her skin.

"There's no hurry," he began. "Why don't you take a break?"

"I need to wash these."

"Do it later; you must be exhausted. I know those guys work you too hard. I'm not like them. Come and sit down. We can talk."

"I need to get this done." Violet made to push past him, but Daniel grabbed her arm, forcing her to drop the clothes. For a moment, he just stared, then he released his grip.

"You better pick those up," he sneered. Violet held his gaze for a moment, and then knelt. As she did, he kicked out, hitting her square in the face and knocking her back. A fountain of blood poured from her nose. Gasping, she held out her hands to try to stop the bleeding. Red liquid trickled through her fingers, and her eyes watered from the pain. Daniel approached her slowly.

"I asked you nicely," he began, his voice low. "Now I'm going to tell you. Stay down and do what I say. Or next time it won't be your nose I make bleed." His face was lit with disturbing glee as he started to unbuckle his belt.

But Violet still had her knife. As he approached, she grabbed it from her waistband and jammed it into his leg.

"You little—"

But the rest of his words were lost. The world around Violet began to soften. The more the blood poured, the softer everything became. Colors and shapes disappeared. All that was left was the beautiful crimson. She knew what was happening, but she didn't try to fight it. This time, she was an observer, watching as the creature she became tore into Daniel's flesh. It ripped out his throat. Within seconds, he was dead. Then it fed.

VIOLET WOKE UP. HER HEAD WAS SPINNING. SHE GLANCED around, the walls of the library eventually coming into focus. Slowly, she got to her feet. Daniel's body was on the ground. Violet bit her lip, tasting the blood there.

Oh crap. Oh crap. This is bad.

Calm down. It could be worse.

She wasn't upset she'd killed him. Should she be? Either way, he was dead now. She had bigger problems than her guilt, and the first was just beginning to wake up. Daniel's grey eyes opened. When he began to breathe the rasping breaths of the dead, Violet slammed her knife into his skull.

Okay, that's one problem dealt with.

Now for the next part.

There was blood on her clothes, blood around her mouth, and blood on the floor. She also had a body to dispose of, and she had to deal with all of that before John or the others came back. Violet grabbed one of the water pots from outside and hurriedly washed her hands and face as best she could. . Her nose had at least stopped bleeding. Then she went back to the body. The bite marks on his neck were large and revealing. If anyone came in, she'd have a hard time explaining how he accidentally chewed his own neck halfway off.

She spotted a jacket on the table. After retrieving it, she brought it over to the body. It took a while—maneuvering a heavy corpse wasn't exactly an easy job—but she managed to get Daniel into the jacket and zip it up high enough to cover the bites. It also covered the teeth marks on his arms. That was an improvement. To anyone not examining the corpse too closely, it seemed like all he had was a stab wound to the head.

Violet heard footsteps, and her heart began to race. She jumped to her feet, heading for the door.

This is it. They're going to find out. They'll kill me!

"Violet?"

It wasn't John or the others. It was Joe, Matt, and Sam. They were soaking wet, studying her curiously.

"Violet, are you—" Matt was taking in her bloodied clothes with wide eyes.

"No, no, I'm fine. It's..." Violet struggled for an explanation. "It's dye from the clothes. I was washing a red sweater."

Clearly none of the men had any experience washing clothes by hand, since they seemed to immediately accept this might cause a person to become spattered with red from head to toe.

Sam nodded. "Okay, how are you?"

Violet, whose heart felt like it was about to explode, forced a smile. "Yeah. Great. Good. Fine. You?"

"You know, the usual," Sam replied. "Just trying not to drown."

Violet laughed. Probably a little too enthusiastically.

Stop acting weird; just for once try to be normal!

Though Sam and Matt seemed slightly concerned about her sudden outburst of maniacal laughter, it was Joe who appeared the most confused. Violet turned her focus on him. "Hey, it feels like I haven't seen you in ages."

Joe nodded. "Yeah, it's good to see you, Violet. Quick question, why is there a corpse on the floor behind you?" He didn't wait for a response, heading straight into the library.

Crap.

The other two followed Joe inside. They stood around the body, looking at Violet for an explanation.

She sighed, making her way over to join them. "I killed Daniel."

"I can see that," Sam muttered.

All three stared at her with expressions of complete shock.

"How?"

"When?"

"Why?"

Violet sucked in her teeth. "It's kind of a long story."

Joe raised an eyebrow. "Can you give us the gist?"

"Okay. Well, I killed him, with my knife, about half an hour ago, and I did it because he was..." She trailed off, not sure how to explain it. For some reason, she felt ashamed. Not of killing him, but of the reason she'd had to. Matt, however, was scowling at the body now.

"Did he hurt you?"

"No. Well, he kicked me in the nose, but I killed him before he could do...what he wanted to do."

Sam and Joe also glared at the corpse on the floor. Sam kicked it angrily.

"Are you all right?" Matt asked, coming a little closer.

"I'm fine."

Sam stepped forward. "We need to get rid of the body. I can make it look like he jumped the wall. We'll leave his corpse for the biters. They'll think he tried to leave and got chewed up." He gestured to Joe. "I need you to help me carry the body. Matt, I need you to check the coast is clear as we go." He addressed Violet. "Vi, I hate to ask—"

"I need to clean the floor."

EVERYTHING WENT FAR SMOOTHER THAN VIOLET could've ever imagined. John and his men immediately believed the story of Daniel jumping the wall. No one had needed to tell them. They'd gone searching for him themselves after he failed to arrive at dinner. Edd had spotted his remains out on the street from the window.

"He was an idiot," John had sighed, shaking his head. "Got what he deserved."

Violet had not been able to look at anyone during dinner, but her heart finally began to return to normal. She'd gotten away with it. Not only had she and her friends managed to cover up Daniel's death at her hands, but zombie-Violet had actually helped her. Maybe being half-dead wasn't so bad?

No, that was a stretch. It was still terrible.

But it could be worse.

ANOTHER WEEK PASSED. IT WAS TIME FOR A SUPPLY RUN, but Violet had been left behind this time. She didn't know why, only that when she, Emily, and Maggie had laid out lunch for everyone, her friends hadn't been there. John casually mentioned he'd sent them out again, not caring one iota that Violet and the others might've actually wanted to know their friends were back outside with no real weapons.

To take her mind off her absent friends, Violet had gone with Maggie to plant some of the seeds they collected on the last supply run. It was a sunny afternoon, and Violet had spent the past hour helping. Though 'helping' might've been putting it too strongly. So far, she'd already opened the first seed packet so roughly that all the seeds flew out in different directions, overfilled the watering can and soaked herself when attempting to lift it, and tripped over the rake and gone head-first into the dirt.

Emily was there too, equally baffled but less obvious about it. Zack had been ordered by John to accompany the three of them, but Violet had no idea why. Did he think Violet and the others were hatching some grand scheme to tunnel under the fence and out? Violet was sure after seeing her attempt to use a shovel, Zack would've worked out by now how unlikely it was, but he still stayed. The good thing about him, at least, was that he didn't really talk, so Violet, Emily, and Maggie spent much of the afternoon acting as though he wasn't even there.

"I'm not sure I have much hope for these," Violet muttered, looking at the overturned ground. "I'm not exactly skilled at growing food. Or gardening in general. In fact, I'm not really 'outdoorsy' at all."

"I can tell." Maggie grinned. "You screamed when you found that worm."

"It was like a *snake*," Violet argued. Maggie raised an eyebrow, gently pressing the seeds into the soil.

"How long have you been into this stuff?" Emily asked, watching the precise way she worked.

Maggie paused. "My dad used to have a vegetable garden. He was always trying to get me to help with it." When she stopped speaking, Violet realized it wasn't something she wanted to talk about. There was a story. There was always a story these days, so Violet simply nodded.

Of course, this was the precise moment Zack decided to speak for the first time.

"Did you? Ever help him, I mean?"

Maggie glanced in his direction. "No," she answered thoughtfully. "I never did."

"Why?"

Shut up, Zack! Violet yelled internally. It didn't take a genius to see this was something she didn't want to talk about. There was some painful memory wrapped up with this, Violet could tell. Emily knew, too, and shot daggers at Zack, but Maggie answered anyway.

Alive?

MAGGIE WOKE UP EARLY, AND HEADED DOWNSTAIRS TO get some breakfast. Her mother was in the kitchen, gazing out the window with a smile on her face. Maggie followed her gaze, though she didn't really need to, and saw her father working in the garden. He stood over his vegetable patch, one foot resting on his shovel, with a huge grin stretched across his lips. He was never happier than when he was working outside.

"It's a shame you never enjoyed being out there," her mother began. "You know he'd love it if you took an interest."

"I know."

"Maybe today you could—"

Maggie sighed. "Mom, you know it's not my thing."

Her mother's face fell. Maggie couldn't help but feel the sting of her comments and relented. "I'm going to see my friends in an hour, but maybe when I get back, I could ask if he needs any help."

Her mother's face broke into a smile. "Oh Maggie, you know that would make him so—" But she never got to finish her sentence, because it was then that Maggie's father began to shout. She and her mother turned back to the window to see three men in the garden. They set upon him within seconds. If Maggie hadn't seen it with her own eyes, she would never have believed it. They were biting him, eating him. Maggie's mother ran to the door and wrenched it open. She charged into the garden without even looking back. Within seconds, the creatures had her, too.

Then there was one in the house. Maggie spun around and ran for the front door, running from the screams of her parents.

"THE SCHOOL WAS THE FIRST PLACE I STOPPED. I'D BEEN running for so long."

Emily reached out, putting a hand on Maggie's shoulder. Violet did the same.

"I'm okay," she said.

They were all silent for at least a minute. But then

Zack, king of saying the wrong thing at the wrong time, spoke up. "So, isn't that the perfect reason to stay away from gardening? I mean, that's how they die—"

He didn't get to finish his sentence, because he finally caught sight of the furious glare Violet was shooting him.

"No," Maggie insisted firmly. "He always wanted me to try it, and I'm doing it now."

BY EIGHT O'CLOCK, THE GROUP WAS SITTING DOWN FOR dinner, but Sam and the others still hadn't come back. The mood in the cafeteria was tense, and Violet could tell she wasn't the only one who felt uneasy. She glanced around the table, trying to figure out what the others were thinking. Zack was silent, as usual, picking solemnly at his pasta.

Probably trying to think of more delightfully invasive questions about Maggie's dead parents.

No, that was cruel of her. He'd been okay today. A big improvement on the other men at the table anyway, and Maggie didn't seem too upset. Zack was definitely the best of John's group, though that hardly meant much. It was like saying diarrhea was better than a broken leg. It was, but that still didn't mean she wanted it.

Maggie was picking at her food, too, continually looking up at the clock on the wall. Edd and Vince were deep in conversation, and Violet didn't have to listen to know they were talking about fighting, drinking, or women. They were their three favorite, and only, topics of conversation. She glanced in their direction. Edd was grinning, waving his fork around as he spoke.

"So then I punched him right between the eyes, downed his drink, and ran off with his sister! He didn't know what to do!"

Oh, he's incorporated all three into one story. That's new.

John wasn't joining in with the conversation today, and was harder to read. Violet was sure he was planning something, but couldn't put her finger on what.

Emily wasn't eating, just staring at the wall with a blank expression on her face. Her eyes were glassy, and Violet could tell that whatever she was thinking about was far away from the rest of them. She'd gone to lie down earlier, and came back looking worse than when she'd left. Violet was worried she was getting sick.

"I'm telling you, they've gone," Edd said loudly. It seemed the conversation had shifted, and Violet sat up a little straighter.

John shook his head. "They wouldn't do that; they wouldn't leave *them*." He pointed with his fork in the direction of Violet, Emily, and Maggie.

We have names, Violet thought angrily, but said nothing.

"How can you be sure?" Vince asked. "None of them are related; they've got no reason to come back."

John shook his head again, but Edd was nodding in agreement. "Exactly, I'm telling you, they've taken whatever they've found and hit the road. Good riddance, I say. We don't need them."

"Oh yeah?" John asked. "And who's going to go out for supplies now? You?"

Edd snorted. "If I had to, but we don't need to do that. We've got Hannah." He pointed at Violet.

Why is my name so hard to remember? It's literally six letters.

Edd continued. "Remember what she said before? 'I can handle myself'." He spoke in a ridiculous high-pitched imitation of Violet's voice, and she scowled, the fork in her hand suddenly feeling very friendly indeed.

John shook his head. "We're not sending Hannah out."

Oh my God, it's Violet!

"We're not sending *any* of the girls out. You three can go next time. We need to keep them here."

Violet rolled her eyes, thinking at first that this was just another example of John's casual sexism. She was just gearing up to roll out her 'anything men can do, we can do' speech, when she found herself halted in her tracks. The moment John spoke about keeping the women in the school, Emily tensed up. Her eyes dropped to the floor, and her whole posture seemed to change. She appeared smaller, more delicate. Violet watched her intently, trying to catch her friend's eye, but Emily wouldn't meet her gaze. Her eyes were red, something Violet had at first put down to tiredness.

Has she been crying?

As she turned her head a little Violet noticed the red mark on her cheek.

Someone has hit her.

Violet's stomach sank, and a horrible realization bubbled.

"Yeah, you're right." Edd grinned. "We don't want them going too far." His eyes were on Emily, and now it all made sense. Emily hadn't been there when she and Maggie had fixed dinner. Violet had assumed she was sleeping—she was supposed to be sleeping. When she finally arrived at dinner, she was red-eyed and didn't talk to anyone.

Violet got to her feet, the chair clattering out from behind her. The table fell silent. She stared John down. Her mind was racing, her cheeks hot, teeth and fists clenched. Emily was the only one not looking at Violet; she had the attention of everyone else at the table.

"What's the matter, Hayley?" Vince asked.

"It's Violet! It's always been Violet!" But she wasn't even mad about that; her blazing eyes were fixed on John.

"Sit down," he said. He didn't speak loudly, but Violet knew he was angry. She didn't care. However mad he might be, she was five times that.

"What did you do to her?" Violet growled, unblinking.

"Sit down."

"What did you do?" She slammed her hands on the table.

John got to his feet, removing the gun from the back of his jeans and raising it. He pointed it at Violet. "I think you need to calm down." He scowled angrily, and she knew he was serious. She would have been more scared, however, if he didn't have a large piece of something green wedged between his teeth.

"Do you think this is a joke?" he growled. "Do you think I won't kill you?"

Don't look at it. Don't look at it.

"It's like you don't understand the situation here. We're in control!"

How does he not feel it? It's like a tree.

Ben, who had been sleeping under the table, suddenly began to whimper loudly. He moved to the fire doors at the side of the cafeteria, scratching at the wood.

"What's he doing?" John asked, his tone irritated, still holding up his gun.

"He can sense them; he warns us," Violet replied through gritted teeth. As much as she feared the dead, right now she was too busy being mad at John to even consider the fact they might be inside the fence.

John glanced from Ben to the door, then to the rest of the group. "Edd, go check the fences."

Edd snorted, picking up another can of beer. "I'm not going out there; get the kid to do it." He meant Zack; Edd hated him.

John nodded at Zack. "Go."

He got up.

"It's not safe to go alone," Violet found herself saying. She hated herself for caring. Zack was one of *them* after all. But he'd been with Maggie and Violet in the kitchen all afternoon while they were preparing dinner. She knew he couldn't have hurt Emily, and she felt fairly certain he wouldn't have even wanted to. She didn't want him to get killed if the dead were actually out there.

But John didn't like being told what to do, and his eyes narrowed.

"Fine, *you* go with him."

Fine with me.

Violet got to her feet, motioning for Maggie to do the same. She moved to Emily, taking her hand.

"No," John said. "Leave her. No reason for her to be punished for your behavior."

Edd was grinning. Violet shook her head, pulling at Emily's hand. "I'm not leaving her here."

John raised his gun again. "Don't you forget who's in charge here!" His voice echoed off the walls of the huge room. All thoughts of the spinach were gone. Violet knew he was serious now. When he next spoke, his voice was little more than a whisper. "I've been very patient. I don't want to spoil our peaceful mood by killing you. But if you push me too far, I'll do it."

"Just go," Emily whispered. "I'll be fine."

"Emily—"

John raised the gun, aiming it at Emily's head now. "Will this work better?" Emily began to shake, and Violet reluctantly let go of her hand. John lowered the gun.

I'm going to kill you.

She didn't know how or when, but she knew she would.

THEY WALKED THE LENGTH OF THE FENCES, WHICH TOOK around forty-five minutes. It was dark now, but luckily there was no sign of any biters. Violet guessed Ben had gotten upset about the raised voices and that was why he'd been acting strangely.

It had started to rain around ten minutes before, just a light shower, but Violet got the feeling it was going to get heavier as the night drew on. It didn't matter; her mind was racing too much to care. She was planning, planning her revenge on John. She knew she could kill him. It would be relatively easy. All she had to do was cut him, just a little, just like she had Daniel. Then the thing that lived inside her would come out, and she'd be able to overpower him. She could kill him and eat him. He wouldn't be able to hurt anyone else ever again.

This is crazy. I sound crazy.

Crazy is okay as long as it's secret. Just keep it to yourself. Secret-crazy is fine.

Maggie walked on her left, Zack on her right. Ben was up ahead. Violet could feel Maggie's eyes on her, but she was too wrapped up in her thoughts to even look in her direction.

Okay, it's decided. We'll kill him. Me and zombie-me. Together. Just keep quiet. Act normal. Don't say anything to make anyone suspicious.

"Violet, are you okay?"

"I'm going to kill him." Violet's eyes widened; she had *not* meant to say that aloud. Maggie looked shocked—not at Violet's words, but at the fact she had said it within earshot of Zack. But now that it was out there, Violet decided she may as well go for it.

"I don't care," she said flatly, eyeing Zack now. "I'm going to kill your friend. Probably all of them. Maybe even you." She paused, thinking. "Well, maybe not you. I haven't decided yet."

It was a reckless thing to say. If Zack decided to tell John, she would be dead by the morning. But he simply shook his head. "You won't. You can't. He won't let you."

"He won't have a choice."

"He's strong."

You don't know what I can do.

But then another thought occurred to her, and she stopped walking, turning to face Zack. "Do you even like him? I've just told you I'm going to kill one of your friends, and you're not even the tiniest bit concerned?"

Zack shrugged. "I'm not their friend. They don't like me. But I owe them."

Violet got the feeling an origin story was coming. And she was right.

ZACK AND ELIZA RAN, TRYING TO IGNORE THE SOUNDS OF chaos around them. People were everywhere, some trying to escape, the rest trying to rip the rest apart. Zack felt like he'd been running for hours, and Eliza pulled back on his hand.

"I can't..." she breathed, her black hair clinging to her sweat-drenched forehead. Zack pulled her behind a car. For a few minutes, the two of them squatted on the sidewalk, just watching the violence surrounding them on all sides. Half the city was burning; the other half was filled with screaming and death.

"What are we going to do?" Eliza asked.

"I don't know."

"Connor, Sarah, Todd...all of them..."

"Don't think about it. We need to get out of here." Zack took hold of Eliza's hand again, pulling her to her feet. Her eyes widened. "Zack!"

Zack spun around just as the foul creature leaned in to bite, and he managed to push the thing back. He pulled the kitchen knife from his pocket, stabbing again and again at the creature's chest. But though he opened countless wounds and dark blood began to flow, the thing just kept coming. Then there was a bang, and the ghoul fell to the ground. Zack stood over its body; a small hole had appeared right in the middle of its temple. He looked up as three men climbed out of a car. One of them, tall and muscular, was holding the gun.

"It's got to be the head," he said. Zack, exhausted, just stared at him wide-eyed. There was a scream from behind him, but Zack turned around too slowly this time. Eliza wrestled with one ghoul as another sank its teeth into her neck. Her scream was loud and piercing, but lasted only seconds before another gunshot rang out. Eliza fell to the ground, a hole opening in the middle of her forehead. Two more shots, and the ghouls went down, too. More approached, but Zack was numb, watching wordlessly as the bodies continued to fall around him. Finally, it was over, and the first man told the other two to search for anything useful. He walked over to Zack, whose eyes were fixed on Eliza.

"She was infected," the man said, his voice low. "That's how it spreads, through the bites."

"I know. I've seen it."

The man looked at his friends, then back to Zack. "Come with us."

"I KNEW JOHN WAS DANGEROUS, BUT HE SAVED MY LIFE, and he and the others protected me this whole time. I just stay quiet and do what he says, and it's kept me breathing this long."

Violet shook her head. "They may have saved you, but

they only care about themselves. They'll only protect you as long as it doesn't put their own lives in danger."

"But what about *your* friends?"

"What about them?"

"If your friends are so great, so selfless, where are they?"

Violet opened her mouth, but realized she couldn't answer. She had no idea. She scowled and continued walking. "Maybe I *will* kill you too," she muttered weakly.

TWELVE

THE STORM OUTSIDE RAGED, AS IT HAD FOR THE PAST few hours, and Violet tried as hard as she could to get some sleep. It was a battle she was losing. All the classroom had to offer was the hard floor with a couple of thin sheets on top. The room was even colder than usual, and Violet could see her breath hanging in the air every time she exhaled.

She got to her feet, stretching and hearing her joints pop from having been curled up in a ball on the floor for so long. It was too cold; she wouldn't sleep tonight. All she could hope for would be the chance to try and escape to the teachers' lounge for a few hours tomorrow. Maggie would be able to prepare lunch without her; she'd done it before.

Violet glanced at Maggie, who was sleeping soundly.

Emily wasn't here.

Violet's mind had been racing all night: half desperately trying to think about what was happening to her friend, half desperately trying not to. She'd been gone for hours. When Violet, Maggie, and Ben had been brought into the classroom for the night and she realized Emily wasn't already inside, she'd tried to fight her way out. Maggie had needed to hold her back as Vince laughed in her face. Violet had eventually stopped fighting; she knew Maggie was right. She was on thin ice with John, and he'd like nothing better than to have a reason to shoot her.

It was strange to live in such close quarters with someone who wanted her dead. The biters were different. It wasn't personal with them; they were just doing what they did. It was horrible and she hated them for it, but she couldn't be angry about it, not really. But having a living person who simply hated her enough to want to kill her was something she couldn't get used to. She knew she'd have to bite her tongue and keep her cool with John and the others. She may not have been much, but if Sam and the rest of her friends didn't come back from the supply run, Violet would be the only one left to keep Maggie and Emily safe. Though she'd hardly done a great job so far.

She walked over to the table beside the window, sitting down and watching the rain hammer heavily on the glass. Her thoughts drifted to her absent friends. Violet found it hard to imagine them purposefully leaving her and the others behind, but what was the alternative? That they'd been ripped apart by a herd of undead? No. If they weren't coming back, Violet was going to tell herself it was because they'd decided not to. Yes, it meant she, Emily, and Maggie were stuck, but at least the others wouldn't have to endure it any longer. Perhaps they'd even find help? Maybe they'd come back to rescue them? They could be thinking of a plan right at that very moment.

She couldn't depend on that. All she could do was try harder to keep Emily and Maggie safe. Violet was still watching the rain. She could barely see the world outside the window. The sky was dark, and the streetlights went off weeks ago.

The sky lit up, just for half a second at a flash of lightning, and the thunder rumbled. Ben raised his head, ears pricked up. Violet shushed him gently before he got the chance to cry, and within moments, he was asleep again.

Another roar of thunder. The storm was getting worse. She wondered if there would be flooding. There had been such bad flooding a few years ago that people had to be rescued from their houses in boats. Would that be such a bad thing now? She couldn't imagine the dead would be too fast if they had to run through water. If the river burst, they might even get washed away?

Come to think of it, a little flooding right now would be pretty good.

There was another flash of lightning, and then Violet saw it; movement by the gate. But everything went dark again, and she lost sight of whatever it was. Still, she had seen something. There was something moving out there, inside the fence. She pressed her hands against the glass, waiting for more lightning. For what felt like an agonizingly long amount of time, the sky remained black. Then, just as she was beginning to doubt herself, lightning struck again.

There it was! Something was heading for the window.

Darkness again, and Violet instinctively dropped to the floor, heart racing.

How did the biters get inside?

She crawled toward Maggie. She knew she had to wake her quickly, get her out of sight before those things reached the glass. But just as Violet's hand was about to touch Maggie's shoulder, she heard the tapping.

The dead don't knock.

Violet swiveled her head toward the window slowly. When lightning struck once more, she saw the faces she had wanted to see more than anything in the world. And Tom. Relief washed over her in waves. She ran to the window, opening it as wide as she could. Sam, Joe, Matt, and Tom climbed inside. Violet hugged each of them tightly, not caring one bit that they were soaking wet. Then she lightly shoved Matt. "I was so worried! Why didn't you come back? Why *did* you come back?"

He looked confused. "What? Of course we came back. We wouldn't leave you behind."

Maggie woke up at the sound of their voices. She got up, flinging her arms around Joe's neck.

"We couldn't come back straight away," Sam explained. "They would've locked us in the teachers' lounge, and we'd be back to square one. This way, we still had the keys to the gate. We knew we could come and get you."

"I'm surprised they didn't leave anyone to guard it," Joe said. "That's pretty stupid."

"*They're* stupid," Violet replied, shrugging. "Probably didn't want to be out in the rain."

"Well, whatever, we're lucky they didn't," Sam said.

"Do you have a car?" Violet asked.

"Yeah, we thought it might be a bit of a squeeze if we all tried to get on my tricycle," Joe replied.

Sam rolled his eyes, glancing around the room. "Where's Em?"

Maggie and Violet stared at each other, both deflated. What would they say? How could Violet tell them what was going on?

"She's with them. They..." She didn't know how to finish, but it seemed she didn't need to. Matt, Sam, and Joe all stood a little straighter, moving for the classroom door.

"It's no good," Violet said. "They've locked us in. We'll need to go around the other way."

Sam nodded. "Okay, you two get in the car. We'll go and get Emily."

Violet shook her head. "No, we need to be smart about this. They're armed, and we're not. We need to get in there quietly and get her out." She took a breath, not liking what she knew she had to do. "I'll go. I'm the quietest."

She wasn't sure why she had said that. It wasn't true. Violet was the clumsiest, and therefore the loudest, but something told her she had to be the one to do it. A big part of her felt so angry that she'd been powerless to stop this happening. She at least had to be the one to put it right.

"You're not going alone," Matt said. "I'll come too."

Violet could see that Sam didn't like the idea, but he reluctantly agreed. "Okay, we'll get Maggie down to the car and wait for you. But if you're not back in ten minutes, I'm coming in."

"Me too," Joe said.

They all climbed out of the window. It was colder outside than Violet had expected, despite the polar classroom. The rain felt like glass crashing down onto her skin, but it didn't matter. She was free, and that was all she cared about. Violet passed Ben to Joe, then headed toward the main doors of the school.

"Please be careful," Joe muttered.

VIOLET WENT BACK INSIDE, WITH MATT CLOSE BEHIND. She was thankful for once that John and the others were wasteful enough to keep the hallways lit with candles.

They approached the library, and Violet slowed down. She tiptoed now as she crossed the room, water dripping from her clothes and hair onto the ground. There were no candles lit in there, but she could see the outlines of the men sleeping not too far away. She tried to count, pretty sure despite the darkness that there were only three of them. Three men in the room meant one somewhere else. They would need to be fast. She scanned the surroundings for Emily, spotting her on the couch closest to them, her back to the rest of the room.

The men snored loudly. Violet could see garbage littering the floor. She made her way carefully, doing her best to avoid the debris. When she reached Emily, she gently shook her on the shoulder. Her friend curled up even tighter.

She thinks I'm John or one of the others.

Emily's clothes were ripped, and there was blood on her leg. It was dry, so Violet was able to remain in control of herself.

"Emily, it's me," Violet whispered. Emily rolled over quickly, eyes puffy and bloodshot. She had a bruise on her cheek and her lip had been split. Violet felt anger boiling inside her, a hateful desire to go over and bash in the heads of the sleeping men, a desire that had nothing to do with being half-dead. But she knew they didn't have time for that, and no real weapons to speak of. She tried to keep calm, squeezing Emily's shoulder.

"We're getting out of here," she whispered. Matt helped her get Emily to her feet, but she soon realized her friend could barely walk. She and Matt each took one of Emily's arms over their shoulders, leading her toward the door.

Halfway across the room, just as she was congratulating herself on how smoothly everything was going, Violet stumbled. Her right arm collided with a tower of beer cans. They clattered heavily to the floor. Violet stopped, jaw clenching, waiting for the sounds of yelling. But there was nothing; the men continued to snore. She caught Matt's eye in the moonlight. He didn't understand either.

"They took some pills," Emily murmured. "They won't wake up for hours."

You are so lucky these men are drug addicts, Violet, or your clumsiness would've got you all killed. You might not survive dying twice.

They headed out of the room. When they were halfway toward the main doors out of the school, they heard whistling. The three of them froze. Violet turned to Matt, fear blossoming inside her. But there was nothing they could do; whoever was whistling was about to come out of the bathrooms a few feet away, and would block their path to the front door.

Please be Zack. Please be Zack.

It was Vince. His eyes widened when he saw Violet and Matt holding up a bruised and broken Emily.

"What the hell do you think you're doing?" he yelled. He was loud, and Violet was sure that even a cocktail of booze and mystery drugs wouldn't keep John and the others sleeping much longer.

"We're leaving," Matt said firmly. "You can have this place, but we're not staying."

Vince reached behind him, pulling out a gun. Violet had only ever seen John with a firearm, and she had no idea whether this was it, or if Vince had one all along.

"Put her down, then go into that classroom." He pointed with the weapon at the door behind them. Matt, Emily, and Violet stayed frozen in place.

"No." Violet's voice was firm, but she sounded far braver than she felt.

"Do it now."

Violet shook her head, her voice cracking a little when she spoke. "She's not yours. None of us are yours. We're leaving."

"You think I won't do it?" Vince spat, but his hand was shaking. Violet knew it had always been John in charge. She wondered if Vince had even fired a gun before.

"Let us pass," Matt said gently but firmly. "You can pretend you didn't see us."

Vince ran one hand through his hair. "Oh yeah, and how's that? I was supposed to be guarding the gate! No, put her down and get into that classroom. If you do, maybe John won't kill you."

Violet shook her head again. "We're going. Get out of our way."

She and Matt moved forward. Surprisingly, Vince stepped aside to let them pass. Violet couldn't believe it was happening, but he was letting them go. She looked sideways at Matt, who stared determinedly forward, and the three of them kept going toward the double doors. Vince did nothing; he didn't shout for backup, didn't chase them, he just watched.

Maybe he's not as bad as the rest of them?

A single gunshot. Suddenly, Emily seemed to weigh twice as much. Violet felt herself lurch forward. Emily had stopped holding herself up, her legs crumpling underneath her. Violet brought her gaze to Emily's face, not wanting to believe what she already knew. Vince had shot Emily. The bullet had hit the back of her head—a clean shot straight through her skull. She was dead.

Violet felt sick. She let her friend's body drop to the floor. Matt's eyes were wide as he gaped at the lifeless corpse.

Vince spluttered from behind them. "I..." He was pale and sweating, unable to even string a full sentence together. "I wasn't trying to..." He pointed at Violet. "It was supposed to be you! Not... I didn't mean..." He dropped the gun as though it burned him. The beautiful smell of Emily's blood began to fill the air, but it all too quickly turned sour. The blood of a dead girl meant nothing, but Violet didn't need it. She glared at Vince, the man who had killed her friend, and felt something stronger than the hunger.

Hate.

It happened fast. She threw herself at Vince, knocking him to the floor. He had been caught off guard, but fought back, trying to throw her off. She could hear Matt yelling, but he may as well have been underwater for she couldn't understand his words. Violet was so angry, but she couldn't do it alone. She needed the monster, and she knew how to make it come out. As Vince tried to push her off, Violet bit his hand.

Then it began.

It bites into his flesh, tearing the fingers off. Chewing some and spitting the rest out. Then it moves onto the neck. He's not fighting as much when it bites there. The blood is sweet, and it feels so strong!

Then there are hands on its shoulders, and even though it is strong, it is pulled away. Pinned down. It is roughly shook, over and over, slapped once across the face, shaken again until things start to come into focus. It fights at first, but slowly the struggling stops. It is kneeling on the floor, the man's blood drying on its chin. Someone is talking, and things are beginning to make sense again.

"Go," Violet croaked, the world around her still blurry. "Get out of here before I hurt you."

Matt's face faded in and out. He got up and moved away.

It's better this way. He'll be safer.

I should find John and the others. Kill them before it completely goes away.

Cold water splashed on Violet's face. She spluttered, blinking rapidly. Matt stood in front of her before slowly lowering to his knees, dropping the empty water bottle. He held a wad of scratchy hand towels from the bathrooms and began to wipe her face, trying to clean the blood away.

"You should go," Violet whispered.

Matt shook his head. When he had finished cleaning her face, he took her hand, helping her up. The gun was on the floor. Violet watched as he picked it up. He carefully tucked it in the back of his jeans. Then he led her into the rain.

SAM AND JOE WERE APPROACHING AS VIOLET AND MATT came outside.

"Where is she?" Sam asked, having to raise his voice to be heard above the storm.

Matt shook his head.

Sam swore loudly. Joe ran his hands through his hair, moving as though he was about to go back inside, then he caught sight of Violet's bloodied clothes.

"Violet, what—"

Another gunshot. Violet and the others turned back to the school. John was standing in the doorway. He'd fired his gun into the air. Edd and Zack were behind him. Edd had a baseball bat, but Zack had a gun.

Where did they get all of those from?

Edd stepped forward. "Where the hell do you think you're going?"

"Just let us go, you can have this place," Matt said calmly, stepping slightly to the right. Joe moved a little to the left, and Violet realized they were trying to block her from sight. She looked over at the car; Tom and Maggie were safely inside with Ben.

"You killed Vince," John said. It didn't sound like he really cared.

Joe and Sam may have been shocked by this, but they took it in stride. Sam stepped forward. "He deserved it," he said simply, taking the blame for something he had no idea Violet had done.

"He killed Emily," Matt growled. Sam and Joe, upon hearing the words aloud, glared at John now with even more anger etched on their faces.

"Well then, I guess we're even." John grinned. He nodded at Violet. "Leave Harriet here; the other one, too. The rest of you can go. *They* belong with us."

"Who's Harriet?" Joe asked.

"He means me," Violet muttered.

Matt stepped forward, holding out Vince's gun. "I don't want to kill you, but if you don't let us go, *all of us,* I will shoot you."

John laughed. "Go on then, I dare you."

"I mean it," Matt threatened. He sounded pretty sure of himself, but Violet knew his heart was racing. Hers was, too.

John stepped closer again, a cruel smile on his face. Violet's stomach churned; she didn't think Matt would do it. She didn't blame him. She may have just killed Vince, but it wasn't like she could take all the credit for that— she at least had the excuse of being half dead. Matt didn't exactly have a zombie version of himself to call upon.

In one smooth move, Sam took the gun from Matt's hand, aimed at John's leg, and then pulled the trigger.

Nothing.

He pulled it again.

Still nothing. Sam quickly popped open the gun's chamber and checked inside. Violet didn't have to see through his eyes to know what he had found.

John and Edd began to laugh viciously.

"Oops," John said. "Vince only had one bullet left, and it's in the skull of the pretty one." He raised his gun, aiming it at Sam. "I, on the other hand, have enough for all of you."

"Please," Violet begged, stepping out from behind Matt and Joe. "Don't hurt them. I'll stay. Just let the others go."

John sneered. "You? You're more trouble than you're worth. We want the redhead; she'll do as she's told." He paused. "Maybe we'll keep you, too, but I think you need a leash, at least until you learn your place." He studied her more carefully. "And you're covered in Vince's blood." An ugly sneer crossed his face. "Why don't you start by taking those bloody clothes off?" He laughed, and Violet's face burned with humiliation. John swept his gun in front of Matt and the others. "As for the rest of you—"

The gunshot rang out before he could finish, louder and clearer than the thunder. Rain beat down, diluting the blood pouring on to the concrete.

THIRTEEN

"WHAT THE HELL ARE YOU DOING?" EDD SCREAMED, dropping to examine John's body. Violet knew it was no good. John had been dead before he hit the ground. Zack had shot hit him in the head. Violet allowed herself to take a breath. Just one.

Edd lunged for John's gun, but Zack quickly kicked it toward Sam, who grabbed it and aimed at Edd.

"You'll pay for that," Edd growled at Zack. His eyes were wild.

"I'm sure," Zack replied sincerely...right before shooting Edd in the leg. Edd fell, crying out in pain as the blood seeped from the wound. Violet turned away; the delicious smell was already dangerously tempting. She was just grateful for the rain, which began to dilute the blood as it pooled on the ground.

"We need to leave," Violet muttered, stumbling a little as she moved toward the car. She could feel Matt watching her, but couldn't look him in the eye.

What does he think of me after what he saw?

"Come on," Sam said to the others. "Let's go."

Matt and Joe went to leave, but Matt paused. He stepped over Edd, who was holding onto his leg and groaning, and halted in front of Zack.

"Come with us," he said. Zack regarded the rest of the group, and Violet saw Sam eyeing the bodies on

146

the floor before giving him a nod. They hurried down to the car. Violet climbed in first, wanting to be as far away from the smell of Edd's blood as possible. It didn't matter that she'd just eaten. She already needed more.

With seven people in the vehicle, as well as a dog, it was a bit of a squeeze. Sam was in the driver's seat, with Joe and Zack sharing the passenger seat, Violet, Maggie, Matt, and Tom squashed into the back, with Ben on Violet's lap. It was tight, but a vacation compared to where she'd just been, so she wasn't complaining.

"Look," Maggie said, pointing to the school gates. They were wide open.

"We wanted to make sure we could get away quickly," Matt explained.

"No," Maggie continued. "Look."

Violet saw it now; just barely visible in the darkness were the silhouettes of the dead. Lots of them. They were heading toward them—fast.

"Should we help him?" Maggie asked. She meant Edd, who was still clutching his leg and shouting obscenities from over by the doors. The biters were getting closer, ignoring the car and heading toward the sound of his voice.

"No." Sam answered.

Violet almost felt bad for not arguing. Almost.

Sam slammed the accelerator, and the car screeched away. Violet turned to watch through the back window, but couldn't see Edd anymore, only the dead swarming around the place he'd fallen. He was gone.

"Hang on!" Sam cried. The car slammed into the creatures that were continuing to pour through the gates. Violet closed her eyes, heart pounding, sweat on her forehead. She felt an unwanted tear slide down her face, and wiped it away before anyone could see the blood. Someone's hand found hers in the dark.

THEY HAD BEEN DRIVING IN SILENCE FOR A FEW MINUTES when Matt finally asked the question on all of their minds.

"So, where are we going?"

"I don't know," Sam replied honestly. "I live in an apartment in the middle of town. I doubt it's the best option right now."

"What about you?" Matt asked Joe.

"I live with Sam."

"Great." Matt sighed. "My place isn't safe. I barely made it out of there in one piece, and I had to smash the glass door to do it."

"I wouldn't even know how to get to my house from here," Zack added. "Those guys found me miles away."

Violet knew what was coming. Her house would probably be the best option. She remembered Maggie's story well enough to know her's wasn't safe. Tom hadn't offered, but it wasn't like she was particularly eager to go to whatever dark hole he called 'home'.

But even though she knew her house was probably okay, it didn't feel right for some reason. She didn't want to go home, but she didn't know why. Still, it wasn't like they had much of a choice.

"What about my place?" she offered quietly.

"Is it safe?" Matt asked.

"I don't know," Violet admitted. "I haven't been there since it started, but it was locked up when I left, so there shouldn't be any of those things inside."

"Parents?" Sam asked.

"Away. They were on vacation."

"Sounds like a good idea," Joe said. "Is it close?"

"About twenty minutes away."

"Or we could go to my house?" Tom suggested. "It's just outside town, so it might be safer. Plus, it's nice."

Violet scowled. *What's that supposed to mean?*

"You think I don't live in a nice house?" she asked.

Tom shrugged. "I don't know."

"Well, that's what you said."

"Read into it whatever you want."

"You literally said—"

"Let's go to Violet's," Joe interrupted.

Sam nodded. "I agree. It's closer anyway. The less time we have to spend traveling in the dark, the better."

Matt seemed to be formulating a plan already. "A couple of us can go in and check it's clear. If it is, then everyone else can come. At least it'll be somewhere to stop and make plans. We need to start thinking long term—"

"*Stop,*" Violet shouted, interrupting Matt and causing Sam to slam on the brakes.

"What?" he asked, his voice sounding almost annoyed.

"Over there." She pointed to the road on their right, where there were at least twenty biters running in their direction.

"That's lovely, Violet, but why are we stopping?" Joe asked quickly.

Running from the biters, leading the undead following, was Toby, the boy from the bike store who had saved her life. Violet reached across Tom, not caring about leaning heavily on his leg, and opened the back door.

"*Toby,*" she yelled.

Toby sped up, charging toward the car. The dead were close behind.

"He's not going to make it," Tom argued, reaching for the handle, but Violet 'accidentally' slipped and elbowed him between the legs. He let go of the door, groaning in pain, and she held it open for Toby.

"*Run,*" Matt shouted. Sam revved the engine, creeping the car forward a little.

The boy was inches from her now. Violet grabbed his hand, pulling him inside. The car screeched away with the door still open. It banged closed against a streetlight. Toby practically collapsed onto the floor in front of her seat. He was drenched and pale, but alive.

"Hi," he panted.

THEY PARKED OUTSIDE VIOLET'S HOUSE. DESPITE HER arguments, Matt and Sam went to check it out alone. She told them about the spare key under the mat. It was an obvious hiding place, but it couldn't be understated how often Violet forgot her key before she became a zombie, and they left the rest of the group in the car.

"What happened?" she asked Toby as he took Matt's place beside her.

"I went out to find food, but my bike got a puncture on some broken glass. I was trying to drag it back when those things found me. I had to leave it behind. I hid in a house for the night, but they got in." He flicked his eyes over Violet's bloodied clothes. "You look terrible."

"You should see the other guy."

The one I ate.

That's so disgusting, Violet.

She glanced up as the back door to her house opened. Sam waved them over.

"We're clear," Violet said to the others. They stepped out into the cool night air. The rain had stopped, and the moon had finally escaped the clouds, giving the group a little silvery light to see by. Sam and Matt had flashlights, but kept them low as they walked with the others to the door.

"We may have a small problem," Matt whispered to Violet.

I have more than one small problem, she thought miserably, but followed him all the same. She saw what he meant when they stepped into the living room. One of the large windows was smashed, with a hole large enough for a person to fit through.

"We checked; there's no one here," Sam whispered. "I'm guessing someone broke in to hide, but they've gone now. We'll need to block up the window."

They used Violet's dad's tools to remove the living room door, then nailed it over the remains of the window. It was not a neat job, and was loud and time consuming to carry out. Violet was sure the dead would hear, but so far, they had been lucky. When the job was finally finished, Sam, Joe, and Matt stood back to admire their work while Maggie lit some candles.

"Do you think it's secure?" Violet asked.

Joe pulled at the door with both hands; it didn't move. "Seems so."

"At least if it comes down, it'll make a lot of noise," Sam added. "We'll have time to get out."

A thought suddenly occurred to Violet. "Why did we take the living room door off? We could've used the dining room one, then closed the door to this room. It'd mean the biters would take longer to get to us."

Everyone was silent for a moment before Joe sighed, wiping the sweat from his brow. "Wow. Really wish you'd said something before we nailed it on, Vi."

"Sorry, didn't think of it until now."

"It'll be fine," Sam insisted. "I'm not taking another damn door off. If the dead get through that, they can have me."

VIOLET HAD ASSUMED THERE WOULD BE FOOD IN THE house since her parents stocked up before they went away. They'd bought far too much for her to get through on her own. Unfortunately, most of that stuff went into the fridge and freezer. With the power off for weeks, none of it was even remotely salvageable. There was still food in the cupboards, but a lot of it was missing. Most that was left needed to be cooked. The camping stove was still at the school.

"We could start a fire?" Joe suggested.

Sam shook his head. "There's no fireplace, and nothing to start it in. I don't want to risk it getting too big and us not being able to put it out."

The others agreed. Violet thought if there was even the slightest chance of her parents coming back, she didn't want them to return to a burned-down house. A zombie daughter was probably enough bad news to have to deal with. Unfortunately, no fire meant no cooking, and so dinner that evening consisted of cold soups and tinned beans. It didn't matter to Violet—all food tasted like the color beige now anyway—but she doubted it was too enjoyable for the others. Still, they were safe and together, which was far more important.

They sat quietly for a long time, whispering in small groups, but mostly just listening for any sounds from outside. So far, there had been none. Eventually, Joe got to his feet and began to walk around the room, picking up the framed photos on the coffee table.

"These are your parents?" he asked.

Violet nodded, taking the picture from him and holding it gently in both hands. It was one of her favorites: she and her parents on vacation in Florida when she was nine.

"Where are they?" Zack asked.

"In Australia, visiting family. They wanted me to come with them, but I never liked the flight, and had loads of stuff to do at school. I told them I'd be fine here."

Joe grinned. "Great judgement, as always, Violet."

"So you were alone when it started?" Zack asked.

She nodded. "On the way back from a party." She didn't go into any more detail. She was tired and worried she might accidentally say something she didn't want them to know. Matt was watching her closely, and she tried not to look at him. He had seen her, seen what she really was. What did he think of her now? More confusingly, why hadn't he told the others? Didn't he realize how dangerous she was?

Violet felt more eyes on her, and realized she'd been quiet for a little too long. She turned back to Joe, deciding to shift the focus to someone else.

"What happened to you?" she asked. "On that first day, I mean. How did you end up at the school? I've never asked."

"Well, that's a particularly cheerful story," Joe began. "Sam and I had gone to a party the night before it all happened, at Fiona Long's house—"

"Me too," Violet interrupted, weirdly excited by this link in their zombie apocalypse origin stories.

"Awesome," Joe replied sarcastically, and Violet hit him with a couch cushion. "Anyway, we didn't arrive until about midnight. By then, we were pretty wasted already. I don't remember much of that night, only drinking this funky-tasting purple drink and ending up face down on the floor."

$\sim\!\!\sqrt{\!\!\sqrt{\!\!\backslash\!\!\backslash}}\!\!\sqrt{\!\!\backslash}\!\!\sim\!\!\sim$ _____

Alive?

JOE WOKE UP TO THE SOUND OF BASS MUSIC. IT MADE THE throbbing in his head feel a million times worse. He decided then and there that he hated bass music more than anything in the whole world. Slowly, carefully, he climbed to his feet, stumbling a little. The music was too loud; he felt like his head was about to explode. He shuffled over to the CD player, pushing various buttons to no avail. He gritted his teeth in frustration before yanking the wire out of the wall. Finally, silence. He took a minute to look around. The place was a mess: drink bottles everywhere, puke, passed-out partygoers. There were more people on the floor. Sam was one of them, sleeping next to a guy with dreadlocks. The guy had his arm around Sam's waist, which made Joe smile. He took a quick picture with his phone and sent it to everyone in his address book before gently nudging Sam with his shoe.

No reaction. When he tried again, he got the same response. He sighed, picking up a beer can from the coffee table and pouring the contents over Sam's head. His friend spluttered awake.

"Hey," he cried, wiping his eyes.

"Oh good, you're up."

"Why's the music stopped?" Sam yawned.

"Partly because the party ended hours ago, partly because my head hurt, but mostly because it was the worst CD ever to be created. I know you brought it here, and I'm sorry to say it, but you have the crappiest musical taste of anyone who's ever existed. Ever."

"Thanks for putting it so kindly," Sam muttered sarcastically.

"Of course."

Sam rolled his eyes, finally noticing the man beside him. "She looked different last night." He laughed. "Hope no one else saw that."

"I'm sure they didn't." Joe's phone was already vibrating in his pocket.

Sam wriggled free and got to his feet. "What time is it?"

"Seven."

"Right... I need to be at work in an hour. We better get

going."

"I'll get my coat." Joe yawned, leaving Sam and heading for the kitchen, where he vaguely remembered throwing it a few hours earlier. He opened the door, spotting it on the floor by the table. There were more people passed out in this room, and what he guessed were puddles of red wine everywhere. It seemed like the party was still going on though; Fiona was pressed against the wall by two men who were kissing her neck. Her eyes widened when she saw him come in, but he covered his eyes playfully, grabbing his coat and closing the door behind him.

"You'll never guess what I saw in there," he said to Sam, who was waiting for him outside.

Sam wasn't listening, rubbing his head gingerly. "I drank way too much. I can barely see straight."

"You're not the only one." Joe fell into step behind him, smiling at an old lady walking her dog into the woods. "I'd never heard of most of the booze Fiona got in. Who knows what was in it?"

"She was really knocking it back last night, wasn't she?"

"She was still partying in the kitchen a minute ago. She had two guys in there."

Sam whistled. "Rather them than me. She's terrifying."

Joe laughed, glancing around. "Quiet this morning, isn't it?" He'd only just noticed how empty the roads seemed to be.

Sam shrugged. "It's early." As he spoke, a load of kids on bikes appeared, all pedaling full speed toward them. He and Joe jumped out of the way. "Whoa, whoa, slow down!"

"Get out of the way!"

"The monsters are coming!"

"Move!"

Sam snorted. "Yeah, all right, thanks for that." They watched the kids disappear into the woods. Sam rubbed his head again. "I do not need that much noise right now."

Joe nodded. He felt better after seeing a few more people. There were cars passing on the road ahead, too, but he couldn't shake the feeling that something wasn't right. Sam nudged him.

"Here comes trouble."

Joe followed his line of sight and smiled. It was Jake, attempting to get into a house across the road. Joe was surprised to see him standing. He'd not been looking so hot the night before.

"Jake," Sam called.

No response. Jake continued to bang on the door.

"That guy's so deaf," Sam muttered. "Jake..." he repeated as he and Joe headed across the road. Jake still didn't respond. Sam picked up a pebble from the ground, and then flung it in his direction.

"Ow!" Jake turned around, rubbing his head. "That hurt."

"You should've answered then," Sam replied, but he was smiling. Jake left the door and headed over. His shirt was untucked, misbuttoned, and stained with something Joe was pretty sure was vomit.

"How's it going?" Jake asked. "Enjoy the party?"

"Yeah, it was all right," Joe replied. "I don't think either of us were having as much fun as you, though."

"Huh?"

Sam grinned. "Oh yeah, you were having a very good time if I remember right."

Jake's eyes widened. "Was I with a girl?"

Joe and Sam glanced at each other, giving Jake a moment before bursting his bubble.

"No," Joe replied. "No, the party didn't slip into another dimension where girls like you."

"Har-har," Jake drawled.

"It wasn't a magical party," Sam agreed.

"Yeah, okay, I get it. So what happened then?"

Joe put on his most serious face. "You took your clothes off and danced on the table."

Jake's eyes widened again. "No, I didn't."

Sam nodded. "You did. You actually had some good moves."

"You're kidding," Jake pleaded. "Tell me you're kidding."

Joe grinned. "We're kidding."

"Oh, thank God."

"You didn't have good moves."

"No..." Sam shook his head. "No, they were just terrible."

Jake put his head in his hands, leaning against the fence. "I want to die."

"People will forget," Joe suggested encouragingly. "I wouldn't worry about it."

Jake lowered his hands. "You wouldn't say that if you were me."

"What are you doing anyway?" Sam asked, clearly feeling a little sorry for him and attempting to change the subject.

"I forgot my key, but my mom's usually up by now. I thought she'd let me in." He turned back to the door, banging on it again. No response. "I know she's in there," he continued. "I'm sure I just saw her. I think she's annoyed; I told her I wouldn't stay out all night."

"Aren't you eighteen?" Sam asked.

Jake shrugged. "Her house, her rules. I'm gonna go around the back." He headed along the side of the house and toward the side gate, jumping over it in one quick motion. Sam and Joe headed back to the road, where Sam glanced at his watch. "We need to get going or I'm going to be late."

A shrill scream cut through the quiet morning. The pair turned back to Jake's house.

"Do you think his mom hit him?" Sam asked.

"Maybe," Joe replied. But he didn't. That scream wasn't from a slap, a punch, or anything like that. It was long and agonizing. Seconds later, the front door opened and Jake stumbled out. He was covered in blood, grasping onto his neck where the crimson liquid poured through the gaps in his fingers.

Joe and Sam were frozen to the spot for a few seconds before they ran to help their friend. Jake had already collapsed outside the door. As Joe and Sam approached the path, a woman in a blue dressing gown came outside. She, too, was bloodied, but didn't appear to be in any pain. She threw herself down on Jake. For one mad moment, Joe thought she was trying to resuscitate him. Then he saw her tear the flesh from his lips. Joe slapped a hand across Sam's chest, blocking him from getting any closer, forcing his friend to look more closely at what he was seeing.

"What the—"

Sam's confusion was interrupted by the woman's head snapping up in their direction. She screamed, scrambled to her feet, and ran toward them.

"Go!" Joe yelled. The woman was fast, but they were faster. They managed to get some distance between them. As they raced down the next street, Joe started to see the world around them a little more clearly; cars were screeching out of town in every direction, people were screaming, houses were on fire, there were bodies on the ground, and crazed maniacs chasing people. He and Sam didn't stop; they just kept running.

It was only when they reached the wall around the school that Sam began to slow, motioning for Joe to do the same. The road was deserted for now. Joe's heart was hammering, sweat pouring from his forehead.

"What was it?" he asked.

Sam shook his head; he had no clue either. They didn't have time to talk. More of the crazed people were coming their way, appearing as if from nowhere. They were all bloodied, and one of them had an arm ripped off. Joe could see the sharp bone protruding from the wound. Sam grabbed a nearby garbage can, then pushed it up against the brick wall surrounding the school.

"Come on," he panted, climbing up. Joe followed suit, kicking the garbage can over once Sam had hold of his hand. They sat up there, watching the psychos crowd around. None of them thought to pick up the can and follow the men up, which was good, because Sam and Joe were both spent.

They spent an hour on the wall, watching the chaos and starting to understand what they were seeing. Climbing down the other side, they went to see what they could find inside the building. They would quickly meet Matt and Amy. Within a few hours, Tom and Maggie would arrive, too.

THE GROUP SAT IN SILENCE FOR A FEW MINUTES. VIOLET

knew that none of them were quite sure how to follow Joe's story. Eventually, she got to her feet.

"We should get some rest," she began. "You guys can have my parent's room; it's the biggest. Maggie, you can have the spare room. I'll sleep in mine, if that's okay?"

"I'll stay down here," Sam added. "Someone needs to be by the window in case anything happens, and it saves me from being spooned by Joe."

Joe showed Sam what he thought of that using a finger gesture. Less than ten minutes later, Violet was in her old room, wearing her old pajamas, and feeling the most peculiar sense of déjà vu she had ever felt. This wasn't right; she shouldn't be back, not now. Not after what she had become. But she didn't have any choice. She needed to keep her friends safe, and this had been their only option.

Well, other than Tom's 'nice house,' of course.

Ugh, you've got to let that go.

Still, after losing control back at the school, having everyone living so close made Violet feel uncomfortable. That was part of the reason she'd opted to sleep alone; at least there was no chance of sleep-eating anyone.

There was a knock at the door, and it opened slowly. Matt stood in the doorway. Violet's heart began to race. She wasn't ready to talk to him yet, she had no idea where to even start.

"Usually when people knock, they wait to be told to come in," she joked weakly.

Matt's lips curved. "I'm not very polite. You're lucky I even remembered to knock." He stepped a little further into the room, closing the door behind him. He considered her for a moment. "Nice PJs."

"Thanks."

"What are they, horses?"

"Unicorns."

"Oh yeah. I like the rainbows."

"Thanks."

"You don't often see pajamas like that in adult size."

"You can still get them."

"And if we have to leave quickly in the middle of the night?"

"Then I'll spend the rest of the zombie apocalypse in unicorn PJs without a single regret."

Matt smiled, then took a final step closer. "We need to talk."

FOURTEEN

"WE NEED TO TALK."

"About what?"

Oh yeah, real casual, Violet. What could he possibly want to talk to you about?

She sat on the bed, having no idea where to even begin this conversation. "Matt..."

Matt shook his head, instantly silencing her. He moved a little closer. "Are you okay?"

The question caught Violet off guard. "Me? Am *I* okay?" Was her mouth hanging open? It certainly felt like it. She spoke slowly. "You saw me attack a man. You saw me... And you're asking if *I'm* okay? Are you stupid?"

Matt looked a little confused. "I was going for 'thoughtful,' but..."

"I'm dangerous," Violet hissed, getting to her feet and trying to keep her voice low, not wanting the others to hear. "I could've killed you back there!"

"But you didn't—"

"Why didn't you leave me behind?"

The confusion was back on Matt's face. "I could never do that," he said, shaking his head.

"Then you're an idiot."

Matt laughed. "Stupid and an idiot? I don't have a lot going for me."

Violet sighed, exasperated. "This isn't a joke. I've

160

killed, and not just today. I've done it before. I'm dangerous." She couldn't help but feel that the unicorn pajamas might not be helping her argument.

Matt moved over to the bed, sitting down. He studied Violet, not with fear, but with some other expression she didn't recognize. Did he feel sorry for her? He didn't need to; she was good enough at feeling that on her own.

"How many?" he asked. "How many people have you killed?"

"Four, I think, including Vince. I'm not sure if there were any others, I have gaps in my memory."

"Four isn't too bad."

"It's not great, Matt."

He smirked, patting the spot beside him. "Sit down, it's hard to take you seriously when you're pacing in those pajamas."

Violet felt her face flush red and sat beside him. "They were a gift," she muttered.

"I'm sure."

Violet knocked him with her shoulder. "Why can't you take this seriously?"

Matt shrugged. "I am, but I just can't be afraid of you."

"Well then, you're—"

"An idiot, I know."

It was Violet's turn to smile, even though she didn't want to.

"Did you mean to kill them?" he asked, quietly enough that if she had wanted to, she could've pretended not to hear.

"I don't know about Vince," Violet admitted. "I was so angry."

"So was I."

"Yeah, but you didn't kill him."

"Maybe only because you did it first," he suggested. "What about the other three?"

"Daniel... I just wanted to make him go away. Hurt him at the most. Not kill him."

"And the others?"

Violet shook her head. "I didn't want to kill them. It was an accident."

Matt waited, and she knew he wanted an explanation. The trouble was she had no idea how to even begin. But she had to try; she owed him that much at the very least for keeping her secret.

"I was bitten at the start, but I didn't die. At least not fully. And I'm not like the others; it's something to do with the blood. It's like I'm a completely normal person, but when I smell fresh blood, something else takes over. I can't control myself. It's like I'm inside my body, just watching everything happen." A horrible thought crossed her mind. "Do you think that's what it's like for the rest of them?" She gestured toward the window. "Do you think the biters are trapped in there, just like I am?"

Matt didn't answer. He couldn't; he knew just as little about the dead as she did. Instead, he asked her a different question. "What happens when you bite them? How do you feel?"

"Do you really want to know?"

He nodded.

"It's like I feel alive. Truly alive. More alive than I've ever felt before. The more I...eat...the better I feel. But then it all gets too much, and I can't handle it. That's usually when I pass out. When I wake up, I'm me again." She met Matt's green eyes, so full of life. So different from her own. "Do you think I'm dead? Like them?"

Matt shook his head, immediately. "No."

"But I eat people. Regular food has no taste, and the blood... It makes me so strong—"

"But you're not rotting," Matt argued. "You're still breathing."

"Maybe that's habit. Those things breathe, too."

Matt took hold of her hand, felt her wrist. "You have a pulse."

"Maybe they do, too."

Matt shook his head. "They're dead. You know they are. They might breathe, but they don't need to. I've seen them walking around with limbs hanging off. And you can still eat our food. Do you drink water? Does it stop you from feeling thirsty?"

"Yes."

"Do you get tired when you run?"

"Literally all the time, I'm super unfit."

Matt grinned. "See, you're not like them. They never get tired. Plus, they still chase *you*. They still want to eat you. They don't do that to each other."

Violet got up, pacing again. "So what am I? Why am I like this?"

"I don't know," Matt admitted. "Maybe whatever turned them into those things didn't work fully on you? Maybe you've got some kind of immunity?"

"But I've turned people before," Violet admitted, finally saying the words aloud. "The first person I killed; he came back, and so did Daniel."

Matt seemed to be taking that in, saying nothing.

Violet continued. "If I'm not completely like the biters, why can I do that?"

"I don't know," Matt repeated. He got to his feet, moving closer and taking her hands in his. "But we'll find out."

"How?"

He bit his lip. "Okay, we might not find out. But I promise I'll keep you safe."

Violet wasn't so sure. "I should leave. You'd all be so much safer without me around."

"Oh, I don't know, our own personal zombie bodyguard might come in handy."

She pulled away and shoved him. Matt held his hands up, huffing out a laugh. "I'm kidding! Whatever this is, we'll deal with it. Together. All of us, I mean."

Violet cocked her head, still not sure she could believe how relaxed he was about the whole thing. Even Amy had looked at her differently when she found out, but Matt was so calm.

"What?" he asked.

"I just don't get it. Why aren't you afraid of me?"

Matt shrugged. "I'll be honest, I'm more afraid of having to sleep in the same bed as Tom tonight." He pulled a disgusted face.

Violet rolled her eyes. "Very funny."

Matt winked, getting up and moving toward the door. She called him back. "Wait."

"What is it?"

"Do you think I should tell the others?"

Matt raised an eyebrow. "That's up to you."

"What do you think?"

"I think...I think we've all been through a lot. Maybe telling them now would add stress we don't need."

"But if something happens, if someone gets cut—"

"I'll keep you away from anything like that. Don't worry." His smile was reassuring, and Violet knew he meant it. He was going to try to keep her from hurting anyone.

She just wished she could believe it would work.

IT WALKS THROUGH THE HALLWAY, STUMBLING AIMLESSLY. It doesn't have a destination, it just walks. It doesn't look at the pictures on the walls or the things on the shelves. Those things don't matter to it. All it cares about is feeding.

There's an open door at the end of the hall, and it can hear sounds from inside. They are in there. It walks a little faster, and it finds them sleeping. Two in the bed, three on the floor.

Don't hurt them!

It moves closer, smelling the air. It can smell them. It knows what it must do.

Stop! They're my friends!

It can see one of them stirring. That one sits up in the bed, looks at it with a smile. Then the smile disappears as it jumps and begins to feed.

Stop! Stop! Leave him alone!

Delicious blood, hot and thick, smearing around its mouth. Then the flesh, juicy and tender. The others are waking. They're making noises, and it forgets its meal. Fresher is better. It runs for the next one. This one is stronger, fights harder, but it always gets what it wants, and soon it is feeding again. The other ones are screaming, throwing things at it. The screaming is louder, more painful. It hurts its throat. Is it the one screaming?

"Violet! Violet, it's me!"

Someone clapped hands over her mouth, and the

screaming stopped. As the room came into focus, Violet realized it had only been a dream. She let out a single sob, feeling like a weight had been lifted off her chest, and threw her arms around whoever had silenced her. It was Matt, and he let her hold onto him. She was afraid at any moment she would slip back into the dream again.

The door to the bedroom burst open, and Joe and Sam appeared. Sam was holding one of the guns. Joe was wearing a T-shirt and no underwear.

Who sleeps like that?

"We heard screaming," Sam said, his eyes scanning the room.

"I...I had a bad dream," Violet choked, her mouth dry.

Sam looked like he didn't altogether believe her. She wondered again just how loudly she had been yelling, but he nodded anyway.

"Sorry," she whispered.

"It's okay," Sam replied. "I'll go check the windows, make sure none of the dead heard it." He left the room. Joe stayed, regarding Violet with a concerned expression.

"You sure you're okay?" he asked.

Violet nodded, starting to feel a little calmer, and still not altogether sure why Joe had no pants on.

"You look really pale, Vi," he added.

Matt held up a hand to shield his eyes. "Joe, I'm going to need you to put on some underwear before we continue this conversation."

Joe glanced down, as if realizing for the first time that he was naked from the waist down. He covered himself up. "Oh, sorry. This is just how I sleep." He grinned sheepishly, though he still didn't leave.

"You want me to stay with you?" he asked Violet. "Obviously, boxers would be put on before I made any attempt to approach you."

Violet smiled, but shook her head. Matt squeezed her hand. "I'll stay with her."

Joe nodded, then sidestepped out of the room. As he walked down the hallway, they heard Tom's voice.

"For Christ's sake, Joe, cover yourself up!"

"My half of the bed, my rules."

"I'm sleeping on the floor with Zack and the kid."

Violet slumped back, realizing for the first time that she was drenched with sweat.

"Bad?" Matt asked.

She nodded.

"It was just a dream."

"It felt so real."

"The worst ones always do." Matt shifted a little so he was beside her. "I'll stay here; you go back to sleep. I'll wake you if it looks like you're having another nightmare."

She shook her head. "I don't think I'll be able to sleep again."

"Just try."

So she did what he said, laying back down. As if her waking moments weren't bad enough, now she had to be scared to go to sleep, too?

VIOLET WOKE UP LATE THE NEXT DAY. MATT WAS GONE, but he had done his job. After she fell asleep, she had begun to dream of that dark hallway again, but just as she was stepping into the room containing her sleeping friends, Matt had shaken her awake. He said she'd been whimpering. After that, she dreamed of nothing.

Violet dressed quickly, grateful to finally be in her own clothes and not a random assortment from the school. She headed downstairs to find everyone busy. Joe, Toby, and Tom were leaning over some paper in the dining room, talking in hushed voices about something. As she approached, Violet realized they were drawing a map of the town. Toby was talking them through it based on his time outside.

"We thought it would be useful," Joe explained. "It's good to know what's out there. We can never be sure about the biters, but Toby knows where the roads are blocked, which buildings we can get into without the dead knowing, places that still have supplies..."

Violet nodded. As much as she could see herself settling back at home, she knew they couldn't stay indefinitely. When it came down to it, they had to get out of town. She followed the route they had begun to mark out. Last night, the group had decided on a destination—Matt's grandparents' house. They lived out in the country, and it seemed at least a good place to start. Violet pointed to part of the route, her brow furrowing.

"Why are we going along the highway? Isn't it too open?" They had agreed to stick to small roads; places where there was as much cover as possible. The highway was wide and offered no concealment from the biters.

Toby shook his head. "It's deserted. My friends and I went out there to get supplies from some of the cars. There's the odd monster, but not many."

"You think they went toward town?" Joe asked.

"That's where the food is," Toby said.

"Thanks for that," Joe replied sarcastically. "Anyway, Toby says it's safe, and it's the quickest route out of here, so we should try it."

That made sense at least. Tom, however, was scowling at the map.

"What?" she asked.

"Don't get him started—" Joe tried to begin, but Tom interrupted.

"They won't listen to me. I'm trying to help, but they won't let me."

"That's because you don't know what you're talking about," Joe replied, not unkindly. "Toby's been out there this whole time, and you've been locked in with us. What could you know about the town that he doesn't?"

"I just don't think we should rule out South road. It's really wide. It can't be completely blocked."

Toby and Joe just stared at Tom blankly, before Toby said, "Well...it is."

But Tom clearly wasn't ready to give in yet. "What if we cut through the 'Save and Buy'? That would give us a chance to get some supplies on the way."

Joe shook his head. "No, that would... Wait, what did you call it?"

"The 'Save and Buy'?"

"It's the 'Buy and Save'."

Tom shook his head, as if Joe had just said the stupidest thing he'd ever heard. "No, it's not."

"Yes, it is," Toby said.

"No, it's not."

"It is," Violet added.

"It's not!" Tom's face was becoming red with anger.

Joe held up his hands in exasperation. "Your name makes no sense at all! The idea is that if you buy your stuff there, you save money. Not that you have to save up to buy—that's ridiculous."

Tom stared them both down, and Violet felt the air get a little frostier.

"Okay, well, have fun," she muttered before making a hasty getaway. No way was she going to get involved in that pointless argument.

Even though Tom was completely wrong.

In the living room, Sam and Zack were examining the guns. On the table in front of them were eight shiny metal bullets. "That's it?" Violet asked, disappointed. She'd hoped for more

"Yeah, but it's better than nothing." Sam sighed.

"Do you have any experience with guns?"

He shrugged. "What you saw at the school was the extent of it."

When she swung her gaze to Zack, he shook his head. "John and the others didn't really let me shoot..."

"Why did you have a gun back at the school?" Violet asked.

"I just happened to grab it before Edd."

"Okay." Violet bit her lip. "We don't want to waste our bullets, or risk any of us getting hurt. I say we only shoot if we have no other choice; otherwise, we use knives and stuff."

Sam gestured toward the kitchen. "I think Matt's working on the weapon situation now."

Violet went into the other room where Matt had laid out an assortment of weapons on the table. Alongside her knife, there were three others, as well as a shovel and a garden fork. "You went into the garage?" Violet asked.

Matt nodded. "Early this morning. There were no

biters, and I was fast."

"You should've told me, I would've come with you."

"You were sleeping. You needed it."

Violet looked at the stuff on the table. "We don't have much."

"I'll keep searching. I'm resourceful." Matt winked. Maggie appeared from the other room with a couple of backpacks. She began filling them with anything in the cupboards they might be able to use: soup, chips, chocolate bars, cereal bars, and a couple of boxes of cookies.

"Not exactly a great selection," Violet murmured, immediately feeling embarrassed about what her home had to offer. "If I'd have known about the zombie apocalypse, I'd have stocked up."

Maggie smiled. "You'll know for next time." She headed back into the other room.

"Did she make a joke?" Matt asked.

"I think so."

"That's new." Matt grinned. "See, things are looking up!"

VIOLET AWOKE EARLY THE NEXT MORNING TO THE SOUND of screaming, only this time it wasn't her who was doing it. She sat bolt upright, listening again for the sound. It sounded like it was coming from close by. She jumped out of bed and ran to the hallway, then into her parent's room, where the others were already getting up and heading to the window. Sunlight was beginning to trickle through the gap in the curtains, and Violet cautiously pulled them aside to see what was happening.

There was a man in overalls not far from the house. There was also a woman in a yellow dress. Both were running from the biters—at least seven or eight of them. It was hard to tell how many. They were moving too fast, and the hedge out front kept blocking them from view. The man had a gun, and the woman had a hammer. Another man appeared holding a crowbar.

"Wait a minute," Matt began, standing at Violet's side.

Suddenly, she knew what he was about to say. The group in the house watched helplessly as the man used the crowbar to break into their car. He climbed inside and disappeared while the other two continued to fight off the dead. Seconds later, the engine roared to life.

"He's hotwired it," Joe exclaimed. The other two members of the group got in, and the car sped away. A few of the biters ran after the vehicle, but the rest remained.

"Oh good, they left their friends behind." Joe groaned, stepping away from the window and throwing the shirt he'd had balled up in his hands onto the bed. Violet was grateful he at least had underwear on today.

"What do we do now?" Zack asked.

Sam ran his fingers through his hair, something he did when he was stressed. He seemed to be doing a lot more of it recently. When he faced the others, his expression was set. "We stick to the plan. We need to get out of this town, with or without a car. We leave tomorrow."

THE GROUP GOT UP EARLY TO GO OVER THE PLANS again. Violet thought they probably talked them through more times than was necessary, probably because none of her friends were overly eager to leave the house, but eventually they had to go. They had a long walk ahead of them. They had initially thought of breaking into one of the other cars in the neighborhood, but still knew nothing about jacking cars. Sam continued to try and open each vehicle they passed, hopeful that someone might've left their keys inside, but they were out of luck.

Violet was grateful they had a plan. Matt's grandparents' house was the best option, yet somehow, she still didn't feel good about it. Yes, they lived in the middle of nowhere, so were less likely to have been overrun by the biters, and yes, they grew a lot of their own food, so would have been able to remain relatively self-sufficient. But did that mean they were safe? In this new world, Violet wasn't sure she held out a lot of hope for two old people. Still, it wasn't like she could say any of this. How would that sound?

"Hey Matt, thanks for telling us about your grandparents' house. By the way, what shall we plan to do with their corpses?" No, she knew they'd just have to deal with events as they unfolded.

As they stepped out into the cold morning air,

FIFTEEN

Violet took one last glance at her house. She had the very real feeling that she would never see it again.

They moved together as a group; Sam and Joe at the front, Tom behind, then Matt and Violet, Maggie, Zack, and Toby behind them. Ben walked at Violet's side, sniffing the air cautiously, ears pricked up. They moved silently, each carrying a weapon of sorts. Sam had a gun, Zack had the other, as well as the shovel, Violet, Maggie, Toby and Tom had knives, Matt had the garden fork, and Joe had a wooden table leg. He hadn't exactly been thrilled with it, but unfortunately, he'd gotten to the offerings last.

The birds were still singing, which didn't exactly feel right. Violet didn't like hearing such a cheerful sound as they passed each corpse lying in the road. She shivered, trying not to look, but found herself doing it anyway. The bodies were all different; some more decomposed than others, some half-eaten. They each told a different story; the woman who'd died early on from a bite to the neck, but cracked her skull on the pavement as she went down; the boy who'd probably died a week ago, whose entire stomach was ripped open; the man who'd died recently from a shot to the head, who didn't seem to have been bitten at all. Violet tried not to think about how easily she could've been one of those bodies.

They passed a crashed car, with other cars parked around it. It appeared as though they had stopped to check that the driver was okay, so it must've happened early on. There were bits of those good Samaritans littered around the open door of the crashed car. The driver was nowhere to be seen.

"Are you all right?" Matt asked quietly. Violet nodded, then shook her head, then shrugged. What answer could she really give? She was still breathing, so that was good enough for now.

Sam and Joe continued to lead the group through countless alleyways and back roads. So far, they seemed to have luck on their side. Though they had passed countless corpses on the ground, they'd yet to encounter a walking one.

IT HAD BEEN SEVERAL HOURS NOW, AND THE GROUP HAD reached the furthest end of town. Violet saw something up ahead, something familiar.

"The car," she exclaimed, forgetting in that instant to keep her voice down. She clapped her hand over her own mouth, looking apologetically at the others. Together, the eight of them moved silently along the wall of the building they had been passing. Sam motioned for everyone to stay there while he went to investigate. He headed closer to a crashed car, and—of course—Joe, Matt, and Violet followed. They knelt beside the burned-out wreck in front of them, peering carefully around the sides. Violet could see their vehicle not too far away. It was parked, not crashed, in the middle of the road, and seemed to be in good condition. The doors were wide open.

"Where are the people who stole it?" she whispered.

Matt shook his head. "I don't know. But it will make this journey a lot easier if we can use it."

Violet got to her feet before she was quickly pulled down again by Joe. He pointed to an area just off to the right-hand side of the car, slightly obscured by an overturned truck. She shifted a little to get a better view, then saw them. There were at least five biters feeding on someone. The wind blew, and there was a flash of yellow material.

I guess we found them.

"Stay behind me," Sam whispered. He motioned for the rest of the group to follow before moving forward. They kept low, hidden by the vehicles along the road. Sam led them silently, and Violet knew that by heading in this direction, they should be able to avoid the biters, at least long enough to get into the car and get moving. Still, her heart was racing, and she felt as though she was just moments away from throwing up. She tried to focus instead on the sound of her feet, keeping her steps as light as possible. It seemed to be working. The dead continued to feed, undisturbed, and Violet and her friends were getting closer to the car.

But of course, nothing ever went as planned. A loud, piercing screech rang out through the silent street. Tom had tripped and fallen heavily onto the ground behind them.

"Ow," he groaned, rubbing his knee. Violet could hear the biters approaching, heard the slap of their feet on the tarmac, their heavy breaths, their hungry cries. She felt her blood boil. For a moment, the group was frozen on the spot. All of them were watching Tom in disbelief.

We're going to get eaten because Tom tripped and grazed his knee?

"Help me up!" Tom ordered.

Leave him. Let them eat him. Let me eat him.

But they didn't. Well, Sam and Matt didn't. Joe looked as though he may have been thinking the same thing as Violet. But the dead weren't far now. There was no time to hold grudges.

"Get to the car," Matt shouted, forcing Violet out of her angry daze as he yanked Tom up. She grabbed Maggie's hand, pulling her in the right direction. Toby was close behind. Violet could hear Ben barking, but he wasn't with her. She glanced back over her shoulder, and saw Joe raise the table leg and knock over the first biter. Zack jammed his knife into its skull.

"Violet!" Maggie pulled back on Violet's hand, and she turned just in time to see the dead woman blocking their path. She snapped her bloodied jaws hungrily, moving toward them. Luckily, half her left foot was missing, so she wasn't exactly speedy.

"This way." Violet veered off to the right, leading Maggie down a narrow street.

"Keep going," Toby cried from behind them, and Violet could hear more biters joining the chase. She headed down an alleyway, and then cut through several backyards. She had no idea where she was taking them, just concentrating on getting away from the dead. As they rounded the corner, she saw a convenience store not too far away.

Please, she thought desperately. *Please let it be unlocked.*

Finally, she caught a break. The door swung open easily, and the three of them ran inside. Just as she closed the door, Violet heard scraping on the glass.

"Ben," she hissed. She hadn't even realized he'd been behind them.

"There's no time—" Toby began, but Violet had already opened the door. The dog ran in, but as she tried to slam it shut again, a single biter managed to get her arm inside.

"Help me," Violet ordered, and Toby and Maggie both threw their weight against the door. They all pushed, crying out in exertion. There was a horrible cracking sound, and then the door closed. Toby turned the lock. There was only the one biter out there. They'd managed to lose the rest of them somewhere along the way. Violet allowed herself to breathe.

Maggie smiled, sweat glistening on her face. She glanced down and frowned. "Violet, you've got something on your foot."

Violet glanced down. The dead woman's arm was on the floor, the hand resting neatly on her shoe. She kicked it away disgustedly. Toby snorted as he caught his breath, then surveyed the store. "We should get supplies."

"We need to find the others," Violet replied, shaking her head.

"Yeah, I know. I'll be fast." He hurriedly moved around the shelves, shoving things into his bag. Maggie glanced at Violet for approval, then headed off, too, filling her own bag. The biter outside continued to bang on the glass with her remaining arm, but she wasn't much of a threat now the door was locked. Violet stepped away, picking up a few things as she moved toward the back of the store. Ben was over by the counter, sniffing the air furiously. He stopped, ears pricked and tail high, still as stone. He let out a single whine. Violet heard the other two stop what they were doing. All eyes were on the dog.

There was an open door behind the counter, and now that they were silent, she was sure there was something moving back there. She held up her hand and dropped to her knees, motioning for Maggie and Toby to get down. She crawled toward the counter as quickly as she could, sitting with her back against it. Maggie and Toby were there seconds later. Violet could hear it now, coming through the doorway behind them. She slipped her bag off, leaving it beside her, and crawled toward the side of the counter, holding her knife tightly in her right hand. As she reached the gap, she could see the biter. It was a man, in good enough condition to suggest he'd succumbed recently. There was a large bloodstain on the shoulder of his shirt. She watched as his head panned the store. It didn't look like he knew they were there. He didn't seem to notice or care about the biter hammering on the door. She could hear his long, rasping breaths, and smell the rotting flesh of his skin. She took a moment to prepare herself, waiting for the opportunity.

The creature turned, showing Violet his back for just a moment. It was her chance. She jumped up and slammed the knife into the back of his head. It was harder than she'd anticipated, but the thing went down all the same. He twitched on the floor for a moment, and then was still. Toby and Maggie got up, watching as Violet wrenched her blade out of the biter's head. There wasn't much blood.

"Let's go," she muttered, nodding to the door from which the biter had come. Maggie and Toby hurried through, with Ben close behind. As Violet went to follow, there was a bang from the other side of the room, and she glanced over at the door. At least five biters were hammering on the glass, which was beginning to crack.

"Hurry," she hissed, breaking into a run as she followed the others.

VIOLET HADN'T REALIZED HOW LUCKY SHE'D BEEN THAT Toby was with her when they'd fled the zombies. He had a fantastic sense of direction, and was able to lead them back to the car within ten minutes. Violet knew if it had been left up to her, they would've walked around in circles for hours, and then ended up living in the store.

They managed to avoid any biters, and the car was soon in sight. Violet quickly opened the back doors for

Toby and Maggie to get in. Ben jumped onto Maggie's lap. The engine was still running. Violet didn't get in yet, watching the street around her anxiously. Her eyes darted back and forth, searching for any sign of movement.

Come on, come on. Where are you?

She knew she wouldn't leave without them, but she, Toby, and Maggie were exposed out in the open. If the rest of the group didn't arrive soon, they would have to take shelter in one of the nearby houses while they waited.

What if they're de—

Lalalala... not listening!

The street was silent except for a single breath of wind, which rustled the leaves of the oak tree nearby. The birds weren't singing now.

Finally, Violet saw movement up ahead.

Please don't be dead people.

It wasn't; it was the others. Sam was out in front, followed by Joe and Matt supporting Tom. Zack was behind. Tom had his arm clutched to his chest, and his shirt was drenched with blood. Violet's heart was racing, and she ran toward the group.

"What happened?" she called.

"No time, get in the car," Sam ordered. Violet looked over his shoulder; there were at least ten biters running at full speed toward them.

"Later is good," Violet gasped, helping Tom get into the car. She paused, not wanting to get in beside him. The smell of his blood would be too dangerous; her head was already starting to spin. Matt grabbed her hand, pulling her to the front of the car with him, while Joe and Zack got in the back. Sam slammed the driver's door at the exact moment the dead arrived. They pounded their bloody hands on the glass, leaving red smears across the surface. One of them pulled the windshield wipers off, while another repeatedly smashed her face against the window.

"Drive," Violet and Matt shouted simultaneously.

Sam slammed the car into reverse and backed away from the biters at full speed before flooring it past the angry group. Violet had her hand over her nose, vaguely aware that Matt was pouring water onto something beside her. Puzzled, she watched as he drenched a sock from his bag. "Put this over your nose," he instructed, passing it to her.

Violet did so. Immediately, the delicious smell of Tom's blood was diluted. The world around her began to lose its soft edge.

"She feels sick," Matt explained, as though this weird solution made perfect sense. Luckily none of the others were paying much attention to Violet, all focused on Tom. Now that she couldn't smell it so badly, Violet chanced a look. It wasn't good. Three of his fingers had been completely ripped off. Maggie removed her sweater, using it to wrap the hand.

"Did he get bitten?" Toby asked.

"No," Sam replied. "Caught his hand in a door when we were trying to get away from the dead. They were all piled up against it on the other side, and the pressure just ripped his fingers clean off."

Everyone in the car seemed to relax a little; at least he wasn't going to turn.

"We need to stop the bleeding," Violet said through the sock, aware of how ridiculous she must have appeared.

"She's right. He could die," Toby agreed.

"We need to find somewhere safe to stop," Sam said. "Then we can take a proper look. What's the quickest way out of town?" he asked Joe. "Do you remember?"

"Yes, which is good because I dropped my bag. The map was inside." Joe pointed to the road ahead. "Go left here."

"He's passed out," Maggie said anxiously. Violet turned to see Tom had his head on Maggie's lap. He was indeed unconscious. She immediately liked him more.

That's terrible. He could be really hurt.

"He'll be okay." Sam took another left. This road was quiet, with no sign of biters.

Matt reached back and touched Tom's forehead. "No, he's burning up. We need to get him some antibiotics or at least something for the pain."

"From where?" Joe asked.

Suddenly, the car screeched to a halt, and the

passengers were thrown forward.

"What the hell, Sam?" Joe complained, rubbing his neck. Sam pointed to his left, and the group followed his gaze. Up ahead was a large sign that said—*Hospital: 3M.*

"We could get some in there," Sam said.

"No way," Violet replied, still holding the damp sock to her nose. "That place would've had thousands of people in it when the dead started walking. Chances are most of them are still in there."

"We don't have a choice," Sam replied, glancing at Tom's hand. He started driving in the direction the sign had pointed them in. "He needs medicine."

Violet started to protest, but she knew he was right. Tom needed help, and the hospital was their best bet for the things they wanted. Still, a huge building full of people, where more would've undoubtedly flocked when people started eating each other? It didn't exactly scream 'safe place'.

It didn't take long to get there. Sam drove into the parking lot and stopped right outside the front of the building, beside an ambulance with its back doors wide open. A trail of dried blood led from the ambulance into the front doors.

"This is a good start," Joe muttered as he climbed out of the car. Sam turned around to the rest of the passengers.

"Tom needs to stay here, and someone should be with him." He inclined his head at Maggie and Toby. "Stay here and keep him safe."

Violet and Matt got out of the car. As Zack joined them, Ben made to climb out, too.

"No, stay," Violet said, holding up her hand. She told Maggie and Toby, "Keep him with you. He can smell them before you see them."

Sam spoke to Maggie. "If anything happens, just drive. Do a couple of circles around the hospital, then come back. That should be enough to lose them."

Sam, Matt, Joe, Violet, and Zack made their way toward the doors.

"We don't have any guns," Sam told Violet as they got closer. "Zack's jammed, and he dropped it when we were fighting off the biters. Mine is out of bullets."

Violet nodded. They would have to make do without them. She tried to tell herself they'd coped well enough so far without guns, and then remembered they hadn't exactly been doing great. Matt didn't have the garden fork. It had been lost in the struggle, too, so he was also currently without a weapon.

The large automatic doors were wide open, and the area inside was dark. Sam flicked on his flashlight, shining it around the large entrance to the emergency room. It was like a war zone inside—pills, syringes, and papers littered the floor. Gurneys lay sideways, computer equipment was smashed, and blood was smeared and splattered across the walls. There were bodies, too, picked clean to the bone.

"At least they're not coming back," Joe said, then he shuddered. "Can you imagine skeleton zombies? Actually, that might be pretty—"

"Shhh," Sam hissed. He pointed them toward the nearest hallway, and they moved in that direction. As they got further into the hospital, it became darker. The smell of death and rot filled the air.

"Anyone else think this is a really bad idea?" Joe whispered. "Watch any horror movie and you'll see that something bad always happens in hospitals. Especially abandoned hospitals."

"This isn't a movie," Sam replied, pausing to look inside an empty patient room. "Maybe we should—"

"Do not say, 'We should split up to cover more ground,'" Joe interrupted. "I'm not getting ripped to pieces so you can live out your *Scooby Doo* fantasy."

Sam grinned. "Fair enough."

They continued to explore the hospital. It soon became clear they hadn't been the first to get the idea. Any time they found a place where pills or medicines might be kept, it had been cleared out already by someone else. Violet was starting to get nervous. She didn't like how long they had been gone or how far they were getting into this labyrinth of a hospital, and she definitely didn't like the fact that she was sure she could hear movement around every corner.

As they continued down another hallway, Sam suddenly held out his hand to block their path.

"What?" Violet whispered. Sam raised a finger to his lips. She listened, and then heard it, too. It was a wet, lip smacking, slurping sound.

This can't be good.

The group stood still for a moment. Sam gestured for them to follow him. The hallway continued ahead, but there was also a turn to the left, which led to another ward. As Violet and the others peered around the corner, they could see one of the dead. It was wearing a doctor's coat and feeding on what appeared to be another doctor. It had its back to them; it hadn't seen them yet. Matt pointed forward, motioning for the others to continue down the hallway. Violet nodded, slowly moving on. She kept her eyes on the creature, terrified it would notice them at any moment.

That was probably why she didn't see the broken glass until she'd already walked over it. The biter's head snapped toward the sound, and it screamed when it saw them.

"*Go*," Matt shouted, and the group split in two. Joe, Zack, and Sam ran back in the direction they had come from, while Violet and Matt went the other way. Violet followed Matt through the maze of hallways, aware now of the other noises around her. There were more biters in the hospital. Matt was fast, but Violet worked hard to keep up, even though her eyes were streaming and her throat was burning. The two of them jumped over corpses and garbage. More than once, Violet saw movement in the rooms they passed.

Just as she was starting to think she might've got the hang of running away without falling over, she fell over. The ground slipped out from beneath her, and Violet felt her knees crack against the hard floor. She raised her hands, finding them covered in blood. But it wasn't hers; she'd slipped in a puddle of the congealed liquid surrounding a corpse beside her. Violet tried to get up, but her legs were shaking with exhaustion. She felt hands grab her shoulders roughly. Matt had come back to help.

He pulled her up, keeping hold of her hand as he led her into a room to the left.

It was empty, save for the skeleton on the bed. There was a large closet, and Matt hastily pulled Violet into it, closing the door behind them. She could hear sounds outside the room, feet pounding along the hallway, hungry cries. There had to be at least three out there. They were searching for them. More than once, the creatures screamed out. For one horrifying minute, she was sure they had come into the room. Then, slowly, the sounds began to fade.

Violet felt something snap.

"Oh no," she breathed.

"Are you okay?" Matt sounded worried.

"No."

"What? Why? Are you hurt?"

"No, my bra strap broke." Violet could feel it flapping against her back.

"Oh."

"That's so annoying."

"Well...yeah, but...you could be hurt, or dead. So..."

"Where am I going to find a decent bra in the zombie apocalypse?"

"I'm sure we could—"

"This is absolutely the worst day ever."

"You're handling this really well."

Violet snorted at the pure ridiculousness of the situation, then erupted into silent giggles. Matt was grinning.

"Sorry," she said when she had stopped laughing.

"No, it's serious. I get it."

Violet smiled, taking a moment to catch her breath. There was no sound from outside. "I think we're okay."

Matt opened the door. The two of them stepped out into the room, listening tentatively. They moved into the hallway, which was deserted again.

"Where do you think the others are?" Violet asked.

Matt shook his head. "I have no idea. Let's just try to find our way out. I'm sure they'll do the same."

They continued through the dark hallways, following

the signs for the hospital exit. As they rounded the corner, Violet caught sight of Zack going through something on the floor up ahead.

"Zack," she half-whispered, half-called.

Zack's head snapped up. Violet's stomach dropped.

That's not Zack. Not anymore.

His grey eyes locked with hers, wet blood smeared around his mouth. He wasn't going through a bag. He was eating someone.

"Oh..." Violet took a wobbly step back. The thing that used to be Zack cried out, sprinting toward them. Matt grabbed Violet's hand again, pulling her back the way they came. They ran, turning down different hallways, heading up some stairs, and then through another maze of dark corridors. Matt suddenly changed direction, yanking Violet to the left and through some double doors.

The large room smelled of dust and decay. As her eyes adjusted to the darkness, Violet realized they were surrounded by beds, many of which contained the remains of more people chewed right down to the bone. The machines were off, and the dark room was silent. There was a crash just outside the door. Violet spun around, realizing there was no other way out of the room. Her mouth felt like the desert, and her heart began to race. Matt, still holding onto her hand, pulled her toward an empty bed.

"Get in," he hissed. Violet didn't need to be told twice, not when she could see movement outside the little window on the door. Quickly, she got under the sheets. Matt lay down beside her, pulling the blankets over their heads.

This is crazy. This is crazy.

But there was no time to move now. The door to the room swung open, and Violet heard the biter come inside.

183

SIXTEEN

THE THING THAT USED TO BE ZACK WAS IN THE ROOM now. Violet could see his outline through the thin sheet covering her face, and could hear heavy steps as he lurched around. She felt as though time had slowed down, having no choice but to watch helplessly through the fabric. He was sniffing the air. Violet could hear the ragged breaths. He moved closer.

Can he smell us?

Slowly, he staggered toward the bed, still sniffing like a dog. He stood beside Violet, leaning a little over the sheet. She felt a wave of sadness at what Zack had become. His mouth was open, and saliva dripped onto the sheet covering her face. She could smell the blood in the thick liquid, mixed with rot and decay. Matt squeezed her hand as the two of them struggled not to breathe. Violet knew they could be about to die. Any moment now, this thing might just rip the sheet off and tear them to shreds. She felt as though her heartbeat was coming through a loudspeaker; so sure the creature would hear it.

But then there was a noise outside the room; the sound of something delicate being dropped. Zack let out a growl and broke into a run, crashing through the doors. Violet finally let out her breath, her whole body shaking. Matt pulled her closer, holding onto her as she shook. For a moment, they stayed like that, stuck together under the sheet in the room that smelled of death.

"We should go," he finally whispered.

Violet nodded, and they lifted the blanket. She listened—silence. The two of them stayed sitting on the bed for a moment, neither confident enough to open the doors, but both knowing they had no choice. Eventually, Matt took the lead, getting off the bed and moving to the end of the room.

Violet got out her knife and held it in front of her, following Matt. He pushed open the door carefully. There was a woman outside. Thankfully, this one was alive. She stared at them, frozen in place. She was halfway through dislodging her weapon—a knife taped to a table leg—from Zack's eye socket. She was small, pale, and had blonde hair tied loosely at the top of her head. Her eyes were a rich brown. Her skin was flecked with specks of blood.

"What are you doing here?" she asked, finishing removing her weapon and wiping the blood from the knife on the leg of her scrubs. Violet wondered if she was a doctor.

"The hospital's dangerous," the woman continued. "It's full of the dead. If you're here, you must be desperate."

"We came for medicine," Violet replied. "One of our friends has lost his fingers."

"Was he bitten?" the woman asked briskly, her eyes unblinking.

Matt shook his head. "No."

"Is he still bleeding?"

Violet nodded. The woman sighed. "You'll need more than medicine. Where is he?"

"Outside," Matt replied.

"Go and get him, then bring him here. I'll help you." There was a noise from a room to the left. The woman rolled her eyes, as if dealing with the dead was a chore rather than a horror. "I'll be back. Go down those stairs behind me. They should be clear."

VIOLET AND MATT COLLECTED MAGGIE, TOM, AND TOBY from the car, and returned to where the woman was waiting. She had more blood on her scrubs now, but offered no explanation and simply led them through several hallways until they reached a large breakroom. Violet felt uneasy; Zack was dead, and they'd seen no sign of Joe or Sam. The pair had been gone for too long. From the way the woman moved through the hallways, it was clear the hospital wasn't exactly the safest place. She wished she'd gotten a better look at whoever it was Zack had been eating, and prayed it hadn't been either of her friends. Still, she knew they had to focus on Tom, who was now conscious again but deathly white and barely able walk. She would just have to hope Sam and Joe could take care of themselves.

The breakroom was much larger than the teachers' lounge at school. It was filled with couches and armchairs. There was a large television, a kitchen, and snack and drink machines. There was also a private bathroom with a shower. Several of the windows were open, and the curtains blew gently. Violet moved over to one of them. She could see the car below, and just make out the shape of Ben stretched out on the backseats. She was sure Sam and Joe weren't down there.

"My name is Lorin," the woman said as she locked the door. She gestured for Tom to lie down on the nearest couch, which he did.

"How long have you been here?" Violet asked.

"Since the beginning. I'm a...I *used to be* a midwife. I was in here on my own, on my break, when it all happened. It was so fast." She began to clean up Tom's hand, something which clearly hurt a lot. Any color left in Tom's face drained away, and he groaned quietly, eyes now closed.

Lorin continued speaking as though a mangled hand was nothing out of the ordinary. "When I saw what was happening outside the room, I panicked. I locked the doors and hid. At first, I thought it was some kind of terrorist attack, and waited for the police or the army to come and help. But they never did. When I saw what they were saying on TV, I didn't want to believe it. Eventually, I made myself look out of the window. I saw those things. They were everywhere, just ripping people apart and eating them. There were so many in the parking lot, but more and more people kept coming to the hospital for help, so more and more got bitten. I couldn't risk going outside, so I stayed here. Luckily, the fridge and cupboards were full. After that, I got the vending machines open, too. I didn't leave this room for over a week." Her face took on an almost lost expression. "It was horrible in here alone, listening to the screams. Every time I thought it was finished, more people would arrive, and it would start all over again." She examined Tom's hand, and then began to go through a bag of medical equipment on the floor beside her.

"After a week or so, the place started to quiet down. Most of the dead had left. I thought I'd try to find any survivors. I was thinking there had to be others who locked themselves in like I did. I came across a few of the dead, but they weren't too hard to avoid. I killed the ones I couldn't hide from." She smiled a little. "And running into the doctor who used to make jokes about how short I was made stabbing him though the head pretty satisfying. *Who's a hobbit now, Jonathan?*" She looked at the others. "He was dead, though. I'm sure. Pretty sure."

"Why did you stay, if there was no one left to help?" Matt asked.

Lorin shrugged. "I thought I'd be more useful here. If anyone was stupid enough to come to a place filled with the dead, they'd have to be desperate. I'm not a doctor, but I know enough to do some good."

"We're grateful you stayed," Violet said, watching as Lorin injected Tom with something. He was asleep now, or passed out.

"Do you know much about what caused this?" Maggie asked. "Why corpses are walking, I mean?"

Lorin shook her head. "It's not exactly my area of expertise." She began to stitch up Tom's hand. "Whatever it is, it kills you. But then it does something to bring you back, but only with the most basic instincts. Those things are like animals; they don't reason or even really think. They just act."

"Do you know if anyone is immune?" Matt asked. Immediately, Violet felt her face flush red, as though Lorin and Maggie would suddenly guess her secret from the simple question.

Lorin raised an eyebrow. "Immune? It's not something I've seen, though I suppose if the dead are walking around, anything is possible." She began to wrap Tom's hand. "I'll have to keep him here for a few days to make sure the wound doesn't get infected."

Violet bit her lip. That didn't exactly fit with the plan, and she certainly wasn't loving the idea of sticking around in the Deadspital. She turned to Matt. "What should we do?"

"I don't know," he replied. "We were trying to get out of town as quickly as possible," he explained to Lorin.

"I can understand that. There seem to be more of those things every day, and they're moving in bigger and bigger herds."

"We can't just leave him," Maggie said, though Violet got the distinct impression she wasn't exactly about to fight them over it. Matt knelt beside Tom, and Violet joined him. Tom didn't appear to be waking up any time soon.

"I wouldn't feel right leaving him behind," Matt said.

"No, me neither," Violet replied, aware that she sounded at least twenty-three percent genuine.

Lorin joined them. "I'm sorry, but I don't have the supplies to keep you all here. I can take care of him, though. Hell, I could do with the company."

Violet was sure Matt scoffed at that, but he immediately covered it with a cough. She felt a smile cross her lips. How long would it be before Lorin realized Tom was about as fun as a yeast infection? Hopefully he'd at least not make any short jokes.

Matt took a sheet of paper and a pen from a table nearby, and wrote an address down. "This is my grandparents' house. It's where we're going. I don't know if it's safe, or if we'll get there, but when he's well, you're both welcome to come there and find us."

Lorin nodded, taking the paper.

The door at the far side of the room rattled. Lorin sprang to her feet, approaching it silently. She peeped through the little window.

"I'm guessing these are your friends," she said as she unlocked the door and pulled it open.

Sam and Joe practically fell inside, and Sam quickly slammed it closed again, locking it. They were both spattered with blood and out of breath. Joe looked relieved to see Violet and the others. "Isn't this place great?"

Sam spun to face Joe, his face angry. "What the hell happened back there?"

Joe raised an eyebrow. "I was distracting the biters so we could sneak past."

"Distracting them?"

"Yeah."

"By throwing a bottle at them?"

Joe held up his hands. "I thought it would smash over by the door, and they'd run off to investigate the sound. Could you think of a better plan?"

"I can think of at least twelve ways I could've done it better. I'm literally counting them up in my head now. None of them start with—throw a bottle directly at the dead, alerting them to exactly where we were, and making them chase us!'"

Joe shrugged. "With that tone, anything sounds ridiculous."

Sam rolled his eyes, turning back to the others. "Is Zack here?" he asked. "We got separated just before Joe's awesome bottle plan."

"He's not coming," Violet murmured. She saw Maggie's shoulders slump, and she moved toward the window. Sam swore, punching the wall.

"What—" Matt began, but he was interrupted by the sounds of hammering on the other side of the door. Sam stepped back, and Violet saw the shapes of the dead just outside.

"We need to go," she breathed. Lorin nodded, heading to a door at the other side of the room and unlocking it.

"Go, run as quickly as you can."

"What about you?" Matt asked.

"We'll be fine," Lorin replied quickly. "They've never gotten in before, but if you don't leave now and the dead find this door, you'll be trapped." She gestured again to the only exit. "Go, those things usually get bored after a few days. Your friend will be fine."

Violet took one last glance at Tom, still sleeping despite the sounds outside, and nodded. They ran from the room, Lorin locking up behind them.

They hurried through the dark hospital, running down the stairs so quickly Violet almost fell more than once. She was so sure the biters were behind them, but when they got outside, they were alone. They piled into the car. Sam started the engine, and Violet leaned back in her seat, finally allowing herself to breathe.

Lorin knows what she's doing. She'll take care of Tom.

As the car pulled away, Violet glanced up at the hospital. She could see movement in one of the windows above them. It took her a few moments to realize what it was—someone with blonde hair being forced against the glass.

"Sam—" Violet whispered.

He'd seen it, too. "We're leaving," he stated, cutting her off. It was too late now.

~~~~~~~~~~~~

THEY'D ONLY BEEN DRIVING FOR AN HOUR OR SO, BUT Violet had drifted off within minutes. The sound of conversation woke her.

"What's happening?" she asked groggily, peering out the window. The car was parked outside a huge pair of iron gates. On either side of them was a tall brick wall, between seven and eight feet high, which seemed to stretch on for miles in either direction.

"Where are we?" Violet asked.

"I've driven past this a few times before," Matt replied. "I think there's a big house in there somewhere. Like a country estate."

"Is that why we stopped?"

Sam nodded. "There's no way the biters could get over those walls. It should be secure." He opened his door, and then got out of the car. Maggie, who'd also been asleep, began to stir.

"What's happening?" she asked.

Violet shrugged. "Wait here." She got out, too, heading over to the gates where Sam and Matt were waiting.

"You want to stay here?" she asked Sam.

"I think so. We just need to find out how to get inside."

"What about the plan?" Matt asked. "We were heading to my grandparents' house."

Sam sighed. "We don't know for sure that it's safe, and I think you would've mentioned if it had protection like this. Besides, we're almost out of fuel. If we keep going, it won't be long before we're on foot."

"Pass," Joe said with a yawn, joining them.

Sam agreed. "Look, if we still want to go on, we'll need more fuel and supplies. If there are people in there, or if it's empty, we might be able to find something. Or we could stay. I know I'd feel more secure with this huge wall around me."

Violet bit her lip. As much as she didn't want to say so, Sam was right. Matt's grandparents were almost certainly gone, one way or another. This was their best option. And there was no way the biters would be able to get inside those walls.

Unless they're already in there.

Matt seemed to read Violet's mind. "What if the people inside have turned?"

Sam put his hands on the bars of the gate, rattling them gently. "Then we'll get rid of them. We've done it before. We'll just take it slow. If there are too many, we'll get out, but we have to try. It's better than roaming the streets, surely, which is our other option once the car runs dry." He shook the gates again, more roughly. "Maybe we could move the car closer. Use it to climb—"

Sam jumped back as a face appeared at the gates. It was an old man, with dirty grey hair that hung raggedly around his cheeks. His face was gaunt and unshaven, and his breath smelled of cigarettes.

"What do you want?" he asked gruffly, his blue eyes darting anxiously to each of them.

"We're looking for a place to stay," Sam said, stepping forward again.

"Keep looking."

"We're good people," Sam continued. "We don't want to hurt anyone or steal anything. We're just trying to find a place to rest, even just for a night."

The man shook his head. "No room."

Joe raised an eyebrow, but Violet moved closer. "Please."

'No room' means more people. Living people. Living people means somewhere safe.

As long as I don't eat any of them, we could be golden!

The man narrowed his eyes, then sighed. "Wait." He moved away from the gate, holding a walkie-talkie to his lips. "Got some people down here, wanting to come in."

There was silence for a moment, and then another man's voice spoke in reply. "Are they alone?"

"Yes."

"Are they bitten?"

The man looked over. "You bitten?"

"No," Sam replied.

"They say no."

Joe raised an eyebrow again. "Well, that's thorough."

The walkie-talkie crackled a little. "Open the gates."

Sam drove the car up a long dirt road, which seemed to go on for miles. There were woods on either side, and it was only when they were clear of those that Violet finally got to see the house. It was easily one of the most beautiful buildings she'd ever seen. It was as large as the main block at school, with white walls and huge windows. Green ivy grew in patches over the brickwork, which made the building look even more like something from an old movie. As they pulled up outside, Violet could see wide marble steps leading up to a grand, white front door. They climbed out of the car, each taking in their surroundings. People were riding horses down on the green lawn. There were barns not too far away, with a herd of cows grazing nearby. Chickens pecked at the ground near the marble steps. There were at least fifteen people in sight, each regarding Violet's group with curious, yet friendly expressions.

"Welcome."

Violet and the others turned around. A man was making his way toward them. He had a walkie-talkie clipped to his belt, and the gait of someone important. He was probably in his late fifties, with greying brown hair and a tired but strong air about him. He gave a wide, genuine smile, and held out his hand to shake Sam's.

"I'm Robert," he said, shaking each of their hands now. "I'm sorry for your reception down at the gate. Harold..." He paused, as though he wasn't sure how to finish his sentence. "Harold has a way with people." He smiled. "But we're happy to have you here."

"Thank you," Violet said.

Robert nodded. "Don't worry. You're safe now."

ROBERT GAVE THEM A TOUR OF THE HOUSE TO GET THEM acquainted with what he was already calling their new home. Violet certainly didn't mind. This whole place felt like a dream compared to everything they'd experienced up until that point. Sam asked, almost half-heartedly, about taking some fuel for the car, but Robert waved this idea off.

"You can't go back out there," he dismissed. "We've lost far too many good people, and every person lost is another muncher outside."

"Why would anyone want to leave here?" Joe asked as they walked through another huge room.

Robert held up his hands. "It's understandable; they wanted to go find their families and friends. Thought they could bring them here, but most never make it back." He looked at each of them. "You've all got each other; don't risk that by going back out there."

Robert led the group around the house, telling them his story. "When the dead began to walk, my family and I were the only ones here. This was our house. Although it's large, we didn't have many staff. Harold at the gates, he was the gardener. We had a driver and a few people who came to clean, but no one who lived on site. Harold came first when the dead started walking, but as things outside got worse, more and more people from the town found our gates. So I left him down there, and told him to let people in as long as they weren't bitten."

"That was very kind of you," Violet said.

"What alternative was there? No one in their right mind would leave those people out there, not with what was happening, and not when we have so much room. As time went on, we became a community. We all work together to make ourselves a life here." They headed up a huge staircase, and Robert continued. "A family from the town used to use my land for farming, so we've got crops, animals, and greenhouses full of food. As more people arrived, they brought canned supplies, so we've got those, too. There's more than enough for everyone, and everyone contributes to the farming and harvesting to make sure it stays that way."

"What about water?" Sam asked.

"We've been storing rainwater since the start, and there's a river at the edge of the woods, so we can boil water from there if needed. We've been using a turbine in the river to draw power from the current, and also have hundreds of solar panels. My plan before the world changed was to be self-sufficient out here, which means we already had a steady source of power when everywhere else ran dry. We can even watch movies once in a while."

Robert led the group through the countless rooms, many of which contained families.

"This isn't just my house anymore," he said earnestly. "It belongs to everyone." He waved to an old woman dusting a lampshade, who smiled in return. Matt caught Violet's eye and raised an eyebrow. She knew what he meant— was this too perfect?

Robert stopped outside a door in the middle of the hallway. "I do apologize, but we've run out of family-sized bedrooms. I can only offer you one of the smaller ones." He swung open the door to reveal a huge room containing a king-sized four-poster bed, two large couches, a television, desk, bookcase, and a closet big enough for the group to fit comfortably inside. There was also a private bathroom.

"I think this will be fine," Violet said, aware her mouth was hanging open.

SEVENTEEN

Violet learned that there were twenty families in the house, alongside a few people who had arrived on their own. Even though the place was huge, there were too many people living there to all be able to eat in the oversized dining room together. Most people prepared their food at set times, and ate in their rooms. Tonight, however, Robert had invited Violet's group to come and eat with his family and a few of their close friends. Everyone had been welcoming and polite, but Violet couldn't help but notice their fantastic ability to talk about everything and anything besides the zompocalypse. She supposed it made sense; when people lived so comfortably away from the danger, they probably didn't want to be reminded about the fact that others were still dying.

Everyone was laughing, joking, telling stories, and generally acting like everything was normal. The reality of the situation was clear enough, though, by the scars on their arms and faces, and the haunted expressions behind most of their eyes.

Violet didn't talk much at dinner. She sat at one end of the table, with Matt to her right and Joe to her left, and simply watched the others. Everything felt so relaxed, so...normal? A mother across the table was quietly scolding her son, who looked about ten. He had blond hair and thick glasses.

"I don't want you hanging around with those boys anymore," she said as she spooned peas onto his plate. "They're too wild for you, and with your asthma—"

"I'm fine, Mom," the boy groaned, but his mother shook her head.

"No, that's final."

The boy sighed, catching Violet's eye and seeming a little embarrassed. She turned away, but a smile crossed her lips. She couldn't help it; she was starting to feel safe here. Her friends felt it, too. Joe and Matt were laughing as they spoke to the people around them, Maggie and Toby were deep in conversation with a couple of kids further down the table, and Sam was talking to a pretty girl who sat opposite him. Even Ben seemed happy, sleeping under the table with a couple of other dogs.

"What's it like?"

Violet raised her head. The man sitting next to the mother opposite had asked the question, and was waiting for a response.

"What?" Violet asked.

"*Out there,*" the man clarified, inclining his head toward the window. "What's it like out there?"

Violet shook her head. "Bad."

What a way with words you have, Violet.

The man nodded, reaching for a plate of carrots. "They don't talk about it here. They don't talk about any of it anymore."

⌁⌁⌁

AFTER DINNER, VIOLET AND HER FRIENDS WENT BACK TO the bedroom. Robert had been telling the truth about having enough power to watch movies, and had let them borrow a box full of DVDs. Though Violet was unsure how sensible it was to waste electricity on something as frivolous as watching TV, they were still excited to spend the evening letting their eyes rot away. There had, however, been some disagreement over which movie to watch. Violet and Maggie had wanted an award-winning fantasy movie, which the others had been all for until

Violet mentioned that it was Spanish.

"Wait, so it has subtitles?" Sam asked.

"Well, yeah," Violet replied.

All four of the guys groaned.

"What?" Maggie asked.

"I don't like movies with subtitles," Joe complained.

Violet raised an eyebrow. "Why, can't you read?"

"Har-har."

"What about this one?" Sam asked, delving into the box and holding up an action film. Violet had no idea what it was about, but the fact the box showed a man jumping from an exploding car and a woman in a string bikini holding a machine gun, suggested it wasn't the movie for her. She raised an eyebrow. "I don't think Maggie and I—"

"That looks great," Maggie interrupted enthusiastically. Sam and the others whooped, and the matter was settled.

Though Violet was excited to do something as normal as watching TV, the novelty soon wore off. The movie itself was just terrible. Violet watched as yet another building blew up, and then got to her feet.

"I'm going for a walk."

No response; her friends were transfixed on the screen.

"Okay, bye then," Violet said, a little louder this time.

Still nothing. Joe laughed as the hero of the movie made another ridiculous pun. "Knew he was gonna say that."

Violet rolled her eyes. "I was thinking I might climb over the gate. Have a walk outside? Maybe find a zombie and let them chew on my arm a little bit?"

"Yeah," Sam said obliviously, waving her off with his hand. Violet huffed and left the room.

The night was mild, and the moon full and bright. She walked down the steps outside the front door, making her way to the pen where the horses were kept. She put both arms on the fence, standing and watching the animals for a while. A little brown pony trotted past with its mother, happily throwing its head around.

She heard movement behind her, turning to see Matt approaching. "Hi," he said, smiling as he leaned on the fence to her right. "What are you doing?"

"Nothing really, just thinking." Violet raised an eyebrow. "You realized I was gone then?"

Matt's grin was sheepish. "Yeah...sorry about that. I got a little caught up with all the explosions and violence. It made me feel like a real man."

"Why did you leave?"

"It got *really* loud."

"Wow, you're so tough."

Matt winked, taking a step back from the fence. They began to walk further away from the house.

"Did I miss anything?" Violet asked.

Matt thought for a moment. "That guy with the eye patch jumped out of a skyscraper and destroyed a helicopter with his bare hands on the way down."

Violet was confused. "Wait, I thought he died already?"

"They rebuilt him."

"From what? He got blown up, didn't he?"

"There were some bits left."

"It's literally the worst movie in the world."

Matt smiled. The two of them walked in amicable silence for a few minutes. Violet could see the woods up ahead.

"How are you doing?" Matt asked.

What you mean is, 'How's the zombie stuff going? Want to eat anyone yet?'

"I'm okay," Violet replied. "Not about to eat anyone if that's what you're thinking."

"It wasn't."

Violet scrunched her nose, and Matt held up his hands. "Okay, it wasn't the *only* thing I was thinking."

"That's more like it."

They stopped walking. Violet got the feeling Matt had something on his mind. He seemed a little nervous.

"Are *you* okay?" she asked.

"What? Yeah. I just... I was thinking about you... No, not about you. Not exactly... I mean, I was thinking about us and that maybe—"

"Wait, shut up."

"Excellent, this was just how I was hoping this would go."

"No, look!" Violet pointed toward the woods. Matt followed her gaze. There was movement just beyond the tree line.

"What is that?"

Violet saw a flash of light. "It's not the dead. It's people. They've got flashlights."

"Where are they going?"

"I don't know."

Without saying a word, Violet and Matt headed toward the entrance to the woods. She could see the flashlights, not too far away, but heading in the other direction.

"Should we follow them?" Matt asked.

"Hmm, mysterious people walking into the woods with flashlights..."

Matt nodded. "We shouldn't. It's a terrible idea."

"They could be crazy," Violet added.

"It would be stupid and dangerous."

"You're right."

His dimples popped. "Let's do it."

"Okay."

The two of them entered the woods. Though Violet knew it was risky, she didn't feel too worried, not yet. She knew they were in a safe place; the grounds of the house were surrounded by the brick wall, and Robert and his people wouldn't be wandering around in the woods if the biters were roaming freely out there. And the people themselves? They all seemed friendly and harmless enough. Sure, walking through the woods at night carrying flashlights didn't exactly scream 'normal and safe behavior,' but what was even normal and safe during the zombie apocalypse?

Matt and Violet continued, following the light and giggling like children as they tripped over rocks and tree roots. Neither of them felt in any real danger. Violet could see the people more clearly now. There were three of them. They were far enough away not to hear the noise she and Matt made as they stumbled along behind, but close enough to be kept in sight.

Eventually, Violet saw a building up ahead. It was in the middle of a clearing but still surrounded by the woods.

It was a barn, clearly unused for some time. It was old and crumbling, with a thick chain locking the doors. The three figures climbed a ladder leaning against the wall, and then entered a window on the upper level. Matt went to follow, but stopped when he noticed Violet had held back.

"What's the matter?" he asked.

"I don't know. I've got a weird feeling."

"A weird feeling about the three mysterious people entering the abandoned barn during the middle of the night?"

"So you're familiar with it?"

Matt smiled. "It's probably just some kids sneaking out to smoke or something. We can go back if you want?"

Violet thought for a moment, then shook her head. They'd come this far. She needed to see what they were doing. Otherwise, she'd just drive herself crazy thinking about it. She made her way over to the ladder, pausing for a moment as her hands rested on the wood, then climbed up. After she crawled through the window, she was met with the confused faces of three people. Two of them were teenagers, one was much younger; it was the boy who had been told off by his mother at dinner.

"What are you doing here?" asked a boy with a mass of ginger hair and freckles, who was probably about fifteen. Violet saw the other two attempting to stealthily slide some beer cans behind a bale of hay behind them.

Underage drinking? Definitely better than I was expecting when I saw the creepy barn.

Violet was just starting to think everything might be totally normal and fine, when Matt tapped her on the shoulder. "Um...Vi..."

She followed his gaze. The upper floor of the barn came to a stop a few feet from where they were sitting. She could see one of the dead down on the lower level. He had long black hair, ripped and bloodied clothes, and what appeared to be a red scarf tied around his neck. There were other strips of red tied around his arms and legs.

"What is *that* doing here?" Violet asked, raising her voice a little as she turned back to the kids.

"Relax, it can't escape," the redhead said, rolling his eyes as if a zombie wandering around below them was the most normal thing in the world. He continued, "No one even knows it's here."

"How reassuring," Matt drawled sarcastically.

"What are you doing with it?" Violet eyed a small pile of red cloth on the floor next to the other teenage boy, who had short black hair. His grin smacked of meanness, and Violet noticed for the first time that he was holding three pieces of straw in his hand.

"Just watch," he said. Silently, the kids each picked a straw. It was the youngest, the blond, who ended up with the shortest one. He looked at the creature once more, then got to his feet, taking a piece of red material and moving toward the window. Silently, he climbed out.

The other two began to shout, drawing the attention of the biter. Violet glanced at Matt, wondering if he was as confused as she was about what was happening. He was watching the barn door, and sure enough, it opened a fraction. The chain was loose enough to allow the small boy to slip through the gap and enter the barn without the biter realizing.

"Oh God," Violet breathed, finally putting the pieces together. The boy snuck up behind the creature.

"What are you doing?" Matt angrily asked the other teens, who were still yelling and taunting the biter.

The ginger one rolled his eyes again, and Violet thought if he did that one more time, she might have to punch him.

"Relax," he said. "We've done it loads of times; that thing is slow." He pointed down, and Violet saw the biter had a severely mangled left leg, which it was dragging as it walked. The boy got closer, holding onto the red cloth. The teens were jeering. The black-haired one was even dangling his leg off the platform to keep the thing occupied. But then, without warning, it spun around and lunged at the boy, knocking him to the ground.

"Help him," Violet cried.

The redhead rolled his eyes again, but Matt grabbed Violet's wrist before she got to act out her fantasy. The kid continued, "He's fine. He just needs to keep out of its way until he can knock it over or it falls on its own. Then he ties the cloth around it." He spoke to her as if she were a child and he an adult.

"Are you crazy?" Violet spat. "That thing will kill him!"

The black-haired teen, who'd been laughing and cheering, was suddenly silent. Violet turned back. The blond boy was struggling with the biter. He'd managed to push it off him and onto its back, but now it had hold of his arms and was trying to pull him toward its snapping jaws. Matt got to his feet and ran toward the window. Violet knew there wasn't time. She scanned for something to use, and saw a pitchfork resting against the wall on the ground floor. After jumping from the platform onto a large hay bale, she got to her feet and grabbed the tool. She kicked the boy out of the biter's grasp none too gently, and then slammed the fork into the creature's face. It stopped moving immediately. Violet's heart was hammering. She heard the chain rattle against the barn door as Matt squeezed through the gap. Leaving the fork in the biter's head, she went to help Matt get the boy off the floor. The kid was rubbing his arm, but there was no bite, no blood.

"It didn't have any teeth," the redhead muttered from above them. "You didn't save him from anything."

Violet felt anger boiling inside her. She glared up at the two of them, pointing to the corpse. "Do you think this is all a joke? That you can play games with these things? They can rip someone apart just using their fingers! All they want to do is kill you, and not having teeth doesn't mean they can't or they won't! Have some respect!"

"Are you okay?" Matt asked.

Violet nodded. "Let's go." She scowled, taking one last glance at the dead biter.

"We weren't playing," the redhead called after them. "We were practicing."

VIOLET AND THE OTHERS HAD BEEN LIVING AT THE HOUSE

for a week, and it was really starting to feel like a home. Aside from the incident in the barn, everyone was friendly, normal, and in no hurry to try to murder them. It was a nice change.

Violet was happy, but it was strange to be surrounded by so many people, especially those who didn't really have any idea of what was going on in the world outside the huge walls. Children played outside long after dark and people didn't worry about making noise or lights being on. It was a safe place. Violet knew they were right to relax. She'd seen the wall. It would take a bulldozer to knock down any part of it, and she was pretty sure the dead weren't driving those around. But inside the grounds, the walls were hidden by acres of fields, and after that, acres of woodland, so it was hard to remember it was there.

In fact, the woods were part of the reason Violet felt anxious. Even though they were filled with bright flowers and what seemed like thousands of adorable bunny rabbits—hardly nightmare-inducing stuff—they were still terrifying. She didn't think it was just the fact the woods were home to the biter-barn. After all, the zombie in there was dead now. She thought it was more to do with what they reminded her of, which was the woods she'd been walking through when it all began. That was where she'd spotted her first zombie. Whenever she was alone outside, Violet kept far away from the tree line, even after a week of feeling safe and secure.

Today, she'd gotten up early to walk Ben through the fields. It was a beautiful day. In fact, it seemed like from the moment they had arrived at the house, the weather had dramatically improved. The sun always seemed to be shining.

Violet shuffled out of her borrowed jacket and slung it over her arm. Ben trotted happily by her side. She threw the tennis ball she'd taken along for the walk, but though he chased it, Ben soon lost interest and began sniffing at the ground. Violet watched as he caught sight of something and froze. She felt her heart begin to beat a little faster, simply out of habit, but relaxed when she realized it was just a squirrel. Ben, however, acted as though he'd never seen one before. He charged off in pursuit, disappearing into the woods. He certainly wasn't afraid of going in there. She didn't follow. She knew he'd come back; he always did.

Violet allowed her mind to wander, thinking about the rest of her group. Everyone had settled in quickly. In fact, she sometimes felt like she was the only one who still thought about what was going on outside. It was almost as though she was expecting something to ruin what they had, like they were all skating on a frozen pond, and she was the only one waiting for the ice to crack.

And by crack, she meant the moment when she would accidentally go crazy and eat someone.

Stop. It's not going to happen. Matt won't let it.

That seemed true enough. Matt had stuck by her side since arriving at the house. He was the only one who knew her secret, and he was pretty dedicated to ensuring she didn't accidentally chew anyone's face off. But he'd made himself useful to Robert, too, along with Joe and Sam, and had begun to help in the fields with the crops. Sam in particular had really settled in, and he seemed to be enjoying a break from taking care of everyone. He had become particularly close with the daughter of one of Robert's friends, and he spent much of his time with her. Joe was also constantly surrounded by at least three young women, and Violet soon realized that women outnumbered men at the house. It seemed Joe, young and new, was the most interesting thing to appear at the gates for many weeks. Matt got a similar amount of attention at first, but was less enthusiastic than Joe, and his admirers soon began to leave him alone.

Toby spent a lot of his time with some of the young boys who lived in the house, and Maggie had formed close friendships with the older women of the group, busying herself most days with household chores. Violet thought at first she'd been roped into it, but realized Maggie liked those kinds of jobs and enjoyed hanging out with the old ladies. Everyone had made friends; it was only Violet who tried to keep to herself as much as possible. It was safer that way.

She looked back at the woods. Still no sign of Ben.

Relax, this place is safe. He's probably waiting at the bottom of a tree for that squirrel.

Violet knew she was right, but still didn't want to leave him alone in there. "Ben," she called, straining her eyes for a flash of white. Nothing. "Ben..." she said, louder this time.

A high-pitched cry in return.

He's hurt!

Violet took off at full speed toward the sound, her own fears forgotten. She moved further and further into the woods, calling out Ben's name. She wasn't thinking about finding her way back out, only about the dog. She began to tire, something that seemed to be happening a lot more quickly these days. She wondered if it was because she hadn't eaten, really eaten, in a while. It was the blood, after all, that seemed to make her strong.

Another whimper, closer this time. She scanned her surroundings; Ben was twenty feet or so away, wagging his tail. Relief flushed over her, and Violet jogged over. Ben tried to move closer, then whimpered again, holding his paw up. She crouched, examining it. A sharp twig had become lodged between two of his toes. She pulled it out gently, and watched as he gingerly put some weight on it. He wagged his tail harder, gratefully licked her hand, before trotting off in the other direction.

Violet got to her feet, realizing now she had absolutely no idea where she was, or which was the quickest way out of the woods. The thing that surprised her most, though, was how calm she felt about it. The woods weren't nearly as frightening as she thought. Though they had appeared dark from the tree line, large rays of sunlight broke through the gaps in the trees and colored the ground below a golden brown. She could hear birds singing. Not far in the distance, a large family of rabbits were grazing on a patch of clover. Violet felt foolish for being so afraid. It was beautiful in there. With a renewed sense of confidence, she followed Ben, knowing he probably had more idea of where he was going than she did anyway.

Alive?

WHEN VIOLET RETURNED TO THE BEDROOM THREE hours later—ironically, Ben's sense of direction was *not* much better than her own—the air was tense. Matt, Joe, and Sam were sitting on the couches talking in hushed voices. Maggie and Toby were cross-legged on the floor. Sitting between Sam and Joe was Sam's friend Rachel.

"What's going on?" Violet asked, closing the door behind her.

Sam got to his feet. "Rachel needs our help."

Rachel had clearly been crying. Her blue eyes were red-rimmed, and she ran her fingers through her blonde hair anxiously.

"I'm sorry," she choked. "I shouldn't have come to you with this, but I didn't know who else to ask."

"What is it?" Violet asked as she moved closer.

"Her brother is sick," Joe explained.

"He has asthma," Rachel began. "He needs refills for his inhaler, but we've run out."

"Have you told Robert?"

Rachel nodded. "Yes, but he says it's too dangerous to go outside. He doesn't think Connor's asthma is severe enough to risk people leaving. He says we can manage it in other ways."

"What ways?" Maggie asked.

"Breathing exercises. We learned to do them for mild attacks if we couldn't get to an inhaler, but it won't work if he has a severe one."

Sam shook his head. "What about your parents?"

Rachel frowned. "They agree with Robert. They think it's too dangerous, and we can handle it without his medicine. They keep saying how he's been doing so well, and as long as he doesn't run or do anything else too athletic, he'll be fine."

Matt and Violet exchanged sideways looks. If this was the same boy who had been attempting to attach scarves to the biter in the barn, he wasn't exactly working hard at 'taking it easy'.

"So," Violet began, not liking where this was heading. "What are you asking, exactly?"

Rachel sighed. "I shouldn't ask, I know I shouldn't, but

your group has been outside more recently than anyone else. You lasted out there, and you took care of yourselves. You can handle the munchers. If we could just get some refills for his inhaler, even just a couple for emergencies, it would make all the difference."

"From where?" Joe asked. "Is there a pharmacy nearby?"

Rachel shook her head. "They've been cleaned out, at least all the ones around here. In the early days, Robert was sending people out for medical supplies until it got too dangerous. There was barely anything then. By now, it'll be gone."

"So...where?"

Rachel bit her lip. "The only place I think we can be sure will still have medicine is the hospital."

Violet's shoulders slumped. "Which hospital?"

"THIS IS GREAT. I WAS SUPER KEEN TO COME BACK here." Joe sighed, glaring at the doors leading into the hospital. "Remind me again why we're doing this?"

"Because we're good people, and we want to help a sick kid?" Sam said.

"I'm not sure that's it."

"Because Sam wants to make out with Rachel?" Violet suggested.

"Ding, ding! I think we have a winner," Joe replied glumly.

"Shut up," Sam groaned. He nodded to the doors. "We'll get in, get out, no problem."

"Are you still talking about Rachel?"

Sam's elbow in Joe's ribs suggested he wasn't a fan of that particular joke.

"It wasn't exactly 'no problem' last time," Violet reminded him.

"It will be easier this time."

"How?" Matt asked, raising an eyebrow.

"We have weapons."

That was true. They each had a knife, and Matt and Sam also had crowbars.

Joe still didn't look so sure. "If I remember right, that place was swarming with zombies. I'm not sure a few knives and crowbars are going to make much of a difference."

"We know what to expect this time, too," Sam added.

"That's not exactly a comfort," Matt retorted.

Sam sounded irritated. "You guys didn't have to come. I offered to do it alone."

"What a hero," Joe said sarcastically. "Listen, mate, we're not about to let you end up as one of those things. But we're gonna make you regret trying to show off to your new girlfriend right up until the moment we get safely back behind those walls, okay?"

"Fine."

Sam, Matt, Joe, and Violet had been crouched behind a car parked not far from the main hospital doors. Now Sam waved over the rest of their party—two guys around Violet's age who'd offered to come along and help. Violet didn't know their names. They'd traveled over in their own car, and had so far made no attempt to engage in conversation. They were friends of Rachel's, and willing to risk their lives to help her brother. Violet wondered if Rachel was aware of how easily she could charm guys into doing whatever she wanted.

Toby and Maggie had wanted to come, too, or at least Toby had wanted to and Maggie had offered, but Sam had made them stay behind.

"We need at least a couple of us back at the house so no one gets suspicious," he had explained, though Violet thought it was more that he didn't want to risk the lives of the youngest members of their group unless necessary.

"Okay, let's go," Sam said. Walking together and trying to look in all directions at once, they headed inside the open doors to the hospital. They made their way through the darkened hallways once more, a destination in mind this time. When they had last been there, Lorin the midwife clearly had a large store of medicine in her living space. It was an area of the hospital they knew how to get to, and would hopefully mean a short trip. Of course, it was almost certain Lorin and Tom were both dead now, and none of the group were overjoyed at the possibility of running into them.

The hospital was quiet as a grave, but Violet knew this was an illusion. The dead were there somewhere. Beside her, Joe whispered, "So how long until we're running for our lives?"

"Shall we make a bet?"

"I've got a Milky Way that says it's within five minutes."

"I'll get in on that," Matt said, joining them. "A box of cookies says it's ten minutes in."

Violet thought for a minute. "Fifteen minutes in, and I've got a pack of gum."

"We'll be fine," Sam insisted through gritted teeth.

Joe ignored him. "Next question, who gets us spotted?"

"Me," Violet said immediately. "I'll step on some glass or something and they'll hear us."

Joe nodded. "Interesting. Matt, what do you think?"

"Oh, it'll be Violet."

Violet slapped him on the shoulder. Matt grinned. "Sorry, but you're so clumsy. It'll definitely be you. I'm gonna go with Violet stumbles into a piece of medical equipment, they hear us, and then chase us."

Joe tapped a finger on his chin. "I'm thinking Violet trips over her own feet, swears loudly, and then they chase us."

"Thanks for your support," Violet said sarcastically.

"We'll be fine," Sam repeated.

"Thank you, Sam."

Sam nodded, but then added, "But if we do get killed, it'll definitely be because they heard Violet."

"Great."

The two strangers were regarding each other with confused expressions, but said nothing. The group made their way up the darkened staircase and toward the breakroom. Sam went in first. It was much the same, other than the huge bloodstain on the couch where Tom had once been. There was no sign of either him or Lorin.

"That's not good. I was hoping his body would still be here," Joe said, pointing to the stain.

"Why, because it would mean he was fully dead and not a zombie?" Violet asked.

Joe didn't blink. "Yeah. Sure. That's what I meant. Obviously. Not because I wanted his watch." He scuttled to the other side of the room.

Sam was rifling through the medical supplies, shoving them into his bag. He got to his feet. "I've grabbed it all, but it's not what we need."

"Wonderful." Violet sighed. That meant they had to keep going.

They stepped back outside, following Sam down the next hallway. As they rounded the next corner, they could see at least ten biters, all facing a door at the end of the corridor. Sam held up his hand to stop the others, and they froze where they were. He gestured for them to back up, and they did. Unfortunately, Sam kept his eye on the biters, which meant he wasn't watching the floor. He put his foot down on a glass vial, smashing it. The dead all looked over, crying out.

"Ha," Violet burst out. "It *wasn't* me!"

Matt grabbed her hand. "Congratulations, run!"

They all charged back in the direction they had come from. Violet could hear the dead close behind, hissing and screaming as they ran.

"Split up," Sam yelled as they came to the stairs.

"What a fuc—" But Joe didn't finish his sentence. More biters poured down the stairs. Joe, Violet, and Matt ran down the other staircase, and Sam and the two new guys continued along the hallway. Violet could hear feet on the stairs behind her, so she knew at least some of the dead were following.

"Run faster," Joe yelled, glancing over his shoulder.

Thanks, Joe, I never thought of that.

Left. Right. Right. Left. Right. They continued through the maze, the sound of the things behind them never waning.

"This way," Matt cried, pulling the two of them into another room. Joe tripped as he ran inside, crying out as he hit the floor. Matt slammed the door closed, locking it behind him. Violet looked around. They were in a disabled bathroom. "Lovely."

Matt shrugged, panting a little. "I thought I'd go before we leave."

Violet felt herself grin despite the sound of hands hammering against the door. Yes, they were trapped, and yes, they were in a bathroom, but they'd been about to fall from exhaustion anyway. At least now they were safe and could catch their breath. But then Violet sniffed, realizing something was wrong.

Oh no.

She swiveled to see Joe pulling a large shard of glass out of his arm. He'd fallen on it when they ran inside. Violet's eyes widened, and she turned to Matt in horror. He glanced at Joe, realizing what was happening. He pointed to the window at the other side of the room. Violet hurried over, wrenching it open and hanging her head outside. It helped, at least a little, but things were starting to get fuzzy. She could hear Matt's voice behind her.

"We need to cover that, now."

"Well, I wasn't planning to just let it bleed."

The sound of rummaging was loud as Matt went through his bag. After what felt like an eternity, there was a gentle hand on her shoulder.

"Are you okay?" Matt asked.

"Is it gone?"

"Yes."

Violet pulled her head inside. Joe's arm was bandaged, but he was staring at her curiously.

"Good view out there?" he asked.

"Great."

There was silence for a minute, then Matt sighed. "We need to talk," he said to Joe.

"Okay, cool. Is it about Violet being a zombie?"

Violet felt like the floor had been pulled out from under her. "What? How did you—"

"You literally came out of the school with blood around your mouth, and then we found out Vince was dead. You freak out and cover your face whenever anyone starts bleeding, and to be honest, you're kind of pale. And your eyes are *really* grey. I almost judge the others for *not* getting it."

"Why didn't you say anything?" Violet asked, still in shock.

Joe shrugged. "I don't know. It didn't seem that important. So how are we getting out of here?"

Violet and Matt gazed at each other, mystified.

"You don't have any questions?" Violet asked.

Joe raised an eyebrow. "I just asked one."

"No, about me being...you know...half dead."

Joe thought for a moment. "Do you have any superpowers?"

"No."

"None?"

Matt raised an eyebrow. "She was bitten by a zombie, not a radioactive spider. She's not like...*Zombiegirl*."

Joe's eyes widened. "That would be such a great movie."

Matt grinned. "She'd have the power of the dead."

"She could shoot out little gravestones!"

"And, like, rot people."

Violet frowned. "Please focus on what's actually happening."

"Okay, then I have no questions."

"Are you going to tell the others?" Violet asked.

Joe's tone immediately became gentler. "I've known for ages, and I haven't said anything. I assumed you didn't want anyone to know. It's not my place to tell them."

Relief washed over Violet. "Thank you."

Joe nodded. "But honestly, I don't think you should worry. We all care about you. It doesn't matter if you're dead or not."

"I'm not. Only half."

"Which half?"

Violet rolled her eyes, but Joe laughed.

"Come on," Matt said, opening the window. "We can climb out and onto the roof outside, make our way along, and then get back in through another window."

"Sounds great," Joe said, getting to his feet. He held out his hands. "Dead ladies first."

THEY MADE THEIR WAY ALONG THE SLOPING ROOF. VIOLET almost lost her footing more than once, but had so far managed to avoid falling to her death.

"Are you okay?" Matt asked when she almost slipped

for the sixth time.

"Fantastic," she replied sarcastically. "Can we go back inside soon?"

Matt peered in the next window. As he reached to pull it open, a biter appeared from nowhere, hammering her fists against the glass. He jumped back as if electrocuted.

"Maybe try the next one?" Joe suggested.

"Yeah, I think so."

At the next window, there were no signs of the dead. Matt slid it open, and they climbed inside.

"We still need to get the medicine," Violet whispered.

Joe didn't sound convinced. "Forget the medicine; we need to find the others."

Matt agreed. "He's right. We're stronger together, and you never know...Sam might already have found it." He pointed to the door out of the room they were in. "Let's go."

They stepped out into the hallway at the same moment Sam and the other men charged past.

"Run," Sam yelled, and Violet could see five biters not far behind. They joined the party, barreling down the dark hallway. Following Sam through the maze, they managed to lose their dead pursuers after a few minutes.

The group stood with their backs against the wall, all trying to catch their breath.

"Please tell us you have the medicine," Matt panted. Sam shook his head, causing Joe and Violet to collectively groan. Sam looked apologetic, and then glanced around. They were in a relatively small ward. "We'll check this one," Sam said quietly. "If there's nothing here, then we'll go back."

They agreed, searching the rooms, cupboards, and anywhere else they thought they might find what they were searching for.

Violet and one of the new guys began to rifle through a large medicine store, while Joe, Matt, and the other man went through some carts. Sam kept watch.

"What's your name?" Violet asked the stranger.

"Luke."

"I'm Violet."

"I know."

Was that rude? It felt rude.

"How long have you been at the house?" Violet asked.

"A few weeks."

"That's cool. It's been about a week for us."

"I know."

Okay, this guy almost certainly doesn't like me.

Still, she persevered with her attempts at conversation. "Are you there with your family?"

"No, they're dead."

"Oh, I'm sorry to hear that."

"Don't be, we weren't close."

Oh well, it's lucky they're dead then. Violet wasn't sure she was going to get on with Luke. She glanced over at Matt; maybe his new friend would be more cheerful? She could just about hear their conversation; the man over there was definitely more chatty.

"—and that's how my second sister died. My brother, on the other hand, that was far more gruesome—"

Joe was listening intently, appearing far more surprised and disgusted than when they'd been talking about Violet eating people not that much earlier. Matt caught her eye, mouth open in disbelief. The man continued, "I mean, I never knew an eye could bleed so much—"

Violet turned back to the cupboard. Maybe Luke wasn't so bad after all.

"The house is great," she continued. "Robert is really nice."

"Yeah."

"And everyone has been really friendly."

"Sure."

Okay, let's just not talk. That's fine, too.

"Yeah, sounds great," Matt was saying over his shoulder as he made his way to Violet. When he reached her, he whispered, "You've got to save me from this guy. All he's done for the last ten minutes is tell me about the different ways his family and friends died."

"How cheerful."

"To be honest, it sounds like half of them had a lucky escape, this man has no conversational skills at all. I think he's grateful to have so many 'dead friend' stories, just so he has something to talk about."

Violet, aware Luke was only a couple of feet away, made one last attempt to bring him into the conversation. "Matt, this is Luke."

Luke inclined his head but ignored the hand Matt held out. It hung in the air awkwardly. Luke had to have seen it, yet he did nothing.

Oh my God, Luke, shake his damn hand. It's just hanging there!

Matt slowly lowered his hand, clearly aware this was going nowhere. Luke returned to what he was doing, and Matt glanced at Violet with wide eyes, which seemed to say—*who are these people?*

Joe appeared, still talking over his shoulder as he walked quickly toward Violet. "Ha-ha, yeah, good one. Can't wait to hear about it, Tony." He turned to Matt, the false smile still stretched on his lips. "Matt, Tony wants to tell us about his girlfriend."

"Is she dead?" Matt asked dryly.

"No."

Matt sounded surprised. "Really?"

"No. Of course she is. Apparently, it's a terrible story."

Matt's shoulders sank. "Great."

There was a crashing sound, and Violet spun toward it. Sam had opened the door to a private room, and a biter had lunged out at him. Matt and Joe seemed to perk up at the distraction from Tony's depressing stories, and ran to help. Violet was close behind. Sam pushed the biter back, and slammed his crowbar into its face. Two more appeared from inside the room, and Violet managed to jump aside just before one grabbed her. Matt forced the thing that used to be a woman into the wall, and Violet plunged her knife into the back of its head.

I bet that looked so tough!

I'm basically Lara Croft!

Focus, Violet.

They were being too noisy. Four more biters appeared at the entrance to the ward. Joe had just managed to kill the last one from the room, and looked up as the others ran toward them. He groaned loudly, pulling out his knife and following Violet and the others further into the ward. Sam and Matt were ahead, but Tony, Luke, and Joe darted into a room to her left. Violet made to follow, but Luke was already trying to close the door! Luckily, Joe wrenched it open and yanked Violet inside before slamming it shut again.

"Thanks for that," he said sarcastically to Luke. "Just for next time, we, you know, try *not* to shut our people outside with the biters." The door vibrated as the dead tried to force their way inside, but it was holding strong for now.

"I thought there wasn't time," Luke muttered sheepishly.

"Do you think Sam and Matt are okay?" Violet asked.

Joe nodded. "I'm sure they are. They were heading for the fire exit. Probably where we should've gone actually." He eyed the door, still rattling. "How are we going to get out of here?" Violet moved over to the window; there was no roof to walk along this time, and they were too high up to jump. She shook her head at Joe.

"Not this way."

Luke sighed, reaching for the door to the private bathroom. "Guess we're in for a long wait." He opened the door, and a biter threw itself onto him. It was a tall man with long skeletal arms. Before the others could even react, it sank its teeth into Luke's cheek, ripping at the skin and tearing off great chunks. Joe pushed Violet behind him, and ran for the man while Tony froze in terror. Joe grabbed the biter from behind, pulling him off Luke. Luke stumbled toward Violet, spraying her with blood as he fell. She tried to stop him landing so hard, holding onto him as he went down. His blood soaked her shirt, and she clamped her hand over her nose and mouth, using the other to try to stop the bleeding.

Oh no.

Just don't breathe, don't breathe.

"Help me," she called to Tony, who still didn't move. Joe was trying to hold the dead man back. "Help me stop the bleeding," she ordered. Tony opened and closed his mouth like a fish, still not moving. She heard Joe cry out in triumph as he stabbed the biter through its eye, letting it fall to the ground. Then he appeared at Violet's side.

"Go into the bathroom," he ordered.

She stumbled to her feet, still not daring to breathe, and ran to the bathroom, slamming the door behind her. Things were spinning, but she was still in control. For now. She wanted to wash her hands, and hurriedly got a bottle of water out of her bag, pouring it over them clumsily and rubbing roughly with a towel. Her head felt heavy, but as the blood diluted and began to disappear down the drain, things slowly came into focus. Her heart was racing. There were sounds of a struggle from the other room. Something smashed, and she heard a heavy object banging into the wall. Joe cried out. Tony did, too, then the door swung open and Joe fell inside, slamming it behind him.

"What happened?" Violet asked.

Joe was out of breath. "Luke turned."

"He got Tony?"

Joe nodded. The two of them were silent for a moment.

"That's a shame," Violet began.

"Yeah."

"Tony seemed really..." She searched for the right word.

"Useless and morbid?"

"Well, I wasn't going to say anything quite as blunt as that."

"No?"

"He had nice hair..."

"You're right, he was a real asset."

"What are we going to do?"

Joe opened his mouth to speak, but there was more noise from outside the room. Crashes and the sounds of a struggle. Then there was silence. Neither Violet nor Joe dared to move. After a few seconds of nothing, there was a knock at the door. Joe and Violet stared at each other.

"Who is it?" Joe asked.

"Who the hell do you think?" came Sam's voice. Violet opened the door. Sam and Matt, both bloodied, were smiling. The bodies of Luke and Tony were on the floor.

"So, how's your day going?" Matt asked.

NINETEEN

SAM, VIOLET, JOE, AND MATT GOT OUT OF THE borrowed car and headed for the gates to the house. It was a couple of hours before sunset.

"This doesn't look good." Violet groaned, picking at her spattered clothes.

Matt shook his head. "You look fine. Great."

She raised an eyebrow. "I'm literally covered in blood."

"It's your color."

Violet peered over at the gates. Would this even work? Rachel had said she'd be waiting for them, and would make sure Harold wasn't around, but where was she? They approached the heavy iron bars, and Sam gave them a gentle rattle. There were a few painfully long moments, but then Rachel appeared, her face flooding with relief first, then concern.

"Are you okay?" she asked, clearly shocked at their bloodstained clothes.

Joe might've been about to speak, but Sam interrupted. "Fine. We have the medicine, but the others didn't make it."

Rachel winced, opening the gates. "We need to be fast. Harold will be back any minute. I didn't think you'd be gone so long."

"Sorry about that," Matt replied sarcastically. Rachel blew past it.

"I've brought you some spare clothes. Get changed over there. I'll wash yours when everyone is asleep."

"What about Luke and Tony?" Violet asked. "Won't they be missed?"

Rachel shook her head. "They didn't have any family here. I'll tell Robert they went out for supplies before anyone could stop them. He won't send anyone to check. He's too afraid."

Sam handed her the bag of medicine he'd found while Violet was hiding in the bathroom trying not to eat anyone. Rachel put her hand on his. "Thank you." She gestured for them to go and change in the privacy of the woods. Violet found a spot behind a large tree, away from Sam and the others. She opened the bag of clothes Rachel had provided. Her stomach dropped. It was a short-sleeved shirt.

Oh no.

She couldn't possibly wear it; everyone would see her bite. She felt her heart begin to race. What could she do? It wasn't like she could say, *No thanks, I'm good,* and head back to the house in her bloodied clothes. But putting on the shirt was like attaching a big sign to her head that said 'zombie'. Minutes ticked by, and she still had no idea how to get out of this.

"Violet, you okay?" Matt asked from somewhere not too far away.

"No," she hissed.

"Can I come around?"

"Yeah."

Matt appeared, already changed into a long-sleeved black sweater and a pair of jeans. "What is it?"

She held up the shirt. He looked a little confused. "You don't like pink?"

"The sleeves, Matt."

"Wha—oh." Realization dawned. "Okay." He took off his sweater, handing it to Violet. "Take this."

"What are you going to wear?" she asked, suddenly aware of the fact she'd never seen Matt without a shirt before, and that it wasn't exactly an unpleasant sight. He was strong; she supposed months spent fighting the dead would probably do that, and tanned from his work outside.

She felt her face flush, averting her eyes awkwardly.

You spend your free time eating people, yet seeing a guy without a shirt makes you uncomfortable?

"I'll wear yours." Matt shrugged, taking the pink shirt and pulling it over his head. It was ridiculously tight.

"Look okay?" he asked, clearly aware it didn't.

"Oh yeah." Violet tried not to laugh.

He winked. "See you in a minute." He headed away. Violet changed hurriedly, pulling on the sweater and tossing her bloodied clothes into the bag. She emerged from the tree line as the guys did, and Rachel eyed Matt's shirt.

"Okay..." she began, clearly unsure whether to ask.

"I like pink," Matt said simply. "Shall we go?"

ANOTHER WEEK PASSED, AND THIS TIME THERE WERE NO suicide missions or temptations to eat anyone. It was clear everyone played their part in the little community, so Violet and her friends pitched in wherever they could. She knew they all enjoyed helping as much as she did. They'd been working so hard over the past few months to keep themselves safe that doing nothing would've felt unnatural. Sam, Joe, and Matt continued to help with the crops. While Rachel didn't work in the fields, she seemed to be spending an awful lot of time down there. When Sam wasn't working, he could often be found walking hand in hand with her around the gardens. Violet was happy; she'd never seen him smile as much as he did these days.

Maggie busied herself around the house, but Violet preferred to work down on the farm with the animals. Toby was there, too. Though he spent time with the other children in the house, it didn't seem like he could fully go back to being a kid. He wanted to be useful. It was hard work; they milked cows, fed animals, collected eggs, took the horses out, cleaned out the barns and pens, and every other farming job imaginable. She still walked Ben every day. She wasn't scared anymore, even venturing down to the river, which was deep within the woods. This place felt safe. Noises in the night weren't something that caused her heart to race, because she knew it was just foxes, or people walking down the hallways. There was laughter here, babies crying, children playing. It was home. She rarely had nightmares anymore. Most of the time, she didn't dream at all. Everything was perfect.

She should've known it wouldn't last.

HAROLD TOOK ANOTHER DRINK FROM HIS THERMOS AND shuddered. While he appreciated the thought behind Mrs. Dowly bringing him coffee each evening, the old woman always made it far too strong. Each night he hoped she'd get it right, and each night he was disappointed. He sighed, emptying the remainder of his whiskey bottle into the thermos. At least he could improve it a little.

He flicked through the newspapers he'd read a thousand times, and stretched his legs inside the small gatehouse. There'd been no newcomers for weeks, yet he still had to sit down there and wait. He didn't mind being alone. In fact, he preferred to be away from the company of others, but the boredom was merciless.

He opened the door, then stepped out into the cool evening air. As usual, he walked to the gate and rattled it gently. Still secure. He held up his flashlight, scanning the road. It was empty. The dead ones rarely came out this far.

The face appeared at the gates so suddenly that Harold fell backward, landing heavily on the floor.

"Help me!" The woman choked, rattling the bars helplessly. She had long red hair, matted with sweat and dirt. There was a small bald patch near her temple, as though a handful of hair had been ripped out from the root. Her clothes were torn and stained with blood. Her head and nose were bleeding, and her skin was caked with dirt. She had no shoes. Harold noticed all of those things in the first few seconds from where he sat frozen in place.

"Please let me in," she sobbed, shaking the gates again. Harold scrambled to his feet, grabbing the walkie-

talkie.

"There's someone at the gates," he stammered. No answer.

"Please," the woman cried. "My head hurts."

"Hello?" Harold tried again. He was supposed to ask first; that had always been the rule. But there was no answer, and the woman was crying. She must have been really hurt.

"Please," she sobbed. "They killed my sister. Please... please let me in."

"Are you bit?"

"I'm fine, let me in."

He couldn't leave her, not outside in the dark. Those things would eat her right down to the bone if they found her. And they would; they could always smell the blood. Harold made up his mind.

"Hang on!" The keys were in the gatehouse, and he sprinted inside despite his bad hip. When he was back, he jammed the key into the lock and pulled the gates open. The woman fell at his feet. And now, with the light from the gatehouse shining down on her, he could see the bites. More than he'd ever seen on a living person before. She wasn't moving. He didn't have long until she turned. His knife was in the gatehouse, too. But as he moved to get it, he heard them coming. He was too late. Harold looked up just in time to see them flood through the gates.

WHEN VIOLET HEARD THE SCREAMING, IT TOOK HER OVER a minute to even register what that meant. It had been a while since she'd heard sounds like that. At first, she was certain it was a nightmare. The noise had to be in her head; no one screamed here.

But then it happened again. The sound was long, drawn out, and agonizing. Within seconds, she was on her feet and running to the bedroom door. More yells now, the sound of movement outside. She heard the others getting up behind her. Violet flung the door open and found chaos. People seemed to be running in all directions down the hallway, all screaming or crying, some bloodied. A mother pulled her two young children in the direction of the stairs, both sobbing and one covered in blood. A group of teenagers charged in the opposite direction, carrying vases, table legs, and other things they had deemed heavy enough to be dangerous. Violet heard glass smashing, things breaking, and more screaming. The walls almost seemed to be shaking. Sam appeared at her side, hurriedly putting his shoes on.

"What's going on?" he asked, eyes scanning the hallway.

"I don't know," Violet replied, though of course she did. They both did. "I think—"

She was cut off by a scream, much louder than the others. It was female and painfully familiar.

"Rachel?" Sam cried, running at full speed toward the sound. Joe followed, grabbing a knife from the table.

Violet swung around, seeing Maggie and Toby behind her.

"We have to go," she said, putting her shoes on, motioning for the other two to do the same. It was only then she noticed the three of them were alone.

"Where's Matt? Where's Ben?"

"I don't know," Maggie replied, dazed. "I think I heard Ben scratching at the door a little while ago; maybe Matt took him out? I was half asleep..."

Violet felt lost. Her friends were scattered, and she had no idea what to do.

"We need to go," Toby said as the screams outside seemed to intensify. "The biters..."

He was right. Violet took Maggie's hand, and Toby took Maggie's other one.

"We stay together," Violet insisted. She grabbed the other knife from the table, held it in her free hand, and led her friends out of the room.

The hallway was crowded, and Violet fought to block out the sounds around her. She hardly recognized the place; tables, chairs and other debris were smashed and scattered everywhere. Blood streaked the walls, and was smeared onto the clothes of the people they passed. There was a body on the floor. Although she tried not to look, she couldn't avoid seeing the blond hair and glasses.

"Matt," Violet called, but could barely hear herself over the screams. He wouldn't be able to hear her even if he were in that very hallway.

As they passed a bedroom door, Violet could hear hands pounding from inside the room.

Are there people trapped in there?

She reached for the handle just as a rotten hand punched clean through the wood. Toby pulled Maggie, and therefore Violet, back just in time, and the dead began to tear through the door as though it were made of tissue paper. The three of them ran toward the stairs, still holding tightly onto each other. Violet tried to keep searching for the others, but there were too many people, too much chaos. She called out their names, but the calls were unanswered. They reached the stairs, and she was so intent on running that she barely noticed what was blocking their way. Thankfully, Maggie and Toby did and pulled her back.

At the bottom of the stairs was a dead body, and clustered around it were five biters feeding. Other people were stopped at the top of the stairs, too, no one daring to go forward. Nervous glances passed between them. Violet knew they didn't have much time; there was more screaming and smashing from behind them. It wouldn't be long before the dead had them boxed in. The ones from the bedroom would be there any minute, and she knew they were probably only delayed now because they were feeding on someone else.

Not my friends, she prayed silently. Violet looked at Maggie and Toby. They both knew what they had to do. She took a breath, and then the three of them ran at full speed down the stairs, splitting up at the last moment to run on either side of the creatures. Violet spun quickly when they were clear, but the dead hadn't even noticed them passing.

"In here," a voice called to them from a room to the left, and Maggie, Toby, and Violet quickly made their way toward it. Once they were inside, someone slammed the door shut. Robert was there, as well as several others she vaguely recognized. Robert and another man moved a couch against the door to secure it.

"How many munchers?" Robert asked the dark room.

"I don't know," began one of the other men. "Could be hundreds."

"Do we know how many people we've lost?"

No one answered for a long time. The screaming outside the door continued. Finally, a woman spoke. "I've seen at least six bodies, but there were so many more injured."

"Bites?" Robert asked.

The woman sighed. "I don't know. Some could've been. I was too busy running to check."

"The Collins' are gone," added a skinny man with glasses. "I saw those things rip them all apart."

Violet felt her stomach drop. That was Rachel's family.

"How did they get in?" the woman asked. "I thought we were secure?"

Robert shook his head. "I don't know..." It seemed as though a thought had occurred to him, though, because he hurriedly pulled out his walkie-talkie. "Harold? Harold, are you there?" There was no answer, but no static either. The batteries were dead. Robert threw the thing to the ground.

"What should we do?" the man with glasses asked.

There was a crash from outside the room. All eyes were on the door as it began to shake.

"What do we do?" the woman repeated, her tone frantic. The screams outside got louder, but Violet realized they sounded less like the living and more like the dead. The door continued to shake, and two men tried to hold the couch in place.

Robert began to speak over the noise. "We can stay and try to fight for our home, or we can run. You need to do what's right for you and your families." He moved toward a desk in the middle of the room, pulled open a drawer, and brought out a handgun. "I'm staying."

The couch shifted forward, and hands began to appear around the side of the opening door. Three men now tried to force the door shut, but it was no good. There were too many biters, and they started to fight their way inside. The woman screamed. Robert began to fire the gun, but though some of the dead fell, the noise drew more, and they continued to break into the room.

Violet frantically surveyed her surroundings. The only way out would be through the windows. She ran to the closest one and tried to open it, but it was locked. She saw Maggie try and fail to open another. Toby went to the desk, picking up a heavy paperweight. He moved to Violet's window and hurled it through the glass. It smashed, and he used his foot to kick out some of the larger pieces that were still in place.

"Let's go," he ordered. Violet pushed Maggie toward the window. Toby helped her out before climbing out himself. Violet followed, catching her hand on a piece of glass that still jutted from the frame. There wasn't time for her to register the pain, though. She briefly glanced back into the room.

The men were fighting to close the door, but it was for nothing. The dead were pushing it wider and wider, and Robert couldn't have many more bullets. Violet dropped from the window, which was higher off the ground than she'd expected. She stumbled a little, but Toby and Maggie helped her to her feet. The three of them ran from the house as the gunshots stopped. They passed the stables, none of them having any idea where they were going.

"The horses are gone," Maggie breathed as they stopped to catch their breath.

"Ben always seemed to sense the biters," Violet suggested. "Maybe the horses did, too." She wished she'd had such foresight. She'd been so sure they were safe. How could she have been so stupid? Now the group was split, and she had no idea what to do or where to go.

"What now?" Maggie asked.

Violet shook her head. She had no clue.

"We can't go to the main gates," Toby said. "If that's how the biters got in, then we want to stay as far from there as possible."

"There has to be another way out." Maggie's voice caught in her throat. "There *has* to be."

Violet closed her eyes for a moment, trying to think. She tried to block out the sounds from the house and the fear of what was happening, so she could just focus on every time she'd walked through the grounds with Ben. It came to her immediately.

"The river!"

"What about it?" Maggie asked uncertainly, but Toby was nodding.

"There's a boat down there," he answered for her. "We can use it to get out!"

Fear filled Maggie's face, and Violet knew why. To get to the river, they would have to go through the woods, at night, when they knew for sure there were biters inside the walls. It wasn't exactly the most attractive option, but there was no other choice. They would just have to hope, however morbid it was, that the dead were too busy in the house to go for a nighttime stroll.

They moved toward the tree line. The woods were even more frightening in the dark. Despite the full moon, Violet could barely see past the first row of trees.

"Stay close," she whispered, moving into the darkness.

They walked together, still holding hands. Violet took slow, deep breaths, trying to ignore the sounds of movement around her. It could've been the dead; it could've been animals; it could've been other survivors. She wasn't going to take the chance by calling out. Would their friends come this way? Should she have stayed to look for them?

She knew Matt and the others wouldn't want her to put herself or Maggie and Toby in danger, but she felt incredibly guilty all the same. If she got out tonight, how could she live knowing she'd left the others behind? She hoped Ben was still with Matt. The dog should've been able to sense the dead and warn him. As she walked, Violet found herself brushing her arm along the bushes and trees. If Ben led Matt this way, she wanted to make it easy for him to follow her.

She felt Maggie pull back on her hand, and she stopped walking immediately.

"What?" Violet whispered, only just loud enough to

hear. Maggie and Toby crouched, and she did the same. Maggie pointed up ahead, to a small clearing in the trees. There was a biter there, standing in a patch of moonlight. It was a little girl. She looked around four years old, maybe five. She had white-blonde curls matted with blood, and swayed dreamily where she stood. She wore a blue party dress. Violet felt sick. She'd never seen one that young before, but at that moment, she realized there must be so many like that. Surely small kids would be the easiest to catch? Out there, in that new world, there had to be thousands of undead children. Violet's skin prickled, and she was unable to take her eyes away from the little girl.

"It's just one," Toby breathed. "We can kill it."

Violet knew that was the right thing. They should end it for the poor creature, but she couldn't make herself move. Maggie and Toby must've felt the same, because they stayed frozen, too. And then, it was too late. Violet heard a sound behind her, nothing more than a twig snapping, but the creature heard it.

The little girl's head rose, a small growl escaping her lips. She moved forward slowly, still listening. Violet held her breath, trying to keep as still as possible. Another noise, louder this time. Something was definitely behind them. The girl hissed hungrily, charging toward Violet and the others. Violet closed her eyes, felt the rush of air as the biter passed inches from her, then nothing. It hadn't noticed them. Maggie and Toby got to their feet, and Violet did the same, her legs still shaking. She took a breath, and they continued silently through the woods toward the river.

They were too late; the boat was gone. Toby swore loudly, and Violet kicked a stone into the water. Maggie dropped onto a log, putting her head in her hands.

"Now what?" she mumbled.

Violet didn't know what to say. She'd been so sure the boat would still be there she hadn't even considered the possibility that someone else would have the same idea. They could go back through the woods and take their chances with the gate, but the idea of that made her feel sick to her stomach.

"Hey!" The voice came from the tree line. Joe and Sam were leaving the woods. Joe was smiling at the sight of them, and Violet pulled him in for a hug.

"Same idea as us!" Joe squeezed her tight. "We have so much in common, Vi."

Violet nodded, but her eyes were now on Sam. He was staring vacantly at the ground, and she saw his shirt was drenched in blood. The blood didn't make her hungry, which meant it wasn't his.

"Rachel?" Violet asked tentatively. Sam met her gaze for just a moment before shaking his head. Joe's smile was gone now.

"Let's just go," Sam muttered. Violet's stomach sank.

"Where's the boat?" Joe asked, only just noticing.

"Gone," Violet replied weakly.

Joe scowled. "Thieving—"

"What happened to your hand?" Sam interrupted. Violet had forgotten all about it. Realizing she still had a piece of glass jammed into the skin between her thumb and forefinger, she pulled it out slowly. Although it hurt, she didn't make a sound.

"Jesus, Violet, what are you made of?" Joe breathed, ripping the sleeve of his shirt and wrapping it around her hand carefully.

"Thanks." She couldn't take her eyes off Sam. He looked distraught. His eyes were red-rimmed, and he seemed to be lost in his thoughts.

There was a rustling from the trees, Violet raised her knife. But the person who stepped out wasn't dead.

"Matt!" Violet flung her arms around him, breathing in his familiar smell.

He's okay. We're all okay.

"You're here, too?" Joe asked. "We've clearly been spending too much time together if we're starting to think the same." He gave Matt a hug. Ben jumped up at each of them, wagging his tail excitedly.

"I took Ben outside," Matt explained, "We walked for a while, then suddenly there was all this screaming. I went back to the house, but you guys were gone."

"What did you see?" Violet asked.

Matt shook his head. "There was no one left." His eyes flicked to Sam, who was now sitting on the log with his head in his hands. Matt's shoulders slumped.

"What's the plan?" he asked Violet.

"We could swim?" she suggested.

"Why don't we just walk?" Maggie asked. "Follow the river as closely as we can until we're clear of the house?"

Sam shook his head. "The river runs through the grounds; the wall meets it on both sides. Robert said the wall only breaks in three places—the two main gates and where the river leaves the property. The only way to get out of this place is to follow the river out on the water."

Violet nodded. "I don't want to walk through the woods any more. But if we swim for a while, we could probably find a spot to climb out as soon as we're clear of the wall."

"Why don't we just use the boat?" Matt asked.

"It's gone."

"It's over there." Matt pointed to the right where the boat floated, half hidden from view by a large bush. It was in the middle of the river, wedged against a rock that jutted out.

Joe raised an eyebrow. "Huh, none of us thought to just take a glance over there."

"How are we going to reach it?" Violet asked. Before she even finished the sentence, Sam was splashing into the water.

"Mate, that's got to be below zero," Joe called helpfully.

"Thanks for that," Sam replied through gritted teeth. Matt followed Sam in. The two of them pulled the boat to the bank before joining the others. Violet, Maggie, Toby, and Joe climbed in.

"This is pretty tight," Violet said.

Matt agreed. "Maybe Sam and I shouldn't get in? We're wet already. We could just push you guys until we're clear of this place, then we could all get out together."

Sam didn't seem altogether thrilled with the idea of swimming for freedom, but he said nothing. Joe, on the other hand, shook his head. "This isn't *Titanic*, and you aren't *Jack*, so get in the bloody boat."

Alive?

VIOLET FELT AS THOUGH THEY'D BEEN TRAVELING all day, though in reality it could only have been an hour or so. They passed the wall not long ago, and had been silent for the entire journey. A sorrier crew had never been seen—each in bloodied pajamas with unkempt hair and tired eyes. Sam stared blankly ahead, focused solely on their destination. The little engine of the boat didn't work, so he and Joe had been using a couple of oars to paddle forward. It took a lot of effort, but Violet supposed Sam was just grateful for something to do. Maggie's eyes were closed, and she rested her head on Toby's shoulder, startling awake at the slightest sound. Ben was on her lap, peering around excitedly, hopping off every now and then to hang his head off the side of the boat, the only one enjoying the journey. Toby was watching the water, occasionally skimming his fingers across the surface.

Matt shook a little from his spot beside her. Violet put her arm around him, his wet clothes immediately soaking her own.

"Are you okay?" she asked quietly.

He nodded. "Robert told me the name of this river. As long as we're going the right way, it should take us really close to my grandparents' house."

That was reassuring at least, though having lived

as they had been for the past few weeks, finding a little cottage which may or may not contain the reanimated corpses of Matt's grandparents couldn't help but seem a little less appealing.

"THERE," MATT SAID, POINTING TO THE RIGHT SOME TIME later. Violet followed his gaze; not far away was a narrow road, with several cottages on each side.

"The one on the end belongs to my grandparents," Matt said. "We can get out here."

Sam immediately swung his legs out of the boat and dropped into the water. He began to pull it to shore. Joe rolled his eyes, motioning for Matt to stay put, and followed Sam out. He clearly wasn't expecting the water to be quite so cold, and swore loudly the second he got in. He and Sam led the boat toward the bank.

"Ow!" Joe cried out suddenly.

"What is it?" Violet asked.

"Something bit me."

Matt shook his head. "You probably caught yourself on a rock."

"No," Joe replied. "It felt like a bite... We don't get piranhas here, right?"

"Of course we don't," Sam said.

"And we're sure the biters don't swim?"

No one answered for what Violet thought was an awkwardly long amount of time. Finally, Matt said, "Yeah, I'm sure."

He doesn't sound sure.

"Let's just get out," Sam muttered, pulling himself onto the bank. Joe followed, and they helped the others onto dry land. They crossed the large open green toward the little road, the house appeared very inviting after spending so long in the cold boat. It was a small, red bricked cottage, surrounded by a white picket fence. The other few houses were relatively similar, with variations like the colors of their front doors or the flowers in their gardens. Each was surrounded by a white fence.

Matt led the way with Ben, followed by Violet, Toby, and Maggie, with Sam and Joe squelching along behind them. The garden gate was open, which Violet didn't think was a particularly positive sign. A pretty important element of surviving the zombie apocalypse was security, and a garden gate swinging in the breeze wasn't a great start. The curtains of the house were drawn. Violet had no idea what they were going to find inside. The back door was, at least, closed. She reached out, putting her hand on Matt's shoulder as he made to open it.

"Matt...if they're inside—"

"I know," he interrupted, but his voice was not unkind. He pushed on the handle, but the door didn't move. He pushed again, then forced the door open with his shoulder.

"That's just how you have to open it," he explained to the others. "My grandad never got around to fixing it."

Ben darted inside first, then the rest of the group followed Matt into the silent building. Sam closed the door behind them.

"We need to check the house," Matt said, pointing to the stairs in front of them, and the door to their left. Sam and Joe headed upstairs with Ben. Matt and Violet went through the door, leaving Maggie and Toby in the kitchen. There were only two rooms downstairs—the kitchen and the living room, both of which were empty. Violet was glad the place seemed to be clear of the dead, but there was no sign of Matt's grandparents either, and that didn't make her feel overly positive. Matt looked at the rotten fruit in the bowl, and the layer of dust over the coffee table.

"I don't think anyone's been here for a while," he muttered. "I don't know whether to feel relieved or not. I wanted to see them, to know they were okay, but two old people out here alone? At least if they're not here...maybe they were rescued?"

Violet nodded. "Maybe." She hoped he was right, but deep down, she just didn't believe it. Joe and Sam joined the two of them in the living room, followed by Maggie and Toby. Violet's head began to swim a little, and she realized Joe was wrapping a bandage around his hand.

The smell of blood began to fade as he covered the wound, and the room came back into focus.

"Everything okay?" Matt asked Sam, whose eyes were still glazed.

"Yeah, there's no one up there."

"Why's he bleeding?"

"Because he's an idiot."

Joe rolled his eyes. "I thought we were going to say I killed a biter?"

"No, *you* were going to say that."

"How did you do it?" Violet asked.

"I broke an ornament. I felt guilty so I tried to pick it up, but I cut myself."

"Smooth."

Sam surveyed the empty room. "They're not here?" Matt shook his head. Sam dropped onto the nearest armchair, a cloud of dust flying up as he did so. "At least this place is safe. We can stay until we decide what to do next." His voice sounded so different to how it used to be, almost robotic. Violet caught Joe's eye, but he gave a little shake of his head.

"I'll find some towels," Matt said, then gestured to the fireplace. "If someone wants to get the wood from the pile outside, we could get a fire going."

"I'll go," Violet said. Joe got up, too. Sam stayed where he was, eyes unfocused, as though he were thinking about something a long way away. There was a packet of cigarettes and a lighter sitting on the table by his chair, and he reached over and lit one up. He took a long drag, blowing the smoke out slowly.

"Stay with him," Violet mouthed to Maggie, who nodded.

"I'll check the greenhouse outside," Toby suggested. "See if there's anything we can eat." He grabbed a walking stick leaning against the wall, which Violet guessed he was intending to use as a weapon, and headed toward the kitchen.

"Call if you need us," Violet said, her eyes coming back to Sam. "Sam...I—"

He shook his head. "Just...just get the wood, Violet.

Please."

They found the woodpile in the garden, stacked up against a crooked shed. Violet and Joe began piling it in their arms. She glanced at his bandaged hand. "Does it hurt?"

He followed her gaze, shaking his head. "Not really."

"It was good you covered it up."

"Well yeah, I didn't want to bleed to death."

Violet rolled her eyes, speaking quietly. "I know, but it's good for me, too."

Joe appeared momentarily confused. "Why? Oh right, the zombie thing."

"Yes, the zombie thing."

"I forgot about that," Joe said with a shrug. He picked up another piece of wood, balanced it precariously on his pile, and then dropped the whole lot. "Sonofa—"

"You're not taking it seriously," Violet interrupted.

"I am! I just wasn't holding it right."

"No..." She shook her head, turning to face him. "I mean *me*. You don't understand."

Joe stopped, giving her his full attention now. Violet sighed. "As soon as there's blood, I become this...this monster."

He shrugged. "I haven't met a woman who doesn't."

"No, I'm dangerous."

"Once an ex-girlfriend hit me with a book because I didn't say I liked her new haircut quickly enough."

"I'm not sure you're getting this..."

"It was a huge book. Left a bruise and everything."

"Joe, focus! Do you hear what I'm telling you? You could wake up one morning to find me chewing on your—" Violet stopped, realizing they weren't alone.

Toby was standing behind them, holding a bunch of carrots and wearing a confused expression.

Joe's eyes widened, but then he plastered a smile on his face. "Listen, Vi, I'm flattered, but why don't we collect this wood first, huh?"

Violet's face flushed, but she nodded.

Look at it this way—whatever Toby thinks, it's better than what we were actually talking about.

Toby smiled awkwardly, heading back to the house.

"That was too close," Violet breathed.

Joe nodded. "Anyway, you were saying how dangerous and scary you are? And I'm really interested to know what you're planning to chew on?"

"I mean it; if I lose control...I could kill you. Any of you."

"Well, before you do, could you help me carry this?" he asked as he dropped another piece of wood. "I feel like I'm losing the battle here."

Violet laughed despite her frustration. Joe had the uncanny ability to make everything seem a whole lot less scary; even conversations about her being a member of the living-dead community. "Fine."

She and Joe brought the wood inside. Soon enough, a fire was roaring. The group sat in the living room, warming up and allowing wet clothes to dry. No one spoke for the longest time. Violet knew they needed the time to process what had happened. Sam had been consistently smoking, and a heavy fog filled the air. She hated the smell. She didn't think the others were fans either, but no one said anything. Ben was asleep in the kitchen; the only one who'd made his feelings clear.

Out of nowhere came the sound of car doors slamming. Maggie, who'd been sitting on the floor, jumped to her feet, cutting her arm on the knife she'd been holding. She cried out, slapping her hand over the wound, which poured crimson blood. Violet stepped away, toward the window, while Joe and Matt moved to Maggie. Violet's heart was racing, and she covered her nose instinctively. She peeked through the blinds to see where the sound was coming from, anything to distract herself from the smell.

"It looks like the army," she said to the others, watching as three men in soldiers' uniforms climbed out of a green truck.

"It's not too deep," Matt said to Joe, holding his hand over Maggie's wound. Joe began to wrap the cut.

"If it's the army, they can help." Sam got to his feet now.

"I think we should stay put," Matt said.

Sam looked confused. "Why?"

"I just think...we don't know these people."

Sam shook his head. "It's the army; they're meant to protect people like us."

Joe moved a little closer to Sam, letting Toby take over with Maggie. "I think Matt's right."

Violet knew what was happening. They were trying to protect her. If the army rescued them, surely they'd check for bites? Even if Violet managed to convince them she wasn't dangerous—which her track record demonstrated wasn't exactly true—it'd be highly unlikely they'd simply pat her on the head and let her go.

Joe continued, taking another step closer to Sam. "We don't know who these people are, mate. They might not be the army at all. We've been doing okay on our own so far."

Sam snorted. "Doing okay? You think we've been doing okay?"

"I just mean—"

"Why don't you tell that to Rachel, Emily, Zack, and Tom. Tell Amy." He eyed Maggie, holding on to her bleeding arm. "Tell *her*. I think we've been pretty damn far from okay for a long time."

Violet turned back to the window. She still felt groggy, but Toby was doing a good job wrapping Maggie's arm, and the smell was starting to fade. She wondered if maybe she was beginning to be able to control herself more, too. That would certainly make life a little easier. Two of the soldiers were heading for the house, while the other stayed with the truck. They each held what she thought were rifles, though Violet knew very little about guns. She could see two more heading into a house on the other side of the street. Whatever her friends were going to do, they had to decide fast.

"Sam, we're not staying here. It won't be safe," Matt insisted, taking Violet's hand but not breaking eye contact with Sam. "Please, trust me."

Sam glared at Matt, Joe, and Violet. After an agonizing few seconds, he broke and nodded. "Okay." He reached for the knife on the table, pointing toward the back door. "Let's go."

With a boom, the front door smashed open, and the two men came inside. They stared at the six muddy, bloody people in the room, not lowering their guns. They wore balaclavas, with only their eyes and mouths visible. The one on the left glanced at Maggie, saw the bandage on her arm, which Toby was now securing, and shot her in the head.

That was it. Done. Maggie fell backward, slamming onto the hard floor. Toby stood frozen, his hands still covered in Maggie's blood.

"Anyone else bitten?" the soldier asked, his eyes settling on Joe's bandaged hand. But there wasn't time to answer, because Sam launched himself at the man, catching him off guard and knocking him to the ground. The other one raised his gun, but Matt and Joe were faster and forced him down, too. A gunshot rang out, and bits of the ceiling rained down on them as they fought with the soldiers. Toby tried to wrench Sam off the first one, who he was still punching repeatedly. He'd managed to pull the balaclava off, and the man's face was already a bloody mess. Ben barked angrily, hopping from side to side and baring his teeth.

"Come on," Matt cried, moving back from the second, who appeared to be unconscious, and taking hold of Violet's hand. Joe managed to dislodge Sam, and the two of them ran from the room and out of the back door with Violet, Matt, and Toby. Outside, they headed for the road behind the house, the sounds from inside getting louder. The soldiers were yelling and swearing, and then there were gunshots all around, ringing in Violet's ears. It sounded like they'd called for backup.

They're going to kill us!

"Keep going," Joe yelled.

They rounded a corner, their shoes hitting the tarmac of the main road, and ran as fast as they could. Matt pulled Violet ahead, leading them through back roads and gardens. She could hear the truck. It was close. It was searching for them.

"In here," Matt hissed, taking them into a house with its front door wide open. Joe slammed it shut, plunging them into relative darkness. All the blinds were drawn, and they stood silently for several minutes trying to catch their breath. Ben panted, dropping onto the wooden floor. Violet's throat felt hot and acidic, and she put her hands on her knees as she sucked in the dusty air.

"Maggie," Joe whispered eventually. "I can't believe it. Just like that..."

"We can't trust anyone," Sam said, his voice low. "Not anymore. I was so stupid. We should've run straight away. That's what you guys wanted to do."

Violet reached out to touch his shoulder. "You didn't know—"

He shrugged her hand off, trudging toward the kitchen. Violet realized she was still holding onto Matt's hand. She looked at him, trying to find the words. What happened to Maggie didn't feel real, and she had no idea how everything had changed so quickly. Matt shook his head; he didn't know what to say either.

She was just with us. She was fine. Now she's dead.

There was the sound of something being knocked over in the kitchen. Violet thought at first that Sam was taking out his frustrations on the crockery, but then she could hear more than one pair of feet moving inside. Joe's eyes widened as he realized the same thing, and they ran to the kitchen door.

Sam was fighting a biter, his back against the kitchen counter. He'd jammed his knife into its neck, but it still held onto him tightly. As Violet stepped through the doorway, she watched its teeth snap at his face, just millimeters from his skin. Matt and Joe hurried into the room, pulling the biter away, but they didn't have their knives. They fought with it. During the scuffle, Violet heard more coming down the stairs.

"Go," Matt yelled. "We'll catch up!"

Violet grabbed Toby's arm, pulling him through the back door and out into the yard. They opened the gate and ran into the street.

Where the truck was waiting.

VIOLET AND TOBY WERE BUNDLED INTO THE BACK OF the truck, despite their best efforts to fight. Inside, sacks were put over their heads, and their hands were restrained. Violet's heart was pounding. She struggled against the person holding her, but was roughly pushed to the floor. She lay in the dark, feeling the truck pulling away, with no idea where they were going, no idea whether Toby was still beside her, no idea whether Matt, Sam, or Joe were even alive. She heard barking fading into the distance as they left Ben behind. The soldiers weren't speaking, and the truck sped on in silence for the longest time. It made left and right turns, but Violet soon lost count of how many. She knew she'd never find her way back to her friends, not now they had gone so far.

If we manage to escape, we'll be on our own now.

But even escape seemed incredibly unlikely— there must've been at least six men in the truck; she remembered counting them earlier. She and Toby stood no chance against six trained soldiers. Eventually, Violet felt the vehicle stop, and she was pulled roughly upright. Still with the sack over her head, she was taken out and marched forward.

"Where am I?" she asked, her voice cracking as she spoke. No response from the person pushing her.

"Toby?"

TWENTY-ONE

Nothing. Either Toby wasn't with her, or they had made it so he couldn't speak.

"Where is my friend?" she persisted. Still no answer.

Violet felt the ground beneath her change. She was inside now, but had no idea where 'inside' was.

"In," a voice said gruffly, pushing her forward. They stood still for a while, the floor seeming to vibrate beneath her feet, and Violet realized they were in an elevator. So wherever they were, the power was still on. She heard doors opening, and was then marched on again. More walking, more doors, until she was finally roughly pushed onto a chair.

"Thank you," said a voice she didn't recognize. It was male. "Where did you find her?"

"Zone C." It was said from behind her, so it must've belonged to one of the soldiers. "She was with others."

"Do you have all of them?"

"No. Just one more."

That's good. Matt, Sam, and Joe are still okay.

As long as they've not been eaten.

Shut up, brain!

"You look angry," said the voice she didn't know. "What happened?"

"Her people attacked us."

"You killed my friend," Violet interrupted, sounding confident despite still having no idea where she was or what was happening.

"She was bitten."

"No, she wasn't!"

"Okay, that's enough, Gobber," the first voice said.

Violet snorted. *Gobber.*

"Something funny?" the one called Gobber asked, an edge to his tone.

"Nope."

"Leave us," insisted the other man.

She heard the soldier leave, and the door close heavily behind him. The man in front of her didn't speak for a while, but she knew he was still there. She could hear him breathing. Eventually, she heard him move forward. The sack was removed from her head, and she was momentarily blinded by the bright light in the room. Her eyes slowly adjusted, and Violet took in her surroundings. It appeared to be an office: white walls, a desk in front of her with a computer, a large potted plant in the corner. The man in front of her wore a white coat, like a doctor, and had greying brown hair. His eyes were the brightest blue she'd ever seen.

"What's your name?" he asked, his voice gentle.

Violet didn't answer, staring him out. What did he want from her? Why was she here?

"What's your name?" he repeated.

Violet kept her face impassive, her tone dry when she finally spoke. "Am I not wearing my name badge? I must've lost it when I was kidnapped and shoved into a dirty old truck."

A smile flickered on the man's face. "Are you going to tell me?"

"My friend," Violet began. "The one I came in with... is he safe?"

"Why don't you start by answering my question, then I'll answer yours?"

"Why do you want to know my name?"

He smiled fully now, and it was almost reassuring. Almost. "I'd like to have a conversation with you. It would be more pleasant if I were able to call you by your first name."

"Violet."

"Pleasure to meet you, Violet. My name is Doctor Jeremy Ross."

"Where is my friend?" Violet asked again.

"I saw the two of you arrive out the window. He was fine. I'm sure he'll be brought to me after you leave."

"Leave?" Violet felt her heart beat a little faster. "I can go?"

The doctor's smile flickered. "I mean when you leave this room. You'll be taken somewhere to rest, and then we need to run a few tests."

Beads of sweat began to appear on Violet's forehead. "What kind of tests?"

"Before we can evacuate you, we need to check you're

okay. Have you been out there the whole time?"

Violet shook her head. "We were in a house...what kind of tests?"

Doctor Ross waved a hand casually. "We'll collect blood and saliva samples. We need to check for any infectious diseases before we take you out of the country. We also need to do a psychiatric evaluation. Being out there for so long...we need to make sure it hasn't had any...adverse effects."

I can think of one or two.

The doctor continued. "You should be out within a few days—"

"I don't want to leave," Violet interrupted.

He looked confused. "You were asking me if you could go just a moment ago."

"I mean I don't want to be evacuated. I want to stay in the country."

Doctor Ross raised an eyebrow. "I'm not sure I believe that. Why would you want to stay here?"

Because my friends are here.

Because I don't trust you.

Because if you do blood tests, you might find out I'm half-zombie.

Because I don't want whatever I have to spread anywhere else.

But she didn't say any of those things. She just stayed silent. Doctor Ross sighed. "I think you should get some rest. I'll see you tomorrow for your tests." He nodded over her shoulder. She hadn't realized one of the soldiers had come back in, and was waiting just behind her. He pulled her to her feet. This one had greasy brown hair and was missing a front tooth.

Is this Gobber? He's a looker.

"Take Violet to her room," Doctor Ross said. "Gently, please. She's been through a lot."

───── ∿⋀⋁⋀⋀∿ ─────

VIOLET WASN'T SURE GOBBER UNDERSTOOD 'GENTLY'. SHE didn't think the doctor meant—*drag her toward the room, then shove her inside and slam the door behind her.* Still, she was glad to be rid of him, at least. She took in her new surroundings. The room used to be an office of some kind, but had been masterfully 'converted' into a bedroom by simply moving the desk and filing cabinet to one side, and putting six cots against the wall. For now, she was on her own. She sat on the edge of a cot, her head in her hands, trying to figure out how she was going to get out of this. Then she stood up, pacing the room.

I don't know where Toby is. I don't know where I am. I have no idea if Matt, Sam, and Joe are even still alive.

What's going to happen when they find out I'm infected? Will they kill me straight away? Will they do tests on me?

She pulled up the sleeve of her left arm, looking at the ugly scar where she was bitten. It was so clearly a bite wound. Even without the blood tests, they'd be able to recognize it a mile off. She sighed, tugging down the sleeve again and glancing out the window. She was high up; the building had to be at least ten stories. What was this place? What was it used for now?

She heard the door open behind her, and saw Toby being led into the room. His wrist restraints were removed, and the door closed behind him. He had a black eye. Violet hurried over, pulling him into a hug, suddenly aware of how young he was.

"Are you okay?" she asked, surveying him at arm's length. "Did they hurt you?"

He shook his head. "No, I'm fine. Did they hurt you?"

"No."

"The doctor said they want to evacuate us. He said they'll take us out of the country." He didn't sound particularly excited.

"What do you think?" Violet asked.

He paused, and then shook his head again. "I don't trust them, and I don't want to go. Not without the others; they're still out there somewhere."

"I agree. We need to get out of here."

"How?"

"That's the problem. I have no idea."

VIOLET AND TOBY WERE BOTH PULLED OUT THE NEXT morning by Gobber and two other soldiers, who led them to a small examination room across the hall. Violet knew this must've been some kind of clinic or research center before; there was too much medical equipment for it to have been anything else.

"You don't have to always point the guns at them," Doctor Ross said as he entered the room followed by two other doctors, one male and one female.

"They're dangerous," one of the soldiers muttered. This one was dark with a shaved head, and he kept his gun aimed squarely at Violet. He had a black eye and a split lip, and she wondered if he might've been the one Matt and Joe had attacked.

The other male doctor snorted. "Dangerous? The girl and the child?"

"Don't underestimate them."

"Fine." Doctor Ross sighed impatiently. "Let's just get on with it." He smiled, moving toward Violet while his female colleague approached Toby.

"We're just going to take some blood," he explained. "It shouldn't hurt too much, and it won't take very long." He made to roll up her sleeve, but Violet kicked out, knocking him back unexpectedly. Following Violet's lead, Toby shoved his doctor away. Immediately, the guns were pointed at their faces, the soldiers yelling.

"Stop," Doctor Ross cried over the noise. He glanced at Violet warily, then at the soldiers. "Wait outside."

"No chance." Gobber shook his greasy head.

"I'm in charge here, and I can't get any work done while you're here pointing those things at my patients. Get out."

Surprisingly, after a few scathing looks, the soldiers left the room. Gobber threw Violet one last scowl, which was slightly less intimidating with his missing front chomper, before following the others. Now there were no guns in the room, Doctor Ross turned back to Violet. "Why did you do that?"

She didn't reply.

"You don't want me to take your blood?"

She shook her head.

"Why?"

What answer could she give?

"I want to help you," Doctor Ross began. "Both of you. But I can only do that—I can only get you out of this nightmare—if I can prove you're fit and well. We can do this the easy way, or we can do it the hard way." He regarded her sympathetically. "Trust me, you don't want it to be the hard way.

He moved closer, the syringe still in his hand, but Violet backed further away. The doctor sighed. "Okay." He headed for the door, and opened it. "Hold them down," he said to the soldiers outside, who immediately came into the room.

Gobber grinned, grabbing Violet roughly by the shoulders and forcing her onto the bed. She and Toby fought against it, but they weren't strong enough, and were held in place by their shoulders and wrists. Violet saw another doctor take Toby's blood. Doctor Ross approached her. He nodded to the soldiers, and the sleeves on both of her arms were pulled up. She closed her eyes, feeling the silence fall on the whole room as they saw her bite. After what felt like an eternity, one of the other soldiers spoke. "She's been bitten!"

Violet opened her eyes and focused her attention on Toby, who was staring at her wound openmouthed.

"She can't have been," the female doctor breathed. "That's impossible."

Another soldier pointed to the bite angrily. "You look at that and tell me it's not a bite!"

He raised his gun to her head, but Doctor Ross called, "No, don't shoot her!"

"She's bitten!"

"She's been here for over eighteen hours," Doctor Ross breathed. "She should've turned by now, or at least be showing symptoms, especially with a bite as deep as that. Look at the coloring around it." He moved closer. "That bite has healed."

"What does that mean?" Gobber asked.

Doctor Ross moved Violet's head, not roughly, but forcing her to lock eyes with him. "When were you bitten?" he asked.

Violet's mouth was a desert. She swallowed thickly.

"*When*?" he repeated.

"At the start," she croaked. "I don't know how long it's been."

The doctor's eyes widened, a smile spreading across his lips. "Take her away, quarantine her." He gestured to Toby. "He can go back to his room."

Toby fought as they strapped Violet onto the bed before wheeling her from the room. She heard him calling out her name, trying to break free of the hands holding him, but she couldn't do anything. She was trapped, and she was numb. What was going to happen now?

AND SO, THINGS FELL INTO A ROUTINE. VIOLET realized that wherever she was, there would always be a routine. At the school, all those months ago, it had involved patrolling the fence, making meals, eating together, finding ways to pass the time until the next patrol, and trying not to eat anyone. When John and his men arrived, her routine became cooking, cleaning, generally trying to keep out of everyone's way, and trying not to eat anyone. At the house, she'd had chores involving the animals, Ben was walked every day, they had a set time to cook in the kitchen, and she had to try not to eat anyone. When they were out there, without walls or fences to protect them, the routine had become simpler—get up, keep moving, stay alive, find somewhere to sleep, and try not to eat anyone. It was easy to remember at least.

This place followed a routine, too. Every morning, she was woken up by soldiers coming into her room with guns pointed at her head. She was tied down on a gurney—even though she was more than capable of walking—and wheeled into a white room two floors down. She was sedated, and she would wake up in her room again. Every day the same, for five days.

Though things were becoming fuzzy in Violet's mind, she made sure to keep track of the days. She made a tally on the wall using a pen she'd found in one of the drawers. She wasn't trying so hard not to eat anyone here. In fact, that might've at least cheered her up a little. Unfortunately, she was surrounded by people who actually realized how dangerous she was, and the opportunity to do a little flesh eating never seemed to present itself.

Today was day six, and as usual, Violet was strapped down on a bed in the white room. She wasn't sure how long she'd been there, probably a few minutes. She hadn't been sedated yet, but still didn't feel right. She had been knocked out so often over the past few days even her moments of consciousness felt strange and dream-like. She was naked, as always, waiting to be poked and prodded by doctors wearing masks. They didn't talk to her. It was like she was already dead, just a cadaver they were practicing on. It felt like every inch of her body had been injected or scraped at some point. In her rare moments of consciousness, Violet found herself daydreaming about breaking free of the table and releasing the thing that lived inside her. She could kill everyone: the ones who bought her here, the ones who pulled and poked and probed, the ones who pointed guns in her face. No one would be safe.

"Violet?"

This was unusual; someone was speaking to her today. Violet's head felt heavy as she lazily turned it to the left. She wasn't in the operating room any longer; she was lying on her cot.

When did they bring me here? I thought I was still on the table?

Violet's eyelids drooped, but she tried to focus on the voice. A woman was watching her. She had red hair tied into a neat plait. She wore a white coat, like the other doctors, but she wasn't wearing a mask. She seemed to actually see Violet as a person, rather than imagining all the ways she could cut her open.

Give it time.

"Violet, can you hear me?" the woman asked.

Violet tried to croak a response, but her voice didn't seem to be working. The woman scowled, looking behind her, where Violet could just make out the shape of another doctor.

"What have you got her on?" the woman asked sharply. "She's barely conscious."

"We have to keep her sedated. We don't know what effect the virus has on her."

"Still? You've had her for almost a week. How can you not know?"

No reply.

"Have you considered *asking* her how it has affected her?"

"That's your job."

"Yes, it is." The woman's tone was cold. "And how am I supposed to do that if she can't even string a sentence together?"

Silence. Finally, the woman spoke again. "No more drugs, not until her next round of tests. Until then, just let the poor girl rest. When she comes around fully, bring her to me."

"But Doctor Ross says—"

"I don't care what he says. Just do it."

TWO DAYS PASSED. FINALLY, VIOLET WAS BEGINNING TO feel like herself again. The objects around her lost their hazy edges, and she could stand up without feeling as though the floor was vibrating beneath her. She had just finished marking the tally on the wall when she heard her door unlocking. Gobber and two other soldiers came into the room. As usual, their guns were pointed at her.

"Drop it," Gobber ordered. For a moment, Violet had no idea what he was talking about. Then she realized she was still holding the pen. She rolled her eyes. "Seriously?"

Gobber stepped closer, the gun still raised. "Don't make me hurt you."

Violet dramatically dropped the pen onto the floor, slapping a hand over her heart. "Thank goodness you're so perceptive. I might've caused serious damage with that biro."

"Move," Gobber demanded, pointing to the door.

No gurney today? That's something at least.

Still, even though walking was a new privilege, Violet couldn't help but try to antagonize the soldier a little more. "I can't stop thinking about that pen," she murmured as they walked, shaking her head a little.

"Shut up."

"Do you have any idea of what might've happened? I could've written a strongly worded letter to your superior officer..."

"I said shut up."

Violet pulled a shocked face. "My God, Gobber...I might've drawn a funny mustache on you."

One of the other soldiers snorted, but Gobber just shoved her on with the end of his gun. "Don't push me."

"I might've made you a name badge with a ridiculous... oh, never mind."

A definite laugh from one of the other men. Gobber had clearly had enough. He grasped Violet by the shoulder, forcing her to turn around.

"Listen, mutant, you have all the jokes you want. We both know your days left walking around like the rest of us are ticking away. Soon, they'll have all they need from you while you're breathing, and you'll be cut open on that table and taken apart piece by piece." He grinned widely at the thought.

Violet met his gaze but stayed silent.

"Nothing to say now, huh?"

She cocked her head to one side. "What happened to your tooth? Was it before all this? Or after? And if it was before, why didn't you get it fixed? Something like that would drive me crazy."

Gobber nodded, as if realizing this was how the conversation was going to go, and then slapped her sharply across the face. Violet hadn't been expecting it, and stumbled back.

"Gobber, what are you doing?" one of the other soldiers muttered. "You know our orders."

Gobber shrugged. "Doc said not to kill her. Didn't say we can't bruise her up a little." He stepped forward, almost nose to nose with Violet. When he spoke, his voice was little more than a whisper. "Remember, mutant, I know where you sleep." His grin was evil when he forced her around and pushed her toward the elevator.

Violet was taken into an office, then strapped to a chair with wrist and ankle restraints. The soldiers stepped back, leaving her to take in her surroundings. This room was warmer than the one belonging to Doctor Ross. It had yellow walls and several framed photos of smiling children on the large oak desk. There were framed paintings, and a comfortable-looking cream couch by the large window. Violet heard the door open behind her. The redheaded doctor appeared, smiling kindly at Violet as she walked in. Her smile flickered as she snapped at the soldiers. "What's wrong with her face?"

I really hope I have a bruise; otherwise, that's a little insulting.

"She resisted, so we had to subdue her," came Gobber's cool reply.

The doctor raised an eyebrow. "She's never resisted before."

"First time for everything."

The doctor clearly didn't believe that in the slightest, but simply nodded. "I see. And why is she restrained?"

"Doctor Ross' orders. She's dangerous."

"I want them removed."

"No can do. We have orders."

The doctor bit her lip. "Fine, then leave."

"We have to—"

"She's restrained; she's no threat. Wait outside, please."

Surprisingly, they did as she asked. The doctor sighed, sitting down and staring at her from across the desk. Her face was kind, and she had an accent Violet hadn't noticed before.

"My name is Frances," the woman began. "And I'm so sorry."

Violet was caught a little off guard. She raised an eyebrow. "For what?"

Frances held up her hands, "For everything. I'm sorry you've been locked away from your friend; I'm sorry you've spent so much time sedated; I'm sorry for what those men did to you... I'm afraid the people here have lost touch with what they're meant to be doing. They think they're here to fight and control, when really that's only a tiny part of it."

"What are *you* here for?"

"I'm here to learn. I'm a psychiatrist. My job is to talk, to listen, and to help. If I can."

"No one has jobs anymore," Violet retorted.

"I think it's important to remember who we are."

"You're thinking about who we *were*. Who we *are* is different."

"Okay." Frances was waiting for Violet to explain, but she wasn't going to. She'd said too much already; she didn't want this woman getting into her head. Frances seemed to sense her hesitation. "You're unsure about me; I can understand that. I don't know how much it means to you, but you do have my word that I'm here to help."

Violet said nothing, so Frances continued. "The doctors and scientists in there—" She gestured across the hall. "They're interested in you because they think your blood holds the cure to the disease."

"It doesn't."

"Why do you say that?"

Violet didn't answer. Frances waited several minutes before speaking again. "That's why *they're* interested in you, but not why I am. You survived out there for months, and how you did that is something I'd like to know about. I'd like to know how it has affected you."

"Why should I tell you anything?"

"Because I can help you."

Violet shook her head. "No one can help me."

$\sim\!\!\!\!\wedge\!\!\wedge\!\!\wedge\!\!\wedge\!\!\!\sim\!\!-$

AND THAT WAS HOW IT WAS FOR A WHILE. VIOLET MET with Frances every other day. Each time, she said nothing. Frances, to her credit, never became frustrated, never yelled, never hit her. She simply waited for Violet to speak, and after a while, sent her back to her room. Those sessions weren't the problem. The problem was what happened in between.

Violet was still taken to the white room, still probed and prodded, only now it seemed to be more vigorous. Whenever she woke up, she found herself scarred and sore. One terrible day, she was unable to walk for hours because her feet felt as though someone had taken a knife to the soles. Which they probably had. Violet didn't know what they were doing, but clearly finding a cure from her blood wasn't as simple as it seemed.

Today, they had tried something new—cutting into her without sedation. They hadn't gone deep, but Violet had screamed until her throat was raw. It seemed to take hours, but she never passed out. She felt every cut. Afterward, when the doctors were cleaning up, Gobber approached the bed. He stared at Violet, who was covered only in a thin sheet, and grinned.

"Nothing clever to say now, huh?"

Violet spoke, despite the pain it caused. "I guess not. Is this what it feels like to be you?"

The grin was wiped from Gobber's face, but he said nothing. He glanced over to the doctors, "Want me to take her back?"

"Yes, please."

"My pleasure." Gobber's smirk was back now, and it didn't take long for Violet to realize what he was planning. The second they were out of the doors to the white room, Gobber pulled the sheet off Violet's body and dropped it to the floor. "You looked like you might be too hot." He grinned wickedly. Violet was now completely naked, but due to her restraints, unable to cover herself up.

This is what he wants. He wants to humiliate you. Just act like you don't care.

So Violet said nothing as she was wheeled through the halls to the elevator, past the soldiers and doctors, some of whom considered her, some whom clearly thought of her as a corpse already and didn't even glance in her direction. Gobber continued to grin at his revenge, but Violet kept her face impassive.

As they waited for the elevator, Gobber leaned in a little closer. "How do you feel now, mutant?"

"Pretty embarrassed actually."

Gobber seemed surprised at her admission. "Oh, really?"

"Yes, please don't stand so close to me. I don't want people to think we're friends. That would be mortifying."

Gobber's face turned a rather unflattering shade of magenta. Before he could react, the elevator doors opened.

"Violet?"

She jerked her eyes over, her heart leaping into her throat. Joe, Sam, and Matt, each bruised and covered in dried blood, were being led out of the elevator by two armed soldiers. Violet didn't care one iota that she was naked; all she wanted was to get off the bed and hug her friends. They, however, looked furious, and Matt immediately tried to reach out and grab her hand. He was pushed roughly away by one of the soldiers.

"Keep moving," he growled, tapping Matt with his gun.

"Get off," Matt protested. Two more soldiers, who were passing in the hall, stepped in to hold him back. "Let her go!" Matt fought against them while Sam and Joe watched helplessly, guns still aimed at their heads.

"It's okay," Violet called. "I'm all right!" But she was wheeled into the elevator before she could see what happened next. The doors closed. Gobber was grinning widely now, and Violet knew he was already planning what to do to her friends.

The elevator doors opened again, and Violet was wheeled out into the hall. From the corner of her eye, she saw Frances heading in the other direction.

"Hey," Violet called.

"Shut up," Gobber growled, but it didn't matter. Frances had heard, and she jogged over to the gurney.

"What are you doing with her?" she asked Gobber accusingly.

"Taking her back to her room; the doctors are done for today."

"Why is she naked?"

"What does it matter? She's a freak."

"I don't think you're in any position to judge that," Frances replied coldly.

"I need to speak to you," Violet interrupted, her eyes pleading. "Now."

Frances nodded. "You heard her. Take her to my office, right this minute." She took off her coat, draping it over Violet to give her some modicum of decency.

IN THE OFFICE, FRANCES ORDER THE SOLDIERS OUTSIDE. The second they were gone, she began to untie Violet's restraints. Then she handed her a blanket to wrap around herself.

"He's a nasty piece of work," Frances muttered, sitting down at her desk. She sighed, running a hand through her red hair. It was down today.

"You said you could help me," Violet said.

Frances considered her for a moment, and then nodded. "Yes."

"How?"

"They're confused about you, about your blood. If we can find out more about what happened to you, about what affect the virus has had on you, they'll start to treat you better. They won't need to keep doing all the things they're doing."

"I don't care about that. I want you to help me in a different way."

"How?"

"My friends just arrived, and I know Gobber and the other soldiers want to hurt them. I want you to stop that from happening."

"They say your people injured some of our soldiers."

"They killed my friend first," Violet retorted. "They killed her for no reason. She wasn't infected, and she wasn't dangerous." She felt a tear on her cheek. "She just had a cut."

Frances nodded, eyes widening slightly at the sight of the blood sliding down Violet's face. "Okay. I can make sure the soldiers don't hurt them. Gobber will listen to Jeremy, and I'll speak to him."

"Can you let them go?"

Frances shook her head. "I'm sorry, but I can't. It's nothing to do with them; the soldiers have their orders—anyone fit and well gets evacuated. Surely that's a good thing, though?"

Violet found herself nodding. "It is."

"And I can make sure they're evacuated as quickly as possible."

"But not me."

Frances nodded sadly. "But not you. You're too valuable."

"I want to be with my friends. Until they're evacuated, I mean."

"I'm not sure the others will agree—"

Violet's expression was hard. "If you want me to speak to you, then you make sure we can be together. If they're being evacuated soon, we need time to say goodbye."

Frances considered this, then got to her feet. "Let me see what I can do."

Violet watched the clock while Frances was gone. Twenty-five minutes later, the woman returned. She sat down with a smile on her face. "It wasn't easy, but I convinced the others to put you and your friends in the same room."

"Really? How did you do it?"

Frances' lips curved slyly. "I'm persuasive."

"Thank you."

"So, are you ready to talk?"

Violet told the woman everything she needed to know—about how they had survived, about who she was, and most importantly, about what had happened to her. She explained what happened when she encountered blood, and, reluctantly, about the people she had killed because of it.

"That's why my blood isn't the answer," she said, shaking her head. "They want my blood for a cure, or a vaccine, but I'm not immune. I'm dangerous, just like those things outside."

Frances hadn't interrupted Violet's story at any point, and simply nodded her head now. "I see." She got to her feet. "Thank you for being so honest with me. I'll talk to the other doctors about what you have told me." She moved to the door, opening it for Violet to leave. Violet was escorted by two soldiers she didn't recognize back to the first room she had shared with Toby. She watched as Frances headed in the other direction. She hoped what she had said would be enough to stop what they were doing. Her blood wasn't the answer.

Violet pushed the door open. Her friends stood up when they saw her, and Matt was the first to pull her into a hug.

"I'm so glad you're okay," Violet breathed into his shoulder. She pulled back, looking closely at him and the others. Sam had certainly got the worst of it; it seemed as if his nose had been broken, but he still smiled at the sight of her, giving her a hug, too.

"What happened?" Violet asked.

"We were trying to find you guys," Joe explained. "We guessed you'd been taken in the truck, so we started searching for it. It took us a week, but it eventually showed up again. We were just thinking of how best to follow without being seen, when Sam blew our cover."

Sam interrupted, shaking his head. "I didn't blow our cover."

"You made that ridiculous noise."

"That was a sneeze!"

Joe raised an eyebrow. "That was *not* a sneeze; it was a fog-horn."

"Anyway," Matt interrupted. "They found us and brought us here."

"Not before giving us a less than friendly welcome with their boots," Joe added.

"Where's Ben?"

Matt and the others shifted a little.

"We don't know," Matt finally said. "I think he followed the truck for a while when they took you, but he was gone when we came out."

"Oh."

"He'll be okay," Joe said. "The biters don't eat animals. He'll be all right."

Sam looked Violet up and down. "What about you?

What have they been doing to you?"

Violet sighed, taking in her group. Joe and Matt knew her secret, and Toby had pretty much heard it all, but Sam still had no idea. It didn't feel right to keep anyone in the dark anymore.

"They've been running tests on me."

"Why?" Sam asked.

"Because I have it."

Toby couldn't meet her eye, but Sam just sounded confused. "Have what?"

"*It*—you know, whatever makes the biters do the things they do."

Sam still looked baffled. Joe piped up. "Show him your mangled arm."

Violet exhaled, removing her arm from the blanket to show her bite. Sam instinctively stepped back, color draining from his face.

"How...how long?" he stuttered.

"Since the start," Violet replied honestly. She glanced at Toby, whose expression was unreadable. Sam, however, was shaking his head. "You couldn't...it's not possible."

"It is," Violet said. "It happened on the first day. I passed out and woke up a week later."

"You're immune?" Sam's voice was disbelieving, happy even, but she knew she had to burst his bubble.

"No. Not completely."

"I don't understand."

Violet searched for the words, but they evaded her. She looked to Joe and Matt for support. Matt ran his hand through his hair. "She still has it, whatever *it* is...but she's not dead, and she doesn't want to hurt anyone."

"*Want* being the key word," Joe added. "If she smells or tastes blood—"

"I lose control," Violet interrupted, knowing she had to take responsibility for explaining it. "When there's blood around, I become one of those things. I can't control it. I usually pass out afterward. When I wake up, I'm back to normal."

Toby's voice came from across the room. "Have you killed anyone?"

Violet nodded. "Yes."

"Did they deserve it?"

"Some of them did. Not all."

Toby nodded. "Okay."

That's it?

Sam was nodding, too. "We're still family, Violet. Nothing has changed." He pulled her in for another hug, and her whole body relaxed. "I'll just go to one of the others the next time I get a paper cut."

She smiled. "Good plan."

Joe grinned, clapping his hands together. "Okay, now that we've got the awkward 'Violet might kill us' conversation out of the way, how are we getting out of here?"

"You don't want to be evacuated?" Violet asked. "They said they were taking you guys out of the country."

"I don't trust anything these people say," Sam said. "And I'm guessing if you're so important to them, they're not planning on getting you out?"

Violet shook her head.

He nodded. "Okay then, so we need to break out of this place. Soon."

THE CONVERSATION DIDN'T TAKE VERY LONG, SEEING AS none of them had the faintest idea how they could escape. They were all exhausted, and went to bed early that evening. Violet had been brought some clothes, so at least she was now decent, but she couldn't sleep. She lay awake, eyes fixed on the ceiling, mind racing. They had all survived this long. Had survived through things that made nightmares feel like a walk in the park. They had to find a way out. She turned onto her side, coming face to face with Matt, who was in the next cot. His eyes were open, too, grey in the darkness.

"Can't sleep?" he asked.

She shook her head.

"Me neither."

Violet kept her voice to a whisper, not wanting to wake

up the others. "If they make a vaccine out of my blood, is that really a good thing?"

Matt thought for a moment. "It would mean no more biters."

"Not really. It would mean more people like me; people who could turn at any moment. Isn't that more dangerous than the ones you know about?"

"I see what you mean."

"The survivors out there right now...They're alive. They're making lives for themselves. They don't have to run out of the room if their friend gets a cut. I don't want anyone to live like I do."

Matt looked at her curiously, so she continued. "I'm always afraid; I'm afraid that something will happen, and I'll kill the people I care about. Food has no taste, and the only food I can enjoy means killing an innocent person." She took a breath, realizing she might be about to cry, and not wanting to inflict that horror on Matt. First because she cried blood, and second because she was not an attractive crier. "This isn't a life anyone should have."

Matt sat up and then moved over to her cot, pushing her gently aside so he could squeeze in, too. He put his arms around her, and she breathed in his familiar, comforting smell.

"I'm glad you are the way you are," he whispered. "If you weren't, then you'd be dead."

"Well, or I'd be alive. I could've avoided being bitten altogether."

"We both know you were pretty much destined to get bitten on the first day."

Violet elbowed him gently, and he grinned. "Seriously, though, I'm just grateful you're still here."

Oh no, we both know you can't handle any kind of sentiment.

This will go one of two ways: tears or a terrible joke.

Joke. Joke. Please joke.

Violet felt the tears on her cheeks.

Oh crap.

"Don't cry," Matt said gently.

"I'm sorry, it's really gross. I cry blood."

"Oh, really? I was just going to say you don't strike me as an attractive crier." Matt laughed again, then gently kissed the top of Violet's head. "We'll fix this. We'll get out of here. Don't worry. I won't let them hurt you."

It's not just them I'm worried about.

TWENTY-THREE

THE NEXT MORNING, VIOLET WAS TAKEN BACK INTO Doctor Ross' office. She was strapped into a chair, which was at least an improvement from being strapped onto a bed. He sat across from her, elbows resting on the shiny desk, fingers together. It had been a while since she'd seen him without a surgical mask. His blue eyes didn't appear quite so bright or welcoming anymore.

"I have excellent news," he began, "and I wanted to share it with you."

Why do I get the feeling this is going to be terrible, terrible news?

The doctor grinned. "We have managed to synthesize some prototype vaccines from your blood. After some tests, we will be able to use them to prevent the spread of further infection."

"How?"

"Well, to put it simply—we're going to make it able to disperse in the air, then we'll drop it."

Violet shook her head. "You shouldn't do that; you'll be infecting healthy people with the virus."

"It will prevent them from succumbing to the full infection. We believe with a few adaptations, we can stop any unwanted side effects."

"Unwanted side effects like eating people?" Violet asked sarcastically.

Doctor Ross smiled, though it didn't quite reach

266

his eyes. "Yes, like that. I thought you might like to see our first test?"

"I don't want to see what my blood does to some poor rats."

"Not rats," the doctor answered, getting to his feet. The soldiers behind Violet stepped forward and untied her from the chair, but then bound her hands together. They pushed her from the room. She followed Doctor Ross, because she had no choice, toward the elevator and down to the bottom floor. They went down a long hallway toward a room at the back, which she had never been in before. As Violet entered, her breath immediately caught in her throat. In here, she could look through a window into the room next door. Sam was tied onto a hospital bed.

"What's going on?" she asked, spinning around to face Doctor Ross.

"The virus doesn't affect animals. All previous tests using mice and rats have provided no useful data. Your friend caused a lot of trouble. He killed several of my men when they caught him, which I'm sure he failed to mention to you. If he proves useful here, then I'll be willing to let that go." He pulled what Violet assumed he thought was a reassuring expression. It wasn't. "We're confident he will experience only minimal discomfort at most."

"Please," Violet began, moving toward the doctor, but she was pulled back by the soldiers. "Please don't do this."

"It's already been done," Doctor Ross replied, nodding over her shoulder. The soldiers forced her around in time to watch as a doctor inside the room with Sam pulled a syringe from his arm. Sam caught sight of Violet though the window. He was scared, she could see that, but he kept his expression set.

Don't panic. Maybe this will work? Maybe this is the thing that will save—

But Violet couldn't even finish reassuring herself. Moments later, Sam's body was writhing on the bed. He seemed to be having some sort of fit, struggling against the restraints keeping him down. White foam flowed from his open mouth, which slowly became pink, and then red.

"Someone help him," Violet ordered, but she was

ignored. Sam shook and thrashed for several minutes, all color draining from his face. His hair clung to his damp forehead, and his fingers curled up until his own nails cut through the skin of his hands. He was screaming. Then he stopped. He became as stiff as a board, eyes wide open. His breathing sped up, his chest moving in and out rapidly. He was like that for around thirty seconds, before he stopped breathing altogether. His body went limp. Violet cried out, slamming her tied hands against the glass, but it was no good. Even from here, she knew he was dead. Doctor Ross sighed, motioning through the window for the other doctor to check Sam. He felt for a pulse before shaking his head.

"You killed him," Violet choked.

"Technically, *you* killed him," Gobber retorted from the corner of the room, satisfaction thick in his voice. Violet hadn't even realized he was there. Before she had a chance to even think of a response, she was interrupted by screaming.

Violet jerked her head up, eyes widening. Sam was off the table. She had no idea how he had done it, but the heavy restraints were torn in half where he had broken free. His white skin seemed to have expanded, his muscles more prominent, straining against the surface. He grabbed the doctor, biting his neck and ripping out chunks of flesh. Blood and viscera escaped in all directions, and Sam continued to rip and claw at the man.

"Get in there," Doctor Ross ordered.

"No, don't," Violet protested, but she still had one of the soldiers holding her back. She didn't know why she protested. The real Sam was gone, but she still didn't want them to kill him. What if a tiny part of him was still in there? What if he was like her? The other soldiers went into the room, immediately opening fire. Sam hit the floor.

Violet watched, just for a moment, then slowly turned to face Doctor Ross. "I told you my blood is dangerous. Now he's dead."

"We have three other variations of the vaccine."

Violet shook her head. "It won't work. You need to—" Then it hit her...

Three more vaccines, three more of her friends.

"No," she began, eyes widening. "No, please don't." But it didn't matter. Violet was pulled away from the doctor, still screaming her pleas, back toward the elevator.

DESPITE WHAT SHE HAD JUST SEEN, VIOLET WAS TAKEN back to her room where the others were waiting. She wondered if there had been a mix up; surely they wouldn't want her telling them what had happened? Perhaps they didn't care? They knew the prisoners had no way to escape. Maybe Doctor Ross thought it would be funny to spend their last few hours together knowing they were about to die? Either way, she was pushed inside, the door locked securely behind her. Toby was lying down on one of the cots, while Joe and Matt were sitting up and having some kind of debate.

Joe shook his head. "I'm telling you, Superman is pretty much invincible."

"The amount of times he's been defeated proves he's not."

"Every time he's been beaten it's because there was kryptonite involved. It's his only weakness."

Matt shrugged. "It just seems to me that there's a hell of a lot of kryptonite available to anyone who wants to fight Superman. Is it literally just growing out of the ground?"

"If you take kryptonite out of the equation, Superman is unbeatable."

"That's not fair. That's like saying if you take money out of the equation, you're really rich." Matt diverted his attention to Violet, the smile on his face flickering. "What's wrong? Did they hurt you?"

Violet shook her head, numb after what she had just seen. "Sam." It was the only word she could say.

"He's been taken for some blood tests," Joe said, getting to his feet.

Violet shook her head. "No."

Matt and Joe came closer. Toby sat up, expression anxious.

"What happened?" Matt asked.

Violet shook her head again, unable to string a sentence together.

"Is he..." Joe couldn't finish. Violet nodded. He let out an angry growl, punching the large closet beside him. Matt put his arms around Violet.

"They used my blood," she said, her voice hollow. "They said it was supposed to be a vaccine, but it didn't work. Sam died. Then he came back."

Joe swore loudly, punching the closet again. Toby lay back down, putting his hands over his face.

"They have more," Violet continued. "Three other variations."

"That's a coincidence," Matt muttered.

Violet's voice hitched, "Doctor Ross said they're going to t-test them."

"When?" Toby asked, sitting up again.

She shook her head. "I don't know."

"It'll be soon," Matt said. "We don't have long."

"How are we going to get out?" Joe asked. He gestured to the window. "Even if we could open that thing, smash it somehow, the fall would kill us." He sat down on the edge of one of the cots, his head in his hands.

"We could fight?" Toby suggested.

Joe shook his head. "We don't have any weapons, and the soldiers are always armed. They'd kill us straight away. It's not like we're actually worth anything to them."

Suddenly, everything became clear to Violet.

Doc said not to kill her. Didn't say we can't bruise her up a little.

Doc said not to kill her.

"I'm worth something to them." The strength in Violet's voice surprised her, but the plan was already forming in her head. "They can't kill me; I'm too valuable. I've heard them say it."

Joe looked confused. "You don't have a weapon."

"She does." Matt ran a hand through his hair, eyes on Violet. "That's what you're thinking, isn't it? To let yourself turn?"

She nodded. "I'll be strong, and they won't expect it. I

can probably kill a couple of them, or at least keep them distracted. Then you guys can get out."

Joe shook his head. "This is a terrible plan. You can't be sure they won't kill you."

Violet shrugged. "I'm worth more to them alive. They'll do everything they can to keep me that way."

Matt didn't look happy. "Okay, say that's true...say we get out. What about you?"

She didn't have an answer, but Toby got up from his cot and made his way over. "If we get out, we can make a plan to free Violet. Right now, all three of us are maybe a few hours away from being killed..."

Violet agreed. "And if you are, then you can't help me. The most important thing is that you are all safe. Later, if it's possible, you can try to come back for me."

"We *will* come back for you," Matt insisted, and the other two nodded.

Ok, now for the hard part.

"How do we do it without me killing you?" she asked.

Joe thought for a moment, then pointed to the large closet he'd been punching. "That thing's pretty big. I think the three of us could fit in there, then get out again when the door's open and you're busy."

Busy eating people. Violet shuddered at the thought.

"How do we get you to..." Toby trailed off.

"A cut should do it," she explained. "Just one of you, and nothing too deep. I only need to smell it, and then you have to get clear. I think we should leave it as late as possible, too."

Matt nodded. "We don't want you to go back to normal before the door's open."

"I was more thinking I don't want to be hammering on that closet for too long. I might eventually get in."

The others were silent for a moment. Joe cleared his throat. "Well, that's a cheerful thought, thanks."

"Who's going to get cut?" Violet asked.

"Me."

Of course it would have to be Matt.

"Okay. How will you do it?"

Matt searched the room for a moment before moving

to the desk. He rifled through the drawers, then came out with a stapler. He opened it, pulled a single staple out, and flattened it until its shape resembled that of a sewing needle. There was a sound from outside; people were coming toward the room.

Wait! We're not ready!

Violet's mind was racing; she hadn't even had time to say goodbye. What if the plan didn't work? It was too late now. Matt gave her a reassuring smile before pushing the wire into his arm and forcing it forward several inches. The red liquid dripped out, and the beautiful smell was in the air. Violet felt herself becoming lightheaded.

"Uhh, we might have a problem."

She turned to see what Joe was talking about, the room around her already beginning to spin. The closet was piled high with boxes and files. There wasn't room for a single person to fit inside, let alone three.

"Get them out," Toby urged, glancing at Violet, who was now swaying slightly. Matt took hold of her, moving her head back to face him.

"Violet, it's okay," he reassured. She could hear Joe and Toby ripping out the boxes from the closet, but it was getting harder and harder to concentrate now the smell was so strong. Matt's green eyes locked with her grey ones, and he put his forehead against hers.

"It's okay, stay with me," he said softly.

"Hurry up," she whispered, her voice slow and thick.

Matt glanced over her shoulder where the sounds of Joe and Toby were fading away. She felt like she could hear her own heartbeat, as well as the sound of the blood leaving Matt's hand. It was a steady, melodic drip. Was that a key in the door, too? Everything seemed to slow down. She watched almost absently as her right arm raised a little, reaching for Matt's face. Her fingers curled toward his skin, a hiss escaping her throat.

"It will be okay." His voice sounded so far away, and Violet was vaguely aware he was now working hard to hold her steady as she fought against him. He took one final look over her shoulder, and then there was the sound of a door opening. Matt kept hold of Violet, but spun her around, toward the door. She saw the soldiers.

It is going to feed.

WHEN VIOLET WOKE UP, SHE WASN'T IN THE ROOM WITH her friends. She was in a different office. Slowly, her head pounding, she sat up. Her hair was wet and matted from lying in a pool of blood. Beside her was the body of a soldier. She didn't recognize him, though that was probably because his head had been ripped clean off his shoulders and was nowhere to be seen. There was a bitter taste in Violet's mouth, and she wiped her lips roughly with the back of her hand as she climbed to her feet.

The office was trashed; there had been a struggle. Slowly, trying not to make a sound, she went into the hallway. The lights flickered on and off, and there was screaming coming from some of the other levels.

Looks like I might've infected a few people.

That was good. It meant she could try to escape while the doctors and soldiers fought the dead, though it also meant more danger for her friends. Instinctively, Violet headed for the room she'd shared with the others. The door was open, and she had to step over a mangled mess of limbs and blood to get inside. There were no bodies, though, which meant whatever was left of the soldiers were probably still walking around somewhere. Hopping over various organs and bits of fingers, she moved to the closet. The door was wide open, but there was no sign of Matt, Joe, or Toby.

That's good. It means they got out.

You should get out, too.

At some point in the struggle, the window had been smashed. Violet took a jagged piece of glass from the floor, then left the room. She moved toward the elevator and pressed the call button. It opened—empty other than the dismembered leg in the corner. She pressed the button for the ground floor. The elevator rumbled down, but it seemed to be faulty. It stopped at each level. On the first two, there were no people, just a mess of blood and general disarray.

On the third stop, Violet saw the fight was still going on. Three doctors were being ripped open by at least ten biters, and two soldiers at the end of the hall were trying to fight the others off with knives. It seemed their bullets had run out. She hurriedly pressed the button to close the doors, wanting to be as far away from this floor as possible, until she saw Joe step out of one of the offices. Her eyes widened, and she waved her arms to try to get his attention. It worked; he caught sight of her and smiled, a reassuring sight despite his bloody lip and black eye. Slowly and silently, he slipped past the dead and moved for the elevator.

But then the doors shut.

"No," Violet cried, banging her fists against them as the metal box rumbled toward the ground floor. She hurriedly pressed the button for Joe's level, groaning as the elevator continued to stop at every stop on the way down. Finally, she was at the bottom. She jabbed at the button to close the doors so she could go back up again. But, of course, it had to stop at every single floor on the way back up, too. Violet swore at the thing with as many words as she could think of, in as many languages as she knew.

After an eternity, the doors opened on the right floor. Joe waited on the other side. The biters behind him were still busy feeding. He stepped in swiftly, pressing the button to close the doors again.

"It might've been polite to hold the elevator for me," he joked.

Violet hugged him. "Are you okay?"

"Yeah."

"Where are the others?"

"We got separated. You turned a few of the soldiers, and they turned others. We tried to run. Somehow, we lost each other."

Violet's heart was racing. "Did you see which way they went?"

"I think they ran up the stairs, to the floor above us."

AFTER NUMEROUS STOPS AT EVERY LEVEL THE ELEVATOR was capable of traveling to, Joe and Violet stepped onto the floor they needed. Violet held on to her shard of glass. Joe had a polished baton. This hallway was deserted, but still wrecked like the others.

"How long has it been going on for?" Violet asked, her voice low.

"About five hours," Joe replied. "It was crazy. We couldn't leave the closet for ages, because there were so many biters outside. Then they started to move around the building, and even more people got infected. They were turning really fast; do you think that's something to do with your blood?"

"What do you mean?"

"Well, if you infected the first lot, then they infected the others, maybe that would explain why they seem to come back quicker."

Violet shrugged. "Maybe, I don't know."

"Something to think about."

"I'd rather not."

Joe grinned. "Good point. Let's just find the others and get out."

"Stop right there."

Violet froze. She knew that voice. She and Joe turned, coming face to face with Gobber. He was bruised and worn down, but unfortunately still alive. His gun was pointed squarely at Violet's face. "Doctor Ross is looking for you," he said.

"Tell him I'm busy right now."

Gobber smirked. "Funny. Get in there." He pointed to a room behind her, another office. It wasn't like they had much of a choice, so Violet and Joe trudged inside. Gobber shut the door behind them, and then moved over to the desk. He sat down on the chair, motioning for Joe and Violet to sit in the seats opposite.

"We'll wait here for a while," he said. "Until backup arrives."

"Just let us go," Violet said. "We should all get out of here."

"You think I'm scared of them?" Gobber asked, pointing to the door with the gun. There was more screaming now, and it was getting louder. The biters were close. "I've got bullets; they don't frighten me. The good doctor needs you, mutant, and he'll pay me extra to bring you to him."

"Is money actually worth anything anymore?" Violet asked.

"It will be when I ship out of here next week." His eyes narrowed at Joe, who'd been sitting silently during their conversation but was staring at Gobber intently. "You got something to say?"

"No, I just...I don't want to be rude or anything, but what's with your tooth?"

Gobber's smile flickered, but he just leaned back in the chair and said nothing.

Violet noticed the door behind him, which she assumed led to a private bathroom, was opening silently.

I should warn him if there's a zombie in there.

I'm definitely not going to.

But it wasn't a zombie; it was Frances. She was in bad shape, but she was alive. Gobber put his feet up on the desk, eyes on Violet. "Listen, sweetheart, don't take this personally. I mean, don't get me wrong, I hate you, but it's not a personal thing. I just hate what you are. And who you are. And everything about you."

"It sort of sounds personal," Joe mused, purposefully keeping his eyes off Frances, who was getting closer. She had a knife in her hand.

Gobber sneered. "You know what? I think you're right. It is personal. Oh well, you two will be dead soon, and then we won't have to worry about—"

He didn't get to finish his sentence because Frances plunged her knife into his neck, practically growling with anger as she did. Gobber twitched for a moment as the blood poured from the wound, spraying the table in front of him. Joe yanked Violet to her feet, pushing her out of the room before things started to spin. Frances followed, holding her side and groaning with every step. She closed the office door behind her, but made no effort to follow them down the hallway.

"Come on," Joe said to her.

She shook her head, moving her hand and showing them the bite that had gone clean through her clothing. The blood meant nothing to Violet; Frances was almost fully infected.

"Get as far away as you can," she breathed. "They're looking for you." She went back into the room and closed the door behind her.

Joe eyed Violet. "Are you okay?"

"I don't know why she helped us"

"Maybe not everyone is bad?"

"Let's just find the others."

Joe agreed. "We need to be prepared for anything; who knows what else they have in this place?"

Violet knew he was right. They continued down the hallway, checking the rooms. Most were empty, but a couple contained corpses so mutilated they stood no chance of getting back up again. Joe opened the door to another room, and then hurriedly shut it again before Violet could see what was inside.

"What is it?" she asked.

"Remember I said we needed to be prepared for anything?"

"Yeah?"

"There are six biters in that room."

"Okay..."

"And Toby is on top of a bookcase."

"On top of a—"

"A bookcase, yeah."

Joe opened the door a fraction, and Violet peeked inside. Six biters were standing around a bookcase by the back wall, each reaching hungrily for Toby who was, as Joe said, curled into a ball on top of it. He glanced up as the door opened, and gave Joe and Violet an awkward wave. Joe closed the door again, turning back to Violet. "How fond are you of the kid, really?"

"He's one of us."

Joe sighed. "I knew you were going to say that."

"Hey!" Matt was heading toward them down the hallway, carrying a large machete. His arm was wrapped up where he had cut it, thankfully, and he pulled Violet into a hug.

"Glad you're okay." He held his hands up at Joe. "I thought the plan was to stay together?"

"Things got complicated."

"True enough," Matt said, then paused. "Where's Toby?"

Joe nodded to the door beside him. "In there."

"What's he doing?"

"He's on a bookcase," Violet answered.

"On a... okay, right."

"And Violet says we definitely have to go in after him," Joe said.

Matt agreed. "We do."

"Damn. Okay then." Joe opened the door, and the three of them hurried inside. They were able to kill the first couple of biters quickly enough because they were still distracted with Toby, but as soon as the rest realized, they had to work a little harder. Matt was almost unstoppable with his machete, though, which was far more useful than Violet's glass or Joe's baton. At one point, Joe was pinned, but Matt seemed to appear from nowhere, slicing the biter's head clean off. Soon, all that was left was a mangled heap of corpses on the floor.

Toby climbed down. "Thanks."

Matt wiped his forehead with the back of his sleeve. "No problem." He looked as though he might be about to say something to Violet, but then his expression changed. Steeling herself, she turned to see why. In that instant, her stomach seemed to fall to her feet.

Joe was bitten.

THE BITE WAS ON HIS SHOULDER, AND HE WIPED THE blood away with the sleeve of his shirt. It wasn't deep, but that didn't matter. A bite was a bite. Face white, he stared at them, his expression a mixture of realization and disappointment.

"Sorry, guys," he muttered. "Didn't see him coming."

Violet could hardly breathe. She moved closer to Joe, pulling him close. The smell of his blood made her slightly dizzy, but the damp scent of infection was already there. He was going to turn, and it wouldn't take long. Matt stabbed his machete into the wood of the table, swearing loudly.

"What should we do?" Toby asked, his voice breaking a little.

"Matt, will you do me a favor?" Joe asked, nodding to the machete.

Matt's eyes filled with tears, and he shook his head. "No. No, no, no..."

Joe smiled weakly. "I can't do it myself. You'd really be helping me out." He spoke so casually, as if he was simply asking for a loan of Matt's car or something. "Come on, mate. You know I'd do it for you."

Matt wiped his eyes. He would do it; Violet knew that. As horrible as it was, he wouldn't let his friend become one of the biters. They had made a pact right

TWENTY-FOUR

279

at the start. He pulled the machete out of the desk, and moved closer to Joe. "Are you sure?" he asked.

"I don't want to turn into one of those things. No offense, Vi. I just can't pull off cute-zombie girl like you."

Violet tried to smile. Matt pulled Joe into a hug, then so did Toby. Violet went last.

"I'm so sorry," she whispered. Joe kissed her cheek. "Take care of him," he said, nodding at Matt. "He's definitely a little bit in love with you."

"Thanks, Joe," Matt said, rolling his watery eyes but smiling.

Joe winked at him. "You were taking too long to say it." He got down on his knees, head down. "Do it quick, okay?"

Matt took a deep breath, then lifted the machete.

"Stop!" Violet cried out suddenly.

Matt froze, the machete hanging in the air just above Joe's head. "What?"

Joe was breathing heavily. "Can this wait, Vi? I'm on the clock here."

"We're so stupid," Violet said, eyes wide.

Joe raised an eyebrow. "I'm just about to die, and you're insulting me? That's cold."

She was barely listening as she pulled Joe to his feet. "The vaccines!"

Joe's eyes widened, too. "You think—"

"Maybe one of them can help?"

Matt didn't sound sure. "We don't know if they'll work; you know what happened to Sam."

Toby added, "And weren't those meant to stop people from getting the virus? If Joe's...if he's already...will it even work?"

Joe shrugged, eyes on the machete in Matt's hand. "If *that's* my only option right now, maybe we could give the drug a try? Let's be honest... by the end of today, I'll be dead, or half-dead like Violet. I know which one I'd prefer."

Matt thought for a moment. "We need to find it. Maybe Joe should stay here with Toby?"

Joe shook his head. "Bad idea."

"Yeah," Toby agreed.

"I don't want you guys risking your lives for me. Let

me come and help," Joe said. He glanced at Toby. "Right?"

"Actually, I was thinking I didn't want to be left alone with you if you were going to become a zombie, but sure."

Violet's heart was racing, but this was good. Five minutes ago, it seemed like all hope was lost, but now they had a chance to save Joe.

"Let's go," she said.

THE GROUP HAD BEEN SEARCHING FOR ABOUT TWENTY minutes. So far, they had no success.

"You think they'd signpost this place better," Joe said impatiently, his breathing becoming heavier by the minute.

Matt shrugged. "I guess a big sign saying 'anti-zombie vaccine this way' might be a little much."

Joe grinned, holding onto his shoulder. They'd covered the wound, but it had stopped bleeding relatively quickly. Violet could already see the veins around it turning black. He was paler than he had been ten minutes ago, and walking seemed to be much harder work than before. He caught her eye.

"Stop checking me out, Violet. We're busy right now."

She fluttered her lashes, pushing him playfully. "I just can't get enough."

"I feel like I'm missing out by not starting a post-apocalyptic love story." Joe sighed, then called over to Matt. "Sorry I outed you to Violet; things must be feeling a little uncomfortable right now."

"A little," Matt replied.

"I just kind of assumed I'd be dead so it wouldn't really matter if I mentioned the whole secret love thing. Now I'm caught up in it, and the tension here is killing me."

Matt's expression was fixed. "Yeah, at least you're not still talking about it."

"That would be awkward," Violet agreed, smothering a laugh.

They took the stairs between floors of the building; Violet did not want to risk the PMSing elevator again. Everything was much quieter now, and she wondered if the dead had gone. Perhaps they'd chased the last survivors out the front doors? That would certainly make things a lot easier for her and the others.

The next level seemed more promising. There was a lot of lab equipment. In one room, there seemed to be hundreds of vials of blood.

"That can't all be mine," Violet said.

Matt shook his head. "Who knows how many survivors they took blood from, or how many of the dead ones they tested."

Toby was examining some of the vials more closely. "They all have codes and dates; how will we know which are the ones we need?"

"We could look for ones with the most recent dates?" Violet suggested.

"Yeah, if only we knew what today is," Joe replied. "I don't know about you, but I've stopped writing in my diary."

"Good point."

"What are you doing here?"

Doctor Ross had come out of a small room to their right. He was bloodied and his coat was ripped, but he seemed okay other than that.

"We've come for the vaccine," Violet said, keeping her tone confident despite the fact she was terrified.

Doctor Ross' eyes swept the group and settled on Joe. "He's been bitten?"

"You can tell?" Joe asked sarcastically, the sweat glistening on his pale forehead.

"Where are the vaccines?" Violet insisted. "You said there were three others."

"There are."

Joe held up his hand. "Well, this is your lucky day; I'd like to test one."

Doctor Ross shook his head. "There's no guarantee it will work on someone who has been bitten."

"There's no guarantee it will work at all," Violet countered. "But we're going to try it anyway. Where are they?"

Doctor Ross paused, surveying each of them carefully.

Then he looked squarely at Violet. "Come with me."

"What?"

"I've just radioed the soldiers I sent out on patrol this morning. They're coming back to extract me. You need to come, too."

"No thanks."

Doctor Ross stepped forward, and Violet saw Matt instinctively move a little closer to her.

"Do you have any idea how important you are?" Doctor Ross asked, his voice almost manic. "Your blood could hold the key to everything!"

"She's not going with you," Toby interrupted, the nine-year-old boy standing between Violet and the doctor.

Doctor Ross seemed to sense the way this was heading, and he eyed the machete in Matt's hand. "How about you all come with us?" he asked. "We can try the vaccine on you," he said to Joe, "And get you all to safety."

Violet shook her head. "We'll never be safe around people like you." She took a step closer to the doctor. "Tell us where the vaccine is, or my friend here is going to lodge that machete into your skull."

Doctor Ross' eyes flicked toward Matt, who smiled.

"In here." He gestured to the door behind him. On the table in the smaller room there were three vials, clearly about to be packed into a laptop-sized case. Joe, whose legs looked like they were threatening to give out, sat on a stool by the table. Violet eyed each of the glass tubes.

"Which one should we use?" Matt asked her.

She had no idea. Violet turned to the doctor. "Which one?"

Doctor Ross shrugged, his whole attitude changing. "How should I know? That's why we run tests."

"Guess."

Ross' eyes flicked to the machete, then he gestured to the left-most vial. "That one. That was the one we thought most likely. We were going to test it next."

"Put it into a syringe," Violet ordered. The doctor moved to the table, filling a syringe with around a quarter of the liquid. Joe stuck out his arm, but Violet held up her hand.

"Wait." She glared at Doctor Ross. "You first."

"What?"

"I don't trust you, *Doctor,* but if this is the one you think is the safest, then you should try it first."

Ross shook his head. "I'm not injecting myself with that."

"But it would be good enough to test on us?" Matt asked, teeth clenched. Ross didn't reply.

Violet stepped closer to him. "Test it. Now."

He stared at the needle, and then shook his head. "Not that one."

I knew it!

"Then which?" Violet asked. Doctor Ross filled up a second syringe from the middle vial. He took one last look at Violet and the others before putting it into his arm.

"How long do we have to wait?" Matt asked.

"Not long," Violet replied. As if on cue, the doctor began to shake. White foam bubbled out of his mouth, and he fell to the floor. He shook, more foam escaping his mouth, this time turning from white, to grey, to black. He writhed in agony, beginning to scream. Then he stopped, his chest still. Violet's voice was low when she spoke to Matt. "Do it."

Matt jammed the machete into the doctor's skull without a second's pause. He was dead.

"That went well." Matt sighed. Violet put her head in her hands, leaning on the table. Then she picked up the middle vial and smashed it onto the floor.

"Two left," she muttered. "And the one the scientist thought was most promising is useless."

"Which one should we choose?" asked Toby.

"I chose that one," Joe said, nodding at the left vial. Violet suddenly realized the syringe Doctor Ross had previously filled was gone.

"Joe...did you—"

Joe held up the empty syringe. She could see a pinprick of blood on his arm where he'd just injected himself.

"Why?" Matt asked.

"Why not?"

Matt gestured to the dead doctor on the floor. "I don't

know, because of what we just saw?"

Joe's voice was casual. "He clearly didn't know what he was talking about, so I thought I may as well try this one."

Violet swung her gaze from Matt back to Joe. "How do you feel?"

"Fine."

"Fine?"

"Kind of tired. A bit hungry maybe?" Joe added.

"Does that mean it worked?" Toby asked.

Violet held up her hands. "I have no idea. It might be slower working than the other one. It could work differently because he's already infected—"

"Or it might be the cure," Joe suggested. "Let's have a little positivity, huh?" He got to his feet. "Shall we go? Or do you want me to roll around a little first?"

THEY HEADED INTO THE QUIET HALLWAY, JOE ALREADY seeming stronger than he was when they walked in. Violet caught Matt's eye, holding back so she could talk to him.

"What do you think?"

Matt glanced at Joe. "He looks better."

"It just feels too easy."

"Let's just keep our eyes open. For now, this is good."

He was right. There wasn't anything they could do except wait. She and Matt hurried to catch up with Joe and Toby. They rounded a corner just in time to see the soldiers getting out of the elevator. Matt grabbed Violet's arm, pulling her back into a small breakroom. Joe and Toby followed. They closed the door silently, moving to hide behind one of the couches.

"I wish you hadn't said it was too easy," Matt whispered. Through the glass door, they could see the soldiers heading past. There had to be at least fifteen of them. They moved toward the room where Doctor Ross was.

"They're going to be looking for us when they find him," Violet whispered.

"Maybe they'll just think he got bitten and was

infected?" Toby asked.

"They might, if I hadn't left my machete in his head," Matt muttered.

Joe sighed. "Yeah, I doubt we can get away with 'he tripped and accidentally stabbed himself in the head'."

"Maybe not," Matt agreed. "We need to leave. Now." He crept around to the door, silently pulling it open. Then he gestured to the others to follow. They stayed low, hurrying out into the hallway.

"He's dead," came a voice from behind. "Someone's killed him!"

"Go," Joe hissed. They ran, stampeding down the hallway toward the stairs. Violet heard feet close behind.

"There," someone shouted. Gunshots rang out just as they broke through the doors to the stairwell.

"Go, go, go," Matt yelled, and they ran as fast as they could down the stairs. They were high up, though, and the stairs seemed to go on forever. Violet could hear the soldiers behind them, but didn't dare look back. The last thing she needed now was to trip and cause herself and her friends to make the last part of the journey backward.

"Violet, if you want to turn into a zombie and kill them right now, that would be fine," Joe puffed as he jumped three steps at a time.

"Maybe you should do it?" she wheezed as Matt took her hand in an attempt to speed her up.

Finally, they reached the bottom, and burst through the double doors to the ground floor. One lone soldier stood by the elevator, straightening with a surprised expression on his face.

"What are you doing here?" he asked. He wasn't raising his gun, but he was holding it.

"Oh...uh...we..."

A voice crackled over the soldier's radio. "...three males, one female....they've killed Ross...think one of them might be the girl he was talking about..." The soldier's eyes widened, and his hand tightened on the gun. Toby was quicker. He grabbed the glass from Violet's hand and jammed it into the man's leg. He went down. In the moments before he raised his weapon again, Violet and the others were out the door and into the street.

"ANY HEADACHES?"

"No."

"Double vision?"

"No."

"Random desire to eat people?"

"Yes... Wait, no."

Violet frowned, but Joe just smirked. "I'm fine, really. I just feel normal."

"I wish there was a way to be sure."

Joe thought for a moment. "You could cut yourself and see if I attack you?"

"I'd rather not," Matt chimed in, coming into the kitchen from the garden. "Let's not encourage any zombie behavior until we absolutely have to."

"Agreed," Violet said. She studied Joe across the kitchen table. She didn't think they needed to test it; Joe was like her now. Sure, he hadn't eaten anyone yet, but he was paler than he'd been before. Grey streaks were beginning to fleck across his eyes, too. Joe knew it, of course—probably Matt and Toby, too—but it didn't matter, not really. They were alive, and they were together.

They'd found an abandoned car outside the facility, and headed as far away as possible. Violet had almost given Matt a heart attack on the way out, screaming for him to stop the car. But it wasn't the soldiers or the dead; it was Ben. She'd seen him sniffing around in a pile of garbage, and launched herself out of the still-moving vehicle to get him.

Family complete—complete as it could be without the ones they'd lost—they'd driven for almost six hours until they found the right place to stop. It was a little cottage, right in the middle of nowhere. There was a garden with vegetables, and a huge fireplace in the living room. There were no walls, just a waist-high fence, but Matt said they could build it up. In any case, they hadn't seen a biter for miles.

"What are you thinking?" Matt asked, and Violet realized she'd not spoken for several minutes.

"Just about us, about how everything has changed," she began. "It feels like there were so many of us before. Amy, Emily, Maggie, Tom, Zack, Sam..."

"All the people at the house," Joe added.

"All my friends," Toby said.

Violet nodded. "So many people are dead."

"I love where this is going so far," Joe said sarcastically.

"It's just strange. Out here, it's so peaceful. It feels like nothing's changed," Violet said. "Do you think things will ever get back to the way they used to be?"

"No," Joe replied immediately. "But that doesn't mean they have to be completely terrible."

Matt agreed. "We're here, and we made it. That means other people did, too."

"Good people," Toby added. "There have to be good people out there."

"No more mad scientists, please," Joe said.

"Do you think we did the right thing?" Violet asked. "Not going with Doctor Ross, I mean? My blood saved Joe... maybe—"

"He never would've let you go," Matt said.

"And we're not one hundred percent sure I'm saved," Joe added. "Let's see what happens when one of you gets a nosebleed."

Matt took Violet's hand. "No matter what happens, whether the world goes back to how it was, or gets even more screwed up, we're all in it together. We're family. If you survived being bitten, maybe other people did, too. Maybe there are others working on a cure right now."

Violet took his words to heart. He was right. He had to be. Still, she knew that no matter what he said, even if he meant it, Matt couldn't guarantee they'd be able to stay together. Or keep each other safe. The new world was too cruel and violent to allow that to happen. But that didn't mean she couldn't enjoy these moments of respite when they came. They were safe right now, and that was the important thing.

She was alive.

Sort of.

MELISSA IS A PRIMARY SCHOOL TEACHER BY DAY AND a writer by night. She grew up in a small town in the UK, and spent most of her time with her nose in a book. Her childhood was filled with R.L Stein, Jacqueline Wilson, and J.K Rowling, and they inspired her to begin creating her own worlds. Melissa has always been fascinated with stories about living through an apocalyptic event, and with characters who feel so real that they become part of the reader long after the book was put away. She wrote the first draft of Alive? at sixteen, and has been hooked on writing ever since.

When she's not writing, Melissa enjoys reading, playing video games, crocheting, and spending time with her two dogs (and occasionally her husband).

THERE ARE SO MANY PEOPLE I WOULD LIKE TO THANK for their role in getting Alive? to where it is now. My husband David, who was never allowed to read the manuscript, but had to pretend to be excited about every new idea that popped into my head - most of which were so terrible they never even made it into the book. Thank you to Lorin and Alice, integral members of my very real zombie survival team, for always being at the end of the phone when I had a living-dead question to discuss in-depth. And to Luke, for all the laughter, terrible documentaries, and second lunches. I couldn't do it without you, duck.

Thank you to my mum, for always knowing the right thing to say, and for your constant support throughout my life; from school plays, to hideously long university events, to writing a book, you never missed a single thing.

Finally I would like to thank Cynthia for her patience and kindness during the editing process, and the wonderful ladies at Clean Teen for their hard work and dedication. You have made my dream a reality. Now let's just hope it's not a nightmare for those who read it!

ACKNOWLEDGEMENTS

CPSIA information can be obtained
at www.ICGtesting.com
Printed in the USA
FFHW01n1119020818
47599118-51108FF